MW01009570

Authors Featured in Skein of Shadows:

Corey Blankenship

Nathan Ellsworth

Brannon Hall

Brannon Hollingsworth

Davis Riddle

Skein of Shadows

Tales from Crown

Edited by

Neal Levin

Additional Editing Provided by

Kelsey Blankenship

Brannon Hollingsworth

Heather Hollingsworth

Joanna G. Hurley

Davis Riddle

Daren Scroggie

Proofreading Provided by

Rob McDonald

Skein of Shadows

Copyright © 2007 Dark Quest, LLC

Dark Quest

Howell, New Jersey 07731

Visit our website at www.darkquest.com

CONTENTS

Dedications/Acknowledgments

Ashy and Lady Purity: He incited creativity. She inspired hope. Both sparked the desire to dream.
                        -Corey

The Wandering Men: Whose friendship and hard work made this possible.
Meg: Who understands the creative impulse, and encourages me to pursue it.
                        -Nathan

To my three best friends:
Christ – without you, there ain't nothin'.
Heather – without you, there ain't nothin' worth wantin'.
Davis – without you, there ain't nothin' worth wantin' to do.
                        -Brannon

To Peredhel, The Council, and the Wandering Men, true brothers in the art,
To Dad who suggested I draw castles instead of robots,
To Camille and Mom for your encouragement.
                        -Davis

To the bonds of friendship that gave rise to this story. May our feet find the trail before us and may the 2 A.M. wake-up calls be forgiven.
And to my wife Janet, who supported me through this adventure and so many like it. Thank you for always being there.
                        -Hall

Acknowledgements

The Wandering Men would like to thank Neal at Dark Quest Games for having faith in us, and Daren Scroggie for all of his creative contributions.

SKEIN OF SHADOWS FOREWORD

By Keith Baker

Dear Reader,

When I was a child, a phonograph recording of *The Hobbit* was my first exposure to worlds of fantasy. It was the start of a long and ongoing journey, one that led me through Narnia and Middle Earth, to Melnibone and the Young Kingdoms. Each world had its own wonders to explore – monsters, magic, heroes, and history. And yet, each followed a linear path, seen through the eyes of a single author.

I was in High School when I discovered *Thieves' World.* Here I found something new... a shared setting. Each author follows a different path, but they are united by a common cast of characters and the backdrop of the city. As a result, the reader has the opportunity to see the world through many different eyes – to follow the path of wizard and rogue, to see something that seems to be a trivial detail in one story become the turning point in another.

Skein of Shadows follows this tradition, weaving a single intricate tale through the experiences of people from all walks of life. An assassin watches a gladiator engage it what might be his final match... and soon enough we discover just what brought the warrior to the pits, and what the battle means to him. As the book opens, we learn of the threat presented by a mysterious ship; but as we delve deeper, we track the eerie voyage of that vessel across the waters. The many threads of *Skein* take us to the miserable common room of The Muddy Man, into the ocean depths of the Alônn realm, and all the way into the ethereal plane in the company of a brave Etherean spy, with each step bringing the greater picture into sharp and disturbing focus.

As a writer, I enjoy the chance to see these different authors bring their own styles to the world. As a reader, I'm fascinated to see each character take center stage. But I enjoy this story on another level. When we play roleplaying games, we are creating shared fiction; each gamemaster is a collaborating author, using the established cast of characters and backdrop to create their own unique tales. When fiction overlaps with a gaming world, I want it to provide inspiration, to give me ideas I could take to my own table. *Skein of Shadows* does just that, as each story follows not just a different hero, but a different *kind* of hero. The tapestry they weave is a fascinating one that paints a grim picture for Crown. But they also pave a path that I could follow, revealing the vast potential hidden in the glorious city of Crown.

Welcome to *Skein of Shadows!*

Keith Baker
October 24, 2007

Vendetta

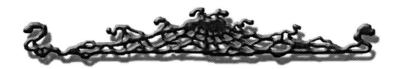

Nathan Ellsworth

VENDETTA

The sun, its morning glow casting everything in red and gold, hadn't yet risen over the rooftops of the Deep Harbor shops and tenements, but Arastin was already waiting at the Glorious Dawn for the breakfast he'd just ordered. He took a table outside. With his back to a wall and his left to the rising sun, he kept a wary eye on the early morning traffic of the Deep Harbor streets - not that there was much. Only a few sailors or dock hands passed by every so often, on their way to the harbor a few blocks away.

Eating at the Glorious Dawn in the morning was a routine for Arastin - something a person in his line of work should never fall into, but he'd grown tired of a life spent looking over his shoulder. If someone took revenge for one of his past deeds while he dined on some of the best grilled skate in Crown, so be it. Plus, Fennah, one of the adventuring owners of the inn, was always good for news and information when she was around.

Fennah didn't have any leads this morning, but Arastin did listen to a few of her latest adventuring tales to keep up the rapport. He smirked to himself as he thought about "adventurers" in general. He'd been alive for just over two centuries, and he still didn't understand the appeal. The streets of Crown had always provided him with enough work, gold, excitement, and - all too often - danger.

It was the latter aspect of his profession that'd he'd been considering a lot lately. He had no problem standing toe to toe with a mark or letting his blade do the talking with a hired thug. But, that was never the real danger in his line of work; it was always more secret or insidious - poison, a turned friend, one of his competitors on a roof with a crossbow, and the list went on. Perhaps adventuring would be safer. The macabre humor brought a smile to his face.

His eyes caught the sight of the morning sun on auburn hair, and his attention shifted. A lithe and attractive tiefling woman sauntered in from the street. Arastin smiled and raised a cup of tea to his lips, while his right hand slid to the knife at his hip.

"Hmmm, to what do I owe the pleasure, El'laa? And it is quite a pleasure, my dear." He took a second to appreciate how the sun accentuated the red in El'laa's hair and how she slid into the seat opposite him.

She flashed him a smile and said, "That's why your hand's resting on your blade?"

"Would you rather I placed my hand on one of your blades?"

El'laa rolled her sea green eyes. "You never stop."

"I'm determined; it's helpful in my line of work." He took another sip from his tea. "And, presumably, that's why you're here."

"You see right through me," she said with a wink. "So you haven't quit, then?"

The rogue arched an eyebrow and asked, "Who or what gave you that impression?"

"You have. Whispers say you haven't taken a job in over a year."

"I'm pickier in my old age. Jobs come, and I take what appeals to me," he said and shrugged. "It's time to enjoy some of my ill-gotten gains, so to speak."

"Well, perhaps my proposition will interest you."

Arastin smiled. "Dinner with you tonight? Absolutely."

The tiefling laughed but shook her head. "Sorry, today I'm all business."

He shrugged and asked, "Moving up in the world?"

"You know, 'friend of a friend of an enemy'," she replied. The elf nodded and began to work at his meal. "That's what I love about you Arastin -- you're such a good listener." He eyed El'laa as he buttered his bread.

The woman shrugged. "A member of the Iceskull League will arrive in Crown soon, and certain parties will pay for you to entertain such an esteemed visitor."

Arastin set down his bread and knife. "You'd better be sure about what your friends are asking."

"My friends are quite sure - and committed." El'laa reached into her verdant colored vest with a gloved hand. She produced a small piece of paper and a pouch that jangled when she set it on the table.

"What else are you hiding beneath that vest?"

"Wouldn't you like to know?" she quipped coyly and motioned towards the bag. "That's for your time. Role reversal -- the meal's on me now. If you're interested in the deal, send a letter with the time and place you'd like to meet for the details. The paper explains how."

El'laa didn't give the rogue time to respond. She stood and sauntered away but paused in mid-stride to glance back towards the table. "Of course, timing is important." The tiefling winked and left Arastin to finish his breakfast.

He ate mechanically. Instead of enjoying the meal, the rogue considered the basic setup needed for any job because, in his mind, he'd already accepted the deal. A smile played across his lips. Whoever El'laa worked for was good -- they knew him and knew he'd take the bait.

If any job would interest him, it'd be one involving the Iceskull League. The white dragons of the north had done enough to his ancestors to earn the ire of any elf. So, decades ago, when Arastin was approached to assassinate a spy the organization had in Crown, he did the job out of a sense of duty. Then, the League made it personal. Since surviving that second encounter, he'd taken every opportunity to wound the organization. The count was seven to nil, in favor of the rogue.

"So much for relaxing," Arastin mumbled to himself.

* * *

It was just after midnight, but the Mud Flats still seethed with activity. The whole district was a collection of shanties and rickety bridges precariously built on stilts above a festering half-swamp. Arastin knew the only people that lived in the Flats were ones that had no other choice; he'd lived there for ten years when he was younger. The Watch didn't visit the district often, for many reasons - the smell just being one. Because of the Watch's absence, certain individuals did business in the Flats, and the Ward's sodden shops and ale houses were constantly abuzz.

The rogue had an appointment at the Muddy Man, and the inn lived up to its name. Deep in the Mud Flats, the rundown inn embraced the squalor of the district. It didn't pay to be ostentatious, and smart visitors followed the same rule. Dressed in threadbare clothes stained too many times by potter's clay, the Arastin that pushed through beggars at the low-slung door to the Muddy Man was not the same elf who sat at the Dawn two days ago.

The inn had a reputation to keep: it was the finest in the Mud Flats - for what that was worth. The food was decent, and the rooms were cleaned semi-regularly. However, most people came to the inn to socialize and get out of the murky air of the district, even if most brought the funk in with them. The inn was a dingy melting pot of the masses.

The Muddy Man was rowdy and packed, but a pair of gentlemen agreed to vacate their table after Arastin's knife had a short conversation with the burlier man's neckline. The late night – really, early morning - patrons of the inn looked harmless - much like he did. He guessed the majority of them were truly benign and kept a wary eye on the handful that might be more than they seemed.

Arastin was half finished with his watery ale when El'laa stormed through the door. She remembered to watch for the low ceilings at the last minute and nearly bowled a patron over as a consequence. The tiefling glared at the simple craftsman and then, true to her fiery character, she unleashed a string of irate profanity that caused the man to wilt and disappear into the crowd.

The elf sighed. He needed information, but El'laa's current state made acquiring it a difficult prospect. The tiefling pounded a stiff drink at the bar before she ordered the house ale and finally approached the rogue. She seethed like a rising thunderhead.

"That light stepping ghost!" she fumed as she fell into her chair.

Arastin sat back. "Problems?"

"Amazing understatement and brilliant deduction," she spat. "No wonder you've been in the business so long; you've such an eye for judging people."

The rogue smirked and took a short drink before he spoke. "I'm willing to let that pass because you're beautiful when you're mad. But keep it up, and you'll upset the one ally you might have." El'laa stared at

Arastin. A laugh escaped her, but she squelched the outburst and hid her smile behind her mug.

"I just had another dance with ol' Stiffshanks!"

"Tenet's on the prowl again? Something's on the wind."

"Longing for company, more likely. Priggish bastard picked me up on a mere whim this time!"

Arastin contemplated his watery brew. "Sure word of our business hasn't traveled?"

El'laa set down her mug and leaned across the table towards the rogue. "My friends aren't the type to talk."

"But you are, my dear."

"I should cut out your tongue!" she hissed and brandished a knife as long as her hand for emphasis.

"Facts are facts, El'laa. We both know the truth. And you may want to hold off relieving me of my tongue - at least until the morning." Arastin's hand darted out and relieved her of the weapon.

El'laa rocked back in her chair. "Incorrigible!"

"Guilty," Arastin agreed and smirked. "But before we discuss what you're doing later, perhaps we should get down to business?" He planted the knife a finger-width into the tabletop.

The tiefling blinked her green eyes a couple of times. "You're still interested in the job then?"

"Your friends know me well enough. I'd love to claim I set up this meeting just to see you, but I do have a reputation to keep up. "

"That you do," she began with a wink. "The individual we'd like you to entertain will be here within ten days. He's the captain of a ship bound from the north; flies the flag of acquaintances of yours. So I've been told."

"It's a love to hate relationship," the rogue began. "I've had the pleasure of meeting a few of his business partners. Late business partners, actually."

"How unfortunate," the tiefling quipped and smiled. "The man's name is Na'akiros. Should you need things to discuss besides his time at sea, I hear he's an able swordsman and has some arcane talent."

"Interesting, I have a feeling the discussion will be lively. But I'm curious about his ship and his reason for visiting. His associates offended a lot of people with their last few deals. Anyone flying their flag is sure to receive a cool welcome, if he just sails into town."

"True," El'laa agreed with a nod. "The captain's not likely to sail a known ship directly into Crown, nor come ashore without a disguise."

"That'll make it tough to be there to greet him. Good thing I asked." Arastin drummed his fingers against the table. "Were you going to offer any of that information?"

She returned his stare in turn. "He's got another meeting to make in eight days time at the *Broken Valor* – it's a bar and arena in the Arm's Crescent."

"Why? And how many people are going to be at the party?"

"You've the time and the place. Why're you curious all of a sudden?"

"I'm a professional. I'm trying to figure out how many guests to plan for, and it's best to know what they might bring to the party. My reputation is on the line, after all."

"I'd love to help more, but I'm the middle woman. I don't know how many to expect."

Arastin scratched his chin and eyed El'laa. He waited for some time before he spoke. "Any specific conditions I should know about for the party? How, when, where?"

"They want the captain entertained as soon as possible. That's all they said."

The elf sighed. "Then, it'd really be nice if you'd tell me when and how he's arriving."

She shook her head. "They only supplied the window. But he has to travel by ship because of the deal, and they claim 'everyone will know when he arrives.' Besides, you've got contacts that can help you with that." The rogue began to drum his fingers on the table again. El'laa frowned, and her eyes darted around the Muddy Man. "Well?"

"I'd like a few more drinks to help mull it over. We can discuss Stiffshank's finer points while you wait for my answer."

El'laa smirked. "The bill's on you then, because I'll need to be seeing triple before I do that."

* * *

Arastin tossed the fruit vendor a bit of coin as he strolled by on his way home. Jalkesh peddled between the Narrows and the Old Temple Ward, but Arastin rarely had the chance to sample his merchandise anymore since he now lived on the Harbor. Pear in hand, he considered the deal he'd accepted as he left the inn-room and El'laa; she had barely acknowledged his departure. The contacts and favors he'd need to call in began to arrange themselves in his mind, but he wanted to catch a few hours of sleep and clean up before he got to the real work.

Hours later, a cleaner and more alert Arastin left his flat. He still couldn't wrap his mind around all the deal's nebulous information. All he had was an identity - Na'akiros, a captain of one of the Iceskull League's numerous pirate vessels, and one fixed date and location - the mark had a deal to make at the *Broken Valor* on the eighth day of the month. The captain had to arrive by ship, so that put him in the harbor before the meeting. However, the wind was fickle, and that meant the mark's arrival time would be an unknown.

It was time to do the grunt work and gather more information, and Deep Harbor was the first stop. He caught up with the old sea-dog he'd bought news from many times before, and then he tracked down Quellon. He routinely swapped favors with the alônn mystic and didn't believe the rumors that Quellon had forsaken his people.

Arastin needed to know when Na'akiros was sailing into port, and the alônn would be able tell him before anyone else. Citizens of the city, but also separate, the alônn lived in water-filled caves under Crown and swam in the harbor. They often ranged farther out to sea to hunt and play, and they had served Crown more than once by providing advanced warning about danger coming from the ocean.

The *Broken Valor* was next. He walked various routes to and from the *Valor* to determine the path the captain might take and which was fastest, and he committed them all to memory. After the sun set, he assessed the establishment in question. The building was really two in the rogue's mind: the tavern and the tower, and the tower commanded his attention. Constructed from rough hewn stone, the formidable edifice was both broad and tall, and the pennants on its peak were higher than almost any other building in Crown. The tavern was just an addendum that abutted the bulk of the tower.

The true nature of the *Valor* was apparent once Arastin plunged into the gloom of the interior. It was an arena for blood sport; the tower's exposed basement had been turned into a fighting pit. And instead of floors, the tower had tiers where patrons could sit or stand and watch the slaughter in the pit. The rogue noted the scent of dried blood blended with the other traditional bar smells of smoke, sweat, and spilt ale.

Compared to the tower, the tavern was mundane, but he did note a long bench for taking and placing bets. A slate board, hung behind the bench, listed the upcoming fights and the current odds. Arastin studied the slate.

Farulazar was the main attraction the night Na'akiros made the deal, and the Fiend Fighter would live up to his epithet: he was scheduled to fight a fiend. That's when he realized the Festival of the Long Night - a night that commemorated the Demon Scourge - was quickly approaching. A shiver shot down his spine as he made the connection, and he contemplated whether it was just a coincidence. Happenstance or not, the professional shelved the information and focused on his job.

He did his best to ingratiate himself with the staff. The rogue relied on charm, and when that didn't work, he dropped some coin. But it always took time to make a good contact, and he didn't press his luck.

The time spent in the *Broken Valor* also gave him a feel for the atmosphere and the patrons of the arena. The blood sport drew a wide variety of people, but everyone was alike when the combatants entered the pit. Cheers, curses, and chants - a cacophony thundered inside the tower. It was possible that pedestrians on the street even heard the clamor through the tower's formidable walls, and the frenetic crowd wore on him as the night progressed.

Arastin left the *Valor* just after midnight. He'd return to keep working on the staff, but after the previous evening, he wanted a night of good sleep. However, old "Stiffshanks" himself – Tenet, the Spymaster of Crown - had other ideas. Tenet waited calmly outside the elf's flat as if he had nowhere else he needed to be in the long hours after midnight.

The assassin closed the distance and nodded to Tenet. "Figured you'd be round to see me; what number am I on your list?"

"You're expecting me? Up to something Arastin?" Tenet asked.

"You could say that. El'laa had a lot to say last night, or maybe it was this morning." The rogue grinned while Tenet frowned. First blood went to him, but the battle with the Spymaster was far from over.

* * *

The next morning Arastin awoke in a malaise - he'd slept wrong. It was more than just Tenet's late night visit; his dreams had been troubled, but he couldn't remember any of them. Outside, the weather matched his mood - clouds cloaked the sky, and a constant chill breeze carried a fine mist. Weather rolling in didn't bode well for the Festival.

Arastin spent some time refining the plan he'd drawn up the day before. He'd have to split his time between the Harbor and the *Valor*, which meant a lot of running around. But the compensation was worth it. The initial retainer he picked up yesterday was more than he'd asked for on "simple jobs" in the past.

He quickly settled into the tedium of waiting, the hardest part of the profession. Only the maid from the *Valor* provided any distraction. Young and wild, Gwen worked the arena, carousing with the fighters, and was quickly drawn to Arastin. The rogue initially resisted, but he found himself spending a lot of his time fraternizing.

* * *

The gray pre-dawn light was just enough for Arastin to maneuver around the cramped room and slip on his boots. "Ugh," he grunted as he bent over to put the first on -- his head reminded him how much wine they'd drunk last night.

"So soon?" Gwen sighed from the bed. She was on her side and blearily gazed at Arastin. "It's only been a couple hours."

"I have to go. You know, love." Arastin stood and walked towards the door.

"No, come back to bed."

The rogue sighed and said, "Can't. No rest for the wicked."

"What do you do?" Gwen asked as she sat up. She didn't bother to cover her figure.

He turned back towards the bed. Arastin took a few seconds to appreciate the young maid's body before he answered. "I do what pays the bills and let's us enjoy good wine, even if it's not so good the next morning."

"Why won't you tell me?"

Arastin wished he'd left sooner. She was fully awake now, and if he just left her, it would greatly damage his ability to work freely at the *Valor*. But the bed had been so comfortable. "I told you, Gwen - I'm nothing but trouble. I get paid for doing bad things, and you really don't want to know more."

"Walk away, Arastin, or at least, take a break. Come back to bed." Gwen pulled back the covers.

For a long moment he was tempted. Finally, he shook his head. "I can't. I made a deal."

"But you don't like it, so why do it?"

The elf arched an eyebrow. "I never said that."

Gwen shrugged. "Not directly. But you've said enough when we drink, and when you fall asleep." Her smile was warm, and Arastin fought against himself.

"When did you turn into a nice girl?" he asked and winked.

"When I'm with someone I care about."

For once the rogue was at a loss for words. After a long moment of staring into Gwen's eyes, he shook his head. "I'm no good, Gwen. I'm not worth it."

"That's not what I think." The young woman rose from the bed and walked towards him. Arastin's heart began to hammer in his chest as she wrapped her arms around his back and pressed close. "You're not who you once were. I think you only do it because you've done it for so long. You don't know what else to do."

Gwen let go and stepped back, but she continued to look into his eyes. She took his hand and pulled him back towards the bed. "But I can help. You just need to be shown that the world is full of opportunity." Arastin's will broke, and the two fell on the bed together.

* * *

Arastin didn't leave Gwen's small flat until after noon. He was divided; his discontent with his course had been growing for a long time, but Gwen exacerbated the matter and gave the indefinite feeling a name and a face. Conversely, his other half knew he was good at his job and enjoyed the thrill. The elf ranged between the harbor and the *Valor* all afternoon, while his two natures warred. As night fell, he came to a decision: no matter the temptation, he was still a professional. He said he'd do the job, and he had taken the money - he had to see it through. But after that, the world was full of opportunity.

The situation with Gwen complicated the days that followed. He still haunted the *Valor,* but he kept to the shadows or went invisible. He couldn't see the young woman anymore - at least not until he finished the deal. That only made the wait harder, which was tough for him to admit.

The environment and conditions also made the days particularly foul. The constant wash of the surf that he heard as he prowled the docks blurred with the murmurs and cries of the patrons of the *Broken Valor*, while the clouds that choked Crown's skies and the perpetual freezing mist created a pall that matched the gloom of the arena.

Lastday, the fifth day of the job, Quellon provided him with the name of the ship: *Frozen Idol*. Arastin didn't bother asking for more; Quellon would have told him more, if the alônn knew. It was meager information, but it gave him hope that his time hadn't been wasted. The next day, the weather got worse. The mist turned into an icy drizzle, and the wind started to pick up, but Arastin also received his reprieve.

The elf headed for the docks to talk to his contact, his last task of an otherwise uneventful day. The weather had brought most of the Harbor to a standstill, and he found the man holed up in a pub. The sea dog nearly left his body when Arastin tapped him on the shoulder.

"Yea, a ship came into port real recent - the *Frozen Idol*. She's battened down at nary the southernmost dock. From the gossip, her papers are clean and say she's a wood, fur, and oil trader from the north." Arastin's informant said as he nodded.

The rogue shrugged and asked, "How are you sure I'd be interested in her, Carson?"

The man smirked. "I took a look at her just before I came for a drink. She ain't much to look at if ya ask me -- more worn an' weathered than I am. But her crew is tough as nails. I watched 'em button her up and disappear below-deck, and no one's visited the local haunts."

"A sailor not getting drunk after he gets into port?"

"I know," Carson agreed as he shook his head. "It's as wrong as a saruulan saint."

The rogue smiled. "You get a look at the captain?"

"No, no sign of him on deck. And only a couple of leather chewin' sea dogs is on watch. The whole harbor's laying low; afraid of what's brewing on the wind."

"Thanks for the word, Carson." Arastin palmed the man some gold, and the sea dog patted the elf on the back as he turned to go.

"Why don't you stay for a drink?"

Arastin stop and half turned. "Thanks, but there's work to be done."

"For an elf, you're always in a hurry. You should enjoy life sometime."

"Carson, I've probably enjoyed more years than you've lived."

Carson shrugged. "I've known you long enough to doubt that, considering your line of work."

The rogue didn't let the man continue; he turned on his heel and walked out into the night. The sea dog had struck an already raw nerve. Arastin was angry because of his situation and because he'd dropped his guard enough for the dock hand to catch a glimpse at what was underneath.

He tried to clear his mind as he headed for the *Idol*. If Carson was right about the ship -- and Arastin had no reason to doubt him -- Na'akiros was holed up inside, so it couldn't hurt to take a look. As he approached the dock, the last drops of his anger ebbed.

The *Frozen Idol* was there. Arastin knew little of ships or sailing, but even he noticed the *Idol's* rough lines and blocky design. It was far different than the rest of the ships he'd gotten to know over the past few days. The *Idol* was meant to haul cargo and plow through the sea.

As he moved closer, a chill dread suddenly pulsed through his veins and caused him to stop. Mingled fear and revulsion clawed up his spine and throat. Arastin hurriedly fell back and slipped into the shadows of the closest building. He searched for anyone, or anything, that may have seen him and caused his instincts to react, but at the back of his mind, he knew the ship was the source of the malaise.

The elf shook his head to clear the last remnants of discomfort and pulled the wand of *alarm* from his belt. One of the best purchases he'd made, the spell allowed him to know when his target was on the move without having to be there. He placed the spell and left the *Idol* to find the nearest inn. Arastin intended to catch whatever sleep he could, because his life was about to get hectic.

* * *

A mental chime roused the rogue from the daze that had overcome him. It'd been a long two days, watching the *Idol* in the rain and sleet, but no one had come or gone from the ship, and he wasn't about to enter the beast's lair. As his watch wore on and the Festival drew closer, the storm got worse. The rain was cold and steady, and wind birthed whitecaps in the bay. Overhead, lightning occasionally lit the cloud choked sky; it'd been many years since Arastin had seen lightning this late in the year.

Finally, on Darkday - the night of the Festival and the night Na'akiros was to make a deal at the *Broken Valor* - the captain stepped from his lair. Even in the dark, Arastin could see the handful of figures milling about on the dock. The rogue stole closer. He was invisible thanks to his ring, but he still kept to the shadows, just in case.

Five people stood on the dock: four humans and a tall, pale, white-haired elf. The elf spoke, gesturing to the four humans, and the professional knew the pallid elf was Na'akiros. Bile welled up in his throat, while flames of anger and hate blossomed in Arastin's brain.

His parents had told him about the dragons of the Iceskull League; how they had ruthlessly attacked the elven lands in the north, destroyed his parents' way of life, and forced the exodus. Not everyone had escaped, though. Some had been captured and forced into slavery, and the elves still mourned their lost kin. Still other families had betrayed their kin, willingly serving their new masters. Na'akiros' family was obviously one of the latter. Arastin struggled with his disgust but kept himself in check. There would be time to repay old vendettas.

The five set out: two in front, Na'akiros in the middle, and two followed. The rogue trailed his quarry and contemplated finishing the deal, but the weather set itself against him. The wind picked up and buffeted him from every angle, while the rain fell so hard it stung his exposed skin. Also, Na'akiros was on guard; he regularly doubled back and always looked over his shoulder. However, the captain's lack of Crown knowledge hindered him - the five always returned to the same route.

Eventually, the *Broken Valor* loomed before Arastin. The captain stopped short and began to issue last minute instructions to his men, but the rogue had endured enough of the weather. He took advantage of another pair of drenched pedestrians and followed them into the *Valor*.

Jeers, garish costumes, shouts, beer, unwashed bodies, bad food, and a hint of old blood accosted his senses as he entered the tavern. Arastin had never seen the *Valor* as busy, and it was tough to find a secluded shadow where he could remove his ring. He'd just managed to do so as Na'akiros and his entourage pushed through the throng to enter the tower and arena proper.

The rogue slid through the crowd after the captain. The five were already seating themselves at a large table situated a quarter turn clockwise around the tower. His frown turned into a grimace. The captain would be meeting some powerful friends if they had a meeting on the first floor and had a table so near the action.

He needed help getting close and knew he had to find Gwen. The rogue spotted her taking orders from a table on the other side of the floor. "Evening, love," Arastin said into her ear as he slid up behind her. He ignored the three at the table and reached around to try to put his hand down the front of the maid's bodice. She squealed and held his hand against her upper chest to stop him. The flat of the coin he had hidden in his hand pressed against her skin.

"You!" Gwen said as she whirled around and pulled him in for a fierce kiss. They separated, and she yanked him away from the table towards the back wall. The coin had already disappeared. "I'm going to get in so much trouble for that! Do you know who that was?"

"I'll make it worth your while."

They reached the wall, and she turned to lean back against it. "You bet you will! In more ways than one." Gwen pulled him in closer, but he resisted.

"Gwen! I'm here on business. I need to get a table, or at least a seat on the other side."

She huffed, set her jaw, and looked away. The crowd roared around them -- a fight had just come to an end. "Come on, Gwen! I told you what kind of relationship this was." He palmed her another coin.

"And I told you there were other options." Gwen looked into his eyes. "What happened?"

Arastin shook his head and pressed the coin upon her. "I'm a professional. It'll all be over tonight. Take this, and if you still want - and I'm still alive - I'll stop by. I could use some more convincing."

"By the Queen, you said you were no good," she sighed as she took the coin.

The rogue smirked. "From my own lips: unfaithful and nothing but trouble." Gwen shook her head, but she did smile.

"Let's see how far I can go before you get me fired!" She gave him a quick kiss on the cheek and led the way around the first floor. "The fight of the year - the Long Night Fight - is coming up next! That's why it's so packed. Farulazar's gonna kill a fiend!" Gwen had to shout over the crowd to be heard.

He pulled her to a stop and whispered in her ear. "I need you to take me past that table," he said and pointed to the one next to Na'akiros'. "Don't sit me there - just take me past it. There'll be a commotion, and I'll need you to step in and pull me away like I'm stumbling drunk."

"Ok," she said and nodded. The rogue picked up a half-finished beer from someone who was too drunk to notice and staggered after Gwen. The distance disappeared in the blink of an eye.

The rogue staggered full speed into the table he'd marked and his stolen, half-finished beer went into the spectator's lap. The man roared and reared up while Arastin crumpled to the floor. He hit the planks and released a *smokestick* that he'd held in the other hand. The cylinder rolled perfectly under Na'akiros' table, but he didn't have the time to see if the elf captain noticed. The beer drenched spectator - a wild-haired man of bigger dimensions than the rogue had realized - loomed over him.

"You damn drunk elf!" The man picked Arastin up by the front of his shirt. "Can't hold on to ya beer? I should shove that tankard down your throat, so you don't lose it!"

"Remy! There you are! You're supposed to follow me!" Gwen said from the hulk's right. "And you! Let go of him this instant!" The brute half turned to look at the diminutive waitress, while the rogue still dangled in the man's grip.

"Why should I?"

"Because Remy will apologize and pay for another round at your table. He's really sorry; aren't you, Remy?" Arastin nodded energetically.

"And if I'd rather see him lick the beer he spilled up off the floor? Whatcha gonna do then lil' miss?" He shook Arastin for emphasis.

"I'm not going to do anything, but Remy might."

"Hah!" the man barked and brought the rogue closer. Arastin smelled hard liquor on the man's breath. The situation wasn't going as planned. "So, cud chewer? What's a drunk featherweight like you gonna do?" The professional's hands struck like snakes: the first into the brute's jugular and the second into the space just below the brute's sternum. He fell to the floor again; the man gasped and staggered back to collapse to his knees.

Gwen pulled Arastin up and the two mock-staggered away as fast as they could. "Horrible," the rogue grumbled. Gwen ignobly dropped him into a chair near the back wall. "Was the white haired elf at the next table watching all that?"

"Arastin, almost everyone around us was watching." He scowled, but didn't reply. Gwen looked around wide-eyed. "These seats are claimed, but the people haven't shown up yet, and as Farulazar's on in a short bit, I doubt they will. This good?"

The rogue covertly glanced at Na'akiros' table. The captain wasn't paying them any attention - another four had already joined them. He looked at Gwen and smiled. "Thanks, love."

"Remember your promise." She kissed him fully again and disappeared.

Arastin quickly mumbled the words to a spell, and suddenly he heard everything as if he stood at the beer-soaked spectator's table. Only snippets of conversation drifted from Na'akiros' table; he had to listen carefully. He didn't dare use the *clairaudience* spell any closer, because he feared one of the nine at Na'akiros' table might detect the magic.

He saw the captain's lips moving and words slipped trough the magical conduit, "...should've warned me...I lost men..." Na'akiros' voice was raspy and deep - not what he'd expected.

One of the four that had just sat down - a wererat - leaned closer to the captain. When his voice carried, it was like a sharp pick to the ear, "Is the relic safe?"

"Of course!"

"Good...suffer the Grey God's wrath," the rat responded. Arastin clenched his jaw, and he tried to listen even harder. The Grey God was an ancient and half forgotten deity that revelled in pain and destruction. If an agent of the god was involved, this deal was dangerous, and the residents of Crown would suffer. The rogue was a killer, but he didn't condone wanton destruction or harming innocent people.

"Don't threaten me, rat! I'm not one of your toadies!" the captain growled. "...business...our money and get this over with." The crowd took that moment to scream, shout, and jump to their feet. Arastin cursed and stood. The nine were seated; they didn't seem to care what transpired around them. He watched the rat push something across the table towards Na'akiros.

It became even harder to hear the exchange as the crowd began chanting "Farulazar!", but the expression on the captain's face spoke volumes.

"...worthless Crown paper! ...not nearly enough!"

"...get more when we finish the deal!" the wererat whined and shook his head.

"...cross the League!" Na'akiros pointed at the wererat.

The rat stood and craned his long neck out threateningly towards the captain. "Don't you threaten me! ...die in a dungeon...Crown is my city!"

Na'akiros shook his pale haired head. "Enough...return to the Claw!"

An electric tingle shot up the rogue's arms and down his neck. The noise, and more importantly, the emotion of the crowd had changed around him. Shouts of dismay, protest, and anger replaced the cries for blood. Patrons pressed away from the main entrance of the tavern where the disturbance seemed focused. Arastin watched someone dart through the crowd and head for the stairs.

A bellow emanated from the door, and suddenly a swath of people was pushed back. It was like a line of dominoes as each person fell over those behind them. A mammoth oltreggan stood at the heart of the chaos. Arastin had to look a second time to make sure: the oltreggan held an anchor before him and was using the broad end like a plow to push through the crowd.

"What's THIS?!" Na'akiros' voice cut through the chaos. The professional whirled back to look at his quarry: the confusion and crush of the crowd had reached their table, and everyone was on their feet. Na'akiros towered over the wererat.

"...NO IDEA! WE MUST FINISH THE DEAL - TONIGHT!" Arastin made a snap decision and slipped through the crowd towards the nine. He sent the mental trigger to the *smokestick* he'd dropped earlier. Enhanced magically, it was yet another handy tool-of-the-trade he'd purchased from a mage that owed him a favor. Smoke as black as the sky outside rapidly filled the vicinity.

"BLADES!" he heard over the magic link and from his own ears. The professional drew his short sword and moved through the jumble of tables and chairs from memory. He found his targets relatively easily - they hadn't moved much. Three lackeys fell. He didn't care which side they were on. But someone finally raised an alarm: "Assassin!"

The rogue discerned the man who shouted through the clearing smoke. He vaulted the table and bull rushed the lanky-haired sailor into the yawning pit. Arastin spun in search of the next foe and locked eyes with Na'akiros, who stood a stone's throw away. The wererat stood next to the captain and had a hand on his shoulder.

"He dares attack! He must pay!" Na'akiros snarled.

"And he shall; they will all pay -- the Grey God will see to it! But we must have the relic first!" the rat whined. The captain scowled and glared at the assassin for a moment longer, but he turned on his heel and pushed through the chaotic throng.

Arastin tried to close the distance, but the wall of people sealed the gap, and he had to push through as well. Thankful that the crowd hindered both of them, the rogue managed to keep Na'akiros's stark white hair in sight.

The captain passed through the *Valor's* entrance, and the assassin followed quickly after. The storm hit him like a wall; its fury had increased. Wind and rain clawed at his clothes and skin, and lightning flickered constantly overhead, but he didn't slow his break-neck pace.

Buildings fell behind the two as they coursed through the rain-soaked byways of Crown. The bursts of illumination from the lightning revealed they were the only people on the streets. Arastin kept pace with his quarry, but he couldn't pull closer.

Na'akiros whirled, his arm outstretched towards the rogue - who recognized at once that the captain was a far more dangerous opponent than he'd assumed. Arastin threw himself into a dive, trying to get out of reach of the wand. He felt the air grow frigid, and needles of cold lanced into his legs, but he hit the ground, rolled, and started running again until he ducked into an alley.

The rogue glanced back into the now empty street and snarled. A thick coat of ice and frost glazed the road and the faces of buildings; he should have expected magic. Arastin took a few seconds to massage feeling back into his legs, thankful he'd escaped the full brunt of the wand's frigid blast. Feeling slowly returned. It was an icy tingling, but it at least meant the damage from the wand wasn't severe.

Sure of his knowledge of the streets and his ability to outrace Na'akiros, the professional contemplated his next move. When he'd been approached ten days earlier for the job, chasing an elf pirate captain and wizard down the streets of Crown wasn't what he'd expected, but he'd taken the contract, and if he was going to survive to retirement, he needed to get sharp. The reality of how soft he'd gotten - thanks to his success - cut like a razor; it fueled the anger that boiled just beneath the surface. Years of training focused the emotion into clarity and determination. The night was far from over.

The deal would continue; the rogue was certain. The timetable would be shortened, due in no small part to his spectacular botch at the *Broken Valor*. His only choice was to head back to the *Frozen Idol* and wait for another opportunity. It galled him, but the thought that the acolyte of the Grey God might get his prize also deeply disturbed Arastin.

He grimaced as he began to run. His legs ached, but the pain was bearable, and the lightning and pouring rain soon became a bigger concern than his sore legs. He wound his way towards Deep Harbor and the *Frozen Idol*.

The distance between the Arms Cresent and Harbor gave him time to think. The assassin had changed his ways since his younger days - he now only accepted contracts on people he felt deserved it. He'd encountered saints and demons in his centuries of life and work; it gave him an amazing breadth of experience in judging someone's character and continuously honed his sense of who "deserves it." Arastin had no problem acting as arbiter, jury, and executioner to the scum that preyed on Crown's population. Crown was home, and he believed his work was a service to the city and its people.

The rogue couldn't think of two people who deserved it more than Na'akiros and the wererat. He desperately wanted to foil the acolyte's machinations, and that's when the plan hit him. If he was indeed going to retire, he'd go out with style. It was so audacious that it just might work - if he was quick enough.

Lightning filled the sky; the blinding flash and the bone shaking thunder snapped the rogue from his reverie. The style and shape of the surrounding buildings were familiar - he'd arrived in Deep Harbor - but the storm crippled his ability to discern any detail beyond a few yards. He continued on memory alone towards the bay and the dock where the *Frozen Idol* lurked.

The scene that the lightning revealed was a study in chaos. Small boats, jetties, and all number of craft lay shattered on the docks and along the road. The wind whipped the sea into a tumultuous froth; waves surged and smashed like hammers upon the docks. Arastin gritted his teeth against the gale and stinging rain and pushed towards the *Idol*. The ship bucked and pitched with every shark-toothed wave. Its massive bulk rose and fell, but with every surge it somehow managed to stay right and not plow into the seawall or the docks.

The rogue again activated his ring and vanished from sight. He walked towards the pitching ship, wondering how he was going to board the wild vessel when he suddenly hit the barrier again. His stomach started to emulate the sea, a cold hand of fear gripped his spine, and waves of nauseous dread flowed through his blood. He knew enough about magic to comprehend the sensation wasn't real and something on the ship was its source, but that didn't stop the desire to turn tail and run screaming into the night.

Even through the stinging rain, the rogue felt tears streaming from his eyes. He asked his ancestors to grant him strength, and he raised his face to take in the whole of the *Frozen Idol*. A howl of defiance burst from his lungs, but the wind ripped it from his lips. Arastin wouldn't be denied; he charged the ship. The hysteria threatened to break him and drive him mad, but then the fear and the wind vanished. It was so spontaneous, he almost lost his balance and fell into the dark harbor waters.

The *Frozen Idol* no longer bucked in the bay before him; something far more horrible rested in the supernaturally calm water. Part ship and part skeleton of some bloated and twisted sea demon, the *Frozen Idol* was simply an arcane phantasm meant to hide the abominable beast that now brooded in Crown's waters. With the aid of the lightning Arastin made out the ship's true name: *Winter's Claw*. But he couldn't spare any moments to stand in awe of the blasphemous vessel - time was short.

The rogue found a moor line and climbed it to reach the deck. The magic that surrounded the *Claw* also tempered the storm's wrath. It was still raining and the wind blew, but it was a simple shower compared to the maelstrom that raged beyond the aura. Arastin was thankful for the small boon as he scouted the deck; it would have been sickening and nearly impossible if the ship was bucking like an unruly stallion.

Below decks, the rogue crept through the ample shadows created by guttering flames within grimy lanterns. Water dripped from the ceilings and ran down Arastin's back like icy claws. Every breath created a billow of condensation that revealed his location. He breathed shallowly and tried to hurry as much as he could. Luck was with him; he only had to dodge two crewmen on his way to the hold where he hoped, from the snippets of conversation he'd overheard, the relic would be.

The rest of the ship was cold, but the hold was freezing. Frost rimed every surface, and even the flames in the lanterns seemed sluggish as they danced and juddered from the occasional arctic gust of wind. Draped in a tarp and isolated, the artifact brooded in the center of the hold. The rogue took a few tentative steps closer. The air continued to drop in temperature, and black images and sinister feelings gnawed at his will. He shook his head and stepped back - he didn't need to see the relic that badly.

The top of the tarp stood a few heads taller than him, and it was at least three times as wide; he wasn't going to carry it out. Thinking on his feet, the professional took stock of the other cargo. Casks lined the hold's forward half, while lumber was stacked high throughout the aft. He removed his knife, ensured no one was in sight, and pierced the top of one of the casks. It came away glistening, and it reeked of whale-oil. The rogue smirked and began to work at piercing every cask.

Shouts and the stomp of feet told Arastin that Na'akiros had arrived. He couldn't discern what was being said through the decks of the ship, but from the apparent volume, the captain wasn't happy. Finished with his first task of sabotage, the rogue slid his knife back in its sheath and set off to see what other mayhem he could cause.

* * *

Arastin thumped down the third keg of alchemist's fire amongst the barrels of whale-oil. The oil would light well enough on its own; the alchemist's fire was just candied fruit on the cake. He'd found the substance in the ship's armory, which would put a small kingdom to shame. It was stocked full of enough nasty solutions, weapons, and devices to wreak months of havoc on the high seas. They may miss the kegs, but he doubted they would find them before he'd had his fun.

Shouts seeped through the ship's walls once more. They came in sharp bursts; the urgency was clear. Something unexpected was happening on deck. The rogue ran to the back of the hold and hid in the shadow of the lumber.

Suddenly the deck covers were thrown back, and Arastin could see all the way up to the storm black sky. Rain came in through the opening, but it turned to snow before it reached the hold's floor. And with the hold open to the top deck, he swore he heard swordplay.

The shuffle of feet brought the rogue's attention back to the hold. Four sailors came into sight and headed for the ominous relic.

One of the four stopped. "Hey, you'z smell something?" The assassin tensed, and his hand went to his sword.

"Yea, it's oil. We'll check it later. We got more important things to do! Get your hide over here!" one of the other three shouted. The first sailor that spoke nodded and joined the group. Rope and chain descended from above, and the four sailors reached up for it. They flipped back the corners of the tarp covering the relic and set about fastening the chain and hooks to the platform the relic sat on.

The four finished their task, and the sailor that'd admonished the first waived his hand at the others. "You three, stay down here and guard this. We'll be rid of her soon."

"What about the fight?" the first asked.

"We can handle the slit-necks, but you boys are here in case they get tricky. So be sharp, got it?" The others nodded, and the sailor stalked off.

Arastin bided his time. He sized up the three sailors and planned. More shouts from the top deck; the three sailors shouted back, and the platform slowly rose off the floor.

The sounds of battle grew, but the relic continued to climb higher inch by inch. Whoever was attacking the *Claw* wasn't strong enough to completely stop the exchange. The professional felt it was time to take advantage of the situation. He slid from behind the stack of timber and charged one of the three guards watching the relic's ascent. Arastin became visible as the sailor felt the knife bite into his neck. Only the final guard had enough time to put up a token resistance. Cognizant something was wrong, he saw his two companions' crumpled bodies and met the assassin's charge with his cutlass, but the sailor's skills weren't a challenge for the assassin.

The rogue leaped up to the relic platform, and with one hand, he whipped the tarp off the profane object. It took a second for Arastin to realize what he was seeing, but when he did, he recoiled and almost stumbled off the platform. The monstrosity looked like a giant ice sculpture of a heart, but the veins and blood vessels were different. Blue or ash gray, they were fleshy, glistening, and quivering as fluids pulsed within. Encased inside it all, beneath the blue tendrils of vein and shell of ice, an elf woman with bone white skin slept, her arms crossed over her chest. As achingly beautiful as she was, and as vile as her prison seemed, he still felt the cold and malignant taint well up from the fell woman.

Arastin shook his head and broke the dark fascination that entangled him. He used a minor spell and lit one of the expanding puddles of oil. The blue flame grew brighter as it danced along the tendril of liquid back towards the cluster of barrels. The rogue swung his blade at the chain and rope that held the platform. The assembly pitched, and its ascent stopped, but the whole thing didn't topple. Arastin saw the flame grow brighter. It blazed amongst the barrels now, and he heard them hiss and creak as they began to expand.

Above, he saw heads peer over the edge of the bay doors, and he recognized the wererat from the *Valor*. The rogue darted to the next closest rope, wrapped his arm around the line just over his head, and swung his sword at its base. He heard the wererat scream something unintelligible. His blade severed the taut rope with an audible, bass "twang," and the platform swung free. Arastin held on for his life as he was whipped one way and then back the other.

The relic toppled to the floor and landed with a crunch, but he didn't spare it a glance. Angry shouts were coming down from above, mixed with the rain, and he heard the distinct sound of chanting.

The rogue put his sword away and began to climb. He reached the top deck, and the mob of angry sailors and wererats wildly swung their weapons at him. Above, a spout of dark liquid at least as wide as he was tall had just appeared in the sky, and below, one the barrels ruptured with a crack. The mob dove for cover, and Arastin swung out of the way. A spray of high pressure, flaming oil soaked the hold, and the torrent of liquid fell past in the space he used to occupy, some of the liquid spraying him and the deck nearby. It was blood.

He heard something heavy careen by within the spout, but its true form was lost in the waterfall of blood. Suddenly, a gore-slicked anchor blew through the deck a few paces away; a yelp of surprise escaped his lips. Strangely, the anchor was familiar, but he had no idea how it had come through the deck - the barrels should have caused more damage if they'd gone up. However, the rogue had no desire to witness his handiwork from so close, and he put distance between him and the hold.

He surveyed the scene as he moved towards the stern. Wererats, sailors, and alônn swarmed the deck. Lightning repeatedly threw the battle into dazzling contrast, and it reminded Arastin that the storm still raged outside the barrier. He could explain the wererats: the acolyte he'd glimpsed earlier had brought more devout worshipers of the Grey God, and many of them wore the god's symbol openly. The presence of the alônn surprised him - certainly the debt his contact owed him didn't account for this - but he was thankful and waded into the fray to help.

The assassin slid through the battle towards the poop deck, where Na'akiros's place would be. His blade struck only when it had to; he didn't want to waste his energy. Arastin had a score to settle with the captain. Suddenly, the ship lurched, and the deck pitched in time with a staccato of explosions. He smiled. He was deeply glad the rain of blood hadn't quenched the fire.

"YOU!" The shout was audible even over the melee, thunder, and wind. The rogue spun and dodged to the right; he felt something split the air. Na'akiros loomed before him, fury etched on every pale feature. The captain held a cutlass that was stained with blood.

"We have a matter to settle," Arastin said.

"That we do. I have to add your finger bones to my collection!" Na'akiros snarled as he swung. The move was a feint, meant to bring the rogue within reach of the dagger the captain wielded in his other hand, but the rogue disappointed him and dodged back. The assassin released a dagger from his off hand, and it grazed Na'akiros's right side. The captain hissed.

"First blood's mine, Na'akiros!" Arastin taunted. "Death will be slow and painful. Just what traitorous scum like you and your kin deserve!"

"I will enjoy carving you up, bit by bit!" Na'akiros spat. The two circled each other once, and then they closed for the real contest. Both were accomplished swordsmen; the captain had strength and reach, but the assassin had speed and control. Na'akiros rained strike after strike down upon the rogue. Finally, he caught one of the furious blows wrong, and it sent an aching numbness shooting down his arm. Arastin grunted and backed off while the captain laughed. "If only your blade was as sharp as your tongue!"

"Come on, then, and you'll see just how sharp my sword is!"

Na'akiros pressed his advantage and closed the distance. The assassin's leg shot out, and his foot slammed into the captain's chest. His fist followed quickly behind, and he landed a left hook against Na'akiros's jaw. The elf staggered and nearly fell backwards. Arastin charged the half-prone captain, but the elf threw the dagger he'd been holding at the assassin's legs. The rogue launched himself into the air with his sword held high. Na'akiros brought his own sword up, but he was too slow.

Arastin's sword fell, and it cleaved through muscle, sinew, and bone; it severed Na'akiros's hand at the wrist. A primal roar of pain and anger escaped the captain as he reared up, while his body melted, twisted, and reshaped itself before the rogue's eyes. Suddenly, and just as surprising, the full fury of the storm hit the ship. The rain and wind battered Arastin, while the frenetic motion of the deck threatened to topple him, but he remained mesmerized by the change that possessed his adversary.

Na'akiros grew larger and bulkier. Bone white scales replaced skin, his now lone hand grew talons, and his face elongated into a draconic muzzle. Two large bat-like wings erupted from his back. Arastin gazed upon the white half-dragon and stood in shock at how deeply an elf could betray his own kind, while Na'akiros took a deep breath, stepped in the rogue's direction, and opened his fanged maw to exhale.

Arastin felt the force of the blast lift him from the deck. The air crystallized and turned white around him. A thousand frozen needles pierced his body, and the pain tripped some primal instinct in his brain - he blacked out. Arastin never even felt it when he hit the water and quickly slipped beneath the surface.

FIEND FIGHTER

Davis Riddle

FIEND FIGHTER

The crowd, its roar muffled by the thick wooden door, the rumble of their feet through the dark passageways, the sickly-sweet smell in the air - they all told a story. Sometimes, the story was one of excitement and thrill, as the handlers led the creature into the arena. Something great would happen, there would be sport. Money would be won and lost. But sometimes, well, sometimes the story was of another sort. And tonight, the story was...Saluthur.

"It is in the arena..." came a low, gravelly voice from behind, followed by the sounds of braces being buckled.

"Aye, it is, and on his wings, I hear a slow night."

Farulazar sighed, stood, and slapped his thick fingered hands together, the sound dying almost as it sprang to life, consumed by the dank, moss-covered walls. He stretched his left hand out expectantly, and into it slid a well-worn gladius, while his right slid into the straps of a wooden shield, its leather re-stretched more times than even he could count. He stamped his iron-shod boots, which alone among all of his gear were new.

With one last stretch, he nodded to his assistant, Korm, a dwarf who, like him, lived on the fringe of acceptance among their people. Their chosen profession, nay, trade, was not something that dwarves considered noble. Indeed, the entire concept they found contemptible. They were not alone, of course; as far as Farulazar knew, the sport was viewed with disdain by all the races of Crown. There had been a time when their scorn bothered him, but that was many years in a past that recorded every rotten, stinking, worthless year on his weathered brow. It had once been a challenge, but now it was...something else.

Farulazar pushed open the heavy wooden door and stalked down the darkened tunnel. The sounds came in waves down the stone corridor, at times muffled, at times clear. Bets were being made, odds determined, money being handled. There was a time when it was all exciting, when the sounds, the smells, the raw energy of the sport made him feel alive. Now, it was just noise, something that had to be endured every Travelday night.

This night would be no better - worse actually, because the take would be small. To some, it was oh so important, for it was Long Night, the 8th day of Layfanil, the first month of winter. Coincidentally, this year it fell on Travelday. Next year, it would fall on the ominous Darkday. To Farulazar, it was really just another day, but to others it was a holiday, celebrating the beginning of the Demon Scourge so many years ago. A great day to them, but just another day, just another fight, and once a year, just another fiend for the dwarf. Perhaps a novice would be in the crowd, one with a large bag of gold that needed lightening.

Of course, a small take would annoy Alfem, his associate, the halfling who ran the wagers. Some small semblance of a grin spread on the grizzled dwarf's leathery face as he imagined the look on the rat of a halfling's face as Saluthur was led into the arena by the summoners. Those greasy whiskers would probably drop to his knees, along with any hopes of wealth beyond count. Alfem was a poor replacement for his father, Falem, a worthy halfling, as halflings went. Where his father had been shrewd, skilled, and worked hard to put up good sport, Alfem was dumb, incompetent, and lazy.

But, it wasn't as if Farulazar was the pillar of dwarvish industriousness. After one-hundred and sixty years of fighting in the pits, the flame had burned down to a dull smolder. There was no glory, no real fame, and no honor among his folk. All that was left was to kill fiends and then spend his winnings at the tavern. And tonight, the fiend would be easy and the money small. So be it. He could use the sleep.

The day had seen several demons summoned into the arena, mostly minor minions of the demonic realm. The lesser fighters were called in early, and they did their work in the daylight hours, though not all could claim a victory. Berwold, a worthy fighter and a veteran of the pits, fought an imp earlier that day. Rumor had it the creature had eviscerated him, and he died with his entrails filling his lap. Alfem must have made money on that one, as he had been chipper when he last spoke to the dwarf. It was a shame that the halfling had not been in the pits instead; Berwold was good for a pint. But, his lot had cast badly. It happened and now, he was part of a history not likely to be written.

Day passed, and evening ruled the city of Crown. The most anticipated battle had come, the one that most waited all year to see. Many held their bets for this match, but many more came only to watch. To them, this once-a-year game was too irresistible to avoid, even at the peril of their own high standing in Crown. They came not to bet, but to watch a true celebrity do what he did so well. They came to watch Farulazar, Fiend Fighter.

The doors opened, the crowd stood, and he stepped into the arena. Before him cringed poor Saluthur, that pitiful soul who knew so well what was soon to happen. A vengeful grin spread across the dwarf's face as the doors closed behind him and the crowd cheered. Spreading his arms wide, as if to embrace the fiend, Farulazar roared to the assembled mass, presenting himself for their approval. The crowd roared back to him and chanted his name while stamping their feet. Satisfying their love of celebrity, he then turned to his foe, beating his gladius against his shield. Saluthur spread his dark wings and tried to look menacing, his cat-like eyes blazing, his sharp teeth bared. Some in the crowd were even fooled as those low-priced, standing-room only portions of the stands became silent. Their collective intake of breath came as a soft hiss as they grasped the rails before them and gazed in fearful apprehension. Would their hero finally fall before this demonic creature? Would this be the end?

The fight began. Farulazar stepped forward and raised his *demon's bane*. For his part, Saluthur shrieked, flexing his intimidating talons. The two combatants then fell upon each other. It was quickly over. He had made it as convincing as possible to those who did not know better. Those who did had already folded their bets and reclined for that which they knew was coming. Many cheered when Saluthur was banished once again to the realm of agony, while others shrugged. To Farulazar, the were-rats dragging the demon's corpse out of the arena was only a sign that one more night was now over. Turning from the scene, he stalked from the arena and back down the darkened tunnel, passing his gear to Korm as he walked. By the time he reached his chambers, he was nearly undressed and ready for a drink.

"You could have made that better," said a tinny, squeaky voice from behind.

Farulazar nodded and grunted as he removed his braces, dropping them to the floor. "Not enough profit tonight, eh?" he asked without looking up.

"It will cost you like it cost me," replied Alfem, with a tone of exasperation.

"It is but gold," replied the dwarf evenly, as he wiped the dark blood from his sword. "What good does it buy?"

"It buys many good things," retorted the halfling, curling a whisker in his nimble fingers. "But that is of no consequence. You could have performed better and brought up the bidding. It was your job."

"Saluthur died like he has in the past," replied Farulazar. "I have sent him to the dark realm more than twenty times. This one was better than most. You should thank me for not killing him with my eyes closed, again."

"Twenty three times," complained Alfem. "And, you have done better."

"Then when you speak next with your dark-robed friends, be certain they conjure up a better fiend," growled the dwarf. "Azabel, Urika, or Mlethic have always been good for a show. You skimped with your bribes, and it has cost you. Blame yourself for your incompetence."

Finished disrobing and not at all interested in further conversation, Farulazar snatched the gear that Korm had left behind and turned towards the door that led into the darkened streets above. "I will expect my cut in the morning and on time," he grumbled, before stepping through the door and disappearing up the stairs.

Alfem glared at the door as it closed. With the passing of each year, his patience with his brooding partner waned ever more. Yet, the dwarf was a useful tool that not only increased his own personal wealth but served his far greater – and darker – calling. Perhaps another gladiator would gain fame, especially one of the humans who were so brash, and so be worth the wagers passed. Perhaps then dwarf-blood could be added to the other fallen. With that, he could end this inconvenient but necessary partnership.

The halfling pushed aside his indulgent thoughts for the time being. Other business waited that required another guise. He closed his eyes and held his hands together as if to pray. His features became waxen, his eyes moving further apart, his face elongating slightly, and his pale skin darkened to a dull gray as fine hairs grew out. His rounded teeth elongated and sharpened, becoming thinner and more yellowed, while his brown, well-groomed hair became mousy and unruly. His form had evolved into that of a were-rat, a common denizen of Crown and another visage he found convenient. In but a moment, Alfem became Szeethe, or, at least, one of two visions of Szeethe. The other form he reserved for truly dark occasions.

When ready, he turned to a second, smaller door, and passed through, walking down a dark corridor that carried with it the sweet stench of new blood. As he walked, he mentally composed the value of the evening's profit. While the gold's take was less than he would have preferred, the real take was far more valuable. It served his purpose to show his irritation to the dwarf, but in truth, he was very pleased. An evil smile spread across his face as he neared the hanging room. It was time to see how they were draining poor Saluthur.

* * *

Another year passed as did the one before, except the gold from the last Long Night fight had not lasted all that long. Sure, the pits paid as they always had, which bought his bread and butter and continued his fame, but there was not the comfortable security provided by the bags of gold normally earned once a year. This year he had actually depended on the weekly fights for his living, the demon gold being spent far too soon.

Yet the pits paid all the same, and another thirty-two warriors had fallen beneath his blade. Of those, more than half died in the heat of battle, when the battle-lust, dim as it seemed these days, arose within him. The rest died at the pleasure of the crowd, their greed for blood shown with the red disc, held up when a defeated warrior asked for quarter; red for the blood that would flow. At uncommon times, the crowd held the white disc aloft, which guaranteed survival to the disgraced fighter lying on the ground, hand held up for mercy. Only eighteen fighters were blessed by white over the last year, making it bloodier than normal.

Frankly, though, Farulazar cared as much this year as the last, which was not much. They knew the risks but had lusted for the wealth and fame his defeat would bring. They chose to step in and face his steel. There was tragedy when their corpses were dragged out by the were-rats who took care of the bodies when their owners no longer needed them. That they fought him at all, or that much gold passed hands after his fights, was beyond his concern. They kept coming in the vain hope for wealth, fame, and glory.

Farulazar never lost. What the other gladiators did not know, and what gave him an edge over many, was that Farulazar would never beg quarter. His dwarvish blood demanded no less of him, which was normally motivation enough for one of his kind. Yet, he also knew that great wagers were placed on his head. Through the years, he had made many people very wealthy, especially those who preyed on the ignorant, but that wealth bought no loyalty. Should he falter in the ring, powerful citizens of Crown would lose money. They would not forgive him their loss, and so, they would exact their price in blood, his blood, which would flow down the pit holes, draining his life into whatever cauldrons awaited below.

And so, he would fight until death claimed him. Though he did not have a death wish, he knew it would come when it came, and likely in the pits. Nothing existed in Crown to make him fear his own mortality. Farulazar made no plans for retirement; had no great future prepared for after the games when he could spend his winnings in relaxation. He only had the next pint at the tavern, and it did not drive him to any more noble desires.

The dwarf enjoyed his ale, as all dwarves did, but he never drank to excess. He always kept his senses keen enough to fend off those too cowardly to face him in the arena. A few had made that mistake, including one semi-professional who should have gotten more practice. They were no real danger. In truth he could have been drunker than a sailor at the beginning of a month's holiday and defeated them all the same. Though jaded from a lifetime's experience in so worthless a world, Farulazar was still too proud to be taken by an assassin.

He looked out one of the Valor's tavern windows, at the streets crowded by citizens of Crown as well as those visitors who came from other parts for the coming games and festivals. Few of these would come to watch him. They were here for the more noble celebrations and feasts. Of course, why anyone would really wish to celebrate the beginning of those bad days when demons rose up and the Scourge began was beyond his reckoning and care. To each his own, he had long decided, and left their reasons alone.

He watched as a few out-of-towner's bought fruit from a seller's cart on the street. The merchants loved this time of year, as much as some of the more enlightening feasts and festivals. Most of the inns were full, and most of the lesser dealers of their wares, like this grocer who peddled his second-quality fruits from his oh-too-pitiful wagon, were doing a brisk business. Though by the looks of the gathering clouds, business for those on the street would likely taper off soon. It seemed they had picked a bad year to come to town.

The dwarf lifted his tankard to his lips, drained it, left a few silver coins on the well-worn wood, and stalked from the tavern. He had a fight tomorrow, a low-end affair that would bring some coin, and he needed to be well rested. As he made his way down the street to his lodgings, he considered the coming fight. Cador, the halfling knife-twister who fancied himself a gladiator, had drawn a bad card, his card, and would be an easy game. Farulazar hoped the crowd would be kind and let Cador live. The small fellow was no real match for him, and the dwarf did not plan on gutting him unless he had to. The trouble was that halflings could be unpredictable, and this one could have greater designs than his ability would allow; if so, more's the pity, but not for Farulazar.

"I expect a clean kill tomorrow," remarked a voice he regarded with mild contempt.

Without turning, he replied, "No challenge, he'll be quick."

Alfem stepped out from a shadowy side-street and slid up next to his partner, his eyes narrowed, his expression neutral. "Make it look good; we've not done well lately."

"It'll be as good as it deserves," growled the dwarf. "There's no money tomorrow, anyway. The real coin will trade next week."

"All coin is real," snorted the tinny voice, aggravation settling into its well-worn path.

"The rain'll keep the crowds away, any crowds looking for poor sport..."

"I don't pay you for poor sport," interrupted the Halfling. "I pay you to make a happy crowd."

"...and none of the real wagers come this week," continued Farulazar, as if speaking to himself, appraising the coming fight. "They never do, not the week before the Long Night."

Alfem scowled and became silent as he kept up with his brooding pawn. He could not counter the argument, as it was common wisdom that fights held the week before the demon fights were never good...for sport, that is. For his own goals, the fights were sometimes the best, as the rank amateurs who drew those billings managed to carve each other up quite nicely. A vain attempt at gaining fame and notoriety, perhaps, but as long as the blood flowed; Alfem cared little for their reasons.

That the great Farulazar, Fiend Fighter, was even fighting was due solely to the halfling's own wrangling. To an accomplished fighter, such a fight was too much a risk with no good benefit. A bad cut could put him out of the pits the next week, where the real money and real fame were to be found. Yet through some cunning maneuvering, Alfem had all but forced the dwarf into the game.

Farulazar was too important to risk being taken this week, which was why Cador's card had been selected, the price being reasonable so soon to the Long Night fights. Nobody believed that the halfling would be anywhere akin to a match, and even if the dwarf tried hard to make it look convincing, few would be convinced. But Alfem's master demanded the quota be filled before the next week, and the morgues had failed to provide much lately. While Cador offered little blood, he was an easy harvest, which was the only real purpose of the fights.

"Be sure you rest well," said Alfem, setting aside his mental calculations and returning his thoughts to his most useful tool.

"I always sleep well," grunted the dwarf. He stopped at a heavy oaken door and fished a great iron key from his pocket, sliding it into an equally heavy lock.

"We need this," said Alfem, as he reached out and grasped the dwarf's arm. Farulazar turned his head, an expression of fatigued annoyance on his face, his eyes moving slowly from his arm to the halfling's eyes. Alfem withdrew his hand and the dwarf continued turning the key.

"Have you no pride left?" Alfem demanded, his tone strange, almost pleading.

Farulazar pocketed the key and regarded his companion. "I am a dwarf who fights in the pits for the pleasure and wealth of other men," he said before turning the bolt and stepping into his apartment.

The door closed and Alfem stood there, regarding the weather-stained wood. Shaking his head, he turned and passed down the street, heading for the darker quarters of Crown. He had many visits to make that evening, beginning with an associate he did business with at the wharves, followed by the rumor that the blood plague had come to town and an entire boat-load of visitors had been quarantined at the docks. Fifty-six people were rumored to be hemorrhaging, which would make a fine haul, if he arrived in time.

But, these next visits were not for Alfem, who would never have business in Deep Harbor. He turned down a deserted alleyway and stepped onto a darkened stoop. In but a moment, he stepped back out, his halfling visage replaced by the were-rat form that was more useful for such dark occasions. He was Szeethe once more.

Passing down the shadowy lower streets, the creature soon found himself in the Deep Harbor district, where ships of every kind docked and unloaded their cargoes of goods and people. He made his way along innumerable warehouses, cheap, dirty inns, smelly fish markets and taverns, shoulder-to-shoulder with every kind of person to be found entering or leaving Crown. Among them were sailors, noblemen with their expensive sedans, common laborers encumbered by every kind of load, and wide-eyed newcomers to the city, sometimes followed by those of the shadowy world who would liberate them of their goods. He had no use for them, save for what they could offer him and his master, and at the present, he already had the promise of a good supply for the day.

Walking through the district, he turned and stepped into the darkened tavern called *The Sailor's Refuge*, passing a huge, rusted anchor at its door. Inside, he looked about the room lit by numerous whale-oil lamps, their sooty-smoke forming a thick cloud near the stained ceiling. In a moment, he found his target, a fiery tiefling sitting at a booth, her eyes regarding him with a mixture of suspicion and interest. Szeethe took a seat opposite of her and folded his hands, his expression neutral.

"What did he say?" he asked.

El'laa's eyes flicked about the room nervously for a moment, as if looking for someone else. She was a wary sort already, most tieflings were. "You were not followed?"

Szeethe smiled, "I am followed only when I wish to be followed." His expression then changed, a mixture of contempt and arrogance that most found amusing while he wore his current were-rat mask. "But, I am very busy and must have your answer now."

The tiefling ran her hand through her short, curly auburn hair and leaned back. "He says he is interested."

"I do not need interested," spat the rat. "I must have a confirmation."

"He is an elf and an assassin. That is the best you'll get," replied El'laa.

She was a fairly recent member of the cult, though she only occasionally worked directly for Szeethe. Not yet knowing his true nature, El'laa had scant respect for the little rat, a feeling shared by most in Crown for one of his kind. Had she known the truth, she would likely have either refused any kind of contact with him or would have treated him with much more caution than she did. In any case, Szeethe did not care. Her contempt helped him keep his cover in the above world, where the workings of his master were not well known. Like Farulazar, she was a useful tool and little more. When he no longer needed her, he would add her life's blood to the others. The were-rat reached into his shirt and withdrew a pouch of silver and written instructions detailing the target and timing.

She slipped the payment into her green waist coat and held up the parchment, "You've given me this already."

Szeethe nodded, "In case you have forgotten."

El'laa's green eyes flashed as her face clouded. "I am no amateur," she snapped. "I still remember the instructions."

"This is too important a job," replied the rat. "I cannot take chances."

The tiefling leaned back. "The target is Na'akiros, the captain of a ship that is coming into port within the week or so. He is a member of the Iceskull League and will be holding a meeting at the *Broken Valor* in the Arms Crescent on Darkday. just before the Fiend Fighter enters the pits."

El'laa leaned forward, her eyes locked with the rat's. "And you want the elf to kill Na'akiros any time between the day he lands and the Long Night."

"Yes, I do," answered Szeethe. "I want him to die. He must die."

"Why?" asked the tiefling.

"My reasons are my own," replied the rat. "And you have been paid your fee."

"I have," she replied, patting her vest while she stood. "And the deal will be made."

Szeethe stood with her. "I must have his name."

El'laa turned towards the door and, just before she disappeared through it, replied over her shoulder, "Arastin."

The name mattered little to him, just something to put back in his memory for some future day when he no longer had the tiefling's service, when her blood had joined the others. He walked to the door and passed through, the arrangements having been made to kill the captain. He held no great animosity towards Na'akiros, who was just another tool, although an important tool. His ship was bringing into Crown a most precious cargo - an ancient, cursed relic of a power only a servant of the Grey God could truly appreciate.

For many years, he had searched for the relic at the bidding of his master, passing through many lands and enduring long suffering paths. He finally found it in the possession of the Iceskull League; though how they came by it, he could not understand. It seemed so contrary to their very nature. They regarded it as something other than it was and did not understand its power. Perhaps that was why they agreed to sell it to him. While they had charged him dearly for it, the price was nowhere near what he would have paid. No price would have been too great. For once he had the relic, money would be utterly worthless.

Killing Na'akiros for delivering the relic was not as overtly evil as it seemed. Szeethe neither loved nor hated the Iceskull, nor their servants. He merely needed a diversion, something to distract the ship's crew, the Crown Watch, or anyone else who might prevent him from achieving his goals. The ceremony must take place the evening of the Long Night celebration, and he would allow nothing to get in his way. Killing the captain might seem unnecessary or even capricious, but Szeethe was taking no chances. Besides, once the relic was in use, most would probably envy poor Na'akiros's fortune.

A wicked grin spread across his rodent features as he considered the mayhem to be unleashed. But, that was still days away, and he had other business at hand. He still had to find the boat full of plague victims. Leaving the tavern, he looked about the harbors, not certain where to find the sloop and its stricken passengers. His informant, a real halfling, did not know where the boat would be found and had not even been certain about the rumor. As he walked, Szeethe swore that the sniveling halfling informant would pay miserably if this journey proved a waste of time.

As the day waned and light fled, both from the gathering storm and the dying sun, he finally noticed a small group of soldiers standing guard near a dilapidated wharf. He immediately recognized the Crown Watch, the elite guardians of the city in their blue tabards wearing their arrogant expressions. The pier was too ramshackle to be the berth of a noble ship, and guards such as these did not waste their time even on valuable cargo. Deciding that was his destination, the creature made his way towards the guards.

As he approached, the captain looked down at him and sneered, "Be off, ratling. We've no scraps for you."

Szeethe nodded in deference to the guard, his head bowed, "If you will forgive, I am not here to beg; I am here to look in on the stricken on yonder boat."

The guard looked disgusted, and glanced back at the sloop, "You're for them, eh?"

"Yes, I am," replied Szeethe. "If you please."

"They're not carrion yet," growled the guard. "Come back later when your services are needed."

"Oh, I know they are not, but I came only to arrange their passage when the time came, so their fever isn't shared with the good folk of Crown. My kindred will need to be careful to protect them and will have to bring...supplies."

The guard frowned and shook his head, "You've no respect for the dying," but then he followed up quickly with a hand gesture, waving him through.

Szeethe walked quickly down the pier, not at all wondering why the Crown Watch, of all the guards and enforcers of Crown, would be wasted on such a menial task as guarding plague victims or why they were even in this district at all. They were not his concern. When he reached the boat, he found not only the initial fifty-six reported when the boat reached the docks, but the entire boatload was disease-ridden - enough that the fight he arranged for Farulazar and Cador was no longer as needed as it had been. Of course, Cador would still die; his blood would still run for the Grey God's glory. Szeethe was not wasteful.

He stepped back from the stricken boat and returned down the pier, bowing respectfully to the angry guards with nothing to do, as none of the other Crown folk would come near. Walking for another hundred yards or so, he stopped at an empty berth that he hoped would soon be occupied by Na'akiros's ship, but in truth it could be any number of docks in the district. The ship had not arrived, and though it was the first possible day in which it could arrive, and though his other contacts had not informed him of its arrival, he was nonetheless disappointed. Szeethe was anxious for the cargo it carried, which was of far greater value to his master than the dying passengers on the sloop across the harbor. Plans long in the making required the precious relic in its hold, and the night on which all things must occur quickly approached. It could not be late, but there was still time.

With no further business at the wharves, Szeethe quickly turned from the water and passed back into the city. He stepped down a nondescript alleyway and in a moment, he emerged as Alfem once more, which was his normal visage in the city. He then returned to the *Broken Valor* where he did most of his business. Inside, he made his way to a small private door and stepped inside a room he rented, an office of sorts where he could be alone. He locked the door by sliding a heavy iron bolt from one side to the other.

Secure from unwanted visitors, he turned and faced the room. At the far side was a wall, behind which lay a passage that wound through the dark under-realms of Crown. Down that winding stair lay other business that was every bit as dark as that above ground.

That business was not for Alfem, but neither was it for the were-rat form he took down at the wharves. The form that was now required was far darker, far more evil, than would be normally tolerated in the higher regions of Crown. The coming meeting required the real Szeethe to emerge.

The creature took a deep breath, chose his form, and allowed his amorphous body to change. His eyes rolled back, his were-rat form became soft and then started to change. The hair absorbed into the skin, the muscles became like knotted cords. His pointed nails became talon-like claws, and his needle-like teeth lengthened until their tips jutted from his lips, while his dark skin took on a pale, corpse-like pallor. He breathed in, his widened rat-like nostrils taking in the morbidly sweet smell, savoring it.

Looking like a nightmare vision of an undead were-rat, Szeethe, the real Szeethe, raised himself to full height, fully half again his former size. His demon-spawned eyes opened, their cat-like pupils opening wide in the darkness of the small room. He was a creature of darkness, part fiend and part were-rat, mixed with just the right measure of hate formed in the cursed cauldrons in the lost years. A forgotten remnant of the demon scourge, he was neither one of the simpleton were-rats, who were useful slaves, nor a halfling as his dwarvish fool knew him. Possessing a power few could understand, he was the high priest who led the cult that worshiped the wicked and chaotic Grey God. They were a shadowy coven of believers of the dark path. For years, they had served their vile master and had done his bidding in so many heinous ways. And soon, very soon, they would claim a great victory in his name.

The changed creature crossed the room and opened the secret door, looking down the dark passage. He listened for a moment, making certain it was empty. He returned to the main entrance and slid the bolt open before retreating quickly into the passage, closing the hidden portal behind him. Leaving the main door unlocked allowed anyone to enter his office, of course, which was his purpose. The hidden passage could not be discovered, and if those looking for Alfem found his office empty, they would look for him elsewhere. None in *The Broken Valor* would even suspect his real nature. But as the secret door closed, he did not notice the small fragment of skin and hair, remnants of his transformation, that fell from his foot and remained on the plain stone floor of his office.

Making his way down the long passage, following it as it wound into what seemed the very bowels of the world; the dark creature reached a small landing before a great door. Szeethe glanced one more time up the stairway to be certain he had not been followed. Satisfied in his secrecy, he turned to the heavy bronze door and grasped the pull with his clawed fingers. As he pulled it open, he was bathed in the red, sanguine light of the chamber where his minions awaited.

As he stepped through the door, a figure silently slipped from one side to bar his way. The demon rat regarded him for a moment. It was a saruulan, one of those half-demon, half-human creatures despised by so many in Crown. His name was Baetor, an he was a warrior trained in the dark passages of the underground. Though he might be guarding this passage for the moment, awaiting Szeethe's arrival, he was no simple guard. Normally, he spent his time protecting the seething cauldron in the center of the temple, its virtual heart, which he would defend it with his life. Only to answer the Cult's higher calls, or when the high priest came, did he leave that most abhorrent place.

He was one among a very small group of cultists whom Szeethe trusted, partially for being kindred of sorts, but more importantly for the role he would play very soon. The high priest trusted none of the were-rats - they were simpletons, mindless tools to carry out his master's plans - and few of the humans, who were the most numerous cultists. There was even a single elf, a twisted, half-insane conjurer named Xigx, counted among the ranks of the followers of the Grey God. He was most certainly not trusted, but for other reasons that only Szeethe knew. As a general rule, it was something not shared among any of the devoted minions, though like Baetor, the strange creature would play a very important part soon.

Baetor's face showed recognition, and he bowed to the high priest. The saruulan then stepped aside, allowing him to pass, before reaching out and closing the secret door. Szeethe heard the bolt slide closed, denying access from the dark passage. Then, the warrior took his position once more in defense of the Cult, the closest thing to a champion they could ever know. Now deep below Crown's streets, the demon rat stepped among his minions and began the night's work.

* * *

The following day had come and gone, and Farulazar found himself, as he always did these fight nights, sitting in *The Broken Valor*, the tavern that connected to, nay, was an integral part of the fighting pits. The pits, really one giant arena with a multitude of preparation rooms connected, were at the base of a great stone tower. As in many buildings in Crown, this tower was the remnant of a much older construction, a fortress built in the early days of the city, at one time an integral part of the defense. But the city grew, its outer wall became merely an interior division, and a new wall was built, which itself became redundant when the current structure was built. What had once been critical to the protection of the Queen had lost its value. But nothing went to waste, and the tower served a new purpose.

Inside the massively-thick stone walls, the main floors of the tower had been removed, replaced by a series of ringed platforms open at the center, where crowds could gather and watch the fight below. The most expensive rings were naturally lower and thus nearer to the pits, with each higher ring being less and less valuable. The very highest ring, where people could barely discern the events below, was reserved for the most common of people.

Light came primarily from a giant chandelier made from the bones of a mammoth balor, one of the most terrible demons that rose up during the Scourge so many years before. The grisly thing, hanging as if in downward flight, stretched out its bony claws as if it were a great raptor after its prey. Perched atop the hooked barbs that at one time jutted out from its head and scaly back were seemingly hundreds of heavy wax candles, their solid drippings running down the dry bones like pale blood frozen in time. The creature's eye sockets were filled with dark red glass that refracted the flickering lights of the candles. Its menacing, snarling jaws were clenched about a heavy chain from which hung a single large oil lamp. Not a few patrons had stepped into the tower only to be driven away in terror of the ornament, unwilling to tempt the demons below with revenge upon any who benefited from its gruesome light.

As it hung in the center of the tower, those spectators in the highest rings were forced to view the fights through its grisly lattice, barely able to discern the fights in the dim light below.

The Broken Valor, as it was known by the locals and often shortened simply to *The Valor*, was at the lowest ring and off to the side so as not to interfere with the sport and to give patrons a place to escape from the action or make their wagers and deals between fights. The name itself was an evolution of sorts. The single, faded, weather-worn sign above its outside door had but one word etched into its hoary surface: "vALOR". The sign originally spelled "Balor," after the great demons, but it had long ago been damaged; the top left corner had broken away, taking the top of the "B" with it.

New patrons who came to the tavern mispronounced it, calling it *Valor* instead of its rightful name. It became a joke to the locals, who cynically referred to it first as *Broken Balor*, then *Broken Valor*. The last name stuck, and even though no new sign was ever erected reflecting the unofficial change, everyone who came knew it by its new name. So many now believed that the name referred to the losers in battle, or perhaps to any who fought in the pits, that its origins were known to only a few. To Farulazar, the name was just a name, and the tavern just a tavern. Had he not fought here, he would likely never visit.

Though a solitary creature, he often came up to the tables where drinks were served and deals made, just to pass the time before fights. If nothing else, the smell was better up here. After all these years, the dwarf was still not acclimated to the putrid, semi-sweet smell of rot and decay, a permanent feature of the pits and the side chambers where the dead were taken and prepared by the were-rats. Half an hour still remained before he needed to descend the steps into his room and gear up for the fight, which was still more than an hour away; not enough time to go somewhere else, but too much time to sit in his chambers.

The tavern itself was rather unremarkable. It lacked the dark, smoky atmosphere of his more comfortable haunts. The smoke-stained ceilings were higher than in most such places, giving the place a somewhat more wholesome air, while the floors were made of heavy wooden planks underneath of which were several anterooms to the pits. Patrons sat around simple tables whose surfaces were stained with over-turned drink, scared from decades of abuse. Though somewhat cleaner than in most such places, no one would be so bold as to eat from their surfaces. It was generally as dark as the tower, though the lead-framed windows, covered with thick, oily grime, peered though much thinner walls. Tall buildings about the Valor cast permanent shadows onto the building and its windows, which in any case were as dark as the night sky outside.

However, none of this interested the dwarf as he sat at an oaken table, hands folded, his face wearing an almost bored expression. Across from him sat Alfem, a look of anxiety usually reserved for the beginning of a bad night's count, smeared across his features. Farulazar knew the halfling's concern for his own well-being was limited to the amount of gold that might be lost should he fall. So, whatever it was that plagued the little rat-fink, it must have something to do with the coming fight. The trouble was, Cador was of little concern and would be an easy win. The dwarf regarded his companion under heavy brows, his elbows on the table, hands folded against his chin. Whatever it was, the rat-fink would tell soon enough.

"Cador is not fighting tonight," said Alfem in tinny exasperation.

"One is as good as the other," replied Farulazar. "Who will it be?"

The halfling breathed in deeply and then let the air escape his lips in a huff. "Visilik."

Farulazar raised his eyebrows and leaned back. Visilik was a saruulan who had fought only twice in the pits and had done his work neatly and quickly. Two months earlier, he had killed one of the better-known gladiators, a dwarf named Berrek, who also was an exile from Dwarfhome. Farulazar had fought Berrek one time, and that was years earlier. The fight had been tough and though Farulazar was victorious, he carried a brown scar on his forehead as a reminder that the pits were never forgiving.

"Your bribes don't carry so much weight these days," observed the dwarf.

"Mine are just fine," retorted the halfling. "The word is that Cador paid Visilik handsomely to be his second and then managed to break his own leg this morning."

Farulazar smiled. "Some of your folk are smarter than I would have assumed."

Alfem frowned and took a sip of a dark liquid from his mug. "I had not planned this."

"Your greed has gotten you into trouble," said the dwarf. "And now coin you thought you could count may not be so easy to grasp, eh?"

"I would rather you not died."

"I will not," said Farulazar. "But I could be spoiled for your big week."

"Don't do that!" squeaked Alfem. "We couldn't afford that!"

The dwarf chuckled. "Should have thought of that before you signed me up for a low match."

He stood, regarding his companion. "But don't fear, my small friend. I will be in good form for the demons next week."

He then turned from the tables and walked to the stairs leading to his dressing chamber. Still too soon for dressing, he decided he preferred the stench below to the company above. It might smell bad, but it was a respite, no matter how brief. Korm would be there already. The other dwarf was seldom good for a long talk, but Farulazar was in no mood for conversation. As he walked, he noticed the halfling looking not at him, but towards the corner.

At that instant, an assassin stepped from behind a column and deftly flung a dagger towards the Fiend Fighter's head. The dwarf immediately spun and raised his arm, allowing the blade to sink into the leather, the tip driving into his thick skin an inch or so. Ignoring the pain, he leaped towards the attacker, ramming his balled fist into the person's neck while jamming his knee into the other's soft gut. Gasping, the stranger staggered back, his eyes wide, his skin pale. Realizing his mortal mistake, the assassin turned to bolt from the room.

Before the man took two steps, though, Farulazar drew the blade from his arm, the tip stained with his blood. In one fluid motion, he raised his arm, wrist stiffened, and flung the dagger back towards the attacker. The blade turned a single time in the air before burying deep into the base of the man's skull. He collapsed like a puppet whose strings had been cut, just falling into a pile of himself. Scowling, the dwarf stepped up to the man's corpse and spat.

At that moment, perhaps a bit too quickly, Alfem stood. "The Fiend Fighter is wounded!" he screamed. "He cannot fight tonight!"

And so he would not. Farulazar regarded the sniveling rat-fink of a halfling. No doubt the little creature could not risk his fighting the saruulan that night, and so he perpetrated this absurd assault to wound him just enough to put off the week. That the assassin was killed, a certainty on which Alfem could rely, prevented any focused investigation. The dwarf felt the beginning embers of a burning rage he had not felt in more years than he could count. Not hot enough to act, not yet, it nonetheless stirred something inside him. He never had liked Alfem, but he had also never garnered enough energy to quite hate him. That was beginning to change.

He made eye contact with the halfling, who quickly turned his gaze. At that moment, Visilik stepped in front of him. "I had hoped to kill you tonight," he said menacingly.

Farulazar nodded, recognizing the tone, something all saruulans exuded. "You would have failed."

"Perhaps," said the creature, "But we will not learn who is the better tonight. Your friend has seen to that."

Visilik did not refer to the nameless assassin who lay on the floor, already being measured by the were-rats who were opening a canvas bag for his body. "But worry not; I know you were not involved."

The dwarf said nothing, only nodded to his potential adversary.

"I know their kind," continued the saruulan, his head cocked towards Alfem. "He wanted to save you for the fights next week when the wagers are good."

Farulazar grunted.

Visilik smiled wryly. "I will at least have someone on whom to place my wagers. I feared there would be no worthy replacements for you."

With that, the dwarf met the eyes of the taller creature. "You speak boldly," he said. "And since neither of us will be fighting this eve, I shall buy you a drink."

He turned and looked one more time at Alfem, who was keeping himself busy with a ledger, unwilling to return the stare. He shook his head and joined the saruulan at a table. Farulazar rarely bought a drink for another and never for one of the cursed saruulans, but he would tonight. At that moment, he had more in common with Visilik, who had planned to kill him that very night, than with any other creature in *The Broken Valor*. Outside, the clouds darkened even more.

Several days later, Farulazar stepped from his living chambers and onto the street and into the rain. For days, the weather had progressively worsened, until now the city was blanketed in a steady, though not quite driving, rain. He covered his head with a weather-stained cloak, pulling it tight about him. As a dwarf, he could endure all kinds of hardships, and this rain was hardly more than a trifle. Yet, why get wet if you could avoid it? There was little to live for in Crown, and a thorough soaking would make it even less appealing to him.

He turned down the cobblestone street and began making his way towards the tavern he most frequented. With days before the Long Night fight, he had little to do except count time and allow his scratch to heal. A warm anger spread briefly through him, like a hot burst of air that came and then was gone. Every time he considered his wound, considered why he had it, the wave of anger came. Not enough to last, not yet, but each time it came, he felt it stronger, felt it last longer. It would continue at least as long as the wound hurt, then perhaps it would fade back into the semi-numb existence that he knew so well. Then again, this sensation was new. It might not fade. What then?

After no more than a dozen steps, he realized he was being followed. No noise alerted him, both because the rain made enough noise to drown out any footfalls and because he suspected the follower was very good at silent travel. But, the Fiend Fighter was very good at what he

did, and he had foiled too many assassins in his day to be caught
unaware. He had developed a sense about these things, and he was
rarely caught off guard. Yet in this case, he had a feeling that his life
was not in danger. Of course, with the assassins he had faced in his
life, it had never been in danger.

Whoever it was, he would have to walk behind a bit. Farulazar
would not forestall breakfast, something he always took with ale. The
food at the tavern was not very good, but neither was it very bad. It
was sufficient, and that was enough for him. The ale, on the other
hand, was to his liking, and that came before all other
considerations. Few places in Crown had seen his shadow across
their thresholds, and so he could not compare the tapped barrels
across the city. Yet this place, the poorly-named *Lord's Court*,
drained a mug to his taste, better than what was offered at *Broken
Valor*, if only because of its less crowded surroundings.

The dwarf reached the groggery and pulled the heavy steel-
banded door open, stepping inside out of the rain. He threw back his
hood and walked to his preferred corner table. He did not claim it
and would not have been angry to find it occupied. Yet, the keeper of
the house seemed to ensure it was always empty. Farulazar was a
good customer after all, who kept to himself and did not fight
needlessly. There were some blood-stained cracks in the stones of
the floor near his table, proof of where cutthroats had met their
failed ends, but they were not noticeable in the dim light.

He sat down, and presently, a tankard was set before him. The
dwarf grunted and reached for it, draining half of it in a single pull.
He set it down and folded his thick fingers in front of him as he
awaited his guest. Very quickly, the door opened again, and the
follower stepped inside, looked about the room, spotted the dwarf,
and made his way towards his booth.

The visitor stepped to the booth, water dripping from his clothes,
and threw back his hood. The dim light revealed a ghastly form. The
creature's skin was thin, almost cadaverous, under which branched
dark veins that seemed to pulse with the rhythm of his breathing,
while his limbs were long and lithe. His head was bald, his eyes
dark, almost lifeless. At his chin was a long, goat-like tuft of black

hair streaked with white, or perhaps white with black, though in either case, he doubtlessly considered it a beard. It might even have passed for one among his kind, often thought of as ghosts by the simpler minds in Crown.

Farulazar recognized his unwelcomed company as an etherean, one of that mysterious species left behind when the gods fled, who was now doomed to remain in this place. Often aloof and mysterious, they were creatures both of this world and not, ghosts who could take form, who were at times solid and at times not. They could pass through locked doors or stone walls as easily as others passed down an empty hall. Some believed they were truly ghosts, cursed spirits forgotten by their former masters.

Their existence mattered little to the dwarf, except they reminded him why he was glad to be a mortal. For him, death would one day relieve him of a life with no real purpose. These things could not die; at least, he did not think they could. Never before had he spoken with one, though he had seen many. In any case, they were better to have about than a great many others in Crown, if only because they never bothered him - at least, not until today.

"Queen's care 'pon you, Farulazar, Fiend Fighter," he said, bowing slightly.

The dwarf did not move. His uninvited guest was polite if nothing else. Nobody was ever simply polite to him unless they wanted something from him. That was true when he dealt with Alfem, certainly. Farulazar regarded the etherean for a moment and then, a moment more.

A quizzical look spread across the etherean's face, his brow arched, and he pressed on. "I am called Tenet and am known as the Queen's Intelligencer."

Without moving, the dwarf considered this revelation. What purpose would one of the Queen's spy masters have with him? The dwarf lived quite the legal life, was involved with no plots nor with any secret societies. Those who died at his hands outside the pits were assassins and, thus, fair game. He neither smuggled contraband nor cheated at the games, even if he did embellish them on occasion. Quite simply, he was not the kind of person who drew the attention of authorities of any kind, save for those who quietly came to the games and wagered money on him.

Tenet regarded the dwarf, seemingly confused at his stoic, stone-like demeanor. Nothing he had heard about this gladiator had prepared him for this. Indeed, nothing in his career serving Crown had. He knew every kind of interrogation, had talked down every kind of creature in the city, from dwarf to were-rat, from other ethereans to elves. They all responded in some way; some had attacked him, others lied to him, others befriended him, and still others fled from him. But none of them out right ignored him. Stepping to one side, he saw the dwarf's keen gaze follow him. So, he was not being completely snubbed. Encouraged, he pressed on.

For some time, Farulazar endured the interrogation, all the while thinking that his ale was probably stale. The etherean tried one tact and then another, trying to pry information from him, but he was in no mood to answer questions that seemed so unimportant to him. Yet the more questions were asked, the more the dwarf understood that he was not the object of interest at all. Someone else was, someone he must know very well. Of course, the only person the dwarf knew beyond the most casual acquaintance was his halfling partner.

Almost as soon as he thought the name, Tenet spoke it. For the briefest instant, Farulazar was caught off guard, and a single brow rose at the sound of it. The interrogator made no sign that he noticed the dwarf's response to the name. Of course, he expected that this professional, who had worked so deftly to pry, had noticed. He was, after all, the Queen's Intelligencer. The dwarf expected no less.

Just as importantly, though, he cared no less. He was hungry, and this meeting had gone far longer than he would have liked. The dwarf cast a gaze over to the keeper, indicating wordlessly that breakfast could be served. The spy master certainly understood this last gesture and backed silently from the table, bowed slightly, and slipped out of the inn and into the rain-soaked streets outside.

Watching the visitor leave, Farulazar raised his mug slightly in salute. If nothing else, he had to acknowledge Tenet's obvious skill. As he drank from the wooden vessel, he wondered, only briefly, just what the ghostly etherean had learned from the conversation. The thought passed, though, driven away by the eggs and pork set before him.

When finished, he mulled over the meeting once more. While having been silent, he was certain he had given much away. Yet, he learned some from his guest, too. Something was happening, something that involved the rat-fink. It must have been something greater than his schemes in the pits, which never attracted the interest of the Crown Watch, much less one of his kind. No, for this etherean to be interested, Alfem was involved with something far more important. Who else was he manipulating?

Familiar feelings of anger welled within him. He thought of his partner, of the depths this creature evidently was willing to go to control him. Might he be involving the dwarf in a scheme far more nefarious, far more treacherous, than cheating at the games?

The thought hammered at him. For a long time, he had known that he was being used by the halfling, that he was nothing more than a valuable tool to bring in the gold. That had suited him fine, as long as he got a decent enough take to fill his cup and plate. But now, it seemed he may have become something else, a pawn in some greater, perhaps even wicked, scheme. Instead of retreating, the anger that now so often welled up within him only grew, blossoming into a sensation he had not felt in a century. Farulazar slammed his tankard down, splitting the wooden cup.

Standing, he dropped an extra piece of silver to cover the damage and stalked from the inn, seeking his own quarters. As he trudged through the rain, he thought more and more of how he was being used, how he was willingly being used, and how his actions in the pits might be serving in a way he not only did not know, but would not tolerate. He could be used to make gold for others, but he refused to be used for more than that.

By the time he reached his own door and fished out his key, he had made his decision. He would no longer be a pawn, a tool - no, a *puppet* - to anyone. Unlocking the door, he stepped inside and out of the rain. Sitting by the small coal-fire, he made up his mind to watch his "partner" in the next few days. Wherever the rat-fink went, he would follow. Whatever the weasel did, the dwarf would know. And before the Long Night fights began, he would know what he had to do with Alfem.

*   *   *

While Farulazar sat, brooding in his sparse apartment, Alfem sat in the Broken Valor checking his figures on a chalk tablet. The fighters' report had arrived earlier that morning while he had breakfast, and he was reviewing the names on the list to determine odds in the Darkday fights a few days away. All of the names he knew, of course, as the once-a-year fights were not open to anyone without a record. Each of their abilities was well known to any who followed the games, with Aflem knowing better than most. The purpose of the report was to give notice of the general health and legal status of the fighters in the register. Those few wounded on the Travelday fights had their conditions reported, as well as any who might have engaged in any bar-room brawls or other intramural fights. Invariably one or two fighters would come down with fever or would be sitting in one of the jails for any number of offenses ranging from unpaid debts to murder. Those sick or wounded might not be up to their normal fighting form on Darkday, and so the odds would have to be adjusted.

It was really for show, for the numbers had no real meaning to him. Whether he made mountains of gold or ended up a debtor mattered very little to him and would matter even less to the rest of Crown following that fateful day. Yet, Alfem was not the only one who took wagers on the fights. All of the bookies would be figuring the odds on this day, and since he was one of the better known in his profession, he had to as well. With great events drawing so close, it would not do to cause needless talk or draw incorrect attention to himself. And so he figured on his tablet, dutifully scratched his head, and even rubbed a bit of chalk under a whisker on his cheek to give the impression of careful study when all he was really doing was passing the time.

In truth, he was considering tomorrow's harvest. Word had come that the plague ship was now a floating morgue. The owner evidently had plans to sell the vessel, but the bodies would have to be removed before he could clean it and make arrangements for an auction. The were-rats would take care of the victims, of course; that was one of their jobs in Crown. What they would do with them was unimportant, as these were foreigners who should have stayed home instead of bringing their disease into port. For the half-demon-in-halfling's-clothing, their arrival was a true convenience. Not only would his followers harvest these poor souls, but he would get a tidy amount of silver for the job. When evening came, he would meet with his minions and plan their next day's macabre, but very profitable, work.

He was interrupted in his musings by one of the serving wenches. Alfem looked up in annoyance at, who was it? Nalcisa? Gwen? No, it was Eva, he remembered. Pretty, but far too talkative for his tastes, and so he always held her in contempt. She was not all that bright and was easily manipulated when needed, usually out of fear. Of little use other than as a servant, she did not deserve any better treatment. Of course, he did have another use for her, on Darkday, but she knew nothing of those plans.

"What?" he asked, testily.

"Excuse me, master Alfem," she said timidly. "But, well, you have a visitor."

"Do I?" asked the halfling, looking about in annoyance. "Where is he?"

"I took him to your office." answered the girl nervously.

"Simple-minded fool!" seethed Alfem. "You are never to take anyone to my office. I pay for that office, not you, not visitors. I show people in there, not you!"

"I am so sorry, master Alfem..." started the girl, but Alfem cut her off.

"I care little for your sorrow," said the halfling, standing. "Get away from me before I have you scheduled for the pits."

The girl backed away, intimidated. Alfem turned from the table and stamped towards his office, his mind filled with a number of bad ends for the worthless wench. She knew that nobody was to enter his office, though she did not know why. That was not important, of course. That he had ordered her more than once never to admit people to his private domain, but rather bring guests to his table should have been enough.

As he neared his office, he composed himself. It would not do to have prospective wagerers see him flustered or angry. He settled on thoughts of Eva, hands and feet bound, lying on the draining table on Darkday night after the fights. He would look into her eyes as he drew the knife across her throat...

A wicked smile crossed his face briefly as he reached the door, thinking not of her demise, but of the power that would come with the words he spoke, with the blood, the relic... He paused for a moment at the door and composed himself. Wearing a mask of mild concern, he turned the handle and stepped inside.

Standing before the desk, arms behind his back, was an etherean.

The feigned concern quickly turned real, surprising the halfling. These were not the kinds of people who entered his world to place bets. Other business was at hand, and that worried him. With events beginning to build towards a long-awaited climax, he could not afford any entanglements.

"Queen's care 'pon you, Alfem, and a fair morn," the visitor said, bowing slightly at the waist.

A needless pleasantry with no meaning, he thought, both because the queen did not know him and certainly would not approve of him, but also because the weather was dreadful. This was no fair morn. Wary, Alfem spoke, "And who might you be?"

The etherean smiled, conveying a quiet menace. "No one of consequence. I am Tenet, and I am humbly in the service of her majesty, Queen Alayarra the Glorious."

Surprise, fear, and repulsion coursed through him at the offered title. He had heard of Tenet, though he knew nothing about him other than he was one to avoid in his own official line of business. It might be something as simple as complaints of cheating among those who lost too much gold, but the coincidence of this one's arrival troubled the halfling. He doubted this man of great consequence was there for petty larceny or extortion. No, he was there for something else. While adept at verbal sparring, Alfem knew this conversation carried with it risks he was not prepared to take so near to his own destiny.

Playing it cool and impassive, treating this most dangerous guest like any other gambler in his midst, he stuck out his hand. "Queen's man, eh? Eva should've told me I was entertaining royalty this morn; I would have brought scones."

The etherean took Alfem's hand and replied, "Never you mind that, my good Alfem. My call is not a social one, but merely routine. In fact, I have only a few moments to spare, if I might impose on you this morning?"

Alfem nodded and motioned to Tenet to take a chair while he stepped around the desk to his own seat. Making himself appear comfortable, even though his mind was racing, he said, "Anything for the Queen. I don't suppose you are here to place a bet for her, eh? If you are interested, my money's on Farulazar, Fiend Fighter, or 'Triple F', as some call him, for the Long Night Fight!"

"Nay, I do not manage her wagers," answered the etherean. "Nor have I time to discuss the fights."

"Then, what can someone like me do for you?" asked Alfem, calming as he faced his opponent.

"A great deal. To begin with, have you noticed any unusual happenings here at the Valor of late?"

Alfem leaned back and smiled, holding his hands out harmlessly. "This is the Valor. Unusual things happen here all the time."

Tenet regarded the halfling, his expression unreadable. "Such as?" he asked, arching a single brow.

The halfling looked to the ceiling as if searching his mind. After a moment, he replied, "Just last evening, a saruulan and two dwarves shared a drink and discussed a building project."

"You know what I mean, good halfling," replied the etherean darkly, his brow furrowed. "Unusual and nefarious. I have reason to believe that the Valor has been, or shall soon be, the hub of some dark dealings."

Alarmed at the other's tone, Alfem straightened himself. "I mean no insult. Tenet, you said? I had never seen a saruulan and dwarf drink, let alone make plans. I do not mean to annoy, but I know of no conspiracies. Certainly, nothing against the queen."

"No insult taken, Alfem," answered the etherean, smiling. "And yes, the name is Tenet, Intelligencer to the Queen." A matter-of-fact expression returned to his face. "So, you've witnessed no strange doings, eh?"

"I take wages and figure odds; that is my business," said Alfem, shrugging theatrically. He then pointed towards the door and the tavern outside. "One of these wenches or the bar keep might know better of dark deeds."

"I see. Thank you then, for your time and patience. I pray your forgiveness for the intrusion; I ask only that you contact me should anything untoward occur," Tenet answered. He paused for a moment, as if working something out in his mind. "Thank you for your suggestion, too, good Alfem. It seems that there are others about to whom I need to speak."

"I serve as I can. But please, I can promise good odds on Darkday, should you wish to wager..."

"Sorry, no, vices other than chance have claimed my soul, good halfling," interrupted Tenet, shaking his head.

Ready to be finished with the conversation, Alfem stood. "Then, I wish you success in what you seek," he said, offering his hand. "Should I hear of any plots against Crown and the Queen, I shall send word to you. I must apologize, but business calls me."

Tenet stood awkwardly, taking the halfling's hand. "Queen's care 'pon you, Alfem..." he said, before making his way back to the door.

"And I am sure to you," said Alfem, following him.

The queen's man stepped through the door. Alfem closed it and locked it behind him. For a moment, panic washed over him as he considered the conversation. This Tenet was a professional and likely very good at what he did .What had he revealed with his words or gestures? Had he been careless to his own ruin? Did this Tenet now know all of his plans? Dread started to mix with his panic.

Alfem forced himself to take a breath and view the conversation objectively. What possible information could this queen's servant have gleaned from a few meaningless words? Certainly, he could not suspect a halfling bookie of dark events in the harbor or under the city. No, halflings might be shrewd businessmen, but their plots were reserved to financial schemes and nothing more.

Certainly, no one in Crown would ever think to connect Alfem with either of Szeethe's guises. He had been very careful to segregate his business in *The Valor* from his dealings elsewhere. Considering it further, he decided the only possible dark or nefarious deed the etherean could suspect was the planned murder of Na'akiros. But even then, that was set up by a were-rat in Deep Harbor, not a halfling in the Valor. Perhaps setting up a meeting between Szeethe and the dear captain in the tavern had not been wise, but that still had nothing to do with Alfem, who, at worst, could be only accused of being conniving.

He took a deep breath and returned to his chair, sitting down and resting his hands in his lap. As he looked at the desk, he regarded the slate tablet he had brought into the room and set upon his ledger. He looked at the meaningless scribbles written in chalk. An evil smile spread across his otherwise harmless features. Soon, very soon, none of these trivial things such as wagers and odds would matter. And no matter what the Queen's Intelligencer discovered, he would be too late to be of any consequence...

The following day, Farulazar arose and made his way through the driving rain to *The Lord's Court* for his customary breakfast. Some in Crown viewed such an utterly fixed routine to be dangerous and foolhardy. But for the dwarf, who was guaranteed to be in *The Broken Valor* promptly in the evenings every Travelday night, it was the way of life. Being predictable in the course of the day was comfortable enough.

As it turned out, being a creature of habit and being known to keep to a steady routine was to his advantage. Of all the denizens of Crown, Alfem would know Farulazar's routine, would himself be very comfortable with the dwarf's actions, and thus would expect nothing else. He most certainly would not expect the dwarf to be following him in his own daily activities.

Once finished with his morning ritual, Farulazar made his way to the Market Ward, turning his cloak to the wind and rain. Even in this foul weather, it teemed with creatures of every kind. There, he walked into one of the many garment shops and looked for a change of clothing, something that the Fiend Fighter would never wear but was still in the current fashion of the merchant class. He picked out a white shirt, a dark blue waistcoat, brown trousers, some rather foppish leather slippers, and a dark blue hat that matched the coat. Over all of it, he slung a dark blue cape to ward off the storm. He paid for the clothes, dressed, and then folded his well-worn garments, stuffing them into a cloth satchel he'd also bought.

Emerging from the emporium, he looked like a middling merchant or a dwarf about the city on business or a holiday. He was unable to change his face, of course, but from fifty paces, most dwarves looked alike, at least to most folks. In any case, he looked nothing like the Fiend Fighter, which was proven after an hour's wandering through the ward without recognition. Satisfied, he made his way towards the Arms Crescent and *The Broken Valor*, where Alfem usually did his daily business.

He reached the colossal tower and looked about. Farulazar stepped down a side alley he knew would afford a good view of the main doorway and leaned against the wall under an overhang that provided shelter against the storm. Arms folded, he turned his head to watch for the halfling. Not knowing the weasel's routine, if he had one, the dwarf knew he might wait hours upon hours for Alfem to arrive. But, he was the patient type, and such a wait in this alley was as good a way to pass his day as anything else.

The day passed, the weather seemed to worsen even more, and the dwarf saw all manner of people enter and exit the building in a rush. He was surprised at the amount of business the otherwise unremarkable tavern received on a day without fights and with this kind of weather. The food was certainly not good enough, nor were the drinks, to entice visitors for their own sake. Without a good fight to bet on, why bother? Of course none of this mattered to the dwarf. What these people did with their time was fine by him. But, he was beginning to hope Alfem would not skip *The Valor* this day. Neither anxious nor bored, he nonetheless would rather not waste an entire day propping up a wall in the alley, forgoing his afternoon tankard.

When he was almost convinced that the halfling would not show up, the small creature stepped from inside the building and onto the street, a green cloak pulled tightly around him. Farulazar wasted no energy wondering what this small little person could have been doing all day in the tavern. When Alfem had walked nearly beyond view, the dwarf stepped from the alley in casual pursuit.

The halfling, with the dwarf following behind, made his way down the streets, through the various wards, heading more or less in the direction of the Deep Harbor district. When nearly there, Alfem turned suddenly and stepped down a narrow alleyway. Surprised, Farulazar quickened his pace, reaching the side-street only a few moments behind his quarry. He stopped at the entrance and peered around the corner. The narrow alley was dark and shadowed, and it took a moment for the dwarf's eyes to adjust. When they did, he scanned the numerous stoops and nooks for the halfling.

After a moment, he found him, standing with his back pressed against a darkened doorway some fifty yards down the alley. At that instant, Alfem clasped his hands together, and to the dwarf's amazement, his features became blurred. Seeming almost to melt into himself, the small creature evolved quickly from halfling into something else. At first, Farulazar could not tell what, until it turned and began making its way down the alleyway towards him. The halfling was now a were-rat. Pulling quickly away from the corner, the dwarf mingled into the miserable crowd in the direction they had come. Watching carefully, he saw the creature he knew as Alfem emerge from the alley and make its way towards the harbor.

Undaunted by the transformation he witnessed, Farulazar pressed forwards, following the creature once again. As he stalked through the rain-soaked streets in stealthy chase, his demeanor darkened. All that he knew about his partner, whatever he might really be, was meaningless. Certainly, this thing was neither halfling nor were-rat, but some creature that was darker and definitely more magical than either. Though he did not know what the ghostly Tenet wanted with the what ever it was he followed, the Fiend Fighter could now understand his interest.

The two passed through the streets of Crown until they reached the Deep Harbor district, where the street widened as it branched into hundreds of docks of every kind. Worried he might be discovered as the paths widened, the dwarf slowed his pace, allowing the rat creature to open the distance between them. He watched as the thing turned down a particularly dilapidated pier that was guarded by members of the Crown Watch. Curious, he followed a short way before turning down another pier and climbing aboard a smelly whaling ship. He made his way to the starboard side and peered over the railing, picking up his quarry once more.

The were-rat climbed aboard a smaller sailing vessel, where numbers of other were-rats were teeming about, busily working with some sort of cargo. The dwarf could not tell much of what they were doing at first. Worse, he lost Alfem among the scores of other rats for a moment. But then, he saw a single rat standing on the bow, motioning to the others, directing them: Alfem, he presumed, or whatever name this creature used.

For several minutes, the dwarf watched the were-rats as they busied themselves with their work, seemingly oblivious to the storm. Gazing through the driving rain, he was unable to tell what they were moving about. Great lumpy sacks or bags of something were being moved towards one side of the boat. Suddenly, two rats appeared on the pier, carrying a litter piled with something, though what it was he still could not tell.

"'Aye, you there," came a voice from behind. "Wat are yeh doin' there?"

Farulazar turned his head to see a man standing at the top of an open hatch, wearing a filthy apron over a buttoned coat and woolen trousers. On his head, the man wore a broad-brimmed cap, out of which stuck a crimson feather, both of which were rain-soaked and drooped over his head. A silver badge was tacked to the front of the hat, indicating rank of some sort. The look on the man's face was a mixture of bewilderment and irritation, both at the weather and the apparent intruder. He stepped from the hatch and walked over to the dwarf.

"I said, wat are yeh doin' on meh boat?" he demanded, as he took the apron off, wiping his hands on it before tossing the soggy garment to the deck.

Farulazar glared at the man, his face wrathful, his hands clenched. With but a look, he conveyed all he needed to the person, presumably the captain of the foul vessel. The man raised his hands, his eyes widening at the look of death from the dwarf, and he stepped back a pace. The Fiend Fighter stepped up to him and scowled, but instead of striking, he merely reached out and pulled a brass spyglass from the man's belt. Wordlessly, he turned back to the were-rats across the water.

Through the telescope, he saw the rats were still busy doing their work. The creature on the bow directing them was the same rat he had followed to the harbors. He turned the glass on the were-rats carrying the litter down the pier, who were now joined by more rats with more bundles. Through the glass, Farulazar could plainly see piles of dead bodies, their skin splotched with angry patches of dark red that oozed blackened blood. Though he never been in a plague house, the dwarf recognized them for what they were. And, they were being taken away by were-rats under the control of the creature he knew as Alfem.

Farulazar turned and thundered from the ship, passing the telescope to the still slack-jawed captain as he left. He made his way down the pier, keeping away from the were-rats and their macabre cargo. Blending into other citizens fighting the driving rain, he disappeared through the maze of streets. An hour later, he found himself back in his abode, sitting dry and comfortable before his small coal grate, the fire burning solemnly.

As he sat in his spartan room, the drenched, new-bought clothes thrown in a corner, never to be worn again, he considered all that he had seen. Though he had witnessed much in his life and was not easily shaken, the afternoon's revelations were much to consider. When he seated himself in the thick wooden chair, the last rays of light were spread through the room. When the first rays of morning began to erode the frost on his small window, after the long night of contemplating all he had seen, he'd made up his mind.

He would enter the arena and face the demon. It would die, be banished, or expelled - whatever. He would earn his share of gold, which would pay for the better part of a year. He would release Korm from his penitent service. Never again would he fight for another man's gold. Never again would he fight in the pits. With his gear in hand, he would leave *The Broken Valor* and the Arms Cresent and never look back.

*   *   *

"It is in the arena..." said Korm, in his low, gravelly voice.

"Aye," said Farulazar, rubbing the fresh knife scar on his forearm before holding it out for Korm to buckle on his braces. "It is..."

The other dwarf raised an eyebrow and regarded his employer, aware of his changed mood. Finished with the first arm, he buckled the armor on the other and then turned and reached for the battered shield. Korm spoke rarely, always keeping his thoughts to himself, and he would not speak now. What demons plagued the Fiend Fighter were none of his concern.

His benefactor stood and turned, regarding him. Seldom had the two made contact with their eyes. They were not truly friends, even in the stoic dwarvish way, and they never held long conversations. Korm had never even been in the other's lodgings before. And so, he was surprised by the sudden attention.

Farulazar looked long and hard into his subordinate's eyes before he spoke. "After this night, I will not fight again in the pits."

Korm merely nodded.

"I release you from my service. Go back to Dwarfhome. You need spend no more days in exile with one like me. Your penance is served, and they will accept you again," said the Fiend Fighter gravely.

Korm handed him the short, thick-bladed gladius and stepped back. "I count my days here with no great pride," he said. "But, I shall not forget them."

The dwarf bowed slightly and then left the room. Never again would the two meet. Farulazar listened to the door close, and then he turned his attention to the door that led to the pits. In moments he would pass through it, down the passage, and into his last fight. When the night was over, he would be a gladiator no more. Whether death claimed him, or he cut the demon down, his days fighting for the wealth of other men, his days of being manipulated by Alfem, were over.

He had reached for the door when a sound, slight and almost unheard through the noise and rumbling of the crowd, told the dwarf that he was suddenly not alone. He stepped to one side, his muscles tensed and ready for battle, but his blade he kept low. Farulazar knew his company.

"Come out of the shadow," he grumbled. "It does not seem to be your way."

"It is not," agreed Tenet. "But my words are for your ears alone."

The etherean stepped from the corner in which he had arrived and approached the dwarf, his expression oddly grim for one of his kind. It took only a moment for the revelations, only a moment for Tenet to tell how deep the treachery ran. Then the etherean left the room, phasing directly through the wall, leaving the dwarf to consider it all. The full understanding, the full appreciation, for what Alfem had done, of the way he had used him, the wickedness of his plans, and of whom he really was began to consume the dwarf.

He now knew the full details, the real name, and the demonic nature of the halfling/were-rat, but none of it was important. He cared nothing for the creature's name, the missing pieces of the puzzle first revealed by the assassin and then laid bare before him at the docks, the details of its real purpose, the wicked Grey God that it served. None of that mattered. The warm anger that came with every thought of the halfling these days was driven away, replaced by a cold, focused rage. At that moment, Farulazar had but one very clear purpose to his life.

He opened the door, and the the sounds of the crowd were carried over the rotten stench of the pits. The demon waited. He would waste very little time with it and then, he would find his "partner." When he did, without a single word, without a warning of any kind, he would kill him.

*   *   *

While the dwarf was meeting with the etherean, Szeethe was sitting at a table for a meeting of his own. Never before had he appeared at the Valor as Szeethe; this was normally Alfem's domain, but tonight was a very important night. He had not intended to be here, had not intended to meet with this ship's captain, though arrangements to negotiate with him were long made. Had his plans gone smoothly, this captain would already be dead and the planned meeting would never happen. The assassin he had hired had failed to act before now, though he was known as one of the best. Of course, Szeethe had made arrangements should the assassin fail, though the prompt killing of the captain would have made things easier for him. In any case, this Arastin would pay for his tardiness.

Around him, he heard the sounds of people milling about, preparing for the match, perhaps wondering where Alfem might be. As he had walked into the tavern, Szeethe had seen one of the other bookies, another halfling, who had settled comfortably into his role as Alfem's replacement. Evidently thinking himself a shrewd opportunist, this little creature knew precious little of the horror to come. None in this room realized what was coming. Soon, all things held dear by these pitiful people would be meaningless.

But other business pressed, now that the assassin had not acted in time. The meeting that Szeethe never planned to attend was at hand, and so he found himself staring across the table at one he had never planned to see at all. Across from him and flanked by his men, sat Na'akiros, the elven captain who had brought the precious relic. Playing his part expertly, the dark creature reached into his tunic, pulled out a flat package wrapped in oil-cloth, and placed it on the table. The captain looked at it and then regarded his companion.

"Is the relic safe?" asked Szeethe.

"Of course," said the captain, his voice deep and gravelly, something unexpected from an elf.

A wicked grin spread across Szeethe's rat-like face. "Good for you," he sneered. "I would hate for you to suffer the Grey God's wrath."

The elf frowned. "Don't threaten me, rat; I'm not one of your toadies," he growled. He leaned back. "I have no more time for you. I have other business here, so give us our money and get this over with."

Szeethe slid the bundle over to the captain, who folded back the cloth to reveal a stack of Crown script. The captain's face clouded over.

"Don't you waste my time with this worthless Crown paper! We agreed for gold. If you are paying in script, it isn't nearly enough!" he roared.

"Be patient," whined Szeethe, maintaining his were-rat persona. "You will get more when we finish the deal!"

"If you cheat me, you will never be safe," Na'akiros threatened as he pointed to the rat. "None survive who cross the League!"

Szeethe stood, his anger boiling, threatening to reveal his true nature. "Don't you threaten me," he hissed, "or you will die in a dungeon of darkest despair! This isn't the League, nor is it the ocean. Crown is my city!"

"Enough of this," said the elf as he stood, shaking his pale-haired head and motioning to his guards. "Return to the *Claw*!"

*   *   *

Farulazar stepped into the pit and regarded his opponent, a fiend he had never before faced. Normally, this would have given him some pleasure; it would at least be an interesting fight. But not today; today, the demon was merely in his way. He focused on the creature, ignoring the crowd, to their disappointment. He would not give them a good show today, no matter what the demon did. They cheered all the same when he lifted his blade, though he did not hear them.

The creature lurched forward, spreading its wings, hunching over, and opening its clawed fingers. This one was ready to fight. Farulazar narrowed his eyes and stepped closer. The demon hissed and advanced, its hellish eyes regarding him with evil purpose. It slid to the center of the pit and leapt forward, its talons clawing for his throat.

The dwarf ducked low and drove upwards with his blade, aiming for the creature's exposed neck. At the last instant, the fiend moved to one side, and the sword merely grazed the rough, shark-like skin, drawing a dark line that trickled foul demon blood. The creature dove forward, over the dwarf, and latched itself on the wall behind him, spinning its head about to scream in bitter anger.

Above, the crowd roared with pleasure and chanted the dwarf's name, cheering him on. Ignoring them, he spun about to press his attack towards the demon that was now backed against the wall. He drove the blade towards the demon's heart, but the creature pushed hard against the stone and leapt over him, landing mere feet behind him. The creature's supernatural speed amazed the dwarf, who had never seen a fiend of any kind move so fast.

But he was fast, too, and before the creature could press an attack, the dwarf fell to his back and pushed hard against the wall with his stout feet, sending him sliding under the demon's spread legs. With precious little room to swing his sword, the best Farulazar could do was jab the creature's exposed thigh. The blade went in deep, and black demon blood sprayed over him, burning his eyes, but he knew that would do nothing more than enrage the fiend.

Screaming, the creature jumped back, pulling itself from the dwarvish blade. As it leapt, it flung its barbed tail down hard, aiming for its tormentor's head. Farulazar rolled nimbly to one side, but not far enough, as the tail slammed hard into his shoulder and arm, the barbs sinking deep into him.

Fire raced through his flesh as several venomous barbs broke loose. Farulazar had never known such pain, and his vision clouded. He bit down hard to suppress a scream of his own and felt a molar crack. Fighting back the searing pain, he spun swiftly, pulled up to one knee, and vengefully sliced the tail cleanly off. The creature roared in agony. Wincing in pain, the dwarf stood and drove his heavy shield into the creature's back, sending it sprawling against the far wall. It turned quickly and hissed.

Allowing the shield to hang on his arm, he reached down and grabbed the bloody tail with his right hand, holding it like a whip. He charged, slapping the creature hard on the side of the face with the tail, breaking more barbs off into its cheek. At the same time, he stabbed towards the creature's gut with his blade, trying to finish off this deadly creature. The fiend dodged the blow but could not get entirely out of the way, and the weapon pierced deep into its soft side, driving through and nicking the stone behind.

More blood sprayed out, but again, the wound would not be mortal, only enraging. With a roar, the creature bit downwards, its needle sharp teeth clamping hard on Farulazar's iron cap, while pushing hard against his chest with its clawed feet, trying to rip his head from his torso. The cap came cleanly off his head, and Farulazar was sent sliding across the room. Hitting the wall hard, he saw spots before his eyes, and the room dimmed. He shook his head hard and leapt to his feet, raising his sword to face his foe once more.

The fiend slowly advanced, and so did he. Both were cautious now, knowing the deadly threat of the other. When it reached the center of the room, the creature stopped, lowered its head, and raised its wings, hissing at the dwarf. Farulazar stopped a few feet away, catching his breath and measuring his opponent, deciding what the creature's next move might be and how he might preempt it.

At that moment, the noise of the crowd above changed from excited cheering and screams for blood to anger and confusion. The dwarf was not so foolish as to look up and take his attention away from his prey, but he could tell something was happening above. He hoped it did not involve Alfem, but in any case, it did not matter. The rat-fink would die soon enough.

*   *   *

While the dwarf faced the fiend below, chaos was breaking out above. The captain whirled about at the sound of breaking and crashing. "What's this?!" he shouted.

Szeethe looked about, confused. "I do not care and have no idea! We must finish the deal tonight!"

Black smoke began billowing out from under the table. The were-rat stepped back in surprise, while two of the captain's guards and one of Szeethe's fell suddenly to the ground, dead. Behind them, the rat could hear a loud groaning followed by a tremendous sound of breaking bone and rending metal as something huge crashed into the pit. One of the other sailors with the captain shouted out but was quickly pushed over the ledge into the pit below, following whatever it was that fell in. The rat turned and saw the attacker, the elven assassin he had hired to kill the captain. He put his hand on the captain's shoulder, as if to point to the desired target.

"He dares attack! He must pay!" shouted the captain.

Szeethe stepped back and in a menacing voice replied, "And he shall. They will all pay; the Grey God will see to it! But we must have the relic first!"

The captain turned and started pushing through the crowd to leave. Not wanting to be near the captain if the assassin struck again, Szeethe made his way to his secret door. He stepped through to the descending passage behind and began making his way through the Sewer City's underground passageways to one of many countless openings above. His minions were at this moment already massing to overtake the ship, now that the captain was not on it. His only purpose now was to reach *The Frozen Idol* and take possession of his prize.

*   *   *

Farulazar heard the crashing noise much closer and felt a few droplets of blood sprinkle over him. The noise suddenly ended as a lumbering form fell through the air and disappeared mere feet from the stone floor behind him. Almost immediately, it was followed by a single, screaming man who smashed into the ground near the wall. The crowd hushed, and in that instant, Farulazar heard a tremendous cracking, groaning noise. Somehow, the demonic chandelier above was breaking loose. In a moment, he suspected it would come crashing down, though he dared not look and see.

The demon's nostrils flared as it prepared to attack again, its eyes focusing on the dwarf's thick, short neck. In its focused rage, it did not seem to notice the fixture above as it began to break free from its mount. Farulazar raised his improvised whip and pulled his sword back as if to lunge, his eyes taking the fiend's and holding them firmly in his gaze. Then, he stepped back calmly as the giant chandelier crashed down. The demon looked up, too late to escape, and was crushed beneath the bony lattice, its wings splayed out from the wreck. A single clawed hand quivered for a moment and then was motionless. Its foul blood drained out and coursed down the channels and holes cut into the floor.

The crowd looked down, aghast at what just happened. The Fiend Fighter ignored them and raced for the door that led up to the tavern, tossing the demon tail aside. As he thundered up the steps, he pulled the demon barbs from his shoulder. He reached *The Valor*'s tavern area, finding mayhem. He saw several dead bodies, over-turned tables, broken crockery, and the chaos of people running this way and that. Looking about, he unexpectedly spotted Tenet. The two locked eyes, and the etherean pointed to the main door.

"To the wharves," he said.

Farulazar nodded and fled from the room, crashing through patrons and knocking them aside as if they were nothing. He barreled into the street, turned, and charged into the maelstrom, not feeling the icy needles of rain against his skin. The path was largely deserted, most folks having long fled for cover from the wicked storm that was lashing the city. He did not notice it. Turning the corner near the wharves, he tore through the broken remnants of a fruit cart, bowling over the wretched merchant who seemed to be in a state of despair. Bits of pulpy fruit, melon rinds, and sticky juice clung to the dwarf as he roared down the street, guided by a cold, determined purpose.

*   *   *

Drenched from the soaking rain, Szeethe reached the harbor and found the warehouse in which his cultist minions had mustered for the attack. He sent a small group to guard the street to prevent anyone from getting through, especially the captain, should Arastin fail in his mission. The rest of the minions he led to board and take the ship. They had to get the relic off the ship and into their sanctuary. There, they would finish their evil plans.

When he arrived, countless alônn were swarming over the sides of the ship, many already on board attacking the crew. With a sudden dread, he realized they must be after the relic, too. Too soon; he was not ready to perform the rites, not here, not yet. Rage filled him, as years of effort hung in the balance. He would not, could not, fail at the end!

With a howl, he followed the cultists as they attacked the ship, and in the confusion, they climbed aboard. He looked like just another rat, and as they were presently aplenty, he made no great target. The creature stepped through the bedlam until he reached the hold, where he was pleased to discover the relic being raised up, though it still remained in the ship's bowels.

However, looking into the hold more carefully, he saw the relic barely above burning streams of oil. Rage consumed him as he also saw the elven assassin within, at the relic, sword raised. Szeethe screamed to the elf in his own cursed language, desperate to prevent an irrevocable act. Suddenly, the elf swung the blade, cutting the rope. The relic fell, tumbling to the side amidst the burning barrels.

The were-rat shrieked in terror. He could not wait to take the relic below ground, and though he did not have sweet Eva from the Broken Valor to be his final living sacrifice, there were plenty about who could take her place. Though this was not the place he had planned, he had to act now or all his efforts would be in vain. Ignoring Arastin as he climbed the rope, he closed his eyes and spread his arms. His body began to change, and the real Szeethe emerged as he hurriedly chanted the words to a curse long planned.

*   *   *

As Farulazar neared the Deep Harbor district, a group of were-rats leapt from a side alley in a feeble attempt to slow him, evidently knowing their attempt was futile. Without missing a step, he cleaved his way through them, cutting them down as if they were empty phantoms. Bits of fur, rat blood, fruit pulp, and smeared demon blood now caked his soaked beard, making him look like an avenging spirit from the ancient days.

He reached the docks, not knowing where his quarry might be. He looked about until he saw hordes of were-rats scrambling about at the end of a pier alongside a berthed ship. The dwarf raced down the dock and found the pier to be a scene of absolute mayhem. The pier was filled with the foul rodents, who were desperately fighting sailors and the watery alônn, the mysterious creatures who inhabited the bays and inlets of Crown. Smoke billowed out of the hold, preceded by some sort of cargo. More of the watery creatures were storming the ship, and even more rats were swarming aboard. The storm was raging, the angry waves were sending a salty spray over everyone, and all the while, the ship bucked and tossed against its moorings.

The dwarf fought his way through the were-rat cultists on the pier, cleaving a path as if they were nothing more than stalks of winter wheat. As he waded through them, bloodied sword swinging, a head would fall, then an arm, a full torso, another head, until the way behind him was littered by blood and fur. Before him, he saw the main gangplank choked with people of every kind, all fighting each other. He saw a single were-rat clinging to a rope, preparing to swing over to the ship, but he sliced the creature in two. Grabbing the rope, he climbed aboard, pulling himself onto the foredeck.

On deck, he saw the rats fighting with even more sailors, who clashed with the rats and the slit-neck alônn, who, in turn, were battling both rats and sailors. He joined the brawl, fighting any who came close, hacking down sailors and rats with a single-minded purpose. Fortunately for the slit-necks, none came close enough to get in his way, and none seemed to care about him as long as he killed only rats and men.

Finally, he spotted his target, the rat Szeethe, whom he had once known as Alfem. The creature was standing on deck before the cargo being lifted out of the hold, his arms raised. He seemed to be chanting something, though the dwarf was too far away to hear clearly. At that moment, the creature began to change yet again. His form softened for a moment as the fur absorbed into the skin, and then the flesh became knotted and hard, the skin a pale, ghostly white. His hands became claws, and his eyes turned a fiery red. Farulazar beheld for the first time Szeethe's true form.

The dwarf narrowed his eyes, not concerned what form his foe took. Whether rat, demon rat, or halfling rat, a rat he remained and would die all the same. He began to make his way towards the creature when fires roared out of the hold, blocking his way. Farulazar swore to himself as he looked for a way around. The rat would not escape now.

*   *   *

The half-demon, Szeethe, chanted the cursed words from a language few living souls knew. He did not call to the relic burning in the fire, but rather to the sanguine cauldron in the deep places under Crown, the holding tank where gallons upon gallons of foul, rotting blood were held in reserve just for this moment. For a long time he had gathered it, and he would have immersed the relic in it at the culmination of the cursed spell had his plans gone well. He required blood, but how he joined blood and relic did not matter. If he could not bring the relic to the cauldron, he would bring the cauldron's contents here.

The creature's eyes rolled back into his upturned head as he was buffeted by the winds and driving rain, his corpse-like arms stretched out. Cursed words flew from his lips, caught on the wind and focused on a point several feet above the relic. With a final shout, the sky opened up, and a river of blood flowed through the torn air. It flowed towards the hold and the relic below, barely missing the incompetent assassin, Arastin, who managed to fling himself to the side at the last instant.

Szeethe continued his chanting as the blood flowed through the rent in the sky. Suddenly, a gigantic beast of a creature poured through the gap, caught up in the sanguine torrent. It wailed as it fell through the sky, dragging along in its hand a great, blood-soaked anchor at the end of a long chain. The half-demon jumped back, startled, as the creature fell into the hold, followed quickly by the unlikely weapon it wielded. Before he could move or even consider what he saw, the gory anchor smashed up from inside the hold and through the deck beneath his feet. Utterly surprised, he was flung high into the air over the burning hold and his precious relic. The half-demon landed hard at the end of the bow on his belly and crumpled, stunned. He gasped as he faced the city of Crown.

*   *   *

Farulazar watched angrily as Szeethe chanted his curse, unable to find a way through the growing flames. It seemed to the dwarf this half-fiend would succeed in the end. The cold anger grew even colder as resolve steeled him. Nothing would stop him, not even flames. But as the dwarf began marching towards the flames, prepared to push through them to reach his foe at any cost, a great form fell through the sky in a waterfall of blood, an anchor trailing behind him at the end of a chain.

He watched in amazement as the tremendous, wailing bulk fell into the hold. Then, he saw the anchor smash up from the deck and into Szeethe, tossing the creature into the air. Anger, mixed with despair, filled him as he watched what he thought was the death of the demon rat. For the briefest instant, he felt cheated out of his rightful vengeance. But suddenly, like a gift delivered on the wings of the wind, the foul creature landed mere feet in front of him. A menacing grin spread across the dwarf's blood-soaked face as he gripped his sword.

Farulazar thundered forward, sword raised; no challenge uttered from his lips, no words of bravado warned of his approach. But the half-demon creature heard his heavy foot falls, and, staggering to his feet, turned about. At first, it did not recognize the dwarf, who looked like a nightmarish revenant, covered as he was by the filth of this battle-strewn night. But realization came, and Szeethe saw death in the face of his former tool.

But the demonic creature was not easy prey, like its brethren summoned to the fighting pits. As the dwarf sliced down towards his head, Szeethe fell back and batted the blade aside with his wiry forearm. He then followed the deflected blow with his other arm, smashing into the side of the dwarf's head.

Farulazar staggered back, eyes narrowing. He stormed back towards his foe, sword raised in cold fury. Szeethe lithely scrambled to his feet and drew a long dagger from his robe, a wicked blade he used on the dead and dying in his cursed rituals. With an unearthly growl, he lunged forward and under the dwarf's incoming blow, driving his stained blade up towards Farulazar's short neck. The Fiend Fighter turned aside, and the blade narrowly missed, drawing a line across his cheek instead.

With tremendous power, the dwarf rammed his head into Szeethe's, sending the rat-demon sprawling against the deck. Szeethe's head hit the thick wood hard, and he saw stars; as they dimmed, he suddenly saw the dwarf's wide blade stabbing towards his chest. The high priest tried to slide to the side, but he was not fast enough, and the blade pinned his shoulder to the deck. The creature howled in agony, and he dropped his wicked executioner's knife; Farulazar immediately stomped on the blade, snapping it into three pieces. Dark steam hissed from the blade's surface as all enchantment fled from its form.

With his other foot, the dwarf pinned down the twisted creature's unwounded shoulder. He drew his *demon bane* gladius from the foul flesh and raised it, preparing the coup de grace. As the blade swept down, one of the were-rat cultists, his oil-soaked fur burning, sprang onto the dwarf's back, sending the sword clattering harmlessly across the deck. The small, singed rodent-creature bit down hard on Farulazar's thick neck and clawed at his face.

With his free hand, the Fiend Fighter reached back and grabbed the smoldering rat and flung him into the fire, ignoring its screams of agony. Seizing the moment of the dwarf's distraction, Szeethe slid away and scrambled to the doomed ship's prow. The dwarf angrily snatched his sword from the deck and turned his bleeding face towards his prey.

Though disarmed, Szeethe was far from helpless. Now that he had some distance between himself and his foe, he raised his good arm and began chanting the words to a cursed spell. With a roar, Farulazar charged up the few steps, sword raised. As the dwarf reached the top, the rat-demon pointed his talons towards him, and half a dozen arcs of green lightning swarmed from their tips. The bolts sliced into the dwarf's chest and head, leaving long, burning gashes.

Ignoring the smell of burned flesh and the searing pain, Farulazar closed the gap quickly. He swung his *demon's bane* and sliced the creature's limply-hanging arm just beneath the shoulder. Bone and flesh parted, and the limb thudded to the deck, spraying both its owner and the dwarf in foul blood. Screaming hysterically, Szeethe fell back and opened his remaining hand. A caustic cloud of ash spewed out of his palm and enveloped the dwarf's face. Grunting and blind, Farulazar stumbled back and onto the deck.

Trembling, Szeethe leaned down and retrieved his severed arm. Pressing flesh to flesh, he uttered arcane words, and a green vapor issued from the wound as the fibers knitted themselves back together. The rat-demon creature screamed in a moment of relived agony and then let go of his wounded arm, which hung lifelessly, but firmly, to his shoulder.

Then, with a malevolence not shown before, Szeethe rose up to his full height and held his one working hand forward, as if presenting something to the dwarf. In the empty space, a glowing sphere appeared, its color that of the rotten blood that had flowed into the hold. Uttering words never before heard in Crown, in a voice from the darkest realms of chaos, Szeethe stepped forward.

Blinking through the ash, Farulazar stood as the demon-rat approached. He watched as the small globe floated above the creature's palm and began to pulse with a heart-like rhythm. Seemingly oblivious to his own peril, Szeethe stood over the dwarf, his strange voice chanting, his eyes closed. The Fiend Fighter felt all strength suddenly fade from his body and felt his hand lose its grip on his blade, which clattered to the deck; he slumped to his knees. Then his head sagged back, and his breathing began to slow as his very essence began to flow from him.

At that moment it seemed his life would be snuffed out completely. When all breath seemed gone from his body, something stirred within him. Whether magic or some force far older, he would never know, but the tiny flame long left smoldering within him ignited and blazed into a consuming fire. Farulazar was filled with a surging power he had never before felt, but that gave him a strength far greater than he had ever felt fighting demons in the pits. His eyes opened.

Surprised and confused, Szeethe stepped back a pace, lowering the pulsing sphere. Farulazar stood as his hand found and tightened about the grip of his short sword. The demon-rat held the cursed globe aloft once more and resumed the chant, but to his dismay, the globe dimmed and then turned black, dropping harmlessly into his opened hand. The creature stepped back in mortal terror as life filled his foe anew, and a flame kindled afresh in his eyes. Wordlessly, the dwarf stepped forward, forcing the half-demon backwards until his back was against the railing.

All the while, Szeethe chanted, desperately calling forth arcane powers that seemed to have fled from him. He uttered spell after spell, followed by curses and incantations of the most wicked kind, but no power would come forth. He stared full into the face of death, a mask he had so often presented to so many victims in the past. Full appreciation washed over the wicked, depraved creature as he saw his own mortality standing before him. The end had come.

"You will die," he hissed, his eyes blazing, his claws splayed in frustrated rage.

"Yes," answered the dwarf. "Someday I will."

In one very fluid motion, an act so much a part of him through years upon years of fighting in the pits, felling foes of every kind, Farulazar swung his sword and cut the creature's head cleanly from its neck. He quickly extended his hand and caught it, holding it as the body crumpled to the deck of the doomed ship. He looked into the eyes as they clouded in death. His purpose fulfilled, he tossed the head into the flames.

Farulazar turned to leave the ship, to find some new life now that the old had passed. Suddenly, before he could leave, the entire vessel seemed to lift up, swallowed by a horrendous rending of wood and metal as countless barrels below exploded, tearing through the deck, ripping out the sides of the ship, and sending sailors, cultists, and alônn flying through the air. The blast caught him and slammed him back, smashing him into the weakened deck, which buckled beneath the tremendous force and sent him plunging into the compartment below. At that moment, the bowsprit broke loose and was pulled up and over the hole as the main mast collapsed back into the wreck of the ship. The bow separated and slid forward in the water while the jib, tack, and ribbing fell over and into the hole, entangling the dwarf.

Struggling against the ropes, the dwarf found he was unable to pull free with his hands. Undaunted, he began hacking at the thick ropes when the water-logged bow suddenly capsized, throwing him against the dank wood. He continued to hack at the ropes while sea water poured in, but he could not compete with the speed of the rising water. In mere moments, the water rose about his knees, then his waist, then his neck, and finally, over his head.

Farulazar released his blade and watched the *demon bane* fall slowly among the debris in the compartment. As the front of the ship sank, it righted itself once more, and the dwarf looked up at the brilliant flames as they consumed the debris above. He smiled, content in the way of his death, pleased to know that as Fiend Fighter, he had an unbeaten record..

SEABORN SENTINEL

Brannon Hall

SEABORN SENTINEL

Tenth Tides
(28th day of Sumborok)

The smooth, twisting shell of the underwater crustacean spiraled outward, increasing in size as it went. Nothing moved within the confines of the shell. Perhaps it was empty, or perhaps the creature within feared discovery, sensing some threat or movement nearby. Silt crabs were, after all, odd creatures. They usually lived in the watery depths, thriving around sea kelp beds or decaying coral reefs. But there was no such habitation here, only a single silt crab shell surrounded by blue waters that deepened gradually into blackness. A lone figure moved gracefully through the beryl brine, intent on the shell. His blue-scaled skin blended perfectly with the water around him. His hand reached down to the shell, plucking it from the sand gently. Grains of sand fell through the webbed fingers of the figure's hands like sands through an hourglass counting down time. The alônn brought the shell close to his face, inspecting it; it seemed empty, yet not. The last grain slowly tumbled from his hand; as it did so, the shell moved. The particle fell, not to the sandy floor, but upon a floor of bloated fish corpses. The alônn gasped as the entire area in which he floated transformed before his eyes into a charnel visage of death.

A twinge of pain drew his attention to the shell in his hand. It now seemed to pulse with life. He tried to drop it, but it clung to him. The water around him grew bitterly cold. He looked down at his hand as his once beautiful blue scales turned pale white.

The shell pulsed like a beating heart, and dark fissures raced across its surface, growing larger with every beat. The alônn tugged violently at it, vainly trying to remove it. The deep blue of the water slowly turned red around him, drawing towards the pulsing shell. The acrid stench of old blood filled his gills, choking him. The moment the blood touched the shell, everything became utterly silent. The alônn's heart raced and his senses screamed, though the area around him remained as calm as the eye of a hurricane. He looked to his hand to discover that a single claw had extended from the shell and pierced his palm. As he tried to remove the pincer, a dark, viscous liquid exploded violently out of it, enveloping his face in blackness.

Kal awoke in a frantic rush, a scream gurgling from his lips. A voice, faintly sounding in the distant trails of his nightmare, whispered a simple warning, *"It is coming."* The alônn druid looked instantly to his hand, where a single drop of blood formed from a pinprick in his palm. There was no shell, and his scales had their customary blue hue to them. He ran his arm across his brow, the image of the exploding shell fresh in his mind. Perhaps the creature within wanted out.

* * *

Seventh Tides
(1st day of Layfanil)

D'yorn found a comfortable perch upon the rim of the great rift. This was his assigned region of the immense ocean, his responsibility. When the council had first "promoted" him to this remote area, the young alônn scout had been insulted. After all, he felt that someone with his combat skills and talent for observation should be serving in the Deep Harbor, not patrolling the outermost rim.

When he had spoken to Kal Strongsurge, a somewhat eclectic alônn - and the head of his druidic order - D'yorn had conveyed his unrest at his assignment. Kal gently reminded him of the level of importance that came with the patrolling of the outer shoals. He had personally passed over several other officers in order to place D'yorn there so that his talents could be best used.

The fact that Kal had also assigned D'yorn to the rim because of his quick temper that had stirred up more than a little trouble among their kindred was not mentioned. There had been no good reason to be completely frank. In any case, the proffered explanation pleased D'yorn, who now took great pride in his position as a first line of defense not only for the Deep Harbor but for the Three-Cities themselves.

Although D'yorn understood well the importance of his station, he had been out here, patrolling alone, for longer than he cared to think - with no activity to show for it. So, to make up for his lack of action, he at least had found plenty of time to investigate some of the ancient and mysterious shipwrecks that were nestled in their final resting places deep below the waves. Here and there, he found a few interesting trinkets, but nothing of value and sadly, very little that could be classified as "exciting."

Most of his dour race would never have disturbed these ghostly ruins, but D'yorn was ever curious about the world around him. A trait reserved for the young, his fascination with the vibrant life that made the ships home was something that his elders never quite appreciated. He often tried to communicate with the many sea creatures using the mysterious methods his kindred had developed, which Kal had taught him. One day, he hoped to develop his abilities to match that of other, greater alônn who could not only communicate with, but could control and guide the marine life, both flora and fauna. Even the inorganic water itself was a servant of the most powerful druids among his people.

D'yorn entered an area of the outer shoals, near a large sea trench, and what he saw there troubled him. Once teeming with life, this forest of coral and kelp was now strangely a place of silent death. Coral, which once colored the oceanic shelf with their bright and vibrant colors, had paled to a sickly white pallor while the kelp forests had turned a dead, mottled-brown. Those creatures that were not anchored down had fled to places unknown. The overall effect transformed this once-resplendent marine canyon into a vast, vacant, ghastly hall.

D'yorn lifted his head. As water filtered through his gills, he sought out any unusual odors that could have warned away the sea life in this area. A strange smell caught his attention. Almost startled, he cocked his head and drew the odor in, almost savoring it. Like nothing he had ever experienced, it was neither rotten nor sweet. Swimming through the ever-silent, shifting currents, he tracked the smell, following it to what he hoped would be its source. After some time, he reached a dark abyss that in all his travels he had never approached.

He peered down into the gloomy chasm and saw a ship that, in its dying plummet to the bottom, had crashed into the deep crevice. The water there was cloudy, almost opaque, making it nearly impossible to see through. Though he had patrolled these waters many times, he had never encountered this wreck before. Curiosity getting the better of him, the young alônn stretched his webbed hands out and dove from his perch on the trench's rim, slowly spiraling downwards towards the mysterious wreck. As he descended, the water changed, becoming much colder and murkier, until he could barely see more than a few feet ahead of him. What had been merely a clouded gloom many feet above had below become an eerily obscuring soup. Undaunted, he plunged deeper.

Suddenly, the murky water swirled before an undertow of icy-cold water, revealing the ship's shattered bow. His heart raced as he neared the unfamiliar hulk. Mere feet away, the muddy silt curtains parted enough for him to make out the ship's bowsprit and the tattered, rotting remnants of one of the jib sails looming above him. He passed down the side of the vessel, cautiously inspecting its ruined hull, until he reached its stern. There, in ornate brass lettering covered in verdigris and barnacle growths, he found the ship's name: *Black Saber.*

D'yorn's blood ran cold as he stared at the ominous plaque. In childhood, he had heard the many stories about the mysterious vessel; he'd learned a great deal of its evil presence. Belonging to a crazed archmage, the ship had set sail from Crown half a century earlier, carrying a strange relic of unimaginable evil. For unknown reasons, the ship, its crew, and the wicked cargo sank. Some said the relic thirsted for the crews' souls and so drowned them, while others believed the crew purposefully scuttled the ship to destroy the relic, while still others spoke of a blood-drenched mutiny. Yet, all the stories agreed that the crew and their chaotic master could still be heard, murmuring and moaning, in the waters surrounding the doomed ship, their tortured souls seeking other ships and passengers to feed the evil relic's hunger.

It was a ghost story told to young alônn as a warning against swimming into unknown waters - else the *Black Saber* might draw them in and swallow their souls. A mildly frightening story when told at the communal table, it was something else entirely now, looming before him in silent menace. For a moment, D'yorn floated at the stern, his eyes riveted to the plaque, his body rigid in fear. All the terrible images he had conjured in his mind as a child flooded his mind, paralyzing him. Would his soul now be consumed by the terrible evil inside? Yet, he seemed powerless to resist the dark lure of the unknown.

Suddenly, movement within the hulk, followed by a long, hollow creaking, jarred him, sending him into motion. In one fluid movement, the alônn scout flexed his muscles, and like a coiled spring released, he rocketed straight up and away from the evil wreck. His legs pumped harder than ever before, and he clawed with his arms for the safer waters above. He dared not look back, fearing the terrible monster he knew would certainly devour him.

He furiously broke the water's surface, bursting out into the night air for a moment before crashing back into the ocean. He frantically scanned about, desperate to discern just how far out of his patrol area he had wandered, but everything was as it should be. His position was right; he had not left his zone. He knew the area well and certainly would never have missed the wreck of the *Black Saber* in his earlier patrols. Something dreadful had happened, punctuated by the appearance of the grisly ship and its wicked cargo. He glanced fearfully down through the seemingly safe expanse of water between him and the ship.

"It should not be there," he protested aloud to himself.

And he was right, he knew it. However it had arrived, its menace was undeniable. Worse, he knew somehow that the relic within was awakening, its macabre will stretching forth. And of all his kindred, he alone knew where it was.

Pleased that he was still alive, and certain the self-conjured monster from his mind was not chasing him, D'yorn rested at the surface for a while, treading water. He closed the gill slits that ran diagonally across his neck and breathed in the cool night air through the small openings above his mouth. The alônn were by nature water breathers, but they were also capable of breathing air for short periods of time. They preferred to remain under the waves, but they would occasionally come to the surface to interact with the air-breathing races above. Few of his kin actually relished their time away from their watery home, and many of the insular race had never left it.

Somewhat smaller than humans, the blue-scaled skin and other unusual features of the alônn made them very easy to spot on land. A small dorsal fin ran from the back of their skulls, down their spines, usually terminating at their lower backs; this fin aided in navigation through their aquatic natural habitat and occasionally varied in size and coloration. Their gills were narrow, shark-like slits that ran diagonally across their necks and were easily closed whenever they ventured above water. A long, spine-like fin, covered by a transparent membrane, could be seen on the back of their forearms, running from the wrist to the elbow. These "forearm fins" could be fanned at will, and they added speed and maneuverability while swimming. Many alônn also adorned these fins with intricate squid-ink tattoos, accented by blotches of phosphorescent blood from deep-sea fishes, which could then be flashed as a sign of identification.

D'yorn steadied himself as he bobbed gently on the surface of the water while he played the experience in his mind. Of all his kindred, he had found the *Black Saber!* That he found it was enough to confirm Kal's trust in him and his vigilance. Yet, his excitement was tempered by the hard reality of the wreck. It was nowhere near where legend placed it, and it definitely should not have been this close to the harbor. He had not imagined the terror, the bitter cold, or the sense of evil that emanated from within its terrible hold. The ship was here below the surface, below him, and it was real.

He suddenly realized he had to inform Kal of his discovery, had to warn of the awakening evil now stirring beneath the waves so close to Crown. As D'yorn reached for a simple coral necklace that hung around his neck, a glint of light on the dark horizon caught his attention. He squinted as he strained to better see the faint light.

'A ship, perhaps?' the scout thought.

Odd for this time of season and not near one of the common trade routes, for this ship came from the north! His mind racing, he fingered the necklace, noticing he had but a single section of coral left. He peered again down into the dark brine below and then to the light on the horizon. A choice was set clearly before him: he could use the necklace now to warn Kal of his discovery, or he could save it and await the approaching light.

He sighed, allowing his excitement to cool. The call of duty was louder than his rash urge to abandon his post. The *Black Saber* would have to wait; besides it was a shipwreck, it wasn't going anywhere any time soon – he hoped. There would be plenty of time for him to warn his kindred of his discovery. D'yorn opened his gills and dove beneath the waves once more and headed out to the mysterious light on the horizon.

A few hours later, D'yorn surfaced to see how far from the light source he was. The ocean currents had been with him this night, and the ship, for the light source had indeed been a ship, loomed in the distance, roughly a mile away. He could not see any details, but the ship's size was considerable even at this distance. From time to time, a flash of lightning behind it on the horizon would outline it for a split second, revealing the vessel against a backdrop of storm clouds. Perhaps that was the light he had seen. By his judgment, a fierce storm was brewing that would likely overtake the ship before it reached the safety of Crown's Deep Harbor. Further, if he was a fair judge of storms, this was a dangerous one; the approaching vessel could soon end up like so many others, resting on the ocean's bottom.

D'yorn decided to assist the ship's captain and offer his aid in navigating these waters, a task that many alônn undertook in order to steer vessels away from danger. While this service was offered as a courtesy to the surface folk, it also provided a valuable service to the sea-dwelling race: it kept the splintered hulls of ships from littering their pristine and protected seabeds. The scout dove, and in moments, he could discern the dark footprint of the ship's hull on the water's surface. He breached the surface, fully prepared to call out to the vessel's occupants.

What D'yorn saw was unlike anything he had ever encountered before. It was so incredible that he at first thought he saw the ghastly remains of some demonic whale and almost fled in panic. The mammoth vessel that bludgeoned its way through the water was encased in ivory white bone formed into the semblance of a giant rib cage. Like wicked claws reaching from the foam, the ribs gripped the ship, arching over the sides and terminating thorn-like several feet above the deck. The ship's sails looked like the veined, out-stretched wings of a great dragon. A fear every bit as powerful as that which gripped him at the wicked wreck below filled the young alônn as he gazed at the demonic craft before him. Crafted by the darkest magic, the perverse ship rode the waves in quiet menace.

Afraid of being spotted by lookouts above, D'yorn slipped quietly beneath the surface, leaving only the slightest ripple on the already frothed surface. As he drifted down, still in shock, he noticed the shriveled corpses of hundreds of fish, their pale, withered bodies being pulled along by the ship's momentum and tossed about like chum it its wake.

The alônn scout watched in stunned disbelief as a large school of sack fish swam lazily toward the ship in a trance-like stupor. Normally, fish swam along the sides of a vessel or sometimes ahead of it, never directly towards it. Once the school reached the hull, the fish shriveled, their vibrant colors fading, and they joined the macabre stew in the ship's wake.

With a sense of horrified urgency, D'yorn yanked the last piece of coral from his necklace and snapped it in two. He released the fragments and they floated for a moment before him. The water around the coral halves swirled and writhed for a moment before slowly congealing around the pieces. The compacted liquid began taking the form of a small, iridescent-scaled creature with large, bulbous black eyes: a water mephit. The aqueous entity glanced at D'yorn and then to the ship's hull. Obviously disturbed by the vessel, the mephit then gazed back to the alônn, awaiting its orders.

D'yorn recited a message of warning about the vessel, including its position and heading to the small creature and then instructed it to find and inform Kal. The mephit burbled its understanding and quickly departed. The young alônn then turned once more to the vessel. His senses screamed for him to swim away from this abomination as fast as he could, but he had to learn more about this ship and its crew. It was his station to do so, it was his responsibility. He would board the ship and discover as much about it as he could.

D'yorn slowly swam toward the ship's hull, hoping that it would neither en-spell nor kill him. He cautiously out-stretched a webbed hand as he neared. Nothing happened; whatever was affecting the fish was not harmful to him. Emboldened, he placed his hand on the ship's hull; while it was cool to the touch, it did not seem to emit any instantly lethal properties. The alônn had little trouble finding foot- and hand-holds, and he quickly scaled the vessel's side. As he climbed, he noticed that the ship's surface became progressively colder, as if its very form was turning into ice. While it didn't numb his fingers like ice normally did, the strange chill did pervade his very core, causing light puffs of vapor to issue from his mouth and nostrils with each breath.

He reached the railing of the vessel, which ran between the rib-like sections of bone, and peered at the deck beyond. In the storm-backed darkness, he could see several short, stocky forms moving about. The alônn could clearly see four forms from his vantage point, but he heard several more voices from the darkness nearby, their owners obscured by night and the grisly bone.

"I swears I saw'd sumfin' there in da waters!" came one gravelly voice.

"Ahhh, you's jus' tryin' ta get out a workin', me thinks!" growled a second. "'Sides we got us a lookout, and you ain't him! Now come on, we got's ta get goin', the Cap'n'll skin us alive if'n we ain't got everythin' ready in time ta see th' harbor!"

The first voice seemed to turn away and in a somewhat muffled tone, added, "Ten days is plenty o' time ta get what's needin' ta be done by th' time we's dockin', me thinks."

The disembodied voices continued their conversation but trailed off as their owners walked from earshot. D'yorn wondered silently what the crew of this awful vessel planned to do in ten days. His musing was interrupted by the first falling drops of water as the storm that had drawn him to this ship began in earnest. A flash of lightning streaked across the night sky, and he flattened his body against the ship, hiding himself in the shadows as best he could. A second bolt flashed, and he stole a glance to the crow's nest but did not see a lookout. Thinking himself fortunate, he began silently making his way along the side of the ship, moving stealthily from one rib to the next. He kept a wary eye trained towards the deck, watching for more crew members; spying none, he continued his careful trek aft.

Tiny bits of sleet soon joined the rain, as D'yorn silently crept towards the stern and the captain's cabin. To his peril, the ticking of the icy stones upon the ship's deck and sides obscured the strange clacking foot falls of an approaching creature. A flash of lightning suddenly revealed a large, bizarre, centipede-like creature that had spotted the alônn scout and was following him along the outside of the ship.

Startled, D'yorn lost his grip on the bone railing and fell back towards the water. Half a dozen pincher-tipped tentacles lashed out from the strange beast and caught him before he plunged into the ocean's safety, mercilessly biting into his flesh. The young alônn caught a solid glimpse of his attacker and gasped: man-sized, the creature was far from human, and it looked nothing like the silhouetted sailors he had seen on deck. Out of the creature's thick, segmented torso sprouted countless tentacle-like limbs, some of which served as legs latching onto the ship, while others clasped him tightly or lashed the air threateningly. The monstrosity's flattened, mostly horizontal body twisted upwards slightly, revealing an alien, bulbous head crowned with a mane that ran the length of its back: this horrible, writhing fringe was composed of hundreds of glaring eyes of every size, each perched on a fleshy stalk of varying length. The eyes' focus was diverted towards every element of motion surrounding the creature: from the falling rain and sleet, to the pitching waves, to D'yorn himself. It was if a crowd of small animals were perched on it, some looking this way, some that, all intensely interested in whatever it was that caught their attention.

Abject terror filled the alônn's soul as he looked into the forest of wicked, supernatural orbs. He felt himself being drawn up towards the creature and knew that if the beast managed to drag him aboard the ship, he would certainly die. D'yorn grasped desperately for the slightest hold on the hull, anything that might afford him some leverage against his attacker so that he could break free of its grasp.

The diabolical creature sensed D'yorn's intent and tightened its grip, lifting the alônn out and away from the ship, hanging him over the churning waters. Then, with tremendous force, it slammed him against the ship's protruding ribs. D'yorn gasped as the breath was blasted from him. He felt a bone crack in his chest and tasted the copper of blood in his mouth. The abomination slammed him against the ship's side once more, his head thumping against the bone and wood. The alônn saw stars and then nothingness, as his body went limp and his mind fell into the dark waters of unconsciousness.

The strange brute hauled its unconscious catch up the side of the ship and onto the deck, cackling with pleasure. Once aboard, it righted itself, twisting about and placing several of its appendages on the deck to steady itself before hefting up its prize. The few members of the crew that were on deck at that late hour gave it a wide berth as it skittered aft.

None of the men felt comfortable around the thing, but none would openly admit their disquiet, either. They certainly would never grumble to their captain, for he had brought the odd creature aboard himself. It served as the lookout for the vessel, and none begrudged it its duty, for it spared them many a cold, lonely night in the highest perches of the ship. For its own part, the beast seemed to enjoy its solitary duty.

The strange creature stopped at the entrance to the captain's cabin. The single door opened as the ship's master stepped out to observe the commotion. "What have we here?" he questioned.

The creature held up the unconscious alônn and clacked in its native language.

"Interesting," the captain muttered as he looked closer at D'yorn. "Interrogate him! Let's see what brought this slit-neck out so far."

The creature's mandibles quivered, an equivalent of a smile, as it slipped below deck with its charge. Within moments, muffled screams could be heard throughout the ship as the creature went about its unholy interrogation. The captain smiled as if listening to sweet music, as he strolled the deck of his ship.

Hours later, the creature emerged from below deck, holding the still-breathing but broken form of D'yorn. He bled from numerous open wounds, one of which was a grisly hole in his skull that the creature had bored in an attempt to draw information directly from his mind. The beast released its grip, and the alônn scout fell to his knees. Turning to the captain, the interrogator began clacking quickly.

The captain regarded the alônn and slowly walked around him. "D'yorn" he said icily, "Tell us how many of your kind are in the waters below us."

D'yorn feebly looked up at the captain, but through his swollen and bloodied eyes, all he was able to make out was the silhouetted outline of something not-quite-human. Though his jaw was shattered and bones grated against one another as he did so, the alônn managed to raise his head and spit. Enraged, the captain grasped D'yorn by the face and lifted him off the deck. The young alônn flailed about, desperately clawing and kicking with all the strength he had left. The captain's taloned hand squeezed.

D'yorn managed a few muffled screams before his skull collapsed with a sickening pop. The crew, observing the scene, chuckled at the sound as the captain snarled with anger. He released his grip, dropping the lifeless body to the deck. Glaring down at it, the captain's eyes narrowed dangerously.

"Skin him! I want his corpse hung where I can see it!" he boomed, as he stalked to his cabin. "Search the area for more of his kind." The doorway to the captain's cabin slammed as the ship instantly sprang to life, with the crew rushing to fulfill their captain's orders.

Ahead, the sun rose slowly in the eastern sky, bringing day once more to the slumbering world. Before them, the golden rays glinted off the ocean like thousands of diamonds strewn upon undulating sand. As the bright rays neared the monstrous vessel, however, they dimmed, swallowed up by the menacing clouds of the closely-trailing tempest; the tempest that they were bringing, the abominable storm that would soon lash Crown with all its fury.

* * *

Fifth Tides
(3rd day of Layfanil)

The soft body of the silt crab skittered across the sand as it searched for a new home. Silt crabs rarely left their shells unless they had outgrown them, which happened once every seventy-five years or so. During that time, the creatures mated and their population swelled. Their bloated numbers would invariably drop, though, from increased predation or disease, and so a delicate balance was maintained. Such was the order of things; the fittest would survive while the weaker were eaten. Even in the higher species, there was an element of survival, based on the ones that were able to adapt to their changing environments or those able to adapt their environments to suit themselves.

Kal Strongsurge intently watched the crab as it moved from shell to shell, searching for a suitable home. Though its outward appearance would change, it would remain the same creature it had always been. The alônn druid reflected on just how similar they were - he and this crustacean.

Kal gazed at the undersea garden that teemed with life, plant and animal alike. It had long been a place of refuge for him. It was here that he met the hermit who had once called this place home. It was here that Kal had learned the hermit's ways, discovering how to command and communicate with the creatures and plants of the sea, as well as those from the land above. It was here that Kal learned that, given enough time, wisdom, and understanding, all parts of the natural world, the inanimate stones, air, and water, would bend their wills to his own.

The hermit had died many years ago, leaving his grove and tunnels, truly his entire world, to his young apprentice. Pleased that someone would remain to protect that which he loved and perhaps teach others to do the same, the hermit had, in effect, left his shell to Kal. One day, when he was old and infirm, Kal knew that he would find another in whom he could trust to leave the garden-grove to; thus, the cycle would continue.

Kal absently rubbed a small spot on the palm of his hand. He had not slept well in the past several days, and during his waking hours, things around him caused him to recall bits and pieces of his past - as if somehow, together, they meant something more. He watched the silt crab nudge a particularly large shell and roll it over, crawling inside. The shell rocked gently side to side as the creature settled inside. As it stood, the shell wobbled as the crab tentatively found its balance within its new, much larger home.

"Steady there, little one." Kal spoke softly to the creature as he smiled. "You shall grow into it soon enough."

His gaze returned to the grove and its adjoining caverns that he had grown into: his shell. The alônn druid wondered if he would ever have to grow into another one, or if there would be someone to take this one when he was gone. The young D'yorn had been one of the few alônn who had shown an interest in Kal's calling, but he was still too young and impulsive to follow. Yet, Kal felt that if his heart and mind found a balance, he might do well. Perhaps, one day he might be able to assume the mantle, if that is, the young alônn's passions did not get him into too much trouble first.

A sudden shift in the demeanor of the animals and plants in the grove alerted Kal to the presence of a visitor. A thought from the druid and a curtain of kelp, tipped with spiral-shelled snails, parted to reveal a young alônn, one of the Council's many messengers. Kal floated over, fanning his forearm fins in greeting.

The lad smiled as he returned the greeting with one of his own and spoke. "Master Kal, the annual Council meeting will convene soon, sir."

Kal nodded in appreciation for the information, though he loathed the meetings. It seemed the Council had little else to do at these largely ineffectual annual gatherings than to deliberate over the matters from the prior year's meeting. Mostly composed of headstrong skeptics, the alônn ruling body could, and usually did, deliberate on the smallest, most insignificant of details for what felt like an eternity.

The mere act of forming the Council to begin with took many cycles of the tides. The original debates over who would be eligible to hold seats, not to mention where they would meet, had bogged down into an endless series of meaningless debates. The location of the meeting itself would likely have still been undecided, these many hundreds of tides later, had it not been for a wise wizard from Crown who provided a secluded, completely neutral location, reachable only by means of a portal.

However, there were a select few of the Council who did not suffer fools well and sought quick action. Many of these outspoken ones had been expelled from the Council for their heated remarks; a few had even been banished from Deep Harbor altogether, ejected from "polite" alônn society. Kal often found himself allied with this latter group, unwilling to waste time on discussing decisions that could be quickly made and acted upon. Though the meetings galled him, the druid was generally content to attend them because he knew they ultimately affected those for whom he cared. Rarely, though, did he suggest topics for discussion or consideration.

The only reason the council had not banished him already was because he headed the border sentinels who protected the outer regions. Not a job relegated to a political hack, he survived not only because most did not seek his position, but also because he was so good at what he did. Kal was a free thinker, which in the alônn society was discouraged. However, this same trait gave him the ability to look beyond the kelp in front of his eyes, to see the greater events and how they might affect Deep Harbor and beyond - a trait that very few of his brethren possessed.

Even so, he did not dispute the Council as openly and verbally as had his brother, Quellon, many years ago, ultimately leading to his banishment. The maverick now resided above the water, maintaining The Sea Shrine in the Deep Harbor District of Crown. Yet Quellon's punishment had not been reserved solely for him, for his entire family had suffered to some degree in his shame. Many were declared forsaken, and forced into the small class of "undesirables" in alônn society.

Kal remembered well the rejection of his loved ones. He had initially protested the act, but he was restrained by his few friends, who finally convinced him that he could do more good as a Council member than among the ranks of the banished. He finally relented and took his Council seat once more. Even so, the event left him jaded and suspicious of those with whom he shared a quorum.

Kal looked outward from his thoughts towards the young alônn lad who stood by, ready to escort him to the Council chambers for which he held so much scorn. He sighed and was about to speak when something caught his attention. He cocked his head, as if he were listening to a conversation across some great distance. After a moment, a relieved look settled onto the druid's face.

"Tell the Council that you could not find me, but discovered that I had been called away on an urgent matter." Kal smirked. "And that I will be unavoidably late..."

"Sir?" the young alônn questioned. "But I..."

Kal stopped the child with an upturned palm and a wink. The boy swam away, confused but relieved that his day's duties would soon end. The alônn turned, and with a short swim, he found himself within an inner alcove in the rear of his grove. Here, a cluster of thick kelp formed a living wall. Kal applied his druidic skills and whispered to the kelp, coaxing it to move. The watery weed began to twist and turn inward, revealing a dark hole that burrowed into the heart of the coral. He continued to whisper, and soon, two large, fearsome looking moray eels appeared; they regarded the druid coolly and then flanked him, undulating in place like twin living pillars. The alônn then re-directed some of the tendrils of kelp, and they reached deep within the hole and produced a shield-sized oyster shell.

One of the last things the hermit had revealed to Kal before he had died, the magical *scrying* shell was but one of the many items that resided within the guarded coral pocket. Though he was aware of all of the items now contained in the secret cache, Kal guessed it was but a pittance of what had once resided there. The Hermit had taken the names of the other wondrous items that had once lain within the coral cache with him to the grave. And while the tight-lipped morays were not the best conversationalists in the deep, they did guard the treasures he had left well.

Kal opened the oyster shell reverently and gazed into the silvery surface of the mirror-like pearl contained within; his reflection peered back at him. His fingertips traced a series of small carvings that lined the edge of the mirror-pearl's surface, each glowing as he did so. As the last rune was activated, they melted into the glassy surface. His reflection wavered for a moment and then was replaced by an image of an entirely different location. A familiar green glow shone through the mirror, bathing the cavern around him. Kal squinted his eyes in the mirror's light and peered into what lay beyond.

"Quellon?" he called. He knew the caretaker of the Shrine was there, for he had just received his *sending*. "Quellon?" he called again, a bit louder.

"Waves peaking, pools speaking! Can't a body simply eat in peace 'round here?" came a muffled voice from somewhere beyond Kal's field of view. "Quellon never bothers a soul when they eat, but it never fails when Quellon eats, water talks. When water talks, Quellon must listen. Lucky Quellon isn't hungry or Quellon might go crazy as a bubble!"

The rambling continued for a short time, sometimes making sense, sometimes not, before the aged alônn finally stepped into the mirror's range of view. Despite his eccentric nature, Quellon was wise and had strong ties to the surface world; his network of informants were well entrenched throughout Crown and were an invaluable resource. The wily alônn had spent many years on the surface, away from his brethren under the waves; many alônn claimed that this made him peculiar. Kal knew otherwise, and no alônn alive knew Quellon as well as him.

Now able to see his brother in the mirror-pearl, Kal called again, "Quellon!"

The alônn mystic jumped as he heard a voice from his pool. "Kal?" he questioned, as he stooped low to view Kal's image floating in the water. "Good timing, Kal, Quellon was just about to *send* for you..." He stated, wagging a chiding finger at Kal through the pool's surface. Kal merely shook his head and smiled. "...after Quellon had finished eating, of course! So perhaps your timing is not as good as you had thought it to be, eh?!"

The old alônn looked around the room as if there were something missing. With a gruff grunt and one hand planted on his hip, Quellon looked towards the kelp-thatched ceiling and snapped his bony fingers. A wide blade of kelp slowly extended, curling its edge a few feet before touching the tiled floor. The elder alônn snorted at the newly formed chair and sat down with a wide smile across his face. In the pool, he saw his brother, "Kal! I see you received Quellon's *sending*."

Still smiling, Kal nodded in agreement. "What can I do for you today, brother?" he asked.

Quellon stood up from his kelp seat and began pacing around the pool, as if locked in deep thought. Kal, knowing his odd elder, patiently waited and watched the image stride around the edge of the mirror-pearl's surface. When Quellon finally stopped pacing, he stopped and again looked for the seat that, by his thought, should have been behind him. Not seeing it, he snapped his fingers a second time and another kelp blade lowered itself to the floor. The old alônn snorted at it again and sat down facing Kal.

"Ah! There you are Kal. What took you so long?"

Kal had grown accustomed to these "conversations" with his brother and took them in stride. "I do apologize for the delay, dear brother. How may I help you this day?" Despite their often disorienting nature, he still preferred having any score of conversations with Quellon over a single hour in session with the Alônn Council.

"Quellon needs information from you *this day*." His brother replied, "You have eyes along the borders watching for ships, do you not?"

"Indeed, I do." Kal replied

"There is a surface elf named Arastin inquiring of a vessel coming in from the north. Many ships come from the north, Quellon told him, but not this time of year. Have your sentries spotted any ships bound for Crown from the north?"

Kal shook his head; nothing had been reported to him recently. That was D'yorn's territory, and while he was uncharacteristically late in his report, this caused little concern to the druid. It was true that the younger alônn had a way of getting in over his head at times, but Kal had no reason yet to be alarmed.

He began to reply when he was interrupted by a sudden rush of bubbles. A water mephit zipped into the cavern and quickly relayed D'yorn's disturbing message of the bizarre ship and its heading.

Worried, Kal turned to the image of Quellon. "It looks as if your ship will be here in five day's time," he stated grimly. "And it sounds none too friendly."

The druid then instructed the mephit to take a new message to the Council. They had to urgently assemble the military committee: something evil was quickly approaching, and preparations had to be made. The tiny aquan creature burbled a reply and sped off on its mission.

Kal turned to Quellon. "Seek out and learn what you can of this ship, brother," he said gravely, "and contact me as soon as you can. I must know why D'yorn has not returned from his patrol and exactly what it is he saw that disturbed him so. I have to convince the Council to allow a war party to intercept this vessel before it reaches Deep Harbor and the docks of Crown."

Quellon nodded as the image of Kal disappeared from the pool. The old mystic stood from his kelp seat and turned to gather the items he would need to seek out the ship, almost stumbling over the first chair. He swatted the kelp and huffed. "Move!" he scolded. The kelp slowly slithered into place in the ceiling of the domed shrine as the alônn scuttled off. Quellon knew the rough location of the vessel and would be able to find it, but it would take at least a day to do so. The mystic hoped there would still be time to do something about it.

Back in the grotto, Kal sent the pearl-mirror away and focused on the task before him. He made a mental list of the underwater creatures he may need to summon to help him. He then gathered together a few herbal potions and components he could use to persuade the ship's captain to listen to him should reason fail. Kal looked at his armor draped over a patch of coral and thought about putting it on. The loose net material looked flimsy and no more than a net that a fisherman would cast. However, the netting was magical, a gift from the hermit along with the strange, string-less bow that stood propped next to it. He decided against taking them - the Council did not allow weapons, and the armor, other than demonstrating the urgency of the situation, would be of little use there. He could collect them afterwards.

Finished with his preparations, Kal swam from his grotto and started for the portal that would lead him to the Council chamber. His mind was made up; he would make them listen to him. If they did not, then he would do what was needed without them. He only hoped he would not have to.

* * *

Fourth Tides
(4th day of Layfanil)

Quellon sat at the edge of his pool, murmuring softly, asking the waves for guidance. The pool rippled as if drops of rain were striking the surface, repeatedly marring the image of the vessel thereupon. He had not slept, having worked straight through the previous night to find the ship. What he had initially found was a violent storm that seemed to be growing worse with each passing hour. At first, he thought that the ship must have been destroyed in that gale. Had that been the case, though, his *scrying* would have had nothing to focus upon, and so he delved deeper.

The storm was so fierce that its rain was actually affecting his pool, causing it to ripple and splash. He could feel the drops as they plopped onto his skin. Puzzled, but undaunted, Quellon pushed deeper through the thick storm clouds, intently focusing his search. A sharp clacking drew his attention from the pool to the floor nearby. To his surprise, it was actually hailing within the Sea Shrine!

Something was not right. Images had never projected physical properties through one of his *scryings* before. Before his eyes, the air within the domed building dropped drastically in temperature, frost lining the walls and slicking the floor. Physical cold did not bother the alônn, as they were used to the deep, cold waters where the sun did not reach. But this coldness was different, almost like the chill of death itself. As he worked, the room darkened, and Quellon began to hear distant rumbles of thunder.

Small bits of hail ticked and tacked across the seashell-tiles, as if it were somehow trying to break Quellon's concentration. Yet the old alônn was a master of his craft, and even in his weary state, few things above or below the waves could divert his focused attention.

The ship slowly came into view through the storm. It seemed to be leading the storm, not threatened by it, navigating the waves boldly and without any evident concern. A casual glance of the vessel revealed that it was a large, bulky ship made to run cargo. Nothing about it indicated violence or malevolence, except the magical black and red aura that swirled about it. That wicked glow looked utterly alive and entirely wicked.

Quellon swallowed hard. He had never seen nor felt anything this powerful before. Alone, the combined forces of the alônn would be hard pressed to overwhelm such power. The alônn mystic pushed his tired mind and body harder, and soon its deck rolled into view, its crew tending to their duties. Quellon strained, trying to glimpse the ship's name as the bow crashed through a massive wave. As the white foam receded, he could momentarily discern the ship's moniker, and an icy chill raced down his spine: *Frozen Idol.*

Pressing further still, Quellon altered the position of his invisible *scrying* eye in order to get a better look at the ship's crew or its captain. The sailors seemed ordinary enough: the rough and leathery sea dogs found on nearly every ship that plied the seas. Standing at the helm, upon the poop deck, was a tall, thin, white-haired elf that was unmistakably the captain, flanked by some kind of strange, centipede-like creature. The aged alônn drove harder, trying to get a better look at the captain and the odd creature beside him. Despite the unnatural cold in the Sea Shrine, stinging sweat forced Quellon to blink, and when he opened his eyes, his gaze immediately locked with the captain's. A primal snarl issued from the pale elf's lips.

"Fool!" was Quellon's only warning as something unseen slammed into him. The blow tossed him like a rag doll across the shrine and into the far wall. The image of the white-haired elf in the pool shifted, becoming something distinctly not elven, and then it changed back into the elf, before fading from view. Quellon saw none of these changes as he slumped against the wall, unconscious.

* * *

Third Tides
(5th day of Layfanil)

Kal swam nervously around the Council chamber like a netted fish. He had spent the greater part of the previous day trying to convince the Council of the dire urgency of the matter at hand. The debate continued steadily, so much so that very few of the members had even slept. The Council could not understand the need or purpose of risking their warriors in a potential battle that seemed in no way to directly affect the alônn. Through endless debates, questions, retorts, and deliberations, the meeting dragged on with no promise of conclusion. It seemed as if the Council members thrived on talk alone, never desiring action. As long as it could be discussed, they seemed content.

Kal's resolve was wearing very thin. He had already riled the Council several times, demanding they put aside their pettiness and act on the situation before it was too late. Instead of initiating action, the outburst served only to spur the Council to deliberate whether or not Kal should remain as a member of the Council. That, in turn, lead to a debate of who, then, would oversee the alônn border scouts if, in fact, Kal was unable to maintain his position. Ultimately, the Council decided against banning Kal and slowly drifted back to the issue of the approaching ship. But to Kal, much precious time had been lost. Then, to his utter amazement, the Council adjourned for a short recess. An hour and a half later, the members re-entered the chamber, the more prominent among them glaring coldly at him.

"Kal," called the Council's head as they all found their seats. The impatient druid looked up, jaw clenched, knowing full well what decision had been surreptitiously reached. "We simply do not see how a war party is warranted to intercept this vessel. First of all, if it means to attack the harbor then that is an issue for Crown and not the alônn. Second, it is merely one vessel! We strongly disagree that a single ship could pose enough of a threat to warrant our attention." Kal flared his forearm fins with anger as his response welled up from within him.

"Is that so?" issued a familiar voice from the Council chamber's entry portal. "Do you not recall a single ship that reeked havoc in our world once before, Aaragos?! Or has your thick-skulled, indecisive mind simply forgotten what the *Black Saber* brought into our realm from the surface?"

Quellon stormed into the council chamber, a gaunt, robed figure in tow. The Council members shot upwards, swirling about the watery chamber, enraged that this outcast would dare intrude on their meeting. Aaragos demanded Quellon leave the chamber, bubbles frothing angrily from his gills. Others called for guards, or for the eccentric alônn to be drug away in chains. One voice, in the rear, shouted out that perhaps he should be cast in the Great Deep with stones tied about him and his gills sealed shut.

Undeterred, the elder alônn swam forcefully into the center of the chamber, his face resolute. Sweeping a finger across the throng in a slow arc, stopping at last on Aaragos, he said, "Quellon thinks it is time for you to be still and silence yourself. You have no idea what you are facing."

Kal was surprised; for Quellon to intrude into the Council chamber, things must be grave indeed...

The alônn mystic continued, "This vessel, the *Frozen Idol* as it is named, heralds doom. It harbors a dark aura about it and seems to be leading a great storm straight into the heart of Deep Harbor."

"I suppose the waves told you this?" Aaragos balked. "This Council does not heed the words of insane outcasts! It is rash thinking like this that almost cost us our very existence long ago." Aaragos was an exceptional speaker and held much of the Council's attention. "When our forefathers first entered the caverns we now call home, it was not a rash thought or wild act, but rather a rational move based on logic. They knew that rash acts, lacking discussion and deliberation, would affect not just themselves but their heirs as well. Such decisions were enacted only after every possible ramification had been considered." The councilman looked around, confident he held the attention of everyone in the room. "Who are we to contradict what our forefathers built our very past upon?"

The room erupted in thunderous, gurgling cheers. Kal, enraged beyond rational thought, stabbed his finger at the pompous delegate. "Mark these words well, Aaragos! The blood that will be shed shall stain **your** hands! May it forever cloud your gills!"

With that, Kal surged out of the chamber before Quellon could stop him. The elder alônn started towards the door to retrieve his friend, but the robed figure touched his arm, keeping him from following.

"Let him go, my friend," the robed figure said, lowering his grey hood. A sapphire-colored stone swam in a lazy circle about his bald head. "He only needs time to calm himself. It falls to us to convince the Council now." The figure turned to address the Council, bowing, "Queen's care 'pon you. I am Tenet, aid to the Queen, and I speak for her and with her authority. I have information about this ship and the evil that it bears."

"Why should we listen to you? You are not alônn, but an etherean - and you come to us in the company of an outcast!" shouted an angry voice from the group.

"What you speak is true, and knowing that I am an etherean, you must also know that I cannot lie. So, I ask only that you weigh this in your deliberation," replied Tenet gravely. He paused, looking at each member before stopping at Aaragos. "The cult of the Grey God and the Iceskull League are in some manner connected to this vessel. All that draws breath, above or below the waves will be affected by its presence."

For several hours, Tenet explained to the Council members the events he had witnessed and what he had discovered. Quellon added, too, the tale of what he had seen while *scrying* the ship. And though they were addressed by an outcast from their realm and one of the strange ethereans, the Council listened.

* * *

Second Tides
(6th day of Layfanil)

Kal had heard nothing after his curse to Aaragos, as he swam angrily from the council chamber. Determined to take action, he had gathered the small force that now floated in formation behind him, under the premise of a rescue mission for D'yorn. Eight strong, each of these alônn were hardly prepared for a protracted fight, but they were fiercely loyal to Kal and willing to follow his commands, regardless of the personal peril. Enraged at the Council's lack of foresight and stubborn immovability, Kal had decided that he would act in their stead. If they would not lead, he would.

The druid sat upon the back of a giant squid, eyes focused on the waters ahead. Occasionally a small fish or squid would dart in and swim beside him, lending valuable intelligence about the waters ahead. The other squid-riders in the hunting pack marveled at his command of these small, but very efficient scouts. Not in vain were these eight loyal to the druid.

This continued for some time, until Kal signaled to his mount to stop, motioning for the rider behind him to come forward. "The dark ship approaches from the northwest. Take three alônn and dive deep," he ordered. "The wreck of the *Black Saber* is not far away. Be wary and do not approach it. I want you to carefully work your way south; await my signal before approaching the vessel. I and the others will approach from the other directions, and we will flank the ship. We will then order D'yorn's return."

The rider nodded and left with two warriors in tow. Kal watched as they moved out of sight and then turned to the four remaining soldiers, ordering them to head northward in a wide circular pattern, towards the great ravine, and then to angle back to the southwest to cut the ship off. They nodded and sank deeper, leaving Kal alone in the dark waters.

He figured the ship's captain would likely retaliate, or at least sound a call of alarm, at the appearance of a large group appearing near his ship. But surely a single alônn would not cause too much concern. Kal swallowed hard. Something seemed wrong about the entire situation, but he could not figure out if it was his sense of trepidation or merely residual anger at the Council. He sent a mental command to his steed, and the druid sped off to intercept the *Frozen Idol.*

Aboard the *Idol,* the multi-eyed, horrific lookout spotted the submerged group with its otherworldly sight. The creature skittered its way up to the forecastle and told the captain all it had seen. The captain ordered his pet out of sight and much of the crew below deck. He'd been wondering if someone might come looking for the slit-neck fool who'd snuck aboard his ship. He gazed fondly past the bow, to his "new" figurehead and smiled. Flesh hung in tattered strips, exposing blood-stained bones beneath. The seagulls had gorged on most of the softer bits, but some semblance of the alônn still remained.

"It looks like someone has missed you, D'yorn..." the captain growled, smiling wickedly. Though the ship's appearance had been magically altered to look like a cargo vessel, temporarily masking its hideous bone hull, the captain had purposefully kept the alônn's remains visible - just in case someone came looking for him. The tall, white-haired elf crossed his deceptively thin arms and glared out in the direction from whence these new alônn came. "I guess your time alone is at an end."

* * *

The surface of the water rolled above Kal's head as he and his mount narrowed the gap between them and the ship. He mentally directed his giant squid, and the beast raised just enough to put its rider above the waves, while keeping its own bulk submerged. The mid-morning sun strained for the sky, but it was obscured by the dark thunderheads that blotted out its light and warmth with driving rain and cold, whipping winds. Even had he not been a druid, Kal would have discerned the unnatural nature of this storm; its fury intensified the closer he came to the ship.

Ignoring the stinging rain and frigid wind, Kal leveled his gaze on the vessel as he stood on the squid's back, fully visible, with his arms crossed over his chest. In his anger, he had forgotten his armor and bow and now felt slightly vulnerable. Yet he was not helpless: he had other means at his disposal.

He called upon his druidic abilities and the ocean itself became his defense. A thin skin of salty water flowed up and around his form, hardening to the touch yet remaining fluid enough to not hinder his movements. Kal hoped the armor would not be necessary, as he was there for a parlay and not a fight. He moved alongside the ship, hailing its captain.

Lightning crackled through the black storm clouds. The vessel's captain glared out at his visitor, a lurid grin widening across his elven features. Strangely, the storm did not seem to bother him or the few sailors who stood on deck at his side.

"What is your destination and from where do you hail?" Kal yelled through the whipping wind.

"We carry cargo to the harbor of Crown," replied the cultured voice of the ship's captain. The wiry elf looked nothing like a sea captain to Kal. His slight frame and long, white hair was a far cry from the tough, deeply tanned skin and sun-bleached hair of most sea-faring folk. "As for our home port, that is none of your concern."

"I cannot allow you to pass into the harbor of Crown with ill intentions-" began Kal, but he was cut short by a clap of thunder, in what seemed a reply to his statement. His patience wearing thin, he snapped, "I will not allow you passage unless I know the nature of your visit." As he spoke, the druid issued a mental command to the giant cephalopod below him. The great beast surged up from the water, bringing Kal's eyes level with the deck of the ship. The squid then snaked tentacle after tentacle upwards, creating a grand, undulating stairway that took him to the ship's rail and eye-to-eye with her captain. Still swimming, the massive sea beast had no problems keeping up with the ship's forward movement.

Shouts of "Sea monster!" rippled through the few crew members on deck, as they reeled from the beast's entwining tentacles. Undaunted, the captain's cold eyes never left the druid's squid-stair.

"I will stop you and let this accursed storm have its way with you and your vessel if I must," Kal stated calmly. "Now, what is your business in my harbor?"

The captain's laughter caught the druid by surprise. "You may try, slit-neck," he said, grinning menacingly. "But you will fail, as did your snooping friend before you." A vile chuckle issued from his lips as he gestured towards the bow with a point of his chin.

Kal's mental command to the squid moved him in the direction the captain indicated. As he neared the forecastle, he began to discern what looked like be a body strung to the prow. The alônn had not given the profile a second thought as he approached, for many sea vessels were adorned with humanoid figureheads. The captain's heartless reference to this one, however, sent chills down the druid's spine. As Kal drew closer to the figurehead, the storm calmed, giving him a better look. The druid's body nearly went limp at the sight. There, on the prow of the vessel, hung the torn remains of his friend, D'yorn.

The murdered scout barely looked like an alônn anymore. Fragments of skin fluttered like torn parchment over bloated muscles and organs. The bits of bone that pushed through this ghastly covering was still vein-coated and blood-stained. D'yorn's mouth hung agape, screaming a silent, eternal wail. The dead alônn's face was bruised and bloodied, evidence of the brutal tortures he must have endured.

Kal felt his stomach twist and thought he was going to be sick. A wave of emotions surged over him like a wave as he looked upon his young apprentice and friend. He fought them all back except one: rage.

With a single thought to his mount, the druid flew into the air, catapulted by the tentacles beneath his feet. The wild-eyed Kal hung motionless in mid-flight, as if time itself had paused. The crew beneath him drew weapons and made ready for battle. Kal did not notice them; his singular focus was the captain. He wanted nothing more at that moment than to strangle the life from the accursed elf.

A dozen seasoned and armed men stood between him and this goal, however. The sailors wondered how this lone, unarmed creature could be so confident as to attack them head on. Their answer only barely preceded their horror as the entire ship suddenly pitched forward with a violent jerk. Two of the crew members, caught completely off guard, were crushed under the flailing, mast-sized tentacles of Kal's giant squid. Another was tossed overboard while yet another was grappled and dragged, screaming, beneath the waves. Both soon became food for the giant cephalopod.

Kal landed among the men as they scattered and scrambled away in mindless terror, his eyes never leaving the captain. A chill shot through his legs as he came in contact with the deck of the ship. He noticed the rain was now changing to flurries about him. The alônn ignored both the chill and the snow as he bolted aft towards the captain.

As he passed the mainsail mast, a thick-shelled appendage shot out, catching him solidly in the face. Kal reeled in pain, dazed by the unexpected attack. Before he could react, the attack intensified, blow after relentless blow causing him to stumble backwards. He swung blindly, wildly but unable to land a blow on his tormentor.

The druid heard a strange clacking sound as his attacker paused long enough for him to regain his footing. Kal's eyes widened at the sight before him. The strange, centipede-like creature looked like nothing he had seen before. Its thick, segmented upper appendages ended in whip-like tentacles that snaked constantly. Kal could already feel his magical armor weakening but knew that without it, he would already be dead.

The creature chattered excitedly, lashing out with two tentacles, grappling Kal in their fierce grip. Again the creature's speed took the druid by surprise, and he was unable to dodge the attack. Immobilized, he heard the captain's laughter and called out to his squid mount for assistance. Sensing no response from the sea creature, he glanced over his shoulder and saw the behemoth tentacles lying lifelessly on the deck of the ship, frozen solid. One of the crew had suffered a similar fate and now stood frozen, locked in an eternal struggle with any icy tentacle.

The captain sauntered up to Kal with a smirk on his elven features. "My, my - this looks familiar," the captain gloated. "Where have I seen this before?" He tapped a slender finger on his chin. "Ah yes! Just before your kin died; D'yorn was it?"

The sound of D'yorn's name pained Kal more than his many wounds, and he struggled to free himself. Despair began to sink into him as he fought, unable to lash out even in futility. The captain's hand shot up and grasped Kal's throat as the centipede creature squeezed the breath out of him.

"I see you have met my pet," the captain cooed, as he stroked the strange creature with his free hand. "It is a scarrock; they make such wonderful lookouts, you see." He slowly ran his fingers through the thick, fleshy stalks that buttressed the creature's many eyes. "And, they have an amazing talent for, shall we say, tearing information from their captives. Sadly, few ever live long after they are done, but it is such an enjoyment to watch. D'yorn begged for his life as my scarrock played with him. I wonder – will your screams be louder than his?"

The bizarre creature began clacking wildly at the thought. Kal looked desperately past the captain and out towards the open ocean.

"Looking for your friends?" he asked coldly. "I don't think they will be helping you any time soon." He roughly twisted the druid's head to where his crew had just hoisted up six frozen alônn corpses. "We saw your little deception long before you even approached my ship." The elf patted his pet and smiled with perverse glee.

Seven lives were now on the druid's conscience, and he again felt his rage flare within him. Feeling returning to his limbs, Kal called forth the heat from the volcanic vents deep below the surface. Channeling that heat through a druidic spell, he spat the searing heat onto the elf's face and arms. Searing welts and blisters leapt onto the elf's exposed skin, and the captain reeled in pain, screaming.

"KILL HIM!"

The scarrock squeezed Kal, blasting breath from his lungs. Again drawing upon his nature-based abilities, the druid shifted form into a small crab and quickly slipped from the creature's grasp. Skittering across the deck towards the railing, with the monster in tow, he knew that he could not out pace the beast. He again shifted forms and forced his limbs to react. He lithely dove to one side, tucking and rolling, before bouncing back to his feet. Growling fiercely, he grabbed a handful of the scarrock's eye-stalks and, using the creature's momentum, flung himself over the ship's railing. He felt the sickening sensation as half-a-dozen eye-stalks ripped away from flesh just before he plunged into the churning brine below. The creature's shrieks of pain from its torn eyes could be heard over the storm's roar and the crashing waves.

Kal drifted into the surging ocean's blackness, his spent limbs now limp and unresponsive. He closed his eyes and concentrated, calling for any aid the ocean might provide. A large shark soon responded to the druid's calls and gently slid under him, stopping his descent. Two sharksucker fish quickly detached from their massive, toothy host and began tending the druid's wounds as the aquatic quartet moved away from the vessel. Soon, the two alônn soldiers who'd escaped the captain's attack joined them and removed their leader's battered form from the shark's back. Kal thanked his rescuer as it and its two paired fish swam away. One of the soldiers applied a healing salve from his kelp bandolier to Kal's wounds.

"We must return to the Council immediately," the druid gasped weakly.

"But what of the others?" one of the alônn inquired. Kal's look told them everything they needed to know, as the three sped off towards the portal to the Council's hidden chambers.

* * *

First Tides
(7th day of Layfanil)

Aaragos floated, cross-armed and cross-legged, in the midst of Council. Tenet had done well in convincing them that action was desperately needed. Quellon had remained behind after the etherean departed to ensure that the assembly remained focused on the current crisis. Though present for the entire discussion, Aaragos was resolved against involvement of any kind. The rest of the council was split evenly between immediate, but considered, action and a swift, reactive strike.

Quellon floated off to one side, not wanting to distract them from their debate with his unwanted presence. After all these years, it still amazed him that the Council could be so ineffective, so lethargic. If only they would listen to his teachings: the waves never argued with one another, and they accomplished so much more than any individual could alone! The portal to the chamber shimmered, and two armed alônn entered, with Kal in tow. Quellon darted to meet them as they gingerly set the druid down.

"What happened?" he asked one of the soldiers, quickly producing salves and healing stones from his woven kelp vest. The Council's debate silenced; they neared the fallen druid in a knot, desiring to hear what had transpired.

"We confronted the *Frozen Idol*, sir. Eight of us, led by Kal, volunteered to mount a rescue for D'yorn...-" one of the alônn replied, "...but only we three returned. Kal nearly died on that accursed ship. As for D'yorn, we are uncertain." Quellon gently placed his brother's head on the sandy floor and turned to the Council, grim-faced.

"Fool!" Aaragos barked.

Quellon's quick backhand stunned even himself. The mystic glared at the pretentious Councilman. "Quellon suggests you hold your tongue before Quellon removes it!" he said, glaring at the stubborn alônn. "While you sit here debating, the first strikes of this war have already fallen. You are fools to think the Founders would have bickered amongst themselves as do you. They would have acted long before the first alônn perished! Now, their blood sullies your hands! You shall tell their families why they died and why the ever-wise Alônn Council did not act sooner! May the waves and tides have mercy on you all!"

Quellon lifted his brother and started for the portal. "How many more will it take?" he spat as he left.

"Quellon!" spouted Aaragos's, a pained look on his face. He turned briefly and addressed his fellows. "Gather the war party," he said simply. He then turned back to the mystic. "Will Kal be able to fight?"

"His injuries are numerous but not fatal," Quellon offered.

"Good, I need him to lead the assault on the *Idol*," Aaragos said, "Only he knows what we face."

Quellon nodded as the Councilmen swam off to alert their soldier-kin.

Aaragos watched as the Council chamber quickly emptied. "Truly, may the waves and tides have mercy," he whispered to himself.

* * *

New Tides
(8th day of Layfanil)

Kal's strength returned quickly under Quellon's care, and in less than a day, he was making preparations for another confrontation. The mystic had returned to his shrine to commune with the waves and try and discern more of the awful ship and its foul captain. Quellon's voice echoed through his pool and into Kal's mirror-pearl, and then his image slowly took shape within it.

"The *Frozen Idol* has docked and this preternatural storm savages Crown. I have never seen a maelstrom like this, Kal. The wind and water are easily enough to push a stout man off his feet. It's as if the waves and tides themselves have been angered by this vessel. Of the aberration you described, there has been no sign. It is, no doubt, below deck along with the whole of her crew. Na'akiros, the captain, along with four of his men have departed and entered into the city." Quellon paused, "The waves speak ill of this storm, of Na'akiros, and of his ship, Kal. Please be wary."

Kal solemnly nodded and waved his hand over the mirror-pearl, darkening its surface. Near his grotto, the war party had already assembled. Once triggered, it had not taken the Council long to gather their forces. The alônn druid pulled the net armor over his body and slipped the bow into its sheath. The magical weapon had neither string nor arrows, but it needed neither.

Kal turned and gazed at his grove, his shell.H He knew full well that he might be seeing it for the last time. He pondered if the silt crab felt this way when it left its home. He wondered if another would come to replace him now that D'yorn was gone. Sadly, he wondered if he even cared.

Covering the doorway to his grotto with a living lattice of coral and kelp, Kal mounted his newly summoned squid, and the two sped off. Within moments, he was floating at the head of a battle-ready alônn assault force. His people's history was in the making. Without a second thought, Kal bolted for the harbor of Crown with the war party close behind: an aquatic spearhead aimed at the heart of darkness itself.

* * *

The storm raged above the waves. Driving winds flung freezing sheets of rain like blankets of needles at the city of Crown. Finger-like lightning streaked through the jet-black, starless night sky, gripping the edges of the storm clouds as if to draw the fierceness of the storm into one focused location directly above the harbor. The flashes of lightning revealed the utter chaos that the storm brought to Crown's havens. Splintered remains of boats and docks alike littered the tumultuous waters about the harbor, flinging themselves against the seawall and into the city itself. The city's inhabitants had taken cover from the violent juggernaut that wailed upon their homes. Mothers held their children close while husbands battened down their shelters. None could remember the last time a storm of this magnitude had hit the city, but everyone felt the fear it lashed down upon them.

Lightning illuminated the inky blackness of the wild waves, and where moments before only the spray from the whipping waves and splinters from broken boats churned, now stood the combined forces of the alônn war party. So dark was the harbor from the storm clouds and tearing rains that were it not for the sudden flashes of lightning, they would have not appeared at all. Like silent, menacing sentinels, they had entered the harbor on their wrathful mission.

Standing on the backs of their mounts, Kal ordered them to circle a particular ship, the only ship in the harbor that seemed mostly unaffected by the tempest. Something was protecting the *Frozen Idol*, a palpable barrier that shielded it from the surrounding storm's violence. Kal had seen the ring of calmer water surrounding the ship from below the waves. He now stood upon the back of his great squid beneath the ship and just inside that ring. The druid slowly drew himself waist high in the calm waters surrounding the vessel.

"Na'akiros!" he roared to the ship's deck above him. Within moments, the white locks of the ship's captain appeared at the railing. Though he could not see the elf's silhouetted face, Kal could feel his lurid grin.

"My, aren't we the resilient one?" Na'akiros called. "I though you'd died and sunk to the bottom of the ocean." He laughed. "Silly me, I should have known - fish float when they die!" The captain narrowed his eyes threateningly at the druid.

"I'm here to finish this, Na'akiros! I'm here to..."

"Revenge?!" Na'akiros barked, interrupting. "Any other time I would be honored, but, as you can see," the captain looked around at the storm and lifted his palms. "I'm detained at the moment. Besides, it looks as if you've already been caught in a fisher's net, slit-neck."

Kal didn't bother looking down at his net armor but remained focused on this vile elf. Now that he knew his foe, he would not waver in his presence. Too many lives demanded revenge for the druid to be daunted by meaningless words.

Na'akiros glared at him, "I tire of you, fish-man." He turned to the members of his crew, who had joined him at the railing. "Finish this irritant once and for all! I want to see his bloated corpse floating in this Wyrm-forsaken harbor!"

The elf began stalking away, paused, and looked back over his shoulder. "On second thought, I want his corpse hanging next to his comrades'!" He turned back to the railing and looked down at the druid once more. "Did you hear that slit-neck?" he spat. "Tell D'yorn when you see him that you both dangle at the tip of my bow!" The elf turned on a heel, pointing to a group of sailors. "You all – kill him! Kill him and hang his sorry carcass next to the other, stinking slit-neck fools!" Na'akiros stormed off. The sailors turned to the ship's edge and glared at their single opponent, alone in the stormy water.

At the mention of D'yorn's name, raged welled within the alônn. Kal closed his eyes and plunged his clutched fists in to the ocean. The water around the druid churned as if it had taken on a life of its own. The briny fluid crawled up his hands and into the net-like armor like a liquid spider, bringing with it a multitude of tiny sea creatures. One by one, they found a resting place within the water that encased Kal's body, as if each knew exactly where it belonged. As the last creature flowed into place, the watery shell around him rippled with a brilliant cerulean light.

A gift from the hermit, the sentient armor was seamless, and if one section of the living shell was damaged, another member of the whole would shift and take its place. Kal stared up at the snarling crew as two hissing eels coiled around his forearms; the druid's visage promised painful death to any who stood against him.

With a mental command, the giant squid flung Kal high into the air. This time, expecting the wild maneuver, the crew's eyes followed the druid as he arced into the ebon sky – exactly as Kal had intended. So focused were the sailors on him that they utterly missed the massed alônn force emerging behind him. As one, they blasted through the mystical barrier that protected the ship from the raging storm outside. Utterly surprised, the crew blanched at this new spectacle. Like a living wave, the alônn crashed - weapons drawn - against the ship, scattering its surprised crew across the deck. Kal's somersault brought him within feet of the captain, who whirled around to face him.

"I trust you remember my pet?" Na'akiros asked with a wicked grin. "I'm sure he remembers you!"

The scarrock appeared from out of nowhere, blasting the breath from Kal as it rammed into him, tossing him across the deck. The alônn smashed into a group of dark robed were-rats, sending them sprawling. Kal tried to discern from whence they had come, but the abomination waded in viciously. An oozing sore marked the spot on its back where he'd torn the clump of eyes in their last encounter. The druid was pleased to note that a dozen or more additional eyes hung limply around the wound, useless and blind.

The scarrock chattered with hatred, each functioning eye tightly trained upon the druid's every movement. An alônn soldier side-stepped into the creature's path, and the abomination drove a dozen pincers into him, eviscerating him and then pushing him to the deck as if he were a meaningless diversion. Nothing would prevent it from taking its revenge. It scuttled over the still-screaming alônn and brought both tentacles down on Kal in a devastating slam meant to finish him.

The druid deftly rolled out from under the beast's massive blow. Boards splintered under the seething rage of the scarrock's attack. As he rolled, Kal slammed a fist into one of the beast's legs, trying to slow it down. In fluid concert, the druid's sentient armor pressed the attack, as an eel, striking from its forearm perch, sent bolts of searing electricity arcing into the creature's flesh. The scarrock screamed, its whole body shuddering beneath the withering assault. Seizing the moment, Kal reached out with his other arm. The second eel sprang out and attached itself firmly to another of the beast's legs, unleashing its own fierce barrage.

The scarrock lashed out at the thing on its leg, swatting frantic to remove it. The eel coiled tighter, jolting the abomination mercilessly. Desperate, the creature screamed, ripping its own leg from its body and flinging the limb and its tormenting eel into the ocean. The seething hatred within the abomination was then replaced with something far more primal as the scarrock lashed Kal with its tentacles. As the beast's appendages wrapped around Kal, the first eel struck again. Remembering the painful attack, the scarrock quickly batted the hated sea creature across the deck. The moment the abomination connected, however, the fierce eel unleashed all its energy into the tentacle, scorching and withering it.

The centipede creature recoiled for a moment, clacking in pain, but then it recovered and charged the druid, almost knocking him overboard. Using the beast's momentum, Kal swung out and over the railing in a giant half-circle. Twisting his lithe, muscled body sideways as he arched back towards the ship, he slipped expertly between the rail's spindles and landed solidly on the deck; ten feet of empty space now stood between him and his foe. The water called from beneath him, and for a moment, he considered a tactical retreat in order to fully regroup. At that moment, the thought of D'yorn, brutally murdered, roared into his mind, shadowed by the burning rage he'd felt before. He turned and faced the creature, an odd grin across his face.

Enraged, the scarrock lashed out with its one good tentacle. Kal stepped into the blow and grasped it inches from his face. With a deft turn, he slipped behind a sailor who was caught up in his own battle with an alônn warrior and wrapped the tentacle around the man's neck. The scarrock jerked to pull its tentacle loose from the druid's grasp, ripping the sailor's head clean from his shoulders. The severed head rolled to a stop several feet away while the body crumpled to the deck. The abomination flexed its mandibles in frustration but was answered only by the fully armored punch of Kal's fist. The creature's shell plating cracked.

"Ya'neese!" Kal yelled. It was the name of one of the alônn soldiers who had been killed during their first encounter with Na'akiros. The scarrock staggered back, but the enraged Kal did not relent. A small pincher-tipped tentacle slipped from beneath the monster's torso scales and jabbed towards the druid's neck, only to be snagged and snipped by an ogre-crab's claw from Kal's armor.

"Rholl, Vas'sier, Sorak!" Kal screamed, recalling the names of his fallen comrades. Each name was married to a staggering blow from his vengeful fists. The alônn could feel the hard shell crack beneath his withering assault. All the while, the abomination danced around defensively, trying to avoid Kal's vengeful blows.

Reeling in pain, the scarrock lashed out first with the small pincer as a feint, followed by a powerful blow with its remaining tentacle, slamming the druid the full width of the ship. Kal slammed into the railing and grinned, despite the pain. Far from surprised, he was pleased. He and the scarrock had changed places, just like he had planned.

Kal's armor slurped as it relocated several of its aquatic inhabitants, filling in the gaping hole from the beast's attack. A vengeful expression passed over the alônn's face as he readied himself, standing and drawing his unusual bow. He grasped at the area where a bowstring should have been and pulled back, whispering a druidic phrase that told the bow what it needed to know. Aiming at the scarrock, Kal yelled the name, "Tal'yorn!" and released his pull on the invisible string. A viscous stream of water jetted from the bow and splashed upon the scarrock's chest. As it struck, the watery arrow used the information that Kal had given it - the weakness of its target - and exploded into a flashing dome of lightning.

The bolt blasted the beast backwards, toward the ship's railing. Smoke trailed from the new blackened fissure in the scarrock's scaly armor. Before the creature could regain its footing, Kal yelled again as he loosed a second arrow. "K'lorn!" The second fusillade almost toppled the beast over the railing, blasting away a great, gooey chunk of the creature's outer shell. The scarrock reeled.

Kal placed his bow back into its sheath, closed his eyes, and focused inward on his druidic powers. The scarrock managed to scramble up to the top of the railing and gathered itself for a leaping attack. Just as the abomination prepared to spring, Kal's eyes suddenly snapped open.

"D'yorn," he whispered.

The scarrock felt the presence before it was actually seen. The abomination's many eyes spun and swiveled around as a wall of water erupted from behind it, and a giant eel rose high above the deck of the ship. The eel's cold, black orbs focused intently on the otherworldly creature; its massive maw opened wide and blue arcs of electric energy danced wildly from tooth to tooth. Stunned, the beast couldn't move or fight in the face of its own imminent demise. With needle-sharp teeth glistening and tongue held back, the gigantic eel crashed down, removing the scarrock and a crescent-shaped chunk of the deck in a single, giant bite.

As Kal watched the wretched scarrock disappear, shouts of alarm and the din of battle drew his attention forward to where smoke billowed out of the hold. Kal bolted from the forecastle towards the smoke to see what he could do. As he ran, an explosion from below rocked the vessel, sending numerous combatants sprawling. The druid steadied himself and then pressed on to learn what was happening below.

Kal weaved in and around alônn, wererats, cultists, and crew alike. His own forces were holding the battle, but only barely. With the appearance of the dark-robed wererats and men, their advantage vanished. What had become a clearly discernible battle had devolved into a chaotic brawl.

One of the rats dove at the druid, screaming a curse in the name of the Grey God. Kal instinctively threw up his hands and encased the stupid creature's head in a sphere of water. Suddenly more concerned with drowning than fighting the druid, the wretched thing stumbled back into the fight, scrabbling at its neck and the bubble of water over his head.

Kal's attention was then drawn to another section of the ship, where he could make out two slender figures locked in battle - two elves, the white hair of one clearly marking him as Na'akiros. As he started towards the two combatants, the elven form that was the ship's captain twisted and changed into something else, something far worse than a mere elf, however evil. The druid watched in horror as the captain's screaming form shifted, becoming bestial, scaled, and white, while sprouting large, bat-like wings: a half-dragon!

The sounds of battle were suddenly drowned out by the titanic roar of the storm as the magical barrier that held it at bay dissolved. At the same instant, the ordinary-looking cargo ship blurred and then changed, becoming a nightmarish form. Bony ribs suddenly sprouted over the deck and the mast, sails, and rigging changed into giant, skeletal, dragon-like wings. Its true form had emerged. Driving rain and wind whipped the ship and all involved in the desperate brawl. His mind reeling, Kal could barely make out the winged creature through the freezing rain as it twisted its head toward its foe and loosed a cone of ice that blasted the other elf from the ship. Before he could react, a loud crack and a demonic scream broke Kal's focus. A blood slicked anchor was wedged into the decking at the lip of the hold; it had blasted upwards from below.

Kal sprinted towards the hatch, and once there, he could see several fire-licked barrels through the smoke and the whirling sleet. He could tell by the smell that they were filled with super-heated whale oil. As he watched, transfixed, first one, and then all of the barrels ruptured in the intense heat. Time seemed to slow for the alônn as the roaring, rushing flames licked hungrily towards him, propelled outwards and upwards by the explosion's force and the spewing, boiling, burning oil from within the barrels.

Kal closed his eyes, knowing it was going to hurt. Calling on his druidic abilities, he placed a wall of water between himself and the coming maelstrom, hoping that he might be able to at least extinguish the flames before the ship exploded out from under them. Just as he saw the flames erupt through the watery barrier, Kal felt a wave of frigid, unnatural cold tear through him. Before he could even scream from the searing, ripping pain, the flames blasted him from his feet. He had not been quick enough.

At that moment, the entire side of the vessel gave way as the massive explosion tore through the ship and rocked the entire harbor district. Windows in nearby buildings and warehouses shattered from the violent concussion. Bodies of sailors, wererats, and alônns alike were ripped apart and catapulted high into the air and into the dark, yawning waters below.

The explosion hurled Kal through a nearby warehouse window, smashing him into a small stockpile of crates. The traumatic force of the landing would have killed a normal man, but luckily, the alônn, used to the crushing depths of the deep ocean, were made of sterner stuff. Yet, unlike a man, an alônn can remain for only so long out of his native element. And so, Kal lay broken and shattered among the ruin of splintered crates and pulverized fruit, unconscious and dying, his gills flaring in vain.

Jalkesh, the now-disillusioned and jaded street vendor who had sought out this warehouse as his last refuge, looked down at the alônn lying amidst his shattered life and livelihood. His mouth and eyes were wide open in sheer disbelief at this being who had come so very close to crushing him and who had managed to destroy his very last crate of produce.

A single, small melon rolled to a stop against his foot. The slack-jawed vendor reached down and lifted it up - the only piece of fruit to have survived the violent crash - and held it before his face. As he gazed upon it, the melon cracked and split into several large pieces, plopping wetly to the floor. The vendor's eyes fluttered in disbelief and then rolled up into the back of his head as he joined his prized wares in a dead faint.

THE BONDS THAT BIND US

Corey Blankenship

BONDS THAT BIND US

The farm boy wore a thick layer of sweat. Mud crusted his boots, bored under his fingernails, and tanned the frayed hem of his pants. The spring never looked more inviting to the farm boy than after a full day of plowing and seeding the first rows of his father's thirty acres. The lad began to remove his tunic before diving in...

"Ah, better leave him be."

The morning exercise was over. Alastar enjoyed watching the lives of common people, and such probes into the sheet of shimmering water also refreshed him to do more taxing divinations. Without such lighter studies, he would wear down the most precious tool he had: his mind. As the only person to survive the transition across the Veil, Alastar was the Order's sole eyes on the other side of Well of Time's domain.

The water's cascade misted his dormitory-sized grotto, thin tendrils of milky air lapping off the pool of liquid that consumed the bulk of the space. Pillars jutted up from the pool's center, forming a tiered landing where Alastar could sit and gaze into the falling, glittering wall of water. When not there, he would immerse himself into the brisk depths of the pool. Alastar would descend through the luminescent water, its azure tint focusing the brilliance of his iridescent scales, to the rocky bottom below: his stone quarry.

He eyed the square slate before him. Thirty two figures stood frozen on the flat surface. Half of them lurked in a coarse midnight, their shapes vaguely discernable upon the smooth stone. "Who shall probe this malady's heart...?" The chant of the water did not say. Turning from the board, the oracle focused two sapphire eyes into the fluid barrier. His glow faded into the whisper of a candle as clouds welled into the twin orbs. Then the storm broke into a center of clarity as he returned to the array upon the rock. His eyes latch to a single piece resting dormant behind a row of pawns. A hazy grey drifted around the crudely shaped horse's head. Stretching out with his will as much has his hand, Alastar dropped his psyche into the aspect of the knight before him; rustling through shadows and phantasmal matter to the sleeping form hidden in the Deep Ethereal. The bond is long enough for him to utter a single phrase. "Tenet, a shadow is coming..."

The oracle then turned his sight to a white chess piece: a bishop, crafted carefully, lovingly, from seashells. Alastar began to turn the piece over in his hands, reaching out with his mind to the waters beyond and below Crown. He knew this piece well, for the blood of the alônn ran through Alastar's veins too; he knew that this piece would be ready and willing to serve, unlike so many of their brethren. Calling out with his mind, the oracle stuck the seashell-formed piece into his pool, piercing the water's surface with the bishop's mitre. Dark liquid spiraled from the point, as if Alastar had drawn blood from the water's surface itself. Nodding, the oracle whispered, "It is coming."

Now, if only Alastar's rook could be located so easily...

* * *

Moss dripped from the drooping jaw. Better than the brick-hard loaves and stagnant mote water, fungus had become a staple of the oltreggan's diet. He reached up a mammoth hand to redirect the olive juice back into his cracked lips. Seven days a week he repeated the same process: sleep, eat, and sleep again. The guards didn't show any leniency toward the muscular creature after the second day of his imprisonment. Though the swarthy oltreggan had been dumped here for his lack of finances, other prisoners sought to jibe the smelly brute at the main mess hall. That is, until he proceeded to yank up the whole lot into the air, hurling their wiry frames against the stone walls and hardwood tables. The guards had to call in a mage who ensorcelled the wailing barbarian before he killed the entire chain-gang bunch.

Now, imprisoned in his double-barred cell, the oltreggan wasted his astounding physique, his revelry for adventure dampened by the dank hole and inactivity. "Gritgut hate diz place."

"As ye should, ye mound o' blubbering garbage."

Gritgut glared at the callous guard, tendons snapping taught in his throat. He no longer lunged at the bars, swiping with his powerful hands in vain. The desire to squash the cruel, wiry sentry hadn't vanished; rather, the restraint to act had only condensed the barbarian's rage.

Giff me un shot 'n he'd be pok'n jibs at ze 'rats.

Guessing the savage's thoughts, the guard leered near the bars and spat out. "Eh, a plague 'pon ya, ye overgrown piss pot. Ya ain't no better than them wererats: rot-hide sewer suckers what foul th' bodies of goodly folk." The guard was close enough that Gritgut could smell his breath: a vile combo of cheap whiskey and smoked sausage; too close. Femur-sized finger bones leading the way, Gritgut unleashed his fury upon the mangy sentry's gullet, shattering the stunned jailer's jaw and larynx in a single swipe.

"Now dee rats'll git u."

Gritgut only lamented that the body, and the jailer's keys, had fallen out of reach once more. How many guards would it take until he was free?

* * *

A much fatter jailer spun the oiled lock open, eyeing the oltreggan with a gruff indifference. "Don't know what friar hooted yer name, but ye'r free...now get outa me cell!"

Rubbing his sore haunches, the bite of an iron-shod whip still cursing his indomitable nature, Gritgut leaned forward to squeeze through the slim seven-foot entryway. Few men could stand next to him for long without growing uneasy, but the jailer merely shrugged and walked away, leading the gruff inmate down the shadowy corridor. The passage slid through the rock walls in a meandering fashion, more confusing due to ill maintenance than design. When the pair reached the oak door, its iron bolts withdrawn, the wispy watchman began tugging at the frame. Gritgut placed two fingers in the crack and lightly slid the barrier wide, generating a sigh of relief from the weary guard. "Thank ye."

The oltreggan shrugged. "Me freed faster tha way."

The plump jailer chuckled heartily as the wiry lad turned bright red, glaring as the brute ambled by him. Gritgut breathed in the open air and stretched his long-cramped limbs. *Freee...* At that moment he noticed the diminutive man standing in navy robes. The figure seemed to hesitate before moving nearer to the massive oltreggan.

"Greetings...you must be Gritgut. Many call me Jerrin. Follow me; your master has orders for you."

"Me master?" Gritgut hadn't heard from his Whispering Lord in a long time. Not since the Voice had led him to becoming a ship's mate.

"Ah, he'll speak with you shortly. As for now, follow me."

The duo wound through the sun-swept streets of the Old Temple Ward, Gritgut's bootless feet slapping loudly against the smooth cobble. He barely ducked beneath a sign of a weeping woman, her eyes filled with omen: the well-known signpost for *The Prophet's Tears*. Gritgut wondered why the lady-in-the-sign looked so sad, but continued following Jerrin through the massive structures of the Ward into the miry alleys of the Flats. Gritgut eagerly sunk his feet into the muck, savoring the sensation of grime running between his toes; too long had stone bruised his heel! The other man enjoyed the sludge far less, eyeing his stained robe with disdain.

Soon they rounded into an open expanse of stagnant water, brown from refuse and silt. Rickety spans of lumber connected the stilted buildings around the rivers edge; they were lifelines of the river-delta community. Gritgut's guide turned toward the left and headed for a spire of gentle, blue stone. The oltreggan had not ventured into this part of the Flats often, but anyone who'd ever spent a day or more in Crown knew of the Moontower, harbor for the infirm.

"Me no sick!" The oltreggan cried in alarm, fearing an examination - which would probably include a bath - was somewhere in his immediate future.

Stifling his mirth, Jerrin paused at the base of the steps. "Your master merely requests you come here. He wanted you to know the way."

"Na hurd ta feend dat glowee towur."

Smiling, Jerrin replied, "Ah, but he had to make sure. Come in and I'm sure your orders will be swiftly delivered."

Gritgut eyed the soaring staircase inside the Moontower with a sense of dread. Its swirling, fluted shaped, coupled with an odd sapphire glow that permeated the air, made his stomach twist. He had never been apt at balancing, so the prospect of careening many feet to a shameful death sparked his ever-ready anger. Thankfully, a familiar, small voice near his ear rendered such a feat unnecessary.

"Greetings, my friend. Glad you made it safely from prison...I hope your stay wasn't too rough."

Despite the relief to again hear his master's soft and confident voice, Gritgut bellowed, "Yu leve mez! Iez du wha ye seez - n'yu leve'd mez!"

"Calm down!" The invisible liege snapped. Then, once more, in a relaxed tone, "Calm down...I had to ensure you were...otherwise pre-occupied. You will suffer no more ill treatments from me. Find Tenet, the Spymaster; he'll be injured and alone by the time you make it into the tunnels below the Market Ward. Bring him here as safely as you can."

Gritgut tried to piece the string of separate conversations together. Thoroughly confused, except that he was to find Tenet, the oltreggan asked. "Uh, Shiny...wharze meh gu t' feend 'em?"

"Head for the Market Ward; your path will become clear from there."

Shrugging his shoulders, Gritgut turned and headed back into the murky realm of the Mud Flats.

* * *

Dropping through the broken Market Ward sewer grate after the wererats, Gritgut peered into the darkness around him. Why Shiny had said to follow the small, hairy beasts, the brawny brute didn't know, but follow he did. The oltreggan's primal instincts kicked in as his eyes dropped into the nocturnal spectrum, illuminating the black world with shades of grey. The semicircle tunnels veered around two bends, cutting his view short. However, he heard the squeaky whispers of the troop as they continued down the right-hand passage. Sloshing after them, Gritgut slapped his bare foot against something hard and cold. "A plague 'pon ya!" He railed at the lumpy object, which he discovered was a cracked chamber pot. Alarm swept through the ratfolks' voices as the squad whirled to see the looming specter of the oltreggan. Crossbow bolts sailed past the lumbering brute, a razor tip nicking his shoulder. Realizing he was under attack, Gritgut bared his teeth and charged the lot, chamber pot in one hand.

The wooden bowl splintered with the skull of the closest rat, while his left hand compacted another's head into its chest. The third and fourth attempted to flank the barbarian, only to find themselves in symmetrical death grips. A juicy pop signaled their breathless demise before silence returned to the darkened tunnels. Mindlessly toting the broken forms, Gritgut continued down the tunnel, attempting to whistle some sea chantey. He was happy to be free.

Gritgut scratched his head with his free hand, the other idly holding the crushed remains of two wererats.

Wheres me go frum heer?

Shrugging, he squatted in the sludge and popped a flask from the belt of one of the corpses. He hadn't tasted ale in many a day, so the bitter nip and budding warmth were a refreshing experience to the liberated barbarian. He could've sat there and drank down the other's wineskin as well, but at that moment a familiar voice chimed in his ear.

"Drinks can wait. Another will perish if you do not make haste. Just follo—"

The rest was drowned out in a thunderous expulsion of alcohol-laced wind. Gritgut wiped the residue of the belch from his lips and chuckled. "Meesh surrey, Shiny. Dezz gud dreenk. Wahzz youz wants me ta do?"

Though the oltreggan couldn't see it, Alastar shook his head. Sighing, the invisible leader decided ethics was another topic that had to wait. "Just follow your nose...The rest will be made plain."

Grunting as he righted his frame, further flattening the wererats in his grip, Gritgut breathed in deeply—and nearly wretched. A far more nauseating stench floated in the tide of rotting matter. Gritting his teeth, Gritgut ambled after the scent, inhaling deep enough to fulfill his body's need for air and to keep true to the path. The fetid decay now flooded the atmosphere as he delved into a low series of tunnels. The walls slowly changed from the semi-worked stone of the sewers to rugged, natural formations. The sewage had worn away certain areas, connecting with underground reservoirs to create a system of polluted waterways. Gritgut stood at the mouth of a particularly large hole, the darkness emanating purified rot. He gulped in a last half-tainted breath and plunged into the gloom.

* * *

The chamber had been a good breeding ground for the young otyugh. It had wandered into the cave long ago, pursuing the elusive reek of sewage and dead flesh. What the creature found was a haven of oozing delight. The ceiling of the dark hollow held a grate, which spit a continuous drizzle of filth, blood, bile, and tissue. Within the span of months, the gluttonous monster had feasted upon this steady, putrid rain, doubling in size. Enraptured by the endless meal, the otyugh was often oblivious to the world around it. Thus, the gorging denizen had no foreknowledge of the oltreggan sloshing straight towards it, a wererat corpse notched in his giant palm as a trebuchet might ready a payload.

* * *

Shiny did not need to warn Gritgut about the presence of the other creature in this stinking hole. The gleeful slurps and gentle splash of frolicking tentacles revealed the other occupant's location long before darkvision outlined it's massive hide. Considering his route, Gritgut realized he had reached a dead end, the only exception being the grate far above. And there was only one way to reach that entrance— mounting the otyugh.

Something within him said the beast wouldn't simply give him a lift, so the barbarian appraised his arsenal of two slain wererats and two fists. Cocking his arm back, the oltreggan hurled himself into the air as he hammered the shambled rats' frames between two rows of teeth, forcing the otyugh to gag on more flesh than it had expected. A tentacle lashed around the stalwart savage, crimping flesh against bone in a sickening squeeze.

Restraint only enraged the captured oltreggan. Blood hammered in every vein as muscles bulged. He gripped the sides of the tentacle as the beast drew him into its voracious mouth. Spurts of fiery blood washed the otyugh's maw, but Gritgut did not notice his pain. Rather, he bore his tooth-shorn fingernails into the creature's rough hide and twisted violently. The sound of liquid release greeted the barbarian's ears as the whole tentacle dislodged from the monster's back. Landing roughly on his feet, Gritgut's left leg locked up around the knee, a sizeable hole bored into the thigh. Despite the wound, the savage oltreggan slammed the recently severed limb across the monster's face as he leapt onto its back.

Two other tentacles blindly sought the menacing foe, only to slam and buckle the rusted grate above. The monster began shaking and thrashing, seeking any way to swat the intruder off its back. The rocking hide tilted just enough for Gritgut to grab the edge of the opened ceiling. Hoisting the severed tentacle and himself upward, the raging oltreggan spat at the giant monster below. "Plague 'pon ya!!"

Gritgut looked around the room and paused. The cave above had a sickly black luminosity. Refracting the preternatural glow were bloated corpses, suspended from the wall by a chitinous layer of obsidian fungus. The dark moss bubbled and oozed over the frames, extending pitchy veins into the dead. Above the alcove of distorted bodies hung a being of horrific design. A lumilon who glowed with a *black* light. The figure's mouth was locked in a silent wail, though it was obviously unconscious.

And directly beneath the comatose living lantern stood four figures, three of which had turned to see the commotion at the grate. Black cloaks enveloping most of their frames, two of them were human, while the third was a planetouched creature Gritgut knew to be a tiefling, its ashen skin and oversized canines declaring its fiendish parentage. The tiefling's amber eyes flicked from the fourth man: a bizarre, wild-haired elf with three, yellow raptor eyes -- to the muscled intruder. Recognizing the swarthy oltreggan, one of this many stooges from the past, the tiefling spat, "Grissgut!" The cultist turned, barbed whips sliding magically out of his palms, to his henchmen and hissed, "Ssstop ze desfiler!"

The robed elf didn't register any of the interruption as his eyes beheld some distant confrontation, locked rigidly into a stony trance. The first human crossed ten paces before completing a return flight on the leading edge of the otyugh tentacle-flail. Gritgut brought the spiked tentacle back again and swatted at the second man, who would've been instantly disemboweled if two metallic vines hadn't deflected the tuberous whip. With a deft twist, the otyugh's severed limb flew from the barbarian's hand. The tiefling snickered, "Ssshouldn't messs with a masster, ssea dog!"

Roaring, the oltreggan rushed the roguish character, memories of betrayal and cruelty flashing through the flames of his rage. Horned whips lashed against unyielding flesh as the barbarian closed the gap and hammered his muscled frame into the tiefling's diminutive form. The creature gyred, barbed chains spinning wildly, into the statuesque form of the entranced mage. The elf's triple eyes dissipated as a grimace of frustration and pain whirled over his now-elven features. A ripple of shadowy rage pulsed from the wild-haired mage, thrusting his lackeys to the fringes of the cave's perimeter.

Gritgut braced himself, withstanding the chilling pressure until it dissipated. The brawny brute eyed the stunned underlings as they shook off the blast's effects, while placing a hand gingerly against two broken ribs; he tried to decide who next to strike. A vicious slap in the back chose for him, careening the large oltreggan into the warped elf wizard. The otyugh, enraged by its loss of a limb, had widened the corroded grate, lashing wildly into upper chamber. Anger piled on anger; Gritgut wailed into the thin figure of the elf who countered with three jolts of frigid, acidic darkness that launched the barbarian toward the pit.

Blood dribbling down his cheek, the elven mage spouted at his guards. "Slyther! End this mutt's distended life!!"

Whips cracking against stone, the tiefling raced forward, flanked by the two guards. Gritgut managed to deflect the sabers of the henchmen, but had two harsh gapes slashed into his shoulder and hip. Impulsively, he grabbed the blade of one of the cultists, twisting the masterwork steel into a useless design, while punching the man's intestines and innards upward through his mouth and nose. A rough backhand shortened the other lackey six inches before a groping tentacle drug the slumping corpse into the hole.

Slyther sidestepped away from the oltreggan. He knew melee would prove disastrous if the barbarian was allowed to close within arm's length. Using his whips defensively, the tiefling rolled to the far edge of the floor, drawing Gritgut closer to the flailing otyugh's tentacles. The oltreggan almost fell for the trap when Shiny's familiar voice screamed, "Dive!"

Reflex leading the way, the barbarian flew forward as a streak of spiraling, shadowy electricity whirled overhead. The bolt caught a bloated corpse, expanding its dimensions to a hideous degree before the flesh erupted in a mass of pitchy acid. The tumble brought Gritgut within reach of the cornered tiefling, whom he quickly seized in a titanic grapple.

* * *

Slyther felt his vessels rupturing from the vice of Gritgut's arms and quickly discerned this would be his end. Even through the haze of pain, he knew his elven master, Xigx, would not spare him even if he survived. Such a realization drew him to his final act. Thumbing the stopper on an ashen-hued flask, the pirate-turned-cultist dropped the bottle of alchemist fire.

* * *

Gritgut's world became a realm of heat and blisters. He drove the wily tiefling into the wall before tumbling into the hole, Slyther still in tow. Both splashed into the desecrated and diseased waters, which was soothing and unnerving in the same instant. The flames subsided as reality crashed into place. The otyugh still sought revenge and had two victims to wreak its malice upon. The gigantic monster ripped into the hides of the tiefling and oltreggan, jerking them into the air. When Gritgut attempted to grab its tentacle again, the beast hurled him against the roof and then the far wall.

The oltreggan frothed at the injuries and charged the monster. "Heez mein!!!"

Slyther's eyes bulged when he found himself torn between two vices: the massive oltreggan gripping his whips and the hungry otyugh, his thighs. The hairy brute seemed oblivious to the hooks flaying his palms, savoring the test of brawn over the mutilation of himself. Hearing his own death knell tolling, the tiefling morbidly appraised his killer. *'The cult could use such as he...'* he thought as his skin, sinew and bones cleaved at the waist. The otyugh gorged on the distended organs and Gritgut whirled the upper torso into a whirlwind of gore.

As the gluttonous beast feasted upon its end of the prize, Gritgut flung the tiefling's torso into the gaping, over-filled maw. The monstrous aberration frothed and seethed as a bundle of flesh and chain lodged in its throat. Gagging and thrashing, the otyugh lurched forward in a vain attempt to spew the contents of its final meal onto the floor. At that moment an iron fist slammed through its eye socket and crushed the monster's brain.

Nausea and darkness flooded Gritgut's mind as he mounted the felled beast. Blood poured readily out of his torn thigh and wrists. Soon he'd have to rest. "But Shiny seys gitz Tin-nit, so izz duz 't." He barely paid attention to the clamor of arcane words and the distorted colors above as he labored to raise his battered frame over the grate's lip.

What Gritgut saw fanned the dying embers of his rage. Two figures faced off in the room: one, his grey skin and gaunt features marking him as an etherean, who writhed on the floor, thousands of frosty, shadowy shards rending his body; while the other was the strange, twisted elf wizard he'd pummeled before. The wild mage roared with feral glee. "You w-w-will die in this hole, Queens-man! I w-w-will add your blood to the cauldrons and your body to my growing army of umbral undead; and once the Cult has succeeded, I w-w-will replace you in the new Dark Order that w-w-will arise. I w-w-will be the Grey God's right-hand and you w-w-will help usher him in!"

Gritgut didn't care for the banter, but he knew the only Queen's man who'd be down here had to be Tenet. And *that* did matter to the oltreggan. Seeing his charge lying almost dead on the floor threw him into a roaring fit, which he channeled into prying grimy bars from the mangled floor. The iron squealed in protest as the brute ripped the grate from its foundations and hurled the broken mass at the cackling wizard. The elf cocked his head sideways in alarm as the hybrid of metal and stone flattened him against the wall. The distended corpses did their first service of protection without effort as their oozing entrails provided a cushion to spare the mage from becoming a humanoid waffle.

The effort drained Gritgut's reservoir of strength, his muscles drooping under their own weight. His knee crashed into the mossy floor. He had to rest, but his charge was dying. "Izz gots tu make it...gotzz to..." The oltreggan was oblivious to the notion that the crazed enemy still lived, his ears and eyes clouded with exhaustion. Thus, he did not realize the etherean had cried out with an incantation until a brilliant shaft of light washed over the ghastly chamber, lining the elf with a revealing glow. Reacting to the radiance, the crazed elf dispersed into a flurry of shadows and rushed through the rot-rankled air of the corpse-filled chamber; straight at Gritgut.

Frost swept through the barbarian's nerves as the twisted elf disappeared into the void below. Gritgut blindly swiped at the phantasmal wizard, but only grasped air. The effort nearly spent the wounded oltreggan's endurance and sense of balance. Hoisting himself back to his feet, the barbarian turned to see the etherean gaze with horror at a black quarter of the wall. The mage's body tensed and stilled in the harsh darklight of the lumilon. Tremors of cold cramped Gritgut's muscles and seared at his flesh as he neared the immobile etherean. "Tin-nit?... Izz yus Tin-nit??"

Unsure as to the problem, Gritgut tried to shake the motionless form, only to feel granite under his palm. The figure toppled and crashed onto the floor, the oltreggan in tow as he lost his feet. The savage hated being clumsy; a fact that the frozen etherean seemed to shout from the numerous cracks in his stony body.

"Mees surreeey!!!", the brute shouted to the deaf etherean.

Scooping up whatever dirt and fragments that lay amid the room's sludge, Gritgut smudged the gooey bits back into the newly formed crevices of the etherean's frozen form. He then grunted under the weight of the solid stone figure and headed for the only exit he could find. Reeling from the wavering black light and the chilly shadows of the room, the oltreggan accidentally tumped Tenet and himself into the lower chamber. When he gathered himself from the cesspool, Gritgut noticed a rock arm jutting from the grime, broken in the fall.

"Aarrghh!!!" The oltreggan bashed another eye into the otyugh's brain to assuage his frustration.

* * *

Gritgut sighed as he stared at the blank walls of the room. He had carried the comatose etherean into the Moontower late in the evening and had to stay through the rest of next day, needing to recover from his extensive wounds as well. Though he griped and mumbled his apologies, Jerrin merely shook his head gravely at the condition of the broken Tenet. The aged human had him carry the fissured statue into a side chamber on the second floor, which didn't arouse any complaints from the vexed oltreggan.

The healer pulled out a piece of stone and set it to the gap between Tenet's shoulder and dismembered arm. With a rheumy chant, the stone liquefied and dribbled into the space, hardening and contouring the ragged breaks. Even the fissures elsewhere seemed to be massaged out by unseen hands, leaving the statue a striking image of a horrified Tenet. Jerrin laid a withered hand on the oltreggan's bicep. "Do not worry...he'll be fine. We'll have him restored soon enough. Now, let's see to those wounds! You look like a wyrmling used you for a plaything." Chuckling softly at his own joke, the healer led the weary barbarian down to a first floor chamber to wash and dress the wounds, Jerrin patiently ignored the grumbles that issued from the brawny brute at the sight of soap and water.

Shiny stick me in hole ag'in...wha he 'spect me do heer?

The massive oltreggan sat on three creaking wood chairs for a moment longer and began to pace the ten-foot spread of the room. Only the bed, with its feverish charge, and a simple dresser adorned the single-windowed apartment. The Order had Tenet placed in this unmarked room in hopes to keep him out of harm; even in the Tower people of various sorts could hamper the care of the healers. Plus, they felt the Spymaster would prefer a quieter abode than what they could otherwise afford him within the tower. So, as an added precaution, Shiny had told Gritgut to watch over the unconscious Intelligencer.

Pausing by the open window, Gritgut allowed the moist breeze wet his dry skin. A storm was brewing in the bay, churning closer to Crown with each passing day. The curtains licked at his arm, tickling the nerves with delight. He almost felt he was back on the open seas, drifting along on the tides of adventure. Too bad the captain did not keep his word and pay Gritgut's debts, but such were the ways of the sea.

Mes gots Shiny stell...

As reality dragged along the gears of time, Gritgut's instincts flared. The vibrations of the obsidian shaft crackled like lightning in the oltreggan's ears. His calloused palm shattered the hollow dart, splattering its mustard contents onto the adjacent wall. Only the elephantine hide of his hand spared him from the toxin's withering potential. Glaring at the dark sill of the window, Gritgut launched his head outside—face to face with a black-suited figure, blowgun still to its lips. The oltreggan threw himself out of the second-story window and at the assassin. The two tumbled through the air, the wiry figure driven face-down into the unforgiving mud below. However, both were stunned and entangled in the grime, the only things which saved the human from instant death.

Since his weight was greater, Gritgut had more trouble prying his frame from the thick mud. The assassin quickly realized the futility of melee with the oltreggan and fled. A guttural roar leading the way, Gritgut erupted out of the mire and nearly swept the swift man from his feet. The oltreggan's blow missed only because the assassin dissipated into a shadowy form and slipped away. Fury pulsed into Gritgut's veins at such a cowardly foe.

"Mes stawmp yu!"

The shade and savage down a series of wooden stairs and over the expanses of swaying bridges. Gritgut's anger hedged out his fear of heights and ledges, allowing him to focus on the quarry. He hurled a score of objects—any sizeable item that he passed—at the lone rogue, with some success. The figure more tumbled than ran forward, aided by the momentum of the resounding blows.

Soon they were nearing the edge of the Flats and ran onto the Byway Bridge, where a cart and its keeper blocked half the path, using the constricted passage to capture as many customers as possible. The fruit glistened in the moisture of fresh rainfall, a sight that would've stopped the ever-hungry oltreggan if only he could see past the vision of blood and smoke that consumed his mind.

The assassin-turned-shadow leapt over the cart, expelling an outcry from the thin, startled merchant. The note of alarm turned into a scream of riled terror as the wagon shattered into a thousand splinters and liquefied fruit. Well-greased and no longer thirsty, the oltreggan continued on with more steam, plucking strands of melon into his mouth. The scent of the fruits and savory taste made his excitement all the more.

Shiny fede mez!

The assassin grew desperate. He had hoped to lose the lumbering guard in the twists and turns, but somehow the brutish oltreggan kept a foul breath's distance away. He suspected something—or someone— unseen was guiding the mad rampager. *How else could he keep up?* The gurgle of water in his ears, the rogue once more adjusted course; he hoped his Dark Liege would honor his prayers.

Gritgut barely heard the arcane mumble before he had to plow into a nearby crate to dodge the fireball. Heat blistered his left cheek. Everything else within twenty feet, included an aged mare on the opposite side of the path, burst into flames and cinders. "Plague 'pon ya!" he choked out through the smoke.

Hustling through the scalding ash, Gritgut glared at the river, seeking his prey. "Where izz yu??!!!"

"Aim for the waves," answered his invisible master.

The oltreggan glimpsed something black slide through some rusty grates by the river's edge. Leaping the ten yards to the main sluice, Gritgut slammed his nine-foot frame against the bars. They held. The oltreggan gripped his bruised side momentarily before backing up and attempting the charge once more. This only deepened the purple on his arm into a rich black. Muttering his favorite curse, Gritgut looked around. Whether by fortune or design, a rusty chain rested two feet away, conjuring memories of the large hawsers aboard the skiff he had once served on.

Maybe eesh weel wurk.

The iron rungs multiplied as he tugged harder on the thick chain before a solid limb of metal dislodged from the mud. The neck was followed by two gray heads, each tipped with a single horn. Gritgut realized what the barnacled token was immediately: an anchor.

Gripping the keelboat's brake by its throat, the oltreggan took a moment to size up the object. Then, as the last sound of sloshing feet disappeared into the tunnel, Gritgut remembered the escaping assassin. Rage flew into his body once more, drawing forth a violent series of hammer blows against the metal grate. Where flesh and blood could not budge the rusty bars, the iron head of the anchor reduced each beam into a shriveled lump of metal. Smiling at his work, Gritgut plunged into the sewers once more.

The sweet tang of drying melon faded into a rancid stench of bile and refuse. The tunnel veered left after sixty feet of southward descent. Gritgut hurried down the sludge-strewn corridor, seeking his foe. He entered an open chamber where a twenty foot vaulted ceiling dripped a continuous mist of river water from the bedrock above. Gritgut discerned the assassin through the drizzle, dangling from pitons and climbing hooks set into the roof. The oltreggan easily crossed the distance to stand underneath the swinging opponent. Fear etched itself into the otherwise professional visage of the man above. He could have been thirty or so, his beard thick and graying; his eyes bespoke of resolution, tinged with irrepressible fear. Gritgut didn't ken the fear to be from any other form than the two-hundred-pound reality staring the assassin the face.

"Mesh gots yu!"

Gritgut whirled the anchor as a knight might his flail, energizing the heavy end with sheer velocity. From behind the brawny brute, a slithering sound intermingled with the *whoosh* of the anchor. At the moment Gritgut released the howling projectile at the suspended rogue, the barbarian's world went dark and wet. Muscles compacted under thick scales, crushing organs in his abdomen and chest. The last sounds that graced Gritgut's ears before water rushed over them was the scream of the assassin, followed by a sickening crack of metal on bone.

Submerged, Gritgut tried to raise his arms, but a thick chord of scaled muscle bound his arms. Water choked him each time he tried to cry out his frustration. Then, another sensation besides the normal rage swept over him. This new fury rose from a more primal source, drawn from the ages when his people roamed the wild crags of the mountains. Vaporous images of feral oltreggans ripping into their foes with frenzied zeal and might slipped through the encroaching blackness. Gritgut's world lost all sound and feeling, narrowing to a rhythmic hum of blood chanting through his veins.

Gritgut awoke some hours later, his head above water and the pressure on his body now only the slack tension of torn ligaments and lifeless ribs. He wiped the liquid from his eyes, a mixture of bile and blood, and surveyed the chamber once more. The assassin hung limply from his harness, mouth and throat painted in a thick layer of blood from his own pulverized chest. What confused the oltreggan most was the addition of pitchy fluid splattered all over the walls and roof. Giant coils of copper and tan floated in the waves, blocking the entrance he had used earlier. Gritgut's gaze drifted along the twisting path of lifeless scales to a mammoth head; the amber eyes leered lifelessly at the mighty barbarian. The monstrous serpent's jaw hung sideways and shattered, the gums torn and bloody from where the teeth had been stripped out by brute force. Gritgut idly rubbed a two-inch incision on his right side and shrugged. Wrapping the anchor's chain around his chest like a bandolier, the oltreggan headed for the only open exit.

* * *

The oltreggan wandered through the vast intersections and byways of the Sewer City. Bands of wererats and other subterranean denizens occasionally attempted to harass the lone adventurer, only to boost the numbers of bloated dead in the ducts. Gritgut ate well on the rations he collected from each ambush and even pocketed several trinkets, though he favored flasks of ale and brandy over indigestible, unusable coin and gems.

By the end of the day, he dimly noticed an alternation in the tunnels. Where he had skirted a few large chambers full of huts and lean-tos hours before, the path ahead opened into an immense cavern of ancient craft. The granite columns and tiered landings hinted to lost grandeur and powerful rulers. Even the oltreggans had heard of the fabled Tal Vorglath, though most had no interest in the crypts of the dead clerics. However, curiosity perked in the adventurous barbarian as he noticed a glow emanating from a large doorway several stories up. The oltreggan realized this was not a normal fire, but rather a glow that only registered in darkvision.

Wat spooky ting dosh dat?, he wondered.

Gritgut found a flight of stairs that spiraled high into the darkness. Clutching the stairway's central column, the oltreggan crept upward to the level of the strange light. "Shiny...me hates dish...whys me alwees climbin' whin mes hates it?"

The oltreggan didn't expect an answer to such a question. Shiny only answered when important things were happening or when he wanted Gritgut to do another task. But the Voice was his master, a fact no oltreggan argued with. However, a rustle of air tickled his pointed ear, forming the words. "Why did you not run, Gritgut?"

"Wha yu means, mashter?"

Silence pervaded for another twenty steps. "That serpent was a child of a gorgon; its glare would've turned your flesh into well-muscled granite."

"But meesh lukked atz it an' nottin app'nd, bosh...yous alright?"

A melodic chuckle bounced in the oltreggan's eardrum. "I've seen better hours, but you are lucky...nay, blessed...it would seem. Perhaps more lurks within your frame than mighty muscle and strong sinew. Most surely, a soul of fire.." The laughter renewed though Gritgut didn't understand much of his master's ramblings; thankfully, Shiny always repeated his demands in simpler terms that Gritgut could remember.

"Never you mind, my friend. More lies before you than simple wandering. The place you seek is a prison-"

Gritgut roared and began running down the stairs, heedless of his diminishing balance. "Plague 'pon ya! Meesh na go'in ta jeil!! Tell me b'for Ies gitz sa close, Shiny!!"

"CALM DOWN!" The thunder of the command nearly popped

Gritgut's eardrum. He froze in terror of his master's anger. He had never heard Shiny get mad, even when the oltreggan had to hear instructions a thousand times over. The ire was like a blast of caustic ice into the young oltreggan's desire to serve. "Surrey, Mashter..."

Weariness tingeing his voice, Shiny answered, "No...I'm sorry, my friend. This plague boils blacker with each passing day...when will the sun's brightness return to a full noon? Yet even it seems dark to me, now, though I have never felt its weightless rays upon my skin..."

Shiny's sigh wiped away the frost from Gritgut's heart. Where could his master be that he never felt the sun? "Mashter...yus en jeil tu?"

Flakes of self-pity drifting in his tone, Shiny replied, "Of a sort. Yet, some must be chained so that others might be free. Do not fear, my friend. I possess a liberty which none other, save the gods of old, can claim. That is why I must ask you to go up..."

"Esh don't lek jail, Master...yous sed Izz ne'er beez jail'd agin!"

"Yes...'no more ill treatments' was the phrase? However, you are here to free an innocent mage; he'll be bound and drugged, so your strength is necessary to free him. Free this mage and more roots of this storm shall be exposed."

Mind clouded by his Master's thousand riddles, Gritgut shook his head and answered, "Ish getz 'im," and began the ascent once more.

* * *

Alastar's forehead wrinkled in a flux of gold and turquoise as his frustration mounted. Days had passed and he had neither seen nor heard from his rook. The knight and bishop, his aquatic charge, were fast at work, but his rook stood inert, shadowed by a tangible shroud. Fearing his rook had fallen into dire straights, Alastar flung his psyche far and wide into the roaming a field of onyx. However, within that dark realm, he could only sense the impending peril of the ever-widening shadow storm around Crown. Then, Alastar began to fear not only for his charge and for his city, but also, for himself...

The Five's divine energy hinders every trick of divination I use!

Alastar slid down the island a bit and reclined so that he could stare at the roof and the watery lens of time. The cool sheet of liquid flowed steadily downward, merging with the eldritch tarn of his alcove. The psionic diviner raised his eyes to stare at a curiosity in the flow. A bubble emerged at the top of the waterfall and began a lazy descent. Alastar, spawn of a lumilon and alônn dove into the waters and surfaced close as he dared to the falls. He ushered his piercing mental theurgy upward and his mind pressed against the floating crystalline sphere. At first, he feared his mental thrust would pop the bubble, but the tactile sense of pressure relieved, leaving the sphere intact.

His vision within was lacteal, a cynosure of cream and color. The cerebral images focused, revealing a cave amid the soft, white blur. Jars, boxes, basins, and containers crammed much of the space, especially along the walls. Two figures lay on the floor, the smaller tensed while the other sprawled out in a mammoth lump. The mound of relaxed muscles and long, matted hair of the larger forced a shout of praise to echo through Alastar's mind.

He lives!

A third figure leaned against the opposite wall; he raised his alabaster face upward, tilting his ear as though to hear something better. The oracle's exultation must have transferred through his telepathy. The lumilon returned his emerald gaze down to the journal in his half-gloved hands, penning haltingly. Alastar could not make out what the crimson-garbed bard wrote, but the loresinger's intense concentration and energetic speech showed it had to be of import.

Ah...if only I could fully hear what he sang...

The oracle turned his attention back to the oltreggan. "Awake in due time, my friend...your companions will utter the truth of this matter yet. And then, we shall disperse this feral skein of shadows."

* * *

The rescued mage, Landon, had developed a fever, which kept Solis busy during the whole of the next day. Befriended in the prison which held Landon, Solis, a lumilon loresinger, had aided Gritgut in the escape; leading them to a hidden hideaway to rest and recuperate. The battle-weary oltreggan's various wounds had dropped the hulking brute soon after they arrived at Solis' secret cave. The loresinger used the lonely grotto as his storage room and the layers of dust revealed how long it had been since the bard had last visited.

The alabaster-skinned loresinger leaned against a cave wall, allowing the canvas satchel to droop against his left thigh. Studying the unconscious oltreggan, clutching his anchor even in the blackness of sleep, and the clammy mage, who had proved stronger than first perceived, Solis Emberheart smiled in contentment. The lumilon bard had indeed found a tale which would pass beyond the veil of time. Humming softly to himself, Solis began what would be his final lay, which he entitled *Ode to Unbroken Valor*.

> *In the bowels of the old cleric's crypts,*
> *Tal Vorglath, where few sojourners' trips*
> *Return unto the homely light of day,*
> *A lone oltreggan stole vile law's prey.*
>
> *His anchored malice, freedom's berth,*
> *Brought to port ol' Penance Arbiter's derth.*
> *Even in the claws of a glabrezu,*
> *The barbarian's ire proved true!*
>
> *He hammered with unarmored fist,*
> *His rage proving a stalwart tempest*
> *To challenge the bleakest storm at sea,*
> *Harbinger of indomitable anarchy!*
>
> *When ten castigators became a score,*
> *And the Cult's machinations we bore,*
> *Landon shattered them with mastery arcane*
> *His victory, thus, bearing no small fame!*
>
> *Even an undead cleric of era passed,*
> *Withered from the mage's hallowed blasts.*
> *Thus, with muscled arm and eldritch mind,*
> *Two surface souls did one path find*
>
> *To walk and war against demon plot*
> *And the twisted inevitable's rot.*
> *United barbarian, bard, and mage,*
> *An' broke the bars of law's crook'd cage.*
>
> *When Gritgut drove Arbiter into roof,*

A hundred paces in the air,
His anger become liberty's proof,
That law to freedom must forebear...

Solis labored, scratching out verses and rewording in the pursuit of the perfect lines. He had nearly composed three pages when another bout of groaning seized the feverish mage. Setting book and quill aside, the lumilon knelt by the injured sorcerer. "Ah, you're fever is breaking, though I'm sure the fire in your skull says otherwise."

The bard mixed a few herbs into a cup before conjuring forth water. Drawing on his arcane reservoirs, the loresinger allowed theurgy to pulse warmth through his palms, heating the cup. The tea raised wisps of steam as silken banners. Slowly trickling the blend into the human's mouth, Solis whispered, "Mend well, my friend. You'll pull through, or I shan't call you Landon Quinntar, steadfast mage of the Arcane Tower."

Solis marveled at how he had come to trust this pupil of the power hungry-institution many miles above.

How often darkness drives unlikely companions along the same path...

Landon awoke in the early morning, his face pale and waxen. Casting a glance at the room's collected contents, the mage spoke huskily, "All you have, eh?...looks like your pockets hold more than I thought."

Solis chuckled lightly. "Ah, this is not mine, though. I am collecting for the Hall of Lyr. So, what I have is what you see—though you are correct to think my pockets hold more than is apparent." He winked at the slowly-stirring oltreggan.

Gritgut rummaged through the various pots and basins for the ever-elusive staple: food. He had not eaten in some time and severely required something to sate his appetite. Solis quickly stopped him from foraging through the fragile trinkets, fearing the brute might break something. But finally, when his stomach's grumbling became too much to bear, the oltreggan turned to Solis, pleading, "Mez hungree! Wherz y' fud??"

The weary bard smiled wanly and answered, "Alas, my friend, I've survived on *ylvas oil* for a long time. It sates quite well, though the mint flavor is not as satisfying the thousandth time as the first."

Gritgut leaned back and sighed. He had already downed twenty of those bottles, most of them in secret, but still longed for sizzling meat and cold brew.

"Now," the lumilon crouched next to Landon's bandaged side. "As you are awake, can you tell me if there is still pain?"

"Only if you mean that the shard of flame in my side isn't natural." Landon grunted as he tried to straighten himself up against the rock wall, his muscles cramping from lying on the stone floor. Before Solis could riposte, the mage hastily uttered, "The Grey God...I think I've found something that speaks of his return."

The loresinger froze in his place, dread clouding his verdant irises. In a whisper more befitting a funeral pyre, Solis asked, "What do you mean?"

Landon swallowed a draught of *ylvas oil*, which flushed his face with relief. "Ah...in the undead cleric's mausoleum, I found an alcove devoted to the destruction of some dark entity; who was severed into parts, which have since been scattered abroad. I cannot remember more...as my notes are hidden in the same hall.

"We could get there quickly, as I can teleport nearby; the hall itself is warded against such, but I remember the place well."

Solis took a moment to digest the information, while Gritgut merely tapped the prow of the anchor against the floor in boredom. The loresinger placed a hand on anchor's head to still the noise and answered, "But are you able to venture?"

Landon smiled, pointing with his chin, "If hairy-head can survive all that he does, I'm sure I can walk a few yards and get my gear."

The loresinger stood and donned his satchel while flitting about various containers, collecting vials and dried herbs. "Alright, but we must be cautious; I do not wish to face the unliving cleric in his own death-chamber."

The trio exited the alcove, which was similarly closed to scrying and translocation by the divine aura of Tal Vorglath. Landon eyed the oltreggan's bounding energy at the mention of leaving with curious humor, wondering if Gritgut truly kenned anything more than appetite or adventure.

At least he keeps swinging true...I wonder why on earth a smelly 'treggan would be contracted for such a mission? Guess I'll have to ask The Five when I meet them.

After a moment of centralized thought, Landon snatched hold of the location in his mind and drew a link through the Astral plane. The three figures winked out of sight, removed many miles deeper into Tal Vorglath.

* * *

The group arrived at the mouth of a vaulted hall, which was easily the size of a cathedral. Columns lined the expanse in several rows, each bearing some long forgotten language. Solis gripped the incarnadine brooch on his tunic. Warm, ruby light stretched outward for twenty feet. Landon also conjured a quadrant of floating lights. He turned to Solis and said, "Just a precaution." Nodding to the mage, Solis allowed Landon to take point with Gritgut following a little off to the side.

The party made its way into the alcove Landon earlier described. The smooth marble walls shimmered in the light of Solis' brooch, refracting a score of pallets and hues. Gritgut stared at the images of a shadowy figure being divided into three pieces—spirit, mind, heart—and secreted to separate, hidden places. He didn't understand what all of the symbols meant, but a chill swept through his body nonetheless.

Dis spooky stuf...

Solis gazed at the pictures as well, running the bare fingers of his half-gloved hands over the etchings, revulsion and awe in his eyes. Only Landon ignored the pictographs, concentrating on something else. His eyes lost an eldritch luster as he said, "Ah, there you are...my old friend."

The mage scooped up a tiny backpack, its iridescent colors somehow harmonizing with the environment. "Many a rogue would've loved to steal this bag...if it had only been in plain sight." Landon grinned as he donned the backpack, which promptly blended into the wine-shade of his cloak. The mage reached back and grabbed something from the pouch: a book.

"This entails the story from these walls; I even made sure to make rubbings of these wall etchings as well." He handed Solis the book before turning to Gritgut. "I'm sorry I don't have any grub in here."

Gritgut snorted at the jest. "Shiny weelz givs me suffin ta ete."

"Not sure I'd want to eat anything from this place...too close to the bones of vile souls to be savory, if you ask me." Landon glanced at Solis, who was oddly silent.

The loresinger had begun humming softly. His song took on an ancient air and style, leaving the other two in bafflement. The bard's mood drooped with each passing moment, until he had to stop singing due to the sorrow in his spirit. Tears ran down his face. "Let us leave this horrid cairn!" Neither Gritgut nor Landon dared to deny the hatred and pain in the lumilon's stare.

As the trio made their way towards the great hall, the whole alcove quickly transmuted into the consistency of water and then solidified again. A low-toned rumble issued afterward, like the thunder of a looming storm. Again the land shifted states as the group sped out into the cathedral-like chamber.

"Cave-ins are frequent in this area!" Solis shouted over the roar. "Make for the nearest tunnel out of here and pray to whatever free gods there are for protection!" No one paused to debate the bard's theology as they ran.

Rushing across the vastness of the pillared hall, Solis stopped dead in his tracks. He threw one hand up to halt his companions, pointing into the gloom with the other. Landon motioned his orbs of light towards the area, revealing a monstrous entity of stone and earth as it slid from the wall. Its twelve-foot height and sleek form appeared reptilian, though it revealed little organic semblances; it bore only a vast chasm for a mouth and a set of vague limbs. However, to the expert loresinger, the creature might as well screamed its name out; Solis certainly did.

"THRUM!!!"

He turned toward the others and shouted over the rumbling vibrations which had now become continuous. "Run! The thrum will collapse this whole chamber if we don't hurry!!"

Even Gritgut didn't doubt Solis' words as two columns dissolved into a pile of rubble. The trio dashed through the long hall of pillars, watching in horror as the ceiling along the edges dripped like rainwater, granite flooding downward in a wave of continuous mutation. The trio had crossed only twenty yards when a spar of stone blasted through the floor and launched Gritgut into the air. Riding on the jut of rock, the oltreggan found himself slammed into the jagged stones of the cavern's roof, air and blood expelling from his mouth. The spar then instantly liquefied and tumbled sideways into a slump of mud, leaving the battered barbarian to fall sixty feet onto hard ground. Gritgut had barely risen up in time to leap away as a section of the now-cracked ceiling crashed to the floor.

Bubbling and seething, the thrum's colossal form slithered through an adjacent wall and out the far side, onyx cables lashing from its giant mouth. The beast of elemental earth exuded a low rumble that shivered the length of its angular hide. The hum sent fissures through the remaining supports. Another roar would completely destroy the hall, crushing every being of flesh within.

Calm flooded the form of Solis as he closed his eyes and tipped his ear in the direction of the monster. He seemed to be awash with the vibrations around him, his body harmonizing to the rhythm. Then, in the most radiant voice Gritgut, and perhaps Landon, had ever heard, the lumilon sang a perfect countermelody to the thrum's violent outburst.

> *Would the world to see*
> *A realm quite free,*
> *Full of untold gallantry*
> *That none could kill,*
> *No, not with vile will,*
> *Or a shadowlord's soul...*

And so the ballad of Scourge Slayer began, a tale composed long ago during the dark times of the Demon Scourge.

Landon rose upward on a mystical buffer of air while drawing a circle of warding around himself. Shards of stone skittered across the ethereal shield, instantly proving its worth. Gritgut shook his matted mane, snarling, and charged the beast. He severed one of the onyx tongues with a swipe of his anchor, though the damage seemed innocuous to the beast. The barbarian brought his anchor to bear a few more times, barely cracking the unyielding hide of the thrum's foreleg.

A wall of stone slammed against Gritgut's chest like a wave from the sea, smashing him hard against a column. The mass of liquid granite hardened around him, immobilizing the oltreggan for a split second, only to instantly reform into a giant flail, which then slammed Landon from the air. Now free, but reeling, Gritgut watched as the massive stone whip crumbled into harmless, inanimate rock as it neared the counter-harmonic stillness that crept outward from Solis.

Solis continued to sing:

Baeor slaughtered all.
Fiends soon did fall
Upon his serrated light.
Thus turned the fight
To breaking the Scourge,
Our fair city shall be purged!

The thrum shook with frustration, riving forty yards of ceiling on its left into a deluge of stone. Still, Solis' sonic barrier held fast, like a feisty maid against the wooing of an undesirable suitor. Both harmonics raised in pitch, trembling the bases of towers leagues above.

A familiar roar split into the mix. Gritgut had unsuccessfully tried covering his ears and yelling to drown out the noise. He opened his eyes, the pupils swallowing in their white edges and wailed once more. The oltreggan charged the thrum and leapt onto a foreleg, pounding feverishly at the beast's side. Cracks and crevices began coursing along its rocky hide, causing the thrum to vibrate with tremors of pain. Gritgut's snarl broke into a smile at the resulting discordant notes. A wide area of the ground stabilized as the thrum's seismic hum was disrupted.

Realizing what Gritgut had done, Landon quickly, through sheer skill alone, broke the laws of magic and re-wrote them, firing two fireballs into the cave-like maw. The thrum's maw-tendrils melted into slag in the wake of the blasts.

The thrum shook its head and released a volley of sonic spears. One caught Gritgut in the throat, mid-roar, shattering his larynx and blasting him backwards through the air. Blood soaked his mane and stained his teeth as the oltreggan reached his fingers into the gurgling hole. Pain lanced into his lungs as the barbarian strove to push the blood from them. The savage's darkvision began to fade, the leering maw of the thrum fading from his sight.

Shiny...need 'elp...mez...surrey.

Solis Emberheart leapt through the air in an intricate tumble, landing within inches from the gaping oltreggan. Breaking off his melodic countersong, the loresinger pressed his hand to the fatal slit in Gritgut's throat. The lumilon conjured up the words of an ancient, divine language--one not heard in centuries--as he harmonized his body to the latent divine energy in the very stone of the hall. If this had not been otherwise engaged, Landon would've realized this was a rare instance of divine magic in use. Not only did the wound disappear, but all other infections and blights--metaphysical and otherwise--swept from the barbarian's body, ushering him into a place of utter calm and intense holiness.

A rare feeling for the amoral race.

As the alabaster cleric stepped back, his brilliant emerald eyes shot open in shock. The moment he paused his countersong, the behemoth elemental's seismic thrumming increased. The thrum, unused to such opponents, was, ravenous to devour this threat. The trembling stone around the lumilon liquefied and rushed like a flash flood towards the bard, hardening at the last moment into hundreds of spikes. Lifted by the granite javelins, Solis' body poured out his eldritch lifeblood from a thousand spouts.   Gritgut, still awash with a sensation of utter *goodness*, watched in horror as the stone liquefied again, forming into a fist which bore his broken friend into the thrum's giant, eager maw. The seed of joy within the oltreggan's heart erupted into a hallowed rage, clear and vibrant. Even his anchor shone with a golden hue as he charged straight toward the vacuum of the monster's throat.

As he ran, the oltreggan could barely believe his eyes. The lumilon's orbs shone with a new light, the emerald irises flaring with a nova of new life. Gritgut noticed that Solis had raised his dagger in both hands, holding the dirk upright and level with his chest. The loresinger's lifeblood orbited slowly, like thousands of tiny crimson moons, around Solis' dying form, drawn in by the magical bodkin. In the dark void of the thrum's mouth, the blade radiated with a brilliant light. The bard smiled wanly and closed his eyes.

"*Se dejur non libri...*" -- *By oath not written...*

The final incantation seemed to drain the last of his strength, his alabaster skin becoming dull. As the mouth slammed shut over the bard, Solis stabbed himself through the heart. An iridescent glow shimmered in the rocky crevices of the closed maw before darkness reigned once more.

Still somewhat in shock, Gritgut leapt into the air. Bearing his anchor over his head, the oltreggan thunked the starboard prong into the muzzle of the thrum. The barbarian continued upward, swinging himself by the anchor's chain, onto the elemental's head. Now upon the base of its skull, the barbarian yanked his anchor free and hammered at a furious rate. "Yus gevs Soles beck!!!", he bellowed.

The thrum boomed and shot stony barbs upward from its back and head. Gritgut deftly side-stepped the spikes, his reflexes honed by divine might, and continued his barrage of fury. The thrum had known few opponents in its long existence, but now found itself enraged at this minute aggravation upon its neck. Many layers of living sediment lie between the anchor and the broken form of the loresinger, but Gritgut did not relent his furious, stone-chipping barrage . Furious, the massive monster drew its seismic energy to a centralized point at the back of its skull and emitted an unprecedented blast of sonic energy. Gritgut went whirling through the air, many bones shaken out of their joints. A giant fist of stone shot from the roof and swatted the barbarian straight into the ground. He lay completely still, far from the fight, close to an exit tunnel.

Landon had watched the whole ordeal in horror. He realized this beast could not be destroyed by their combined strength, let alone a solo battle. Grabbing Solis' satchel, the mage aimed upward and shot a verdant beam toward the roof. A huge portion crumbled and collapsed upon the thrum. The massive slab buckled the elemental's back, jarring its concentration. The mage flew swiftly toward his friend, trying to outrace the monster's stone shaping abilities.

Javelins and cudgels of rock zipped past Landon's frame as his warding circle began to fray. Soon, he would be unprotected and he knew that he was in grave danger. He glanced back and saw the thrum slide through the slab. The far end of the chamber had collapsed, with more sections tumbling into ruin.

'Almost there...', Landon hoped. A sharp pain lanced through his side; a stony razor glanced off a rib, spilling blood throughout his tunic. He spiraled into blackness.

* * *

As Gritgut slowly righted himself, the world was full of bells and seemed to be suffering from an earthquake.

Wherez em I?

A horrendous pain flared in his skull, while his right side was as stiff as the stone beneath him. He looked around and didn't recognize anything; he could not fathom where he was, why he was hurt, or even who "he" was... He glanced about and oddly, saw the anchor a few feet away. Ambling through the tremors, the oltreggan bent down and picked up the weight. The texture of the keelboat brake felt familiar and comfortable, drawing him to immediately cherish the newly found trinket.

Dez ez m' ship... He smiled in satisfaction at the endearing title.

A new buzz joined the clanging bells in his head. Raising his gaze from the barnacled haft and prongs, he saw the unbelievable: a human soaring through the air! The man dodged a literal storm of rocks and dust and cried out frantically. One of his hands clutched a seeping blotch on his side while the other swung a bag. The omnipresent hum around the oltreggan sifted a bit, allowing words to drift in. "Gritgut!...Take this!!"

The airborne human dropped a small pouch into the satchel and spun about in the air, his momentum sending the satchel hurtling towards the stunned oltreggan. The barbarian only caught the item on reflex, staring blankly at the bag before looking up at the oncoming mage. "Howez yu knew me nem?!"

The mage waved his confusion as he sent a blast of force upward, cleaving a stone fist into fine dust. "Just go! Crown needs to be spared!"

A guttural hum echoed through the area, ominously reinforcing the mage's statement. The sonic pulse dissolved the remaining pillars, toppling the columns and ceiling onto the floor below. Gritgut saw realization, followed by solemnity flood the human's face; he righted himself and waved. Though he could not hear the mage's voice, the amnesiac barbarian understood what the man meant as the stones swallowed the man whole.

"Farewell."

* * *

Gritgut left the collapsed cathedral-cavern, wondering why he felt so sad. He had seen many people die before, but a novel pang of loneliness began eating at the oltreggan's heart.

Mez lonely...

The satchel's strap would not fit over his shoulder, so the oltreggan carried it in the crook of his elbow. He barely noticed the clink of the bottles against his side anymore. His earlier examination of the satchel had revealed some books and bottles, none of which seemed to promise food. The grey liquid inside tasted like watery ash, but he was somewhat nourished. Still, after several bottles, he could not help longing for grilled meat and bitter stout. He'd also found a small vial, its emerald glass strangely familiar. He took a sniff and sip, and nearly dropped the flask as an eerie sensation tickled his side. His muscles instantly began to lose their swelling and bruises completely vanished. He quickly downed the bottle and belched happily as the massaging sensation swept through his whole body.

Dez is gud!!

* * *

Izket was the youngest of his family and adored by both his siblings and parents. Like any youngling, kobold or human, he delighted in wandering into areas where he shouldn't have been to begin with. "Izzy", as his family called him, had done that very thing by creeping out into the main tunnels. Many dark yards away from the communal kobold den, the main tunnels were prone to wandering predators and other dangers. Izzy knew, however, that the older kobolds often went running through these larger, more exciting tunnels without harm, enjoying themselves thoroughly. So, he scampered along the main thoroughfare and soon climbed to a high ledge that held wild *ravrak,* a rare and delicious moss native to Tal Vorglath.

As he sat, feasting upon *ravrak,* Izzy gazed out over the ledge and into the dark passages beyond. Though kobolds themselves were not known for cleanliness, he soon caught a scent far more unpleasant than any he'd ever encountered. The aroma was a putrid mix of at least sweat, ale, bile, and blood – all combined in the worst possible manner. Curious, but whimpering quietly, the little kobold started to creep toward the ledge's lip.

"Wa'r ye doin', Izzy?!"

The youngling kobold turned, startled, to see his elder sister, claws on each hip. Two bright almond eyes bore down upon him without mercy.

"Kiki....tumper tink down der." Izzy replied, pointing toward the passageway below. Both kobolds turned their gaze toward the rock-strewn tunnel; while *Izzy* merely stared in awe, Kiki gasped.

Beneath them, a massive creature was hunched over, scooping up handfuls of fungus and stuffing them alternatively into his mouth and a small pouch that dangled from its forearm. Long ropes of blood-matted fur fell from its head, draping over its powerful shoulders. The elder kobold crinkled her nose at the stench and screamed.

* * *

Gritgut nabbed the last of the pleasant-tasting, orange toadstools when he heard the shriek from above. Glancing upward as his free hand readied his anchor, the oltreggan spied two minute, scaled figures. The smaller one clung to the other, confusion and fear etched onto both their faces. Their cries had alerted their kin, who soon gathered around them. One scarlet-scaled kobold wrapped her arms around the younglings, while another, obviously the father, brandished a jagged spear.

The brawny barbarian recognized the warning and grinned toothily. Wanting no quarrel with the group, Gritgut reached into his satchel and produced a handful of the orange fungi and a scarlet Tal Vorglath flower that smelled like fruit, but tasted awful and dropped them at the family's feet. Even despite his memory loss, Gritgut knew that giving food was a sure sign of peace. Satisfied with his offering, the brute then turned on a heel and began the slow trek through the gloomy halls.

The navy-scaled kobold patron eyed the hulking savage until he was far beyond two spear throws' distance before turning to his clan. Izzy was squeaking and yammering about how he had come to see the mighty monster, how he was about to drop a rock on it, and how he would become a great warrior like his dad just when Kiki had screamed. The tiny clan tried to keep a straight face before the enthusiastically babbling child, only to break down into laughter at the youngling's animated faces and exaggerated gestures.

Gritgut was too far away to hear anything more than a scramble of yips and yaps. The group appeared to have forgotten his sojourning presence, because they were now even laughing sporadically. However, over the din he heard the oft' repeated refrain, "...tumper tink..."

Sniffing under his arm, the swarthy oltreggan shrugged and continued onward until the kobold's den was long distant to mind and body.

* * *

Gritgut continued his wild ambling for many hours without harm or hassle from any other creatures. He once would've enjoyed this freedom, and did for the most part, but a nagging sense of purpose and loss pervaded his simple thoughts. He felt like part of his existence had ended with the mage in those large halls. Though not an introspective creature, the oltreggan found himself returning often to that mental wound as he walked in isolation.

Long after his food and hope had dwindled, he caught the echoes of a sound he hadn't heard in days. He quickened his pace and followed the sharp squeaks and hisses. When he finally caught up to the sound's origin, he instinctually dropped into a crouch. A band of cloaked figures, a mixture of tieflings and wererats, ventured in a small knot. A lone sarulaan, it's form accentuated by hooks and shards of oddly gleaming metal, strode ten paces ahead. The group seemed unaware of Gritgut's presence and chatted easily among themselves.

A high-pitched voice, probably that of a wererat, said, "...Cannae waitz ta get to the Shady Rose! There'll be plenty of lassies, an' wez'll celebrate our winz!"

Another, harsher voice broke in, "Ourz, eh? I think you better talk it over with da' glabby."

A chorus of snickers followed before a third voice, silken and oily, said, "Ah...but the food that awaits us! None of the Crown Watch will dine better than we, all bought by loot from Arbiter's vaults. The poor iron-skulled fool didn't know how to spend his gold!"

And on the conversation went, with the muscled sarulaan keeping his silent vigil and Gritgut trailing behind the bawdy crew. The tunnels slowly altered from natural stone to worked cobble. Even the atmosphere changed, becoming damp and fetid. Before long, the troupe had entered running sewage, the slosh of water further masking the oltreggan's curious and careful pursuit. Gritgut was pleased to hear the constant reference to food and ale, but something within him warned to not stray too close to the group.

At the mouth of three tunnels, the sarulaan halted and turned to the group. Fortunately, Gritgut found himself hidden by a deluge of waste. The crew seemed utterly terrified of the sarulaan warrior and bobbed their heads energetically at everything he said. The oltreggan couldn't comprehend anything over the roar of water, but watched as the sarulaan exited through a different tunnel than the others, who seemed all-too-thankful for his departure. Deciding the motley crew was headed toward a warm meal, Gritgut didn't hesitate to follow them.

*　*　*

The "Shady Rose" turned out to be *The Shadow Rose* in the Narrows. The rogue bar featured a false and magically trapped surface entrance, though the true entryway into the tavern lay below, from the Sewer City. The tavern was cramped and shadowy, with only a few tables and a small bar. A few scattered candles gave off a weak, sparse light amid the smoky gloom, as the bulk of the clientele had no need of light to see. All of this was unknown and unimportant to Gritgut as he wandered in on the heels of the scraggy troupe. The oltreggan drew many eyes from around the pub, most of them leery and unfriendly.

A lithe sarulaan female walked up to Gritgut, quickly eyeing his anchor-and-chain weapon before locking eyes with him. "What d'ya want, 'treggan? Not many of yer ilk make their way inta me establishment."

Gritgut shot her a toothy grin and began rummaging through his satchel. Since he couldn't find any coin, he tried offering her a sapphire vial. The bartender's face twisted in disdain at the attempted bartering. "I want none of yer junk. If ya don't have any crowns, den ye better git out! I'll 'ave na trouble in me place."

The oltreggan glared at her and muttered, "Iez no truble...jiss wanna eatz suffin."

The sarulaan glanced over her shoulder as she returned to the bar and spat, "Then get a job, ye addle-brained oaf!"

Gritgut growled at the insults, but turned from the bar-mistress as he caught a savory aroma. Grilled and spiced, the roasted pork ribs of the nearby table beckoned to nearly all of his senses. He loped over and dropped himself into an empty chair, the wood squealing in protest. The table's rightful occupant, an aged tiefling, sneered at him. When Gritgut snapped up three ribs and stuffed them into his mouth, the shocked fellow leapt from his seat and shouted, "Fool! What're'ya doin!!"

Gritgut merely lowered his head to the plate, spat out a few bones, and reloaded his gullet with another handful of juicy meat. The tiefling rushed around the table and latched on to the oltreggan's barrel-sized bicep and yanked, trying to dislodge the oaf from his meal. The burly barbarian, totally ignoring the aged tiefling's words and actions, pulled hard to dislodge several stubbornly-attached ribs. The bones finally snapped their sinews and gave way with a pop; Gritgut's arm snapped back and the tiefling found himself tumbling through the air.

The tiefling landed hard, flipping over a card table; the players leapt up, grabbing coins and shivs. The four interrupted card players pounced over the dizzy tiefling and began slicing into him, and each other. Chaos erupted all across the Shadow Rose as the bartender reached for her hand crossbow and waded into the fray, spitting curses at the combatants. Seizing the opportunity, the sarulaans quickly began picking the lockbox, hoping to drain the tavern's coffers; they quickly found themselves pitted against a band of human sell-swords with a similar idea.

Gritgut simply finished his appetizer and drained the pitcher of ale before moving to another table that housed a beef roast with apples, alongside a cup of bourbon and a bottle of wine. The occupants, a halfling and half-elf, leapt up and flanked the oltreggan, both drawing rapiers and long-knives. The barbarian stared at the duo for a moment, cocking an eyebrow in amusement. Twin hammer-like fists chopped downwards, shattering two skulls like crockery. Gritgut didn't bother to clean the pithy blood from the beef, finding the hint of half-elf brains not so displeasing to the overall texture.

Tables, chairs, plates, cutlery, mugs, crossbow bolts, throwing knives, and curses began soaring through the air as everyone found themselves embroiled in a fight. The tavern that was usually a haven for displaced rogues was transformed into a battleground or a death bed. Few dared to assail the lumbering oltreggan who moved from the roast and wine to a fine, light course of ale cakes and brandy. What the burly brute could not stuff into his gullet, he plopped into his bag for safe keeping. Gritgut did not hesitate from scooping a leg of lamb from the floor and devouring the dirty meat, occasionally bashing a few heads with the meaty limb.

Gritgut went to place a greasy chicken breast in his satchel when his hand bumped another. He jerked around to see a stunned gnome, a book in one hand and a sausage in the other. Thinking nothing of the book, the barbarian saw only his precious pork being pilfered. This awoke the slumbering flames of the oltreggan's ire, who swung a ham-sized fist towards the thieving gnome. The wily creature zipped away at a surprising rate towards the street-level door. For a moment, Gritgut marveled at the little thief's preternatural speed, but quickly charged after him.

"Iz sqush yu, letle beest!"

The gnome glanced back briefly before muttering an arcane password. The locks spun open and allowed the runt to quickly slide through before slamming the door. All the magical latches fell back into place with an audible *clink*. Gritgut didn't even slow at the closed door, bringing his anchor forward as a massive spearhead.

Gritgut burst into Crown's open streets amid a cloud of lashing splinters and twanging arrows. While many of the bolts missed their mark, the few that struck true did little to faze the barbarian. The whole of Crown lay under a sooty darkness spawned by enormous storm clouds that bellowed their primal might; lightning arched between thunderheads and rain fell in icy sheets. The barbarian spotted the skittering rogue as he rushed toward the Mud Flats. Roaring with the primeval lust for the hunt, the oltreggan pounded through the frosty rain after his quarry.

The gnome, with tremendous speed, raced over rickety bridges which spanned the Mud Flats. Gritgut struggled to keep him in sight and almost lost the thief a time or two. At those tense moments, a soft voice would whisper into his ear, "Go left!" or "Head right!" At first, the oltreggan thought someone followed him, but he had little time to sort it all out. Instead, he went with his gut instinct and heeded the voice as long as it aided him in his chase.

Hajorn had never faced such a determined foe. The gnome knew that he should have lost the plodding brute long ago; something was not right. The sagging bridges and miry lanes of the Flats usually proved a bane for anyone chasing him without magical aid. The gnome knew his dweomered boots were still working, but could not discern where the oltreggan was getting his help.

Fear crept into the rogue's pounding heart as he dashed onward; he knew that soon he'd need to rest. The next series of double-backs and bridge-leaps did little to hinder the charging brute; he merely shattered most obstructions whenever they hindered his path, and deftly dodged the others.   The oltreggan proved an impressive—and terrifying—opponent. His eyes were blacked with rage, yet a sense of unnerving awareness flowed within those irises. Hajorn knew he had few options left. Perhaps slipping into the sewer tunnels would work, but the gnome knew this beast had come from the sewers.

He fretted, *'He might know them better than I do - and then I'd be doomed!'*

As he ran, Hajorn clutched the book tighter; the sausage, grabbed entirely by mistake, had been dropped long ago. The rogue buzzed past the old fruit vendor, noting that his once fine cart had been replaced with a smaller, shoddier version.

'The man must truly be desperate', the gnome thought, *'to try and sell fruit in this weather with a lousy cart like that!'*

Jalkesh had time to see the lumbering oltreggan crest the rise after the gnome splashed past. The barbarian toted an anchor now, his form blotched with grime and stains. The canny vendor recognized the brute from before and was determined, this time, to withstand the beast. The seasoned man crossed his arms and stood resolutely before his cart.

He shouted above the wind and rain, "Ye wanna smash some melons - go bash your own!"

Gritgut smirked at the indignant merchant, doubling his pace as he sped towards him.

Jalkesh's eyes narrowed with disgust and then widened with shock as the oltreggan, at the last moment, lightly sidestepped and twirled wistfully away. A smile of satisfaction blossomed on the vendor's visage, which quickly soured into anger as he watched the brutish barbarian snag a couple of melons.

"Ye rock-fer-brains-no-good-thievin-cur!!   I'll have your head for this!!"

The vendor's faded into the pelting rain as the oltreggan ran on after the fleeing gnome.

* * *

Hajorn now hastened through the cobbled streets of the Old Temple Ward, past the regal homes and guild houses, which looked like brooding tyrants beneath the maelstrom's dark shroud. As he zipped by, he heard the gasps of the few other brave souls who'd braved the storm this Long Night, which was normally an eve of intense festivities. The streets were nearly empty instead, which made speed his only advantage. Yet, he still could not shake the feral oltreggan who ran behind him.

Gritgut barely ducked as he rounded the corner, missing the marble feet of *The Prophet's Tears'* sign. The lumilon's face appeared somber, foretelling doom for anyone beneath her storm-stained gaze. The burly barbarian had come within a few scant yards of the gnome, who was showing signs of fatigue. Even hasted, the rogue was not as used to sustained marches as was the barbarian, whose heritage derived from loping across unforgiving mountains. In desperation, the gnome thief had altered his path once more, bearing north for the Arms Crescent, a ward where swords and hammers often clashed in a continual song of conflict. Tonight the smithies were stilled, but the blades rung with a fatal song, for the pit fighters in *The Broken Valor*, a tavern tower nestled on the edge of the Crescent.

The gnome, panting and wheezing, entered the looming structure. Gritgut rushed in, anchor held at the ready. People balked at the image of the filthy oltreggan, coated in a sheen of rain, blood, sweat and grime. Gritgut snarled and dove into the mob, driving squads of screaming patrons away with each stroke. Most people backed out of reach; the few who drew weapons soon regretted their painful mistake.

Gritgut spotted the gnome, slouched against a wall half-a-flight up, trying to calm its erratic pulse. Blood singing in glorious fury, the oltreggan charged up the sloping steps, trying not to stumble and fall down into the fighting pit far below. The gnome groaned and began quickly limping up the stairway.

At the third rung of the stairs, Gritgut closed with the exasperated gnome. The runt shivered with fatigue and terror, though the thief drew a green-hued short sword in defense. The barbarian bore downward with the barnacled weapon, forcing the defender to sidestep and withdraw. Gritgut surged forward, his retribution at hand. He altered his hold on the anchor, weaving a sequence of cruel strokes to press the squat criminal nearer to the balcony's ledge. His huge shadow fell on the small thief, gloom darkening the gnome's despairing eyes.

A fanged smile broke over the savage's face, "Yous ded, tief."

* * *

Hajorn gulped and placed his free hand into his vest. He could barely think with the blood pounding through his skull. Fear did nothing to calm his mind; his entire profession had been based on stealth and speed. Now, with the end near, he noted his folly: he never had a backup plan. His fingers fell to a pilfered potion which he chugged as the anchor arced downward to cleave his skull.

* * *

Gritgut's eyes bulged as the gnome's form wavered into smoke. The anchor slipped through the once solid head, continued on, pulling a surprised barbarian over the balcony. He twisted in mid-air and launched his anchor at the devilish thief, cursing the gnome's cowardly act. The keelboat brake missed and slammed into a massive bone chandelier. Dusty bone splintered, striking Gritgut above the eye, spraying blood out into the void. The anchor locked into the smoke-stained lattice, tugging the massive construction down with the oltreggan. Gritgut glimpsed the whole form of the balor skeleton as it descended with him toward the pit below.

Knowing his death was upon him, the powerful barbarian roared his beloved invective. "Plague 'pon ya!"

With a liquid crack, blackness erupted in his sight. Velvet warmth enveloped his body. When he opened his mouth to yell, viscous blood rushed into the empty cavity.

Gar! Gritgut ded!

Gritgut only doubted the assumption when his guts wrenched the sanguineous fluid out of his stomach. Besides, this didn't taste like his blood. Rushing air and the gurgle of his clogged throat deafened him. He was able to swipe enough blood from his eyes to see the rim of a mountainous plunge ahead, which dropped into labyrinthine abyss. In Gritgut's mind, he had fallen into the river of death.

* * *

The dark, blood-filled chute threw the oltreggan through a series of intense drops and harsh veers. He could not halt his descent, since the anchor was also slicked with blood. Barely bobbing above the sanguineous flood, Gritgut tried to regulate his breathing when a light approached far below him.   He soon found himself free-falling once more.

He blindly tried to flail around and hook his anchor on anything, but the pouring blood and darkness seemed to thwart even his darkvision. Pulled along by the inexorable flow, the brawny barbarian soon spied a ruddy glow ahead.   The flow increased as the passage constricted and Gritgut found himself racing towards a roaring bloodfall.   Holding tightly onto his anchor, he barely had time for one sanguine-laced breath before plunging into hell.

* * *

Ghals and Snede hated the Ritual of Replenishing.   They always had to ferry buckets from the cathedral's cistern, a literal blood bath at the base of the sanguiducts.   Nothing exciting ever occurred on this detail. Usually, all the major events happened before or after the two completed their task, leaving them effectively out of the inner circle.   They vowed to one day to earn renown in the Cult.

* * *

Gritgut kicked hard to surface from the deep vat of blood.   When his head breached the surface, he gasped in a refreshing breath of cool air. Some process kept the sickening fluid the consistency and warmth of the lifeblood inside a person.   This roiling miasma nearly made the oltreggan wretch on several occasions.   Finally, he was able to open his eyes to something more than dark ooze.

Two figures in black robes stood before him, staring in horror and reverence.   Gritgut recognized the symbol of the Grey God as the sign of traitorous pigs and enemies.   He surged forward to the lip of the pool and stepped out.   Rivulets of blood poured down his form, painting sigils of crimson over his skin.   The dog hide of his clothes had soiled into a solid burgundy with darker patches throughout.   His gore-drenched teeth jutted in a fierce snarl leer as his eyes burned like two glowing coals beneath his brow.   With his brown hair also blackened and matted, he looked like the monstrous embodiment of the cultists' gruesome deity.

"Hail The Grey God He has risen!!"

The two fell upon their faces, whimpering and praying for mercy. The sight disgusted Gritgut, though revulsion at morality was something novel to him. The untended seed planted by Solis' divine healing remained and now sprouted another shoot of pious fury. The oltreggan gripped both their skulls and roared, "Yus wrong! Mez no god!!!" With a deft squeeze, his fingers slid into the center of grey tissue, instantly stilling the two bucket bearers.

Gritgut raised his head and saw where he stood. The room around the caldron was smoothed and contoured into an amorphous dome. If he'd understood more of the bodies he so frequently broke, the barbarian would've realized the shape as a heart. Twisted and fluted columns snaked down to the floor at various intervals, thick obsidian veins flowing through the marble pillars and walls. Some malign theurgy allowed the vaulted alcove to pulse as though blood churned in each vessel and artery. The overall effect was ghastly and a rancid taste rose in Gritgut's mouth.

"Dez is a devul 'eart!" His voice felt damp and leaden in the churning, yet still, room. Its frosty chill congealed the blood on his clothes and body.

"No, it's a deity's heart, Desecrator."

Gritgut leveled his gaze across the room. The other voice sounded as vital as a maggot-filled corpse. A single form stood in the ventricle archway. With two casual strides, the humanoid-shaped shadow turned into the image of a well-toned sarulaan, his skin taut and yet lifeless. Several of his bones were oddly exposed and strangely, encased with mithril. The most freakish element of this champion of the Grey God were the deep gouges in his face, throat and chest, the badges of that chaotic deity.

The oltreggan leered at the apathetic fiend. "Whuz yu?"

"I am of no import," said the champion as he curled mithril talons, "'cept that I must slay you...but I am thankful to have that kill without your cohorts."

Gritgut snorted. "Mez gots na frinds."

The champion was mystified by the brute's incomprehension and answer. This was surely the same warrior who had unknowingly helped the Cult overthrow the construct's dominion in Tal Vorglath. How did the brute not recognize him?

The answer drew a smirk to the otherwise emotionless face. *'He doesn't remember...'*

"Oh, you had friends, fool. They were soiled hogs ready for the butcher. Were you the one to kill them?" The sarulaan grinned wickedly, "Of course you were...you're covered in the guilt of bloodshed."

The sarulaan was mocking him, its amber orbs scorched in hellfire. Gritgut's eyes flared as his veins pounded with wrath. "Yus lie! Iez kells unly munstars!"

"Really?" The cult warrior stepped carefully through the warped shadows of the pillars, circling the oltreggan where he stood. *'Time to draw his pain out; cause him to lose his control.'*

"Oh, they were worms deserving of death. I'm sure you savored the taste of human flesh—or is it lumilon blood that sates you?"

Vague images of alabaster smiles and quiet laughter fluttered in the black dimensions of Gritgut's memory: the faces and voices of those who had been deeply important to him. Another stem of golden rage blossomed. Sparks of luminous ire flickered into the savage's onyx glare. "Yus know nuffin."

The sarulaan paused at the fatal calm of the oltreggan only to find himself flung backwards as the column in front of him exploded. Marble chunks and sheer force propelled him across the floor as an anchor head slid inches away. The whole side of the marble pillar gushed scree and viscid ooze as the stone bled with a demonic fluid. Through the oily spray, the champion saw the barbarian, his stance and visage one of pure and radiant ire.

'When did oltreggans care about anything but destruction? This one wants retribution...'

Another marble spire splintered along its side as a second blow landed. Gritgut had more in mind than simple revenge. He would bring this whole cavern down upon the foul creature and its damnable god. Taking a few strides forward, the oltreggan swung the anchor in a high arch to flatten the sarulaan, who easily dove aside. The warrior turned his dive into a roll as a third column shrieked in protest, sprinkling marble dust and blood upon his unholy flesh. The fiend seized the opportunity and charged as Gritgut hauled in his chain.

The barbarian saw the oncoming foe and wrapped his hands in iron links. The champion slashed out with his claws but missed as Gritgut slid under his blow. But the demon-spawn was too close and would inevitably strike with his deadly talons.   Urgently, the oltreggan crouched and twisted, flinging the massive weight into the air.   The sailing iron hurled passed the half-demon to the right while Gritgut dove to his left, the coupled momentum yanking the lithe fighter off his feet. The sarulaan crashed into a pillar, his face battering hard against smooth stone.

Gritgut quickly retrieved his anchor, smiling at his successful attack.   He almost missed the soft shuffle of running feet as he turned, bringing his anchor to block the warrior's metallic claws.   The creature hissed, as though he seemed oblivious to his shattered nose and broken cheek.   Two pits of brimstone seethed over the locked weapons.

"You're a fool, 'treggan.   Desecrating the Grey God's heart and defying his champion shall be your end or I'm not His servant, Baetor!"

Between the flashes of mithril and swoosh of iron, Gritgut glimpsed places other than this diabolic pit.   He saw a red-attired lumilon sitting in a jail, mirth and exhaustion on his face.   The bard raised a blue vial in offering.   Then reality slid into being as two gouges rent across his side.

"Might want to wake up, fool, before you die sleeping!"   Baetor sneered as he lunged for Gritgut's throat.   The oltreggan fell backward, lugging the anchor in an uppercut.   The sarulaan gasped as the air expelled from its lungs, a prong shattering bone.   Baetor stood and easily returned his breathing to normal.   Gazing at the puncture wound, the sarulaan frowned at the sight of its dark grey blood.   "You may yet prove challenging, 'treggan."

Gritgut rose and stepped forward.   Another image of the alabaster figure again came into being.   This time the lumilon flew through the air, wracked by a lightning bolt from Baetor's hand.   "Daz fer Soles..."

"Ah, so now you remember—and what else did he say before you chewed his arse?" taunted Baetor.

Gritgut bared his fangs and roared.   Blind fury threatened to efface his clarity.   He struck hard, riving a column in half where the sarulaan once stood.   Blood flowed over him, washing into his mouth and eyes as he recoiled from a savage punch.   The blow sent him into the crumbling support, broken marble raining onto his head and shoulders.   Gritgut sputtered and crawled from the wreckage, blowing globules of caked blood from his nose.

A soft voice tried to break into his concentration, but Gritgut wasn't listening to anyone anymore. He barreled forward, heedless that he raised unarmed fists against the hard-edged foe. Blow after blow he bashed Baetor, but at a dreadful cost as with each counterstrike, more of Gritgut's blood mixed with the congealed mess already on his skin. His vest soon became tattered and his breaths ragged. White gleamed through the flowing streams of blood as flesh was stripped from his ribs. Compared to the barely dented sarulaan, Gritgut looked more like a feral zombie than an oltreggan.

Gritgut stepped back wearily, wiping away the warm fluid from a gash in his cheek. Exhaustion swept over him, the cool air lapping softly against his fiery wounds. Baetor flexed his claws in agitation and disappointment.

"Done so soon? Is this the awaited Desecrator who was prophesied? Surely you are not he who will awaken my master with his blood!"

A soft voice slipped through the oltreggan's tired defenses, sounding sharp and crisp in the room's cold air. "Speak truth or perish..."

Wearily, Gritgut closed his heavy lids. A golden orb with four tendrils or perhaps a glowing person, floated in the darkness and whispered "...preserve the light...spare us all."

The seed within Gritgut's soul had fully sprouted and now wreathed his spirit with joy. Its roots bore deep into the essence of his forefathers, the warrior-savages who cared only for freedom. There, in the core of his heart, the eldritch bond found a kindred longing for liberty; a hatred for restraint.

Blackness swelled around the oltreggan, blinding and deafening him. He heard nothing, felt nothing, feared nothing. Then there came a pulse, golden and rich, inside his chest. The faint thrum became a continuous pounding, like war drums upon a distant slope. Fire and zeal coursed through his veins, joy filling his mind with the song of battle. He opened his eyes to reveal orbs of polished gold and miraculously in hands rested his beloved anchor.

And Gritgut knew how to hurt his foe.

Looking at the puncture wound in Baetor's side, the oltreggan unveiled his stained fangs. "Yus gots soft bitz."

Baetor cocked an eyebrow at the spectacle. At first, the shadows seemed to converge and roll over the oltreggan, wrapping him in a shroud of darkness. Then, when the lumbering brute had been totally engulfed, the cover shattered in a flash of brilliant sunlight. Though bloodied and ragged, the barbarian stood tall and stout, his muscles rippling with new strength. The champion of the Grey God could not stare into the solid sheen of the savage's gilded eyes. Before he could reply, the oltreggan was upon him.

Each swing now focused on the prongs instead of the head of the anchor, driving the tips into Baetor's flesh. Gritgut yanked and twisted every time a blow landed, stripping skin and tendons from mithril bones. The tactic threw Baetor on the full defensive after his right arm ceased to function below the shoulder, the bicep and ligaments shredded into thin fibers. He tried to lurk in the shadows, using the pillars as cover, but the oltreggan's power appeared unlimited. The beast rent columns into splinters with devastating blows, stepping through to once more assail the warrior.

As the Grey God's champion, Baetor wasn't powerless. The warrior dug the claws of his left hand into his right palm, trickling blood down his hand. Shadows slid into his wounds, empowering him with the essence of his god, adding a new glint to the flames of his amber gaze. Snarling, the demon leapt over the next blow and slashed at the oltreggan's throat. Gritgut reached up with his left hand and caught the fiend by its own neck, clamping his fingers together. The two were locked in a titanic clash, each desiring to rip the head from his foe.

Despite the vice around his throat and the destruction all around, Baetor smiled. The heart-chamber lay in ruins, blood gushing from every wall. Only handful of pillars remained, and each bore wounds from base to cornice. He **had** found the Desecrator! This was his moment to conquer and prevail, spilling the oltreggan's blood in homage to his liege. Yet, his claws could no longer slice through the oltreggan's thick layers of muscle. A strange new essence, stronger than mithril, hardened the oltreggan's hide.

Baetor glared at the brute; his leer contorting into confusion. The oltreggan was *smiling!* Gritgut's golden orbs stared, unwavering, into the sarulaan's glare. The savage didn't appear vexed or hindered by his opponent's death grip. Rather, he appeared to be waiting for something. Baetor's faith began to waver...

* * *

Warmth slipped slowly from Gritgut's feet to his knees as the blood rose higher. Soon the chamber would fill with the burgundy mire. He would enjoy the sound of Baetor gasping and gurgling as the half-demon gulped in the remains of the slaughtered. Gritgut did not care whether he died or not; this was the moment of glorious death in battle his people spoke of. He only hoped his master would share the tale.

Just before the fluid finally crested over his face, forcing him to hold his breath, Gritgut raised his gilded eyes toward the dark roof and said, "Fer yu, Shiny..."

* * *

Interminable midnight flowed around the oltreggan as he clutched Baetor's throat. Gritgut only knew the sarulaan still lived because he could feel the pulse slowing beneath his fingers. Darkvision could not pierce the solid gloom of the blood, which had leveled out at the roof. The two warriors floated somewhere in the heart chamber, locked in melee for eternity.

Suddenly, the stasis of the submerged warriors ended as something unseen tugged downwards on the fluid around them. They were dragged, still grappling, toward the caldron many feet below. Despite the surrounding gloom, the mouth of the vat glowed luridly, like a sickly, bloody moon. The two passed into the globe, a sense of dread creeping into both fighters' hearts.

Gravity dumped the duo through a frigid breeze, the scent of saltwater and burning oil clashing with the iron tinge of blood. They were able to breathe for a moment before they crashed onto a blood-slicked wooden surface. The impact tore them apart, bouncing their tensed bodies into wooden barrels. Gritgut recovered quickly and saw, by the room's construction and the flaming cargo within, that they were within a burning ship's hold. He returned to his attention to the gasping sarulaan as the fiendish creature stood, clutching his throat.

To their right lay an odd ice sculpture, formed into a heart. Veins of grey and black slithered through the frozen mold, connecting at the center with a pale elf, her skin wan and ashen like the half-demon. A sense of malice and torment filled Gritgut's mind as he stepped away from the thing.

'Iez wantz na'ttin tad u wit dat!'

The lumbering brute dodged aside as the champion launched a

harpoon from the hold's wall. The oltreggan flung his anchor at Baetor, but the creature ducked. The weight soared upward and slammed into the deck above, followed by a curiously softer thump. Gritgut snapped up the sarulaan with both hands and slammed him repeatedly into the bulkhead. Finishing with a guttural roar, the barbarian launched Baetor against the ice heart's side.

The strange sculpture latched onto him and several veins groped hungrily before jabbing into his back. The half-demon's eyes bulged as his usually numb senses flared to life with terror and pain. The inferno of his stare dimmed into embers and then to ash as Baetor dissolved into screaming nothingness.

Inside the cocoon of frost, the form of the sleeping elf was perfectly motionless. However, Gritgut could tell that something had changed. Drawn inexorably to look, he narrowed his eyes and then, he saw it. Now, she was smiling.

Gritgut stumbled backward, vainly searching for an escape. The smoke in the room condensed around him, further concealing any exodus. Gritgut reared his head and bellowed, "Shiny, getz mez outta heer!!!"

A bass rumble of a massive explosion sounded in the hold, searing tongues of flame answering his cry. Gritgut was blasted through the heavy planks and into a raging storm. As his body fell towards the coarse oak of the dock, Gritgut realized: he had not felt the incinerating heat of the flames. Rather, a being of light flashed into existence, drinking in the fire.

'Whoz dus 'dat?'

The sudden crack of the dock against his skull ended his limited questions, drowning the oltreggan in perpetual night.

* * *

Erillon went rigid as a deep rumble vibrated the Moontower at its base. The diviner lowered an inked quill and quickly descended into the hidden basal regions. After rushing through a maze of secret passages, she found herself facing the pale visages of Uonis and Hellen, the Wardens of the Oracle. They merely pointed a shaking finger towards the antechamber that led to the Well. Erillon cried aloud as she entered.

Blasted and scorched, the alcove that once was concealed by the flowing waterfall was now a jagged crater. The sheet of water was gone, blasted away into mist, while at the center of the crater was a set of natural stone, jutting out above a pool's edge, which was now draining away. On top lay the shattered remains of a slate slab and strangely-shaped pebbles. Sprawled upon the rock face was an odd creature, a lumilon with webbing between his digits and iridescent scaled sections over the body's extremities.

His body was suffused with golden energy, though somewhat faded. His face appeared slack, as though his cognizance had been assailed in the eruption, along with his body. Severe burns, puckered and oozing black, blemished his gold and blue hide. Clutched in his right hand, which lay across his chest, was a single chess piece: a rook.

Erillon, Uonis, and Hellen quickly and carefully began the process of tending to the torn figure who must have been the Order's secret guide for many generations. As they worked, they wondered just how blind they had become now that their Eye was excised. Peering into the surprisingly youthful face, a cold dread gripped the diviner in a way she had never imagined.

How could the Order continue, now that their Oracle was gone?

Tenet's Tale

Brannon Hollingsworth

TENET'S TALE

Lastday, 28th of Sumborok, just past midnight
Temple of the Lost, Ethereal Citadel

My thinly-lidded eyes fluttered open; I could rest no more. Technically, we ethereans do not sleep as do the mortal races. We grow weary, yes, but we do not sleep. Some say this has to do with our intrinsic, divine ties to the banished gods; others name it a curse and a burden that my kind must bear. Who may be right, I think, we shall never know.

Nevertheless, it is true that my kind must periodically return to our place of origin, the Ethereal Plane or we *fade.* In Feridar, the etherean's native tongue, this fading is called *yil'ya a'feth,* or bond trance. It is a condition that abandons ethereans, unconscious and defenseless, in the physical world. We remain thusly until drawn home by the Ethereal Plane itself or by the act of someone in the physical realm.

Regardless, I could rest no more, nor could I continue to hide. The times are rare, but occasionally, I wish I could lie, if only to myself. Ethereans cannot lie – something within our deific cores prevents it. The truth was I was tired of hiding – from myself, my vision, and my love.

I cast my eyes over the forsaken scene of the Temple of the Lost and pondered how many times the vision, or her face, had come unbidden to me. The scintillating light from the ethereal curtain, that which divides my world from hers, played hide and seek amongst the sinuous pillars that drifted smoke-like through the vacuous space around me. I lowered my head, seeking the guidance of Truth. Many deemed my dedication foolish, my time and efforts wasted. They could not have been more wrong. Truth had always guided and driven me. The moment I closed my dark orbs, the vision rose again to my mind's eye:

I hear the musical harmony of falling water and smell the comforting scents of cool earth and damp moss. I can feel the brush of leafy ferns and the waterfall's spray as it playfully leaps over and rushes about rounded stones. I like it here; things are simple, and all is what it seems. There is truth in this place. I am standing in an ancient grotto, surrounded by earth, stone, water, and plants that extend into wispy shadow. A massive sheet of dazzling fluid falls, bisecting the entire grotto; from whence the waterfall descends, I cannot tell. It matters little, as I am content to merely...exist...in this magnificent, peaceful place.

It is hard to tell through the mirror-like cascade, but beyond its surface there is a being whose form gives hints of light and scales. The faceless figure moves quickly, shoving its lightly-scaled hand directly through the fall's torrent, dividing it. I am rooted to the spot, my eyes drawn towards this hand as if by magic. It trembles, as if carrying a heavy burden, and rotates upward. Its fingers open like the petals of a slowly blooming flower. In the center of the palm rests a roughly carved, stone figurine. Despite its crude craftsmanship, I know what it is: the knight – in chess, the queen's defender.

I am drawn to it. I stretch forth my hand to claim it. When my fingers meet cold, wet stone, the being speaks to me through the veil of water.

"Tenet, a shadow is coming..."

I could rest or hide no longer. Something foul was coming to my city, and I had to stop it...

* * *

Lastday, 28th of Sumborok, pre-dawn
eastern battlements, Market Ward

I stood shivering atop the battlements of the eastern wall and waited for the sun to rise over Crown. The fleeting night, one of autumn's last, had been dark and frigid. Soon, winter would creep in like an old crone and overtake us. My breath came in wisps of mist that slithered away to join the vast haze that seemed to swallow the entire world.

At first, the gulf was a vast plane of unending, undulating grey, much like my home, but ever so slowly, a miraculous thing occurred. Color began to seep into the world around me, the grey gulf gradually giving way to lighter shades of smoke and fog, finally surrendering altogether to a rosy color. The pale light lasted for a few fleeting, but breathtaking, moments and then, as the sun crested the horizon behind me, it exploded into a deep, burnished gold. The city shone like a hundred-thousand polished brass shields.

The stone battlements around me breathed trails of steam as the heavy frost began to recoil before the dawn's mighty light. My shadow fell long and thin over the rooftops of the city that I had sworn to protect one hundred and sixty years ago: Crown, the greatest city in the world.

Many wonder why ethereans have such a thirst for the physical world, the Material Plane. If they had known only the endless grey expanse of the Ethereal for the bulk of their lives and then seen this, they would have their answer.

It felt good to be back.

* * *

"Hark! Who goes there?" barked a stern, strong voice, snapping me from my reverie. I turned to see a familiar face and smiled. The young corporal stopped short, saluting sharply when he recognized me. A smile flashed across his stubble-covered lips, and he removed his hand from his blade's hilt.

"Lord Tenet! I didn't know t'was you. It's been many days since you graced my wall. What news from the Queen?"

The lad, though barely twenty summers, did his job well; I could tell that he had been up through the night by his frosted boots and the dark patches beneath his eyes. However, he still seemed unable to grasp my unique position within Crown's political and military hierarchy. As the Queen's Intelligencer, I was neither a noble nor part of the military, yet I was afforded the rights and ability to operate freely throughout those structures. I was bound by none of them, save the Queen herself or her Champion, Lady Kyrrava. A hobbled Spymaster, a term I loathed, was of little good when it came to insuring the safety of Crown and her ruler.

"Corporal Simms, how many times have I asked you to call me familiar? I am no lord, merely a humble servant of Truth," I chided him, arching a brow in mock ire.

"The Queen fares well, as best I can gather. She's busily readying her court for the Festival of The Long Night, so I would expect. The whole city seems to hold its breath in anticipation."

The Festival, ten days off, was the largest and most celebrated holiday in the whole of Crown. It marked the day on which the Demon Scourge began, one hundred and sixty-nine years ago. Ironically, it was that same event – the Demon Scourge – that ultimately made me into what I was today.

"What of you, Corporal? What news from the Eastern Watch?"

Simms was a good contact to have, honest and forthright as long as I'd known him. He held Crown and her safety in the highest regard. Many were the times that his words, or those of his comrades-in-arms, had prevented disasters from befalling the city. Simms swiftly informed me of all that he knew. One item was of particular interest to me: scores of completely bloodless bodies had been found all across Crown. To date, the only two witnesses were Jalkesh, the traveling peddler who frequented the bridges between the Narrows and Old Temple Ward, and Jomo, the brigand pirate of the *Fool's Folly*.

Simms's words joined forces with my disturbing vision and further clouded my thoughts; something was truly amiss in Crown.

* * *

Several score birds twittered into view and circled three times around a small, ramshackle home along a narrow alley a half-block from where I stood. I knew then that Alynna and her druidic sisters were nearing completion of their early morning ritual, part of which summoned all of their feathered "messengers" back to their roosts. Like Corporal Simms, the elven druid was an excellent source of information in Crown – if one could meet her price.

Luckily for me, Alynna was fascinated by my familiar, Isil. For even the slightest chance that she could observe and examine the rare etherwasp, she would reveal a veritable treasure trove of rumors and tidings of what was stirring all across the city. Knowing that I had many miles to cover this day and just as many contacts to pursue, I quickly made my way down the still-frosty battlement, pulling my ashen cloak tighter around me to ward away the chill.

* * *

Lastday, 28th of Sumborok, midday
The Crossroads, Market Ward

Even with the sun at its peak, *The Crossroads* was dim and shadowy. One of the oldest inns in the Market Ward, the cramped, smoky space had not changed much since its founding. The low, dingy ceilings, stained from decades of candle, hearth, and pipe smoke, along with the dark, pitted ceiling beams and doors, gave the whole establishment the feel of being in a cave more so than a man-made building. Small, lead-lined windows strangled the light as it tried to enter and brighten the grubby stone walls; a few hooded lanterns dangling from rusty chains here and there added to the wan, mediocre light.

While *The Crossroads* was not necessarily a dangerous place to enjoy a pint, it was not exactly the safest place, either. Only a block from the Sailor's Ward, it was frequented by salty sea merchants, crafty captains, and dubious mercenaries - all seeking refuge. Generally, the sellers and buyers that trolled the Merchant Ward drank elsewhere. It was just the sort of place that those in my line of work do their best business; eroding inns, hazy with pipe smoke and the sounds of poorly played pipes are the stage upon which shady deals are oft made.

One of Alynna's ravens had been frequenting *The Crossroads* for the past several weeks, delivering messages to my quarry, so I knew that sooner or later he would turn up here. Jomo was an old business associate of mine, a dark-skinned human pirate captain who owed me a hefty sum from our last game of bones, which I had purposefully not yet collected upon. Debts can be repaid in ways other than coin, I've always said...

As I dove into the gloom, waving my thin hand before me to ward away the haze, a dark form across the room bolted from a table of smoke-wreathed patrons and fled into the street.

"Jomo," I growled, slamming my fist into my palm. I sent a silent, mental request to Isil and turned, speaking the words to a spell that sundered the very fabric of time and space. An ebon doorway appeared before me, and I stepped through without a moment's pause.

Isil served me well by pinpointing my quarry; Jomo had only thought he could escape my grasp. The man's look of surprise was complete as a doorway as black as his skin coalesced before him and I stepped forth.

The captain tried desperately to skid to a stop, but he slid helplessly into my hands. He instantly began fast-talking.

"Ten-net, m'friend! Long time no see, mon. Hey if dis is 'bout 'dat gold Jomo owes you, Ten-net, Jomo can pay up - quick, mon!"

Isil lit upon my shoulder, gleaming silver mandibles the size of long-knives opening and closing slowly. Jomo's eyes widened in fear; I decided to let my silence hang in the air for a few moments longer, heightening that fear. Finally, I could bear it no more and let out a slight chuckle. "Jomo," I said, unable to disguise my budding grin.

The captain never took his eyes from my etherwasp's razor sharp mouthparts. "Eh? Ten-net, you feelin' well an' all, mon? Jomo t'inks you gettin' a bit too much in da rumdrum!"

"Jomo. I am not here for money."

Jomo finally tore his eyes from Isil. He saw my grin and reacted in kind. He glanced to where I was holding him and pointed with his scraggly bearded chin. "'Den you let Jomo go, eh?"

"Aye," I replied, letting the captain go. "But I need to know something from you, and I need the straight and true." I furrowed my brow, letting him know I was completely serious.

Jomo shrugged and lifted his palms towards me. "Hey, dis be Jomo you talkin' to! Jomo, Captain o' de *Fool's Folly*! Jomo always tells de truf! I be de man who-"

I held up my hand, cutting off the tirade before it began; I'd heard all of this before. "Aye, Jomo, and if you do not, then the *Fool's Folly* will be needing a new captain – one who has all of his...bits." Isil read me perfectly and snipped her mandibles repeatedly. "If you get my meaning, Jomo..."

He did.

* * *

Lastday, 28th of Sumborok, sundown
The Black Well Market, Market Ward

My breath came in ragged gasps. I knew in my bones that I'd not had enough time to truly prepare for my impending foray, but that mattered little. The moment that Jomo's secrets tumbled out, I'd known that I had to come to this now-cursed place and do the unthinkable. Jomo had witnessed several dark robed figures dumping bodies into a once pristine well in the Market Ward now known as the Black Well.

The Black Well Market had not always been cursed. In the past, it had bustled with activity and commerce, drawing merchants and customers from the whole of Crown. Then, it was lovely and serene: a large, rectangular pool, open to the sky, flanked on three sides by stately elms, knee-high, wrought-iron fences, and large, flower-studded planters. The fourth side was dominated by an elaborately carved fountain of Anaedin the Brave, the first champion and Queen of Crown.

Now, it was a twisted and accursed place. The elms now bowed like skeletal reapers over the decaying courtyard that was cluttered with refuse, filth, and litter. The beautiful monument to Crown's first Queen now stood broken and blemished, overrun with scraggly weeds and voracious vines.

The reason for this diametric change lay in the well. Deep beneath that malodorous pool lurked a foul denizen of Tal Vorglath, the perilous underpinnings of Crown itself. Tal Vorglath was a dark place, filled with depravation, deceit, and demonic-spawns from the dark ages of my city's past. No one really knew what the horror was that lurked at the bottom of the Black Well. Its night-black tentacles would randomly slip out of the well's cloudy murk to snatch those foolish or unfortunate enough to wander too close and drag them down to their dooms.

The brigand captain had revealed that a bloodthirsty tiefling – a race whose parentage originated on the lower planes - by the name of Slyther was one of the body-dumpers at the Black Well. Jomo had recognized the back-stabbing former crew member by his unmistakable, hissing speech. Slyther led a knot of dark-robed figures, Grey God cultists from the sounds of them, into the courtyard and called out to the beast from the well while holding a silver amulet aloft. As if on cue, the ebon tentacles appeared and dragged the bodies beneath the murk. The cultists then sliced their palms, transformed into shadow, and glided down the well after them. If the nightmare from the Well was now answering to the Cult of the Grey God, it did not bode well for Crown.

Isil and I slipped the Shroud together and descended slowly into the filth-filled aquifer. We had not gone far when Isil began to drone her silver-veined wings in alarm – something was near to us on the Material Plane – something big. A rolling, boiling form larger than a house filled my entire field of view. What I could discern of its bulk seemed to be nothing more than a massive core of constantly moving, shifting, and changing flesh as black and as fluid as pitch. A wall of slithering, undulating forms pressed down upon me, and from within this horrific tapestry bubbled all manner of terribly foul and evil body parts: eyes, ears, mouths, hands, claws, pinchers, horns – each remaining only for a moment and then succumbing to the riptide beneath the next massive wave of roiling, twisting ebony flesh.

Each of the parts was wholly different but equally terrible. Red, cat-like demon eyes glared with equal hate and revulsion as did the dead-white and bloated fish eyes. Horrific, tooth-lined lamprey maws yearned for blood and bone as much as did the gigantic, rasping, file-like tongue-mouths.

Instinctively, we recoiled from the massive wall of awaiting death and began to take in the enormity of the monstrosity. From the beast's colossal, repulsive core stretched yards of black tentacles, each of them vanishing into the dark abyss around us. My eyes followed a score or more of these tree-trunk-like appendages, and I gasped. The horror was slowly, methodically devouring six lily-white bodies.

Devouring was perhaps too clean a word for what the awful beast did to the bodies. It seemed that its very touch literally dissolved their forms into a thick, ropy slurry that was then consumed by its innumerable gaping orifices. Mouths, ears, hands, eyes: each of them gobbled, snatched, or slurped a portion of the once-living goo and drew it in as the parts themselves were absorbed into the creature's immense black mass.

At that moment, the attitude of the beast shifted, and I saw several trios of predatory yellow eyes, like those of a raptor, roll out from beneath a wave of gibbering simian mouths and clacking, serrated beaks. The sets of eyes glared at me balefully, and somehow, I knew that the beast could see us even as we floated in the Border Ethereal! I called to Isil, to tell her to depart for the Deep, but she buzzed excitedly. My excellent etherwasp had discovered a grate, through which I quickly sought refuge. Any barrier that I could lay between myself and this horror was a good thing. I then directed Isil to flee to the fastness of the Temple of the Lost, unsure of the nature of the strange beast that drifted, still glaring, nearby.

Beyond the grate, a large tunnel curved upwards. I followed and soon found myself above the water's surface in a bell-shaped chamber. Through the Shroud, the sounds of battle and spell-fire instantly reached my ears. Cautiously, I slipped down the sloping tunnel towards the sounds of screams and cracking bones.

* * *

Lastday, 28th of Sumborok, evening
somewhere beneath the Market Ward

The sight that awaited me at the end of that tunnel will haunt me until my last days: a large, dome-shaped chamber seeped with water the color of rotten blood. An obscene glow – not so much light as the actual glow and emanation of continuous waves of negative energy – washed the room with a blunted, wan luminescence.

The source of the glow shocked me to my core and stole the breath from my lungs. A night black being composed of pure negative energy was strung spread-eagle across the domed room's apex! This being was a lumillon – normally a being of light and positive energy – that had been twisted, perverted, and altered in such a way as to exude the exact opposite! The dark lumillon's mouth hung agape, as if frozen in an un-ending scream of abject agony.

My eyes roamed downwards from this grisly chandelier to the walls, which had their own gory dressing. Lining them, from floor to nearly the roof's apex, were long-dead, pale bodies that shone forth from the darkness like bloated moons. Carpet-like moss, black as tar, slithered hungrily across the pale forms, impaling them to the walls with jagged spars. Many of the bodies bore at least one dagger scar, marking the manner of their death, but something odd and evil resonated from those dry, drained wounds: spidery veins of shadowy darkness.

The chamber smelled of charred flesh and spilled blood. The broken form of a human cultist of the Grey God lay in a crumpled heap to my far right. His abdomen had exploded outward and upward, his entrails spilling from his chest, mouth, and nose. Not far from the body lay a twitching, horn-tipped tentacle nearly as long as a rowboat; purple ichor still squirted from one end. The ghastly thing had been ripped out of something that was once alive. The chamber's floor spilled away from me, ending in a blood-slicked fissure. Shattered rock and twisted metal lay strewn about this hole, and the ground smoked and bubbled. I could hear the muffled sounds of combat from below.

In the chamber's center stood a spindly elf with skin as pale as the corpses with which he'd surrounded himself. A shock of black hair sprouted from his pasty brow and stood askew in every direction. Bits of bone, scraps of animal skins, feathers, beads, and baubles of all kinds adorned his spiky, jutting hair, and a feral snarl was plastered across his pointed, but weak and recently-bloodied, chin. The elf was nearly naked, his skeletal frame covered only by a long, tattered and frayed robe, worn toga-like across his right shoulder and down to his knees. The Grey God's symbol he bore openly upon his left breast, branded into the flesh itself. Three baleful raptor's eyes, the same eyes I'd seen staring at me earlier from the creature in the Well, completed this visage of madness and evil.

"W...w...welcome Spymaster!" giggle-murmured the elf in a frenetic voice. "I do hope you like w...w...what I've done w...w...with the place!" Fresh blood spattered out of the elf's mouth as he spoke, staining his chin.

'*How could this crazed cultist be expecting me? How can he see me?*' I wondered.

"You have me at a disadvantage, it seems," I replied, "as you seem familiar with me, yet of you, I have no knowledge."

The wild-eyed elf cackled madly, tossing his head back, "Oh, I have you at so much more than a disadvantage, Stiffshanks. So..."

He raised his right hand, curling it into a claw-like formation.

"Much..." His left land ascended in an inwardly slashing motion, his fingers fused together like a knife blade.

"More!" Both hands twisted as the dark-robed elf leaped nearly six feet towards me. Talons of emerald energy lanced forth from his hands, rending the planar fabric of both the Material and Ethereal Planes simultaneously. Jagged sears of pain ripped across my ethereal flesh, and like water from a shredded bladder, I tumbled, bloody and screaming, into the Material Plane. The scent of lilacs filled my nostrils, and the familiar smell hit me like a bag of bricks: El'laa.

I had suffered the effects of this spell once before, from the very woman who had shattered my soul and driven me into hiding. She was once my love, but now, she hated me. Through an onyx rod, El'laa had unleashed this spell upon me, which robbed me of my ultimate defense: my ethereal form. The fact that this insane-acting elf, who I'd never seen before, had just used the same spell against me did not bode well.

Blood pattered from my body like a light afternoon rain, staining the stone beneath where I knelt on all fours. I gritted my teeth through the pain and tried to tune out the elf's maniac cackling. A drop of fouled water fell onto my bald pate from somewhere above me, and I grinned. Honestly, at that moment, with raw emotion and scalding pain having its way with me, I think I felt a little insane myself. I grabbed a handful of dirt in my right hand and pushed myself to my knees. I dabbed my fingers into the wetness on my head and locked eyes with the elf. His eyes had returned to normal. Apparently, he no longer needed his "seeing" spell to detect me in the ethereal.

"Who are you?" I spat, blood filling my mouth.

The elf cocked one of his shaved brows, a quizzical look dancing over his visage. "I am Xigx, he that surpasses you, Queen's-man. Do you desire to name your doom?"

"No. I need to know what to tell them to put on your headstone," I replied, dryly.

At that moment, my ice storm screamed into existence. With the force of a hurricane, the tempest slammed into Xigx, launching him from his feet and bashing him back down to the stone floor. Hailstones the size of melons hammered the elf, flaying and freezing skin from bone. Ice formed on Xigx's body, and frosty clouds billowed from the cultist's mouth with each blood-curdling scream. Through blood-stained teeth, I grinned - this was a little better.

The violence of my assault quickly waned, and Xigx mumbled arcane syllables through chattering teeth. As the frost and ice receded, his form melted into wispy darkness and then flitted away into the alien half-light-and-darkness that filled the chamber.

"Now w-w-we shall see w-w-who is the true master and w-w-who is the apprentice!"

I immediately went on the defensive, snatching a glass bead from my bonded *girdle of pockets*. I spoke the words and felt the magic begin to unlock and unhinge itself around me. I quickly drew my hands horizontally through the air before me until my palms touched. Then, I drew my hands apart and grinned as the bead hung motionless in the air. By the Bound Gods, I love what I do.

I reversed the flow of my hands, spinning them a half-turn counter-clockwise and increasing the force, and then I slammed my palms together again, completing the incantation. A shimmering, alabaster globe of pure magical energy burned between my palms. As I drew my palms diagonally apart, the globe grew between them. When my arms could reach no further, I blew lightly on the sphere. It immediately leapt from my hands and doubled in size around me.

Five magical crystalline missiles shattered against my globe, leaving only an oily black substance that popped and sizzled like acid. Xigx's voice cursed from the darkness, and I replied with a hearty laugh.

"What were you saying, pupil?" I chided. I wanted him angry, needed him to make a mistake. I had to know what was happening down here and how this mongrel's son was connected to El'laa. I activated my *cresentring*, a gift from friends at the Moontower, and felt many of my lesser ills magically fade. I was still badly wounded, but with my globe now in place, I knew I could play my hand differently.

Xigx erupted from his shadow form thirty yards away, now to my left. He gyrated obscenely with the chaotic, shadowy energies that swirled around him. His bloodshot, amber eyes glared at me with hatred, and the elf spewed a magical lexis laced with frothy blood. Xigx's casting collapsed into mad cackling, and the shadows in the room changed, gaining sharp, gleaming edges.

Then, they exploded.

I dove in vain, trying to escape the wall of swirling, serrated shadows. It did little good. I started to scream as the razor thin slices began to carve my meat from my bones. The scream died in my throat as sheer pain drove the breath from my lungs. I buried my face into the mucky floor of the cavern chamber; if someone was going to find my body down here, I at least wanted them to know who I was.

"You w-w-will die in this hole, Queen's-man!" Xigx cackled. "I w-w-will add your blood to the cauldrons and your body to my growing army of umbral undead. And once the Cult has succeeded, I shall replace you in the new Dark Order that arises. I w-w-will be the Grey God's right-hand, and you w-w-will help usher him in!"

A loud screeching noise interrupted the elf's maniacal ranting. I shifted my head to the right just enough to get a glimpse through the whirling, cutting shadows and tried to focus through the crimson haze. The largest oltreggan I'd ever seen had ripped a large section of rusted, metal grate out of the floor. The hairy brute bled from many wounds, but his eyes smoldered with feral anger and hatred. With a roar that seemed to expel all of that anger, the oltreggan flung the metal grate across the room towards the elf cultist.

Xigx heard the roar and turned just in time to catch the grate broadside in the chest. The blow disrupted Xigx's concentration, and the rotating razors ceased to exist. I felt like one of Fennah's beloved sausages: neatly sliced and ready to be devoured.

Now, I was mad.

I dug deep into my psyche, calling up the most powerful magic that I could command. A spell of my own creation holding the power of Truth itself, the incantation brought the sheer, undeniable light of irrefutability down upon the target. It was time for Xigx to see the light.

I rolled over, groaning, and stifled a scream as I felt the skin on my back and legs tear like worn cloth. I pointed a shaking finger towards Xigx, who was crawling out from under the grate, his face bloodied. I spoke a single, arcane fragment, and the world shuddered.

A column of cool, white light lanced down through the domed ceiling of the chamber, surrounding Xigx. The elf's face twisted in the dawn of this new revelation. I knew that through the light of Truth, he was being shone the actuality of who he really was. In this truism, all perceptions and prejudices are utterly blown away. You have no more excuses and are faced with the responsibility and repercussions of every single act you have ever performed. I don't use this power often; it usually makes the target's head explode. If they're lucky, they only go mad.

The light winked out of existence, and Xigx screamed, clutching the sides of his head. He wailed, gnashed his teeth, and pulled plugs of his own hair out until his scalp began to bleed. He snapped his head towards me and shot me a glance of utter hatred and revulsion. Then, he laughed again, a laugh that sent chills racing down my spine.

"You w-w-will die here, Tenet! For I command a force far greater than one you could ever summon. Have you forgotten my little pet outside? My w-w-wonderfully perverted chaos beast has served me well, Tenet, more so after I twisted it to my liking! Don't you see? I called it and control it, you fool!"

Xigx's eyes rolled back in his head for a moment, and his mouth began silently moving. The ground began to tremble, and I heard a deep, basal sound, something like a gurgling roar. I gasped and whipped my head towards the downward sloping tunnel through which I had entered. My mind and soul screamed in terror, and I began to crawl as quickly as my enfeebled legs and arms could carry me towards the opening.

Behind me, the insane elf hooted and screeched in madcap joy, "And so, the mighty Tenet crawls towards his own doom!" I glanced over my shoulder and saw the elf's form dissolve into shadow and flit away into the pervading gloom. I cursed myself for letting him escape, but I knew that I had much worse issues to deal with.

As I neared the tunnel, I could already see the first of the monster's tentacles, boiling and plopping, quickly filling the entire space. I had only moments. I reached into my *girdle* again, drawing forth some crushed diamond dust. I normally used it for other spells, but I was desperate. If I failed now, I was dead. On my wobbling knees, I ground the powder between my palms and recited phrases more ancient than I, flinging my hands out and apart. The dust sparkled and vanished, and in its place appeared a massive wall of shimmering force the color of lightening.

At that moment, the titanic chaos beast slammed into my wall of force from the other side. The ground thrummed beneath my feet, and several large stones dropped from the ceiling. The monstrous creature roared and slammed its immeasurable bulk against the arcane bulwark again, but the magic held. I sighed and stood, shakily.

I shook my head, trying to dislodge the haze of sanguine cobwebs that danced behind my eyes. My weakened arms dropped in exhaustion, and I looked towards my captive. At that moment, several score eyes, all blazing with hatred, bubbled up and out of the monstrosity's oil hide.

I felt my breath catch in my chest. My skin, all over my body, instantly became painfully tight and fiery. Then I felt a cold sensation fill my belly, and the world went completely dark...

* * *

Travelday, 30th of Sumborok, early morning
The Moontower, The Narrows

I awoke to the gentle sounds of rain and distant thunder. Groggily, I pried my stiff eyes open and tried to focus on my surroundings. I was in a plain, non-descript room occupied by only an unadorned wooden dresser, the bed in which I reclined, and an oddly open window. It was the window that drew my attention and forced me to focus. Outside, it was either early morning or late afternoon; the light was grey and diffused by the storm clouds above, so I could not discern the time. I had no idea where I was, what day it was, but oddly, I did not feel overly alarmed; I only had a mild sense of mixed curiosity and concern. My mind whirled with all that had happened to me previously, but I could not restrain a single thought for more than a heartbeat. I was utterly drained.

I tried to rise, but multihued stars swam before my eyes, and my stomach lurched. I thought better of it and laid my head back upon the straw-and-feather pillow. I was clothed in only a loincloth, but otherwise, I was clean, dry, and completely healed. My right arm ached deeply, like an old scar or a naturally-healed bone break on a rainy day. I was terribly weary and tired. My body told me in no uncertain terms that the *yil'ya a'feth* was near. I was about to slip the Shroud when the door to wherever I was opened.

A lumillon, dressed in the simple robes of the Order of the Benevolent Moon, gave me my first clue. Somehow, I was in the Moontower. The moment I saw him, an image of the horrifically altered member of his race hanging bound in Xigx's torture chamber flashed through my mind. Thankfully, the vile vision was dispelled as quickly as it was conjured. The kind face of the lumillon shone with benevolence as he stood over me, hands clasped before his chest. He inclined his head towards me and spoke, "Arastin?"

The name was known to me, but it being asked here and in the connotation of a question seemed utterly surreal. I knitted my brows and soured my expression, "Excuse me?"

"Arastin?" he asked again, a bit louder and leaning closer.

I shook my head and shrugged slightly, "I'm sorry but I do not understand the question."

Suddenly, something changed. I had the distinct feeling that I had just awoken from a dream, but everything around me was the same: the room, the rain, the open window, the dresser – except the lumillon was gone, replaced now by a human who looked nearly identical to him. The feeling that overwhelmed me at that moment was the same as after my vision; something was afoot.

"I merely asked, 'Are ya restin'?'" the man said gently, a hint of confusion creeping into his voice.

I nodded mutely, and thunder echoed ominously in the distance.

* * *

Travelday, 30th of Sumborok, morning
The Glorious Dawn, **Deep Harbor District**

I teleported to the Silver Lyre College, a block south of my target, *The Glorious Dawn,* and quickly slipped into the ethereal borderlands. I needed desperately to talk to Fennah, but knew that I could not simply walk through the front doors of her inn. I did not want to alert any potential prying eyes to my presence. When the "Queen's Man" is on the move in Crown, word spreads like wildfire. Best to let my enemies think I was dead for awhile. My soul screamed for me to take a dip into the Deep Ethereal, to get some true rest, but I could not, not yet.

I had quickly gathered a great deal of information from the human healer in my room at the Moontower, a man called Marrick. He'd told me that the mysterious Oracle of the Moontower had seen what would happen to me in the Black Well and sent me some help. The huge oltreggan, whose name was apparently Gritgut, had been sent to save me.

As best as the Order could tell, Xigx had escaped, and the chaos beast had turned me to stone. Afterwards, the burly brute, Gritgut, had brought me back to the Moontower and stood guard over me. At least, that was, until an assassination attempt was made on my life before I awoke this very morning.

Learning this, I quickly had gathered my gear and weapons from the dresser and left. My head still pounded, and my right arm throbbed dully, but it didn't matter. I'd unearthed something major, and whatever it was, the Cult of the Grey God did not want me pursuing it any further.

I knew from my encounter with Xigx that El'laa was at least tangentially involved, and now from my recent "vision" this morning, I had the distinct impression that the elf, Arastin, was as well. Arastin was an assassin who had lived in Crown even longer than I. At his chosen "craft," he was once one of the best, though recently, he'd gotten lackadaisical and lax.

To further complicate matters, Arastin and El'laa had once been "an item." It was from that sordid life and ruinous relationship that I'd attempted to save her. Needless to say, I'd failed - miserably. If the two of them were mixed up in something together, then the message from the gut-wrenching knot in my belly was not only right, it was understated.

The current common thread between the two eluded me, taunting me from afar and yet gnawing on the base of my skull like a manticore on a thighbone. While their past was obviously a piece of the puzzle, it wasn't enough to make the sort of foul glue that would connect Arastin and El'laa in whatever dire business was afoot. There was something else hidden to me. The strange words from my dream echoed again in the recesses of my mind, *"Tenet, a shadow is coming..."*

I had to find out how those two were mixed up in all of this, but later would have to do; I was fading quickly - literally. I knew I had to talk to Fennah and set some events in motion, and then I would slip into the well-known folds of fore-matter. I floated through the crowd and into the innards of *The Glorious Dawn*. I passed through the wooden secret door and entered into Fennah's undisclosed and opulent chambers. I slipped the Shroud back into the Material plane as she downed her last piece of sausage. The dwarven bard almost choked.

"Gah! A curse upon your slick head, Ghost!" she spouted, bits of half-chewed pork flying. Why she obsessed about my clean-shaven head had always puzzled me.

I dipped my head slightly, too weary to bow, and returned her greeting, "Queen's care 'pon you, Fennah Stonethroat. Forgive my intrusion; I haven't much time."

Concern crept into her voice, "What ill's befallen the Queen's Man this or'cast mornin'?"

I shook my head, "No ill, Fennah, but by the grace of Truth and Goodness do I yet breathe. I am worn to the bones and am in need of a dip in the Deep. I do require a favor of you before I go, however."

"Speak it and if it can be done by song or deed, it shall be, Ghost." She smiled, again using the nickname she had given me so long ago.

"Two old friends, well known to us both, have some plot stirring betwixt them. Arastin and El'laa are up to something." The words fell from my mouth, lead-laden. It seemed somehow more real once I had given it voice.

"Gah! You know as well as I, Ghost, that the most likely thing a'stirring betwixt those two are sheets! What care has the Queen's Man for that, if it were not for his heart only?"

Her words bit me deeper than an arrowhead. I gritted my teeth and tried hard to focus my still-spinning, fatigued mind. "There is more than that, Fennah, or my master's not Truth. Please, see what your contacts can unearth." It was a statement, not a question, but I could tell she took it as the latter.

"Aye, I will for you, Ghost. Now, go. You look like shite."

It was not the first time I'd been called that, but I think it was the first time I'd taken it as a compliment. I thankfully slipped into the beckoning embrace of the Deep Ethereal and knew only the vast bleakness of ultimate potential.

* * *

Travelday, 30th of Sumborok, near midnight
The Rowdy Goblin, Old Temple District

The *'Goblin* was glum tonight. Maybe it was an echo of the brooding, seething skies above – or maybe it was the feeling that I got every time I thought about seeing her again. I scanned the inn's main room and caught only glimpses of faces and forms between the half-shadows cast by flickering flames and the spidery movements of dampened frivolity.

Despite this, the long years of my experience aided me. As if by magic, barely-seen profiles blossomed into full faces, and fireplace-flung silhouettes emerged into the full light of knowledge. Through my honed observation skills, fragmented glances merged themselves into stained-glass representations of scoundrels both celebrated and suspected. I thanked Goodness and Truth for my skills and for the long years that I've spent honing them.

Even though that honing had taken three deaths and over a century and a half, it was still worth it. Being able to identify potential targets from beyond the Shroud was a skill many would kill for. If they only knew that it was not a killing, but rather, a dying, that made it possible, I wonder how many would have desired the prize.

The telltale tingle of magic, accompanied by a sudden movement from across the Shroud, yanked me from my musing and let me know that my target was on to me. I should've known better than to get distracted; El'laa was no neophyte. She'd grown up on the streets, conning people and becoming what they wanted her to be, something she was incredibly good at. She knew me just as well as I knew her. She was after all, the love of my life.

The inn was too crowded for the rogue to openly act against me; there were countless witnesses. The stunning, auburn-haired tiefling was far too wily and intelligent for that. She was headed for the street, for her territory. I followed with a mere thought, drifting through the crumbly limestone walls and unwashed windows of *The Rowdy Goblin* and into the storm-cloud laden night.

Instantly, jags of searing agony bloomed like angry flowers across my legs and back. The hazy, murmuring curtains of the ethereal borderlands were, for less than a heartbeat, sundered by a brutal intrusion of actuality. Spastic blobs of smoking proto-matter, mixed with my blood, spattered into the surrounding ethereal murk.

I glanced over my shoulder and gritted my teeth; the tiefling rogue had planned ahead this time. She must have known that I'd come looking for her. El'laa's sea-green eyes were already entombed in a pair of ashen goggles, and she whipped out a wand tipped with a thistle of ruby shards.

I quickly slid through the Shroud and into the Material like water through oil, as the wand disgorged twin rays of crimson force. My world was instantly awash with scarlet pain. I screamed as the flesh on the right side of my skull was peeled back by her magic. Woozy, I blinked past the literal and figurative sanguine haze before my eyes. Practiced arcane phrases hastened from my pale lips, and my palms glowed with a sickly green aura. As magical beryl chains streamed from the tiefling's frame, ending in massive emerald-colored anchors, I ripped off her goggles and knocked the wand from her hand.

"Looks like you'll be staying with me a while, m'love," I stated flatly, drizzle and blood running over my right ear and dripping onto my ash-colored robes.

Those sea-green eyes fluttered and then focused on my pale visage, my dark, fathomless eyes. She snarled a curse at me, "Maelthorin take your soul, Tenet! To the Pit with you!"

I shook my head, like a schoolmaster chiding a heedless student, "Even if it wanted, it could not have me, El'laa. I am bound to a higher power and calling, which the Shadow Realm cannot overcome."

She screamed and spat in my face. I was thankful that whatever fiend sired her did not have acid in its belly; I pretended that her actions made me angry and slipped into mock fury. "So, it seems you want the hard way then, eh?" I growled, shaking her.

"I would die before aiding you, Tenet!" she shrieked at me, wriggling like a fish on the end of my hook. Her expensive lilac perfume, as usual, barely covered her constant scent of cloying death. The smell, and her closeness to me, made me light-headed with desire.

I sensed that we had gained an audience. The tiefling's cries had brought lantern-bearing onlookers, and a call for the Watch echoed from the ancient stone walls of the Old Temple Ward. A pool of firelight, filled with a crowd, spilled out of *The 'Goblin*; cries and gasps leaped from their lips. I quickly focused my will into the task of immobilizing the tiefling rogue with an enchantment and had soon powered through El'laa's formidable willpower. My quarry frozen for the moment, I stood as I heard a troop of the Watch clatter down the cobbles.

The captain of the guard saluted sharply, sounding off, "Lord Tenet! You are wounded... How may we assist?"

I shook my head at the incorrect title and merely pointed with a finger towards the held tiefling. "I've need to interrogate this enemy of the Queen's Peace forthwith. My wounds can wait. There is little time..."

* * *

Darkday, 1st of Layfanil, late morning
Byway Bridge, The Mud Flats

El'laa was hiding something from me; I knew this in my bones. It was apparent that she was growing resistant to my usual spells and methods. I could only blame myself. This was the price for getting too close to one of your informers. The moment a weakness was exposed, the edge of fear and revulsion that is critical to survival on the street was utterly lost. It was simple, really; you can not intimidate someone for whom you truly care.

I let her go. I'd never intended on slapping her in chains anyway. The only thing she was guilty of was buying a spell from a cultist, which was not a crime by any means. Right now, I needed information, not prisoners. Fortunately, there were many ways to get information that didn't require interrogation, chains, or imprisonment. One of my favorites was a false sense of confidence. Let the offender go, and invariably, all but the sharpest would betray their wrong-doings in some manner: a slip of an ale-loosened tongue, a visit to the wrong place at the wrong time, or the lure of an even larger payoff. Regardless, the light of Truth would eventually shine upon their nefariousness and expose them for what they genuinely were.

The tiefling had openly admitted that she'd paid Xigx to craft the ethereal rip spell. She had leered at me and mocked me when I'd questioned her about it. She'd become as silent as the grave when I mentioned the name "Arastin," however; I thought I even detected a hint of fear in her eyes. I decided at that moment that I'd be paying the elf assassin a visit very soon. For now, however, I had to speak with the only other solid lead I had: an old friend, Jalkesh the peddler.

As I slogged through the slurry of mud and frost, picking my way around those braving the weather and the pre-lunch traffic on the Byway Bridge, my thoughts began flowing together like the muddy waters of the Gorge River beneath me. In less than the three days since my return from the Deep Ethereal, I had somehow gotten drawn into a vortex that involved a rash of mysterious murders, the cult of the Grey God, a twisted chaos beast, an insane elf wizard cultist, an army of umbral undead, an elven assassin, and the love of my life - who still loathed me. Never let it be said that Crown was a quiet place to settle down and retire. How all these pieces joined together I could not yet tell, but I was determined to find out.

As I neared one of Jalkesh's usual spots – the narrow "Y" that gave the Byway Bridge its name – I spied the soaking wet, thin, balding man standing in the chilly rain amidst the residue of splinters and souring fruit. He held a small basket of mostly bruised produce, and it looked as if he was having a difficult time trying to sell any of it. The man cursed as he simmered over the remains of his ruined cart and livelihood, "By the Bound Gods, is there no justice in this city?"

"Of course there is, or my master's not Truth," I stated flatly as I surveyed the damage. "What happened here, Jalkesh?"

"Ruffians! Law-breakers! Make it so an honest man can't make a livin', I tell ya! A great hairy lout of an oltreggan came a'barrlin' up th' Byway yesterday morn, and th' ox-headed lummox ran right through my cart!"

The cart-pushing peddler ranted on for some time, and I listened carefully. Often, one must give first in order to collect after. Oddly, throughout the entirety of the man's rant, my right arm ached horribly.

* * *

Darkday, 1st of Layfanil, afternoon
Crownmeet Castle, Queenshold Library, Old Temple Ward

I closed the last tome with a puff of dust and ran my fingers across my bald pate. If Jalkesh had only known the latent power in the words he'd spoken to me...if I had only known. I was now relieved that I'd given my peddler friend a safe spot to lay low for the time being. With what he had witnessed, he might soon find himself on the end of an assassin's blade. Luckily, I owned a small warehouse in the Deep Harbor District to which I had given Jalkesh the keys. I knew it was not much recompense for the destruction of his cart and goods, but perhaps it was a place where he could begin rebuilding.

The lonesome cart-peddler had witnessed much more than a mere killing in the alleyways of the Narrows, even though he had no idea. He had, in fact, witnessed the culmination of a black ritual from the time of the Demon Scourge. So far, I'd identified the method, the words used, and the enchanted dagger used in the killings; all of them were clearly laid out in several sources of esoteric arcane knowledge. The only thing that was missing was the purpose, but the signs seemed blatantly clear. The timing of these records, as well the fragments of a single Shadow Walker's journal from one hundred and seventy years ago, clearly indicated that this same ritual was used in Crown during the time leading up to the release of the Demon Hordes upon the unsuspecting city.

My conversation with Corporal Simms immediately jumped to memory; the Festival of Long Night was but a week away! I darted across the room, flipping through age-old tomes and tossing scrolls hither and yon. I soon located the source of my search and unrolled the leather-backed scroll out upon a table. The archaic astrological charts were difficult to read, but I soon divined the answer I sought and yet dreaded with all my heart. Each of the five moons would wan new on Darkday, seven days from now. The night sky would know no light, exactly the same as on that first Long Night, one hundred and sixty-nine years ago. Exactly the same as on the night the Demon Scourge began...

* * *

Darkday, 1st of Layfanil, evening
Greyspur Castle, Lady Kyrrava's chambers, Arm's Crescent

"Enter, Queen's Man."

The weakness in Lorelei's voice shocked me as I entered her opulent chambers, bowing. "Forgive me, Mistress, I realize the lateness of the hour. Only the urgency of my news brings me to darken your door." Although many in Crown assumed from my title, Queen's Intelligencer, that I reported directly to the reigning regent of Crown, the truth was that my superior was instead her sister and Champion, Lady Kyrrava, a skilled warrior and one of the greatest wizards in the known world. I was honored to serve Crown under her guidance and tutelage.

She laughed, a straining, scrawny sound that seemed more like a cough. "You are always welcome, Tenet. I again give you leave to call me familiar. It has been too long since my eyes beheld your face and yours, mine. Look at me, Tenet."

I raised my eyes, and only my decades of training allowed me to maintain my composure. Lady Lorelei Kyrrava looked nearly dead. The strange sickness that had befallen her was progressing quicker than I'd imagined it could. Her flowing mane of chestnut hair was thin and matted. Her eyes, which were once like sparkling grey gems, now held only a glimmer. Her once tan skin now looked thin and sallow. Her hands and arms were covered with mummy-like wrappings that restricted their movement. I noticed her fingertips looked black. I dipped my head in respect, "Lorelei, it is good to see you again."

She turned her head towards me weakly, and I saw a flash of the proud, strong woman who had been my master and teacher for the past two years. "I know you cannot lie, etherean! Tell me, how do I look, truly?"

Thunder boomed outside, and rain spattered hard against Lorelei's stained–glass windows as my very nature spoke words of truth to her. A single flash of lightening illuminated her tear-streaked face as my words ended, and silence invaded the space between us. "But, it is good to see you again, Lorelei." My bloodless lips pursed.

She smiled a small smile and did not bother to wipe the tears away, but merely asked, "So what do you have to report, my dear, ever-truthful Tenet?"

As I spoke of all I'd learned, her face grew ever more fearful and concerned. Occasionally, she glanced down to her bandaged hands, but I did not have the heart to pry further. Even before my lengthy absence, it had been determined that no known magic could stave off this vile malady. When at last my tale was told, she sucked in a deep breath and replied, "Tenet, you have all authority that can be given by my name. None save the Queen herself must stand in your way. Discover what is at the root of this foulness. The Queen and Crown must be protected at all costs."

I nodded, and then, exhausted, slipped the Shroud into the Deep.

* * *

Halfday, 2ⁿᵈ of Layfanil, wee hours of the morning
outside Arastin's flat, Deep Harbor District

It was shortly after midnight when I slipped out of the Deep Ethereal and back into the vibrant reality that is Crown. I'd not rested as long as I should, but I'd rested long enough. I was determined to set Arastin off balance and learn as much as I could about his part in this mounting madness. Something in the back of my skull screamed that time was hastening away from me. To make things worse, I knew in my bones that I'd only scratched the surface of whatever foulness was looming.

Nature herself reflected my suspicions; dark clouds that delivered icy rain clotted the sky, dooming the weak morning light to oblivion. I waited outside Arastin's flat and tried to hide my weariness. I could not let the crafty elven assassin sense my fatigue. If there was a hint of blood in the water, this shark would strike. Of that I had little doubt.

If he was surprised by my presence outside his home, the elf did not let it show. A smarmy smirk slowly dawned on his visage as he sauntered up. "Figured you be 'round to see me. What number am I on your list?" he quipped.

I arched a dark brow ever so slightly and replied, nonplussed, "You're expecting me? Up to something, Arastin?"

"You could say that. El'laa had a lot to say last night, or maybe it was this morning." Arastin grinned, obviously enjoying the cut he'd just scored.

I frowned, furrowing my brow, and decided to join him hilt-to-hilt in this game of verbal swordplay. "I understand. She talks a lot when she's unsatisfied."

This time, it was the elf's turn to frown. Despite my vocal victory, Arastin had me over a barrel. He'd not done anything illegal, yet, and he knew that I had nothing on him. He danced all around my questions and savored every ounce of perverse pleasure he could from my pathetic floundering. There was something about this "dance" that was different, however.

In the past, when I'd investigated the elven assassin, he had never displayed the air of righteous indignation that now laced his words. Whoever his mark was this time, Arastin felt that he was justified in taking him – or her – out. Whether or not he'd intended to was immaterial; the assassin had given me a powerful clue despite his veiled words. This job was personal.

Furthermore, Arastin had unknowingly confirmed one of my suspicions. El'laa was indeed involved with his job. It was time to pay yet another visit to the tiefling who had stolen - and broken - my heart.

I left the elf to his dark works and slipped away into the pre-dawn glow. The clouds had added a steady, chilling north wind to their arsenal of now constant mist and bouts of rain. I grimaced at the weather's foulness and made my way to a darkened alley a couple of blocks from Arastin's flat. Once there, I made certain that I'd not been followed, and I called out to Isil. She must have been hovering nearby in the Border Ethereal, for she materialized instantly.

Quietly instructing her in Feridar, I told her to follow and watch Arastin's every step. I would call her soon to see what the elf had been up to. I cautioned her not to be seen, nor to interact with the assassin in any manner. Isil indicated that she understood, and she faded back into etherealness.

* * *

Halfday, 2nd of Layfanil, dusk
The Black Gypsy, Sailor's Ward

It had taken me all day to find out where El'laa was hiding. I'd cashed in more favors than I'd cared to, but I figured it was unavoidable. I had to unearth a solid lead if I was ever going to determine who or what was at the root of this pervading sense of evil that had befallen Crown. The tiefling rogue could not have been holed up in a worse section of the city. Not only was the Sailor's Ward one of Crown's most ramshackle areas, but the tumble-down dive called *The Black Gypsy* was one of its most depraved and immoral.

Located a mere arrow's flight from the massive crater known as the Ditch, *The Black Gypsy* was a miserable little inn that stank of fetid water, bad booze, and rank bodies. In truth, it was more of a community hovel and storehouse than an actual inn. It had no true proprietor or innkeeper, but rather was governed by whichever cult, gang, or bully held sway that day. It was a rough place that had the potential to become lethal in a heartbeat. Needless to say, I was not welcome there. Likely knowing that I would come looking for her, El'laa had picked her hiding place well.

I'd never been much for sneaking around, and disguises don't really work for me. After all, I can't even lie about my name. So, I elected for the direct approach. The shocked looks on the faces of the gathered rogues as I blasted their front door to splinters with a magically enhanced shout of "EL'LAA!" let me know that I'd chosen the right tactic.

Through the haze of frigid mist and rain, I could see about twenty toughs scattered throughout the bottled-strewn drinker's den. Twelve of them screamed and grabbed their blood-spurting ears, while three collapsed in dead faints. The five unharmed roughs glanced to El'laa, who hissed, "Kill him! Bring me the bastard's bald head, and you'll want for nothing!"

I grinned, drew my bonded blade, *Sicol,* and rushed into the room...

* * *

Halfday, 2nd of Layfanil, night
The Ditch, Sailor's Ward

Despite his fervent declaration that we would get nothing from him, El'laa's sole surviving thug could not have been more wrong. I got the tiefling's destination, and Smokey, a celestial bear that I'd summoned, got a snack.

Now in my ethereal form, I slipped through the secret door El'laa had used and floated quickly down the hidden tunnel. Even though I'd already used my *cresentring,* the wound in my lung and most of my burns still remained. The siren's call of the Deep Ethereal was painfully hard to resist. I knew from the thug's words and the twist in the tunnel that my path was taking me ever closer to the Ditch, that massive sinkhole in the northern part of the Sailor's Ward. It was a dangerous area, prone to mudslides, cave-ins, and worse. It was also a well-known entrance to the Sewer City beneath Crown. It was, without doubt, to this dark and shadowy place that my tiefling love now ran. I had to catch her before she slipped through my fingers again.

I rounded yet another bend in the serpentine tunnel and saw her.

She seemed to be desperately trying to open a newly-placed lock that sealed the iron grate over her escape tunnel. Her slender arms had slipped through the grate's gaps, and her long, deft fingers expertly worked the masterwork lock. She was distracted, and now was my chance to act!

I summoned the magic to bolster my wisdom, swallowing an owl's feather as part of the spell, and drew my curved, silver blade. Then, I slipped through the Shroud, entering the Material Plane in such a way that my blade would rest easily, gently upon the tiefling's shoulder. I barked, "I have you El'laa! Do – Not - Move!"

My sudden appearance behind her and the sensation of cold metal upon her neck caused the tiefling to go ramrod straight. That moment of hesitation was all that I needed. I cast my spell, praying that my magically bolstered willpower could overcome hers. A heartbeat flashed between us, and I almost began to cry - the spell had worked! I lowered my blade and spoke softly to the rogue who had stolen my heart.

"El'laa, turn around please." She did as commanded – an effect of the spell – and her lilac perfume almost buckled my knees. She was there before me, but her eyes were vacant and far away. A part of me screamed and said that this was a hollow victory, but I gritted my teeth and steeled myself to do my job. After all, Crown was in danger.

"El'laa, tell me everything you know of Xigx and Arastin and of their plots that might threaten Crown." Again, zombie-like, the tiefling intoned all she knew. She had no choice. The powerful magic had invaded her mind and forced her to tell me things that she would have never said willingly. My soul cried, "Victory," as the horrific facts tumbled to light, but my heart cried, "Rout."

I continued to question her, until I knew that I had learned all that I could, all that I needed to save Crown. Then, just before the spell dissipated, I issued one last demand, one that I needed, not for Crown, but for me.

"El'laa, tell me that you love me..."

* * *

Prayerday, 4th of Layfanil, early morning
The Temple of the Lost, Ethereal Citadel

I was nearly exhausted. I'd spent the last thirty hours expending every single resource I had – physical and otherwise – in an attempt to piece together the fragmented puzzle of what was approaching my beloved city. It was a tangle of half-truths, names, and unknowns - a literal skein of shadows that made my blood run cold with its implications.

A rash of bloody, ritualistic murders had been growing across the city, murders that precisely followed a historical precedent for ushering in the Demon Scourge. The cultist, Xigx, had openly admitted that he was building an army of umbral undead that would be used when the Grey God rose again to power, an event that his words seemed to indicate was near at hand. El'laa had recently been affiliated with Xigx, paying him to craft a spell that would incapacitate me. She'd also been hired by a were-rat, Szeethe, who'd used her as a go-between to contract an assassination. The assassin in question was none other than Arastin, and he and El'laa had been seen together at least once since the deal was made with Szeethe. As such, I tentatively assumed the elf had taken the deal.

Isil had confirmed that Arastin had been spending quite a lot of time lately at an Arm's Cresent tavern known as *The Broken Valor*. That implied *The 'Valor* was a possible location for the intended assassination attempt, which would occur within four days, before Darkday, the Festival of the Long Night. That was the night of the commemoration of the Demon Scourge, the night that just happened to fall under the same astrological conditions of complete and utter darkness as when the Demon Scourge began one hundred and sixty-nine years ago.

So far, all signs pointed towards *The 'Valor*. I'd already completed an initial scout of the exterior of the building, and the only records or legends I could locate about the building indicated that it dated back to the time of the Demon Scourge. A balor had been summoned there, and its magically preserved skeleton still served as a grotesque chandelier. While definitely unusual, that was no cause for concern. Currently, the tavern served simply as a pit-fighting location with an adjoining bar. Still, I'd determined to have a closer look for myself, as well as speak to as many of its regulars as possible.

The three things that did not add up were the reasoning, the target, and the were-rat. While it was true that if the captain were a member of the hated and feared Iceskull League, then that reason alone might be enough to prompt an assassination attempt. However, things did not seem to be that simple. Perhaps it was merely an issue of timing, with the captain coming into Crown, but that theory, as well, had its holes, for a shipment from the north at this time of year was very odd, costly, and dangerous. The captain was not visiting Crown merely on a whim. Regardless, I was either missing some vital pieces of the puzzle, or this was merely some form of old vendetta. Finally, and most vexing, was El'laa's employer, the were-rat called Szeethe. The name had never been heard by any of my contacts, and this struck me as tremendously discordant.

In what I do, the discordant things are usually the ones that will get you killed...

* * *

Prayerday, 4th of Layfanil, morning
The Lord's Court, Arm's Crescent

I'd decided that it was time to begin talking to the 'Valor's natives. The dwarf was the easiest to find; it seemed that his routine never wavered. I slipped the Shroud right outside his tenement building and followed Farulazar through the frigid rain, letting him know I was there, but giving him plenty of lead to do as he wanted.

This dwarf was an unusual sort, even for his dour kin. I was unable to read him, unable to perceive his motivations, his desires, or his fears. Most folk wore these things as brooches upon their cloaks, but not Farulazar. We trudged through the slate gray, cold rain like two forlorn specters. Finally, the dwarf selected an inn, the *Lord's Court,* and vanished inside.

I waited for a score of heartbeats before entering. I had planned on waiting longer, but my toes were nearly frozen as it was, so I crossed the threshold without a further moment. Upon entering, I scanned the room, suddenly realizing that the establishment's name was no doubt some perverse joke – this was not at all what I expected. My icy feet yearned for a large, crackling fire and a warm hearth, but this "Lord's Court" offered no such luxury. I spotted my quarry sitting at a corner table, tankard before him and fingers laced; he did not look surprised to see me.

I made my way to his booth, still dripping from the rain, and pulled back my hood. Normally, etherean appearance unsettles folk. We are odd-looking, after all: pale, almost translucent skin through which dark veins can be seen, what many consider to be a thin, gaunt, or sickly look about us, and often accompanied by dark eyes and hair. I am even stranger looking than most of my kin (or so Fennah has told me, on many occasions) with solid black orbs, a smooth, shaven head, and a goat-like beard of black and white streaks upon my chin. If Farulazar found my appearance unsettling, I could detect no sign.

I bowed to him slightly and spoke, "Queen's care 'pon you, Farulazar Fiend Fighter." The dwarf looked at me as if I was no more than a statue. He did not speak, and he did not act as if he intended to speak. I wondered for a moment if he had even heard me. I cleared my throat politely and decided to forge ahead. I straightened, arched an eyebrow, and continued, "I am called Tenet and am known as the Queen's Intelligencer."

Farulazar did not even blink.

Taken aback, I was struck speechless for a moment and half-stepped to the right. The dwarf's keen eyes tracked my motion precisely. I smiled. So, the dwarf had not been petrified, after all. With that fact in mind, I spent the next quarter hour relaying what I had learned and mentally battling the dwarf for even the slightest fragment of a syllable. I failed utterly. I had never interviewed a witness like this dwarf. Even the most hardened and hateful fiends replied in some manner. Only the slightest arching of a single bushy brow by Farulazar gave me the next clue along this sordid and twisted path of fragmented and scattered truth: the name of "Alfem," the halfling bookie.

* * *

Prayerday, 4th of Layfanil, mid-morning
The Broken Valor, Arm's Crescent

The tavern known as *The Broken Valor* was massive and imposing, but at least it boasted several large and crackling fires. I stood alone, warming my hands and trying to thaw out my frozen feet when a lovely young maid sauntered up to me, grinning.

"Early riser, eh?"

I dipped my head slightly and replied, "Aye, you could say that." I put a finger to my thin, pale lips, trying to recall all of the names and descriptions of the *Valor's* wait-staff that I'd memorized. I arrived at a conclusion quickly and pointed in the maid's direction. "You must be Gwen, yes?"

The maid laughed musically, but she shook her head, "Nay, Gwen's risin' a bit late this morn, you could say. Why, d'ya be one of her old suitors? 'Cause if ya are, I'd tell ya to point yer pinin' elsewhere. Since her dapper elf came about an' swept her off'n her feet, she's had eyes nor lips for none other!"

I shook my head slightly, indicating that I was not one of Gwen's beaus and then inquired, "Her dapper elf?"

The maid, only too happy to avoid her early cleaning duties and to have someone with whom to converse, went on excitedly, "Aye, Arastin! I tell ya, Gwen talks of none other. Ya'd think this elf hung th' moons an' stars!"

The maid, whose name was Eva, went on for some time. Finally she realized that I had not come to gab or to drink and asked me what I needed. She never even asked me my name. I told her I had come to conduct some personal business with the bookie Alfem, and she blanched slightly, her demeanor dampening. She gave me directions to the halfling's office and told me that she would inform Alfem that he had a visitor.

The halfling's office was located below street level, adjacent to the massive basement-turned-fighting pit, and seemed unremarkable. A half-sized writing desk, chair, and two other human-sized chairs dominated the room, which was otherwise filled with two tidy bookshelves jammed full of ledgers and record books. I did not sit right away, but rather took this opportunity to learn as much as I could about the halfling. All the while I kept a keen ear towards the door.

Flipping through some ledgers at random, I found it odd that many of them were not full. Rather, only the first score or so of pages were filled with what I assumed to be Alfem's jagged ink marks. The desk was locked tight with a built-in lock of fine quality, a luxury that one with Alfem's income would be hard-pressed to afford. Near the halfling's chair I spied a long, thin, black whisker. While this was not in and of itself odd, as some halflings are known to have such whiskers, I pocketed it for later examination. For some reason, silent alarms were ringing in the back of my skull. Things seemed to be a little more than they actually were here.

I silently mouthed the words to a spell that would allow me to visually discern magical dweomers, and I was startled as a large, door-shaped section of Alfem's back wall began to seethe with a combination of crimson and ebon. Several spells of protection and evocation, tinged with the dark magic of necromancy, had been woven across these ancient stones! I followed the line of the door to the floor and caught sight of something peculiar. It looked like little more than a decayed fragment of a rat's carcass at first, but I was drawn to it. I reached for it and heard tiny footfalls on the stairs.

* * *

Alfem, who was a rather non-descript looking halfling, seemed taken aback to see me waiting for him in his office, hands clasped behind my back. I bowed slightly at the waist as he entered, "Queen's care 'pon you, Alfem, and fair morn." I tried desperately to keep a straight face, but the hunk of hairy flesh I'd palmed felt like hair-and ice-filled, jellied pudding in my hands.

"And who might you be?" the halfling replied, his voice smooth but slightly tense; he was instantly on the defensive.

I smiled dangerously. "No one of consequence. I am called Tenet and am humbly in the service of her majesty, Queen Alayarra, the Glorious."

Alfem's face flashed through several emotions in quick succession: surprise, fear, and repulsion. His visage finally came to rest on impassivity, and he stuck out his hand, "Queen's Man, eh? Eva should've told me I was entertaining royalty this morn. I would've brought scones."

I quickly flopped the lump of congealed filth into my left hand behind my back, bowed again, wiping my hand on my robe as I did so, and took the halfling's tiny proffered palm in my own. "Never you mind that, my good Alfem. My call is not a social one, but merely routine. In fact, I have only a few moments to spare, if I might impose on you this morning?"

Alfem nodded, motioning towards one of the larger sized chairs while he took his own. "Anything for the Queen. I don't suppose you are here to place a bet for her, eh? If you are interested, my money's on Farulazar, Fiend Fighter, or 'Triple F,' as some call him, for the Long Night Fight!"

* * *

I did not stay long with the halfling. Normally, I might have placed a bet in favor of the dwarven gladiator, but my detection spell was still active, and I greatly desired to see what other secrets *The Broken 'Valor* held. Furthermore, the halfling bookie made my skin crawl. There was no doubt in my mind that Alfem was somehow mixed up in the tangle of foulness that I'd uncovered. The only question was what part he was playing. I was determined to find out. All of the general questions I'd asked him had been deftly deflected or denied; there was no question in my mind that Alfem was hiding something.

I strode through the *'Valor* as quickly as I could without seeming conspicuous, letting my magically-enhanced eyes rove over the building as quickly as possible. The structure's main section was a large stone tower – an ancient defensive structure from Crown's distant past – that, in its morning desertion, seemed dark and cavernous. The tower soared several stories into the air; at its apex hung the massive balor skeleton, which formed the *'Valor's* well-known and grisly chandelier. The chandelier shone with some protective and restorative magics, obviously to keep the horrid thing from falling to dust, but otherwise, it seemed harmless.

Each floor above the basement level was crafted with a central, circular opening, ringed with a waist-high railing, and each floor sat pitched at a downward angle. This unusual tiered construction allowed for the patrons to view the fights in the basement-pit below, much like an amphitheater, but it also caused a terrific sense of vertigo. As I looked over the railing, I nearly fell, but whether it was from the stomach-twisting sensation of the tower's strange construction or the glaring glow of the metal grate that served as the basement floor, I could not tell.

I had never before seen such a complex and intricate collection of magical formulae and runes traced upon a floor. To make matters worse, the whole nest of swirling sigils seethed with foul necromantic and twisted conjuration dweomers like a smudged seal. It could take me weeks to puzzle out the seal's purpose, trigger, or use – a week that I did not have. I tried to commit as much as I could to memory. I had to get to Galsarius as quickly as possible. With this particular problem, I knew I needed all the help to which I could lay hands.

As I exited the tomb-like gloom of *The Broken Valor* and stepped into the icy wind and pelting rain, something like a mental war hammer slammed into the interior of my skull. A vision of my trusted friend, Quellon, flashed behind my eyes. I did not know how I knew, nor did I know why, but the alônn was hurt. I heard the sound of rushing, falling water – the same as from my vision of the grotto - and my eyes swirled among black and white stars. I was forced to lean against the ancient, rugged stone of the 'Valor, so strong was the sense of impending doom and danger. Again, the voice that I'd heard from beyond the waterfall echoed in my head, *"Tenet, a shadow is coming..."*

I teleported to the Sea Shrine without a moment's hesitation. My visit to Galsarius would have to wait...

* * *

Prayerday, 4ᵗʰ of Layfanil, noon
The Sea Shrine, Deep Harbor District

Quellon lay slumped against the wall, eyes closed and breathing shallow. A trail of thin blood oozed from my old friend's nostrils and ears. Otherwise, I saw no signs of bodily harm, so I began to discern what magical threats laid in wait within the domed Sea Shrine. My dweomer did not reveal any immediate threats, but a pall of tainted divination magic hung in the air, eddying slowly about the pool in the Shrine's center.

I knelt beside my friend and drew a healing draught from my *girdle of pockets*, forcing the liquid past his lips. Quellon's eyes fluttered, and his breathing instantly deepened. It took a moment for the alônn to get his bearings.

"Quellon feels like electric eels had a fight in Quellon's head!" He placed a webbed palm to his forehead as he tried to stand; I helped him. "What brings Tenet to Quellon's home, eh?"

I blinked, trying to determine the answer for myself before handing it over. "I am not sure, Quellon. I somehow knew that you were in danger. What happened to you?"

The eccentric alônn, in his surreptitious manner, imparted to me his tale of encountering a white-haired elven captain aboard a boat approaching Crown. The ship exuded an abominable, evil stigma and sailed upon the winds of a colossal, savage tempest. As he told his tale, relaying facts about trouble among the alônn, their council, and his brother, the druid Kal Strongsurge, my mind whirled as I tried to calculate and pinpoint all of the various connections and possibilities.

I now knew that the captain Szeethe wanted dead was an elf, and his pale hair and fair skin likely marked him as one of the betrayer elves who sided with the white dragons against their own kind so long ago. I also knew from his magical attack upon Quellon that he was an able, if not accomplished, wizard. The knowledge of the captain's probable history also nicely filled a gaping whole in Arastin's motivation and involvement. There was no love between the elves who had been forced out of the northlands and their betrayer kin.

As I mused, Quellon continued in his usual rambling, half-sane way of speaking. I listened with one ear until I heard the name "Arastin."

"Arastin!" I interrupted. "The elven assassin from Deep Harbor?"

The aged alônn nodded, stunned into muteness by my verbal intrusion.

"You say he asked you to search for the ship, as well as Kal?"

"Quellon, did Quellon say that?" The alônn mulled over the self-imposed question for a moment, scratching his smooth chin. Finally he nodded. "Yes, Quellon! Quellon did just say that. Quellon should drain the water from Quellon's ears and listen more closely!"

I nodded and chuckled at the alônn mystic's words. Then, I told him of all that I knew, of the shadowy entanglements into which Kal and the other alônn were likely being drawn. Quellon's eyes grew so large that I thought they would fall from his skull. Once I had finished, he requested that I to go and tell the same tale to the Alônn Council on the morrow. I agreed and warned my old friend to remain hidden until then and to speak to no one of what I'd told him.

Then I departed the Sea Shrine, calling Isil to my side. There was much to do...

* * *

Lastday, 5th of Layfanil, pre-dawn
The Blue Crystal, The Street of Hands, Twospire

"There is still so much to do and so little time!" I was nearly at my wit's end, and Galsarlus could tell, he likely knew me better than any man alive. The wizard who was so well known in Crown for his ioun stones laughed, his cerulean eyes sparkling like one of his magic-granting gems.

"You never did cope well with deadlines..." Referring to our time together as apprentices, Galsarius, who was far older than his appearance led most to believe, shook his wooly head as a smile split his bearded lips.

I almost threw something at him, but I knew that I'd likely shatter some of the priceless magical items that his shop, *The Blue Crystal,* held. On second thought, that might not have been that bad of an idea, after all.

"Speaking of deadlines, have you unraveled the mystery of *The 'Valor's* floor, yet, genius?" Galsarius and I were like brothers, and it was often said by those who knew us that we acted as such.

"Nay, but I cannot claim fault for it, seeing as how poor my initial intelligence was..." Galsarius shot me a look of mock disdain, and we both collapsed into a bought of fatigue-born laughter.

We had been working steadily, side by side, since my meeting with Quellon. Methodically, we approached the clues from every conceivable angle, but we still did not seem to have all of the pieces. We had sent and received countless messages via Fennah's contacts and Alynna's living messenger service, and Isil had likely flown the length and breadth of Crown countless times throughout the night. We had initially examined the whisker and gobbet of hairy flesh that I'd discovered in Alfem's office, and we had consumed untold hours trying to decipher the complex layers of theurgy that covered the floor of *The 'Valor's* fighting pit.

While the whisker was quickly identified as a wererat's, the gob of skin and hair was beyond the spheres of our specialties. We utilized a few of Galsarius's connections to the Arcane Tower to have it quickly identified. Galsarius tackled the magical floor puzzle, which was his forte, while I continually polled my network of contacts and informants for more fragmented pieces of the ever-widening puzzle.

Despite Galsarius's continual urges, I flatly refused to rest in any form, physical or ethereal. I pushed through the fatigue and struggled to focus. Before I knew what had happened, I had received a mental summons from the Alônn Council. Galsarius produced a slender reed wand and a cobalt stone from one of his dark brown robe's hidden pockets. He waved the wand over me, and I instantly felt physically refreshed, as if I'd rested on the Material Plane. Deep down I was still weary, but it was as if a splash of cold water had been dashed in my face. Then, my friend handed me the gemstone.

"Here, Tenet. Release this, and it will circle your body at all times. Its power will allow you to breathe, speak, and move underwater just as if you were on land."

I smiled, knowing that this was truly a treasure, and clasped the hand of my friend and "brother."

"Thank you, Galsarius. Thank you!"

"Queen's care, Tenet."

"Queen's care 'pon you, my friend."

* * *

Lastday, 5th of Layfanil, late afternoon
Deep Harbor District

It had taken nearly all day to finally convince the Alônn Council to simply make the decision to act, but at last, they had done so. They would aid Kal Strongsurge in his attempt to slow or halt the *Frozen Idol*. I exited the portal that led from the hidden location of the chamber and stepped onto the afternoon streets of Deep Harbor. The icy rain and blustery wind stung my eyes and drew tears from the corners of my dark orbs. At least the water in the Alônn Council's extra-planar meeting chamber had been warm...

As I passed the Silver Lyre College, an unhappy-looking, sodden thrush, one of Alynna's, lit upon my soaking-wet shoulder. The bird bore a wax-coated and sealed note upon its leg, tied with a soggy blue string. The note read:

Brother,

We finally received word from the Tower about the gobbet of skin. As we suspected, it is extra-planar, but there is more. The creature that shed this skin is steeped in ancient, fiendish evil, and the flesh also bears properties attributed to natural shapeshifters! Beware, Brother; I fear Alfem is far worse than what he seems!

Also, I think I've unlocked the secret of the Valor's enchanted floor! We were looking at it incorrectly. We assumed the dweomered layers were there to keep something out, but that could not be more wrong! This magical seal was crafted to keep something in. Disable it from the outside moving inward, and it should work. Furthermore, the magic that allows

*passage through the barriers is triggered by a single keyword, "plague."
Given your suspected involvement of the Grey God, Tenet, I fear what
might lie within. Be wary.*

*Lastly, Isil was so weary she could barely hold herself up. I
dismissed her back to the Ethereal. I hope you don't mind... She would
not go when asked, so I forced her for her own good. She's nearly as
hard-headed as her master!*

*Take care of yourself, and may Truth guide you and Goodness
watch over you...*

Your smarter, stronger, and more handsome brother,
Galsarius

I folded the note and slipped it into my magical *girdle*, nodding
grimly to myself. Now I was getting somewhere. It was time to pay yet
another visit to my "friend," Alfem, the halfling at *The Broken Valor*. I
sundered time and space with a thought and stepped through the rent
into the Arms Crescent.

* * *

Lastday, 5th of Layfanil, late afternoon
The Broken Valor, Arm's Crescent

I waltzed into the fighting pit of *The 'Valor* with no resistance
whatsoever; the whole of the tavern above and the arena below seemed
eerily deserted. Quickly casting every spell at my disposal to aid me in
unraveling the magical mystery that covered the arena's floor, I began
carefully picking apart the complex, interwoven sigils.

I would be the first to admit that this sort of thing is far from my
forte. In fact, this meticulously precise form of dispersing and dispelling
magical wards and bindings is more along Galsarius's specialty.
Personally, I've always loathed this type of magic.

Which is why, after nearly two hours of attempting to unravel the
knot, I threw up my hands in surrender. I was glad Isil was not here to
see me, but I figured that her eyes, like thousands of faceted
moonstones, were likely watching me from somewhere along the Border
Ethereal. I had only dispelled one major ward and a handful of minor
enchantments - pitiful. I was not sure if I had cracked open the door to

let something in or out, but nevertheless, the door was now ajar.

The door...

Realization dawned over me like the rising sun over Crown: the door! The magical, hidden door in Alfem's office! I sprinted across the arena floor, and in moments, I had wound my way down to the halfling's office I had inspected a little more than a day ago. I listened at the oaken door, and hearing nothing, I slipped the Shroud and passed through as easily as would a specter. Moments later, I was again in the physical realm and had unhinged and unlocked all of the magical wards surrounding the magical door, which seemed like child's play compared to the wards on the pit's floor. Then, the craftily hidden stone portal slid quietly open.

A ruddy light flickered from somewhere far below, and I heard rustles of casual movement. The passageway angled down, gradually, and it eventually gave way to an ancient stone stair. I padded down the steps, flitting from one shadow to the next as best I could, and I was contemplating slipping the Shroud when I heard a perverted giggle that made my blood run cold.

"W...w...welcome, Spymaster..."

I looked up, seeing Xigx floating above me. He leered at me like I was a beetle about to be squashed.

I raised my hand to launch a volley of *magic missiles,* when the ceiling seemed to crash down upon the back of my head. I saw only a flash of ruby-tinted light that was quickly swallowed by utter blackness...

* * *

Darkday, 8th of Layfanil, dusk
Xigx's Torture Chamber, Sewer City

Instantly, I knew that it had been several days since I'd last felt the embrace of the Ethereal. I felt like I was floating, disembodied, through a hazy fog. I heard voices. Briefly, I wondered if I were again experiencing the *aer'vachti,* or re-birth, that all ethereans, upon death, go through.

"Is everything in place and ready?" A woman's voice, vaguely familiar, echoed in a vast space. I heard and smelt dank, dripping water.

Snickering, quiet laughter, and shuffling, followed by a reply, "Oh yes...all is nearing completion – my master, Szeethe, w...w...will be most pleased w...w...with w...w...what w...w...we have w...w...wrought."

The familiar stuttering of Xigx forced clarity into my thoughts. Unfortunately, this lucidity also accentuated the extreme pain wracking my body. The pain was unlike any that I'd ever known before; it had driven my mind totally numb. Now, however, my every sense was alive and completely awash with blazing, fiery agony. I could not stifle the teeth-clenched moan that escaped my lips.

"Leave us! He is awakening!" the woman's voice snapped.

"W...w...watch to w...w...who you speak, w...w...woman! You hold no power over me!" Xigx barked in reply. I could hear the mad hiss underlying his voice.

Instantly, the woman's voice changed, taking on a smooth, sultry, and yet apologetic tone. The moment I heard it, I groaned again – this time, from inward pain. It was El'laa.

"You're right, my love. I am sorry, but this dreary work vexes me so...can you forgive me?" What could only be the sounds of kissing followed.

I thought I was going to retch.

Xigx must have left, because the next thing I knew, El'laa was standing over me. Cool liquid dribbled over my hairless head and down into my swollen eyes. I felt the healing energies ripple into my skull and shoulders. My lids fluttered open.

El'laa looked like a fiery angel: scowling and beautiful at the same time. A plain, worked-stone room wrapped around us. I was chained, arms spread wide to one wall. Bloody torture implements of every sort stood in a haphazard pile on the wall opposite. A nearby table was filled with bloody bandages and what looked like healer's tools. My entire body ached and simmered with pain.

I tried to speak, but only a weak croak came out. El'laa gave me a quick swig of the cool fluid, and it felt like quicksilver running down my throat. Again, the healing energies coursed through my innards, giving me strength enough to draw breath and speak, "What happened here?"

Her sea-green eyes looked towards the floor – a sign that she was lying – and then locked with mine. "Xigx had his fun with you and has left you to my tender mercies." Her lips tightened, "But I intend to free you, Tenet."

Hearing her speak my name sent arcs of lightening up my spine, but I had to focus. "And to what do I owe this honor?" I managed a smirk and a cocked eyebrow, but that was the best that I could do.

Her eyes narrowed dangerously, "Do not think that I do this out of care for you, Queen's Man!" she hissed. Glancing towards the room's single exit, she paused before continuing, her voice lowered even more. "I do this for my sake only. A rat within a snake's den does not question an exit when she sees it. I will get you out of here, but you must do me something in return, Tenet."

Outwardly, I regarded her coolly. Inside, I wanted nothing more than to embrace her, to save her.

"I need your help, Tenet. Please help me." She was pleading now, her fingertips touching my cheek, and her forehead was upon my bloodied shoulder.

Like a giant-breached wall, my resolve crumbled. "I will, my love. Anything for you."

El'laa smiled...

* * *

Darkday, 8th of Layfanil, early evening
Warehouse Row, Deep Harbor District

I sighed quietly. At least El'laa had been telling the truth about Xigx's location. She'd asked me to kill him. I would have done it anyway, but after she told me about what he'd done to her – and forced her to do – there was no question in my mind that this would be Xigx's last night to draw breath. The auburn-haired tiefling had even inadvertently given me a vital piece of my puzzle: Szeethe was *the* high priest of the Grey God – a half-demon who had been groomed for his position for years. He was a shapeshifter as well and often posed as a wererat to conduct his "above ground" dealings in Crown. Xigx was his lackey – a chaotic magical force that Szeethe wielded like the blunt instrument the insane elf truly was. Twisted, evil, and unpredictable, Xigx was a necessary asset to the hierarchy of the cult.

El'laa had further shown her loyalty by managing to hide my robes and *cresentring* during my torture, both of which I now wore again. My love even managed to provide some additional healing draughts. While I was not totally without injury or wound, I was certainly well enough to slay the mongrel that cowered in the shadows a half-block away.

A part of me wanted to slip the Shroud and simply appear behind him, *Sicol* already buried in his back, but I did not dare. I was so weary, so close to the *yil'ya a'feth,* that I knew the moment I slipped the Shroud, I could not return for many hours.

This needed doing now.

The storm was fully upon Crown now. The rain, which was more ice than wet, was driving mostly sideways. I could hear the waves pounding the docks from two blocks away, and lightening constantly danced from one boiling black cloud to another. I stood in the freezing, slamming rain for a few heartbeats more, watching Xigx. He was leading a large number of Grey God cultists – mostly wererats, but also a few humans – and they all seemed to be waiting for something. I had no idea for what, and I did not really care; the justified cries for revenge sang in my ears. Killing Xigx would aid many and likely cripple one of the most heinous cults in my beloved city.

This time, I could save El'laa and Crown at the same time. I would not have to choose again.

In response to some unseen or unheard signal, Xigx and his toadies began slipping from shadow to shadow, working their way ever-closer to the harbor. I noted their general direction and smiled, the plan forming itself in my mind. Slipping into the shadows, I worked my way behind and around them. They were so intent on the harbor that they never even looked back my way - perfect.

* * *

"Do you understand, Jalkesh?" I asked fervently.

Jalkesh bobbed his head and let his actions speak for his compliance, as he wheeled his ramshackle fruit cart out into one of the most vicious storms to hit Crown in the last century.

* * *

"W...w...we don't w...w...want any of your fruit, old man!" Xigx yelled, trying to overpower the whipping wind, the crackling thunder, and the thick skull of the fruit vendor who'd parked his shoddy cart in the worst possible location.

It was hard to stifle my laugh. Jalkesh had performed perfectly, and he had bottled the cultists up in a makeshift alleyway of wooden shipping crates. I could see from my vantage point that the number of cultists was far greater than I'd originally seen – and most of them were standing in water up to their ankles. Perfect.

"But fruit is good for you!" Jalkesh screamed back to the crazed cultist, who was near boiling with rage. At that moment, an apple joined the falling, icy rain and plopped to the sodden ground at Xigx's feet. "See!" Jalkesh continued, "It even falls from the heavens!" As he spoke, the thin peddler quickly clambered upon his cart and lay down flat upon his precious fruit. Xigx stopped in mid-motion from glancing upwards and stared incredulously at the obviously insane man.

At that moment, my lightening bolt, which was easily the size of a wine cask, slammed into the ground beside him. Xigx screamed and danced an electrically quickened, jerky jig and then was instantly incinerated, quickly followed by a third of the cultists in the flooded alleyway. Dark robed forms burst into smoldering flame, and the alleyway filled with the stench of burning flesh and cooking rat.

Jalkesh's broken-down cart exploded, throwing the shattered cart fully across the street. Slivers of smoking wood shot into the air like arrows, and fragments of pulpy fruit and juice fell like tangy rain and sleet. Jalkesh himself was flung high up into the air. Flying, I was prepared for this and caught him mid-plummet. As I deposited him near the wreckage of his cart, I could not tell if he was laughing or crying; he kept keening about his last bit of fruit.

I had no time to help him, however, as I had to get to Farulazar and warn him about his partner, who was far more than a mere halfling bookie. If I could get there in time, I knew that I might be able to catch Szeethe and end this madness.

* * *

Darkday, 8th of Layfanil, evening
The Broken Valor, Arms Cresent

Slipping into *The 'Valor* was easy; the Long Night Fight was usually one of the largest draws across Crown on this holiday, and the raging storm outside had driven even more folk than usual northward to the Arm's Crescent tavern. I kept my hood drawn and quietly slipped down the stairs leading below street level, to the fighting pit. I did not have to wait long for the dwarf to appear; the time for his fight was nigh. Somehow, he sensed me hiding in the shadows and spoke.

"Come out of the shadow," he grumbled. "It does not seem to be your way."

"It is not," I agreed. "But my words are for your ears alone." I quickly informed Farulazar of all that I'd discovered and saw his face shift slightly. Even knowing the little I did of this stoic, dour dwarf, I knew that something fundamental had just changed within him. I quickly conjured another inky dimensional doorway within the shadows and stepped through, arriving one floor up and several yards away, at the fireplace where I'd met Eva.

* * *

The first thing I noticed was that I smelt lilacs. The second thing I noticed was a knife point in my ribs. "Do not move, Tenet," El'laa hissed. "Do not shift the Shroud, or whatever it is that you call it. My blade is coated with *kyn'taas*, and I will cut you with it before you can breathe, if you do not do exactly as I tell you. Do you understand me, Stiffshanks?!?"

Indeed I did. I understood all too well. In fact, I had been the one to introduce El'laa to this substance. *Kyn'taas* was a rare and exceedingly lethal poison, and few were those who survived its touch. It was also one of the few known natural substances that could prevent an ethereal from experiencing their re-birth, or *aer'vachti*, after dying on the Material Plane. My mind whirled, for obvious reasons. The substance was lethal to me, not to mention tightly controlled and highly illegal in Crown. El'laa only knew of it because I had used it against Vaxx, an etherean serial killer who'd been after El'laa when I'd first met her.

I had little choice, so I nodded my head once and asked, "So what is it you want, m'love?"

She leaned in close to me. She wanted the other patrons in the packed tavern to think we were lovers. I would have liked that as well, but the blade between us bespoke other intentions. "Your bald head on a platter might be nice, to start with." Before I could reply in confusion, a large commotion, followed by several screams, drew our attention aside.

From across the room, a dwarf was blasted, bellowing, into the air. He flew straight towards El'laa and I, and the swift tiefling rolled out and away from me. I caught the brunt of the dwarf's considerable bulk full in my chest. We slammed into the stone fireplace and toppled to the floor in a heap. All around me, the room was erupting into chaos. Chairs were flying, patrons screaming and flying, glass breaking, and wood splintering. I quickly scanned the room and saw an enormous oltreggan wielding, of all things, an anchor. His ire seemed focused one moment and then scattered the next - the burly brute seemed to be searching for something. For a moment, I thought I recognized the mammoth creature, but then, a twang of pain deep in my shoulder drew my thoughts inward.

Before I could assess my wound, El'laa dove at me from out of the throng, screaming a curse and with her sea-green eyes blazing. Her *kyn'taas*-stained blade jabbed down once, but I rolled quickly to my left. A small, blurred form zipped past the attacking tiefling at that moment, clipping her right side and spinning her around. I seized that fortunate moment and blasted her across the room with a bone-rattling cone of *telekinesis*. I watched as my love soared through the air, wincing as she happened to connect with the swatting anchor of the oltreggan. A sickening crunch, followed by her cry of pain told me that, at least, El'laa was still alive.

I waded through the mounting chaos in the room, ducking swings from swords, fists, and flung crockery. So great was the chaos and my focus upon El'laa that the thought to slip the Shroud never even entered my mind. I found her beneath the broken remains of an oaken table, broken, torn, and bleeding. Thankfully, she was still breathing.

The moment she saw me, she screamed and slashed at me with the dagger she still clenched with bloodied fingers. The strike was desperate, clumsy, and born of quickly failing strength. I stomped the dagger from her hand and flung it across the room into the fireplace's cracking fire. El'laa cried out in frustration and pain.

As I turned my head from the fireplace towards El'laa, my sight exploded into a world of complete, flat, whiteness. As I reeled from the punch to the face, I heard a rough, gravelly voice shout, "Hey, don't 'cha be treatin' ladies like 'at!"

* * *

Some moments later, my vision cleared, and I rose painfully to my feet. The right side of my face throbbed painfully with each heartbeat, and I wondered if my nose might be broken. I glanced around and grimaced. El'laa was gone, and the tavern around me was a complete loss. Dead bodies, shattered crockery and furniture, smoke from sundered lanterns, and people running hither and yon like mindless sheep filled the tavern.

Thundering footsteps on the stairs alerted me, and my gaze fell to the top of the flight of stairs. Farulazar, "the Fiend Fighter," appeared from the darkness, looking a little worse for wear from his fight with the demon in the pit. Regardless, the look on his face told me that he was more than able to put an end to this madness. Somehow, I knew that he was looking for Szeethe, and if the dwarf had not found him below, then I knew one of the few places that he would be: with the cultists at the docks.

I locked eyes with the dwarf and pointed towards *the 'Valor's* main door, which led out into the howling storm.

"To the wharves," I said.

Farulazar nodded and rushed from the tavern, barreling past patrons as if they were nothing more than shadows.

I heard the alarm bells of the Watch toll and instantly slipped the Shroud; I could not waste time explaining this chaos to Crown's finest now. I had to get to the docks.

The moment I was fully in the Ethereal, my soul exploded into white-hot agony...

* * *

Darkday, 8th of Layfanil, nearing midnight
The Dying Lands, Ethereal Plane

There is a reason why the *aer'vachti* works on only ethereans. At our cores, we are made up of proto-matter, the stuff that constitutes the entirety of the Ethereal Plane. So, regardless of how many times our physical forms might be slain, the souls of we ethereans will survive so long as does the plane that sired us. Simply put, deep down, we are the Ethereal Plane; our souls are the very stuff of ultimate potential.

Apparently, it was that same reason that was about to utterly destroy me...

The moment I coalesced into the ethereal borderlands, I felt a horrific explosion in the core of my being. Instantly, gaping holes appeared in my ghostly flesh and out ripped long, lashing tendrils of inky darkness. The dark tentacles spider-webbed their way out of my writhing, screaming body and instantly dove into the globs of floating proto-matter around me. The once-perfectly white bits of pure potential began warping and twisting into slithering dollops of stinking black pus.

Through my miasma of choking, gut-wrenching pain, I realized the true horror of this event. Whatever was inside of me was physical – real – and it was infecting, altering, and effectively destroying every mote of ethereal-ness that it touched. Somehow, I had become the carrier of the sole disease that could kill not only me, but my entire plane.

And my entire race...

The Ethereal space around me literally growled and darkened like an angry storm cloud. Like a massive whirlpool, the plane began to fold inwards upon itself, drawing as much of its essence as it could away from me and the horrible plague that I'd foolishly brought. Arcs of silver, ethereal lightening began vibrating and arching from one congealed mass of proto-matter to another, and I began to feel twin, inexorable tugs. The part of my form that was ethereal was quickly slipping away from me, spiraling out into tiny, mercury rivulets, while those bits of my body that had already been altered to the physical were twisting, warping, and corrupting everything around them.

I hung in the fractured balance and could do nothing but scream...

* * *

Black and silver lightening shot through my agonized form, and the ethereal whirlpool to my right began to roar like a thousand dragons. If I'd had any ears left, they would have exploded from the sheer sound long ago. In my splintering mind, I heard voices as they tossed about in what was left of my consciousness like so much flotsam. Whispered words that held only fragments of meaning floated through my being. I wondered if this was what oblivion was like.

Then, the words rang like behemoth brass bells around me! Words that resounded with such ancient power that I knew, without thinking, that their roots sank deep into the foundations of the Bound Gods' powers. Dark phrases, filled with venom and bound up with unspeakable chaos and might! The words drew me like a lodestone, and before me a horrific scene unfolded.

Blinking through ash, the dwarf, Farulazar, stood as what could only be the creature Szeethe approached him. The horrific thing was nearly double the Fiend Fighter's height, and it commanded a pulsing sphere that hovered over the dwarf, beating like a malevolent heart. Szeethe's chanted words were growing in power and cadence with each echoing thump.

I saw doom fall upon Farulazar as the strength drained away from his body. To my own cries of agony, I added a scream of denial. The dwarf could not fail! He must not fail! I summoned all of my remaining willpower and flung it across the ruined void between us. If my death was to be final, at least it would be worth something. I gave him my all.

* * *

Darkday, 8th of Layfanil, midnight
somewhere In-Between

A cosmic cord snapped, and I found myself in a strange place where I had never before been. It was as if I existed in a narrow gap between two worlds: the world of the physical and the world of the ethereal. I could perceive both worlds with equal clarity.

In the ethereal, a dark stain was spreading outwards from where I could only assume that I had just been, a stain that was slowly, relentlessly trying to devour the very fabric of my home plane. The ethereal maelstrom grew ever larger as it raced away from the encroaching stain, drawing every mote of etherealness into itself as it went.

On the material, I was witness to a climatic, dramatic battle. A ship rocked and rode upon the storm-driven waves in Crown's Deep Harbor. Scores of combatants swarmed across its decks and riggings: cultists, human, and were-rat alike clashed with alônn - led by Kal Strongsurge - who in turn battled fierce pirates, who also stained their blades with alônn and cultists' blood. Fires raged all across the ship, and smoke billowed out of the hold and the portholes. I saw Arastin fighting a white-haired elf - the captain, I presumed - while Farulazar finished the fiendish Szeethe with a single stroke.

Finally, a seething, dark presence drew me down and into the hold. It was there that I witnessed...horror. A massive, bloody, heart-shaped thing brooded in the hold. A blood-coated oltreggan and sarulaan were locked in mortal combat nearby. This thing, though...it *called* to me. With a sibilant voice, I heard its whispering laughter, taunting me, mocking me. It was then that I noticed the trail. A dark line, like clotted, dried blood, ran from the heart, through me, to the stain in the ethereal beyond.

And then I knew.

And then the world exploded.

EPILOGUE

EPILOGUE

On board the doomed *Winter's Claw,* Na'akiros stomped to a burning glob of oil and stuck his mutilated arm into the flame. Pain streaked through his body anew as the whale oil bubbled on the jagged wound. He roared into the night; the sound rivaled the rolling thunder.

'That accursed elf!' he seethed. The half-dragon took stock of the situation. His missing hand, his battered and slowly sinking ship, the vermin and fish-men swarming the decks, and the loss of his cargo and the deal made him seethe.

He bellowed aloud, "Bastard elf!"

Na'akiros did not even know the name of the assassin he had just blasted into the sea to rot amongst the crabs. He did not know the other's motivations other than the obvious hatred between elves and the League. But he knew the quick death was too good for him, and he wished he had more time to properly repay the elf.

A blue-skinned slit-neck charged, and he ran the fool through with his cutlass. He spat as he kicked the alônn from his blade, disgusted by their persistence. The captain spun about, looking for another of the fish-men to disembowel and so continue what small retribution he could, but none were close at hand. He clenched his remaining hand into a clawed fist, almost consumed by the fierce rage that burned inside him. There was no hope of salvaging anything from this catastrophe. Na'akiros leapt into the air. He circled once and exhaled a wave of frozen death, not caring who suffered the brunt of the deadly attack.

His wings struggled, but the storm's rage was spent, and the winds were quickly dying. The half-dragon considered his route and knew he only had one choice: north. The League had a few outposts hidden in seldom used coves along the cost. One of those would welcome him and allow him to rest and recover. Na'akiros took a last look at Crown as he passed over, and he vowed the city had not seen the last of him or the Iceskull League...

*   *   *

She had bravely come to the battle with no intention of joining the fray. Many of her fellow alônn were fighting valiantly against the foul minions of the dragons. Some would die and would find peace in the long halls, where the toils of this world could be shed and all care would be gone. Many more would be wounded, both grievously and mildly. They were the ones Asliana came to serve. In all battles, there were the warriors and those who dealt with the damages. She and her sisters were the latter, and they would comfort and revive the valiant wounded in what ways they could. They were trained in the old arts of their people, and many a soul thought doomed to death had found life at their hands.

Many already had fallen beneath the waves and were being tended by her sisters. Those who were not alônn, who could not breathe the life water, were taken to the dry over-world where their kindred might tend to them. Almost all were cared for, even the wicked seamen who manned the vile ship above. Only the strange were-rats were allowed to sink to the bottom, and only then because they were followers of the accursed one who had the vile relic brought into these peaceable waters.

Hers was a life of sadness, as it was her lot to deal with so many who suffered so profoundly. There were those who could not find salvation in her touch, no matter what she or her sisters could do. This night, with the terrible storm above, had already brought much sadness, and more would come in the following days as those who were not slain would die of their terrible wounds. Yet without her efforts, many more would die. And so, she would continue to serve.

When the headless body of the accursed one dipped beneath the waves, she did not mourn, but nor did she rejoice. It would have been better had he never come to the harbor or brought the wicked relic to disturb the waves. She watched the body settle to the murky bottom, knowing that the crabs would feast in the coming days. It pleased her that even that horrible creature would bring life and sustenance to others.

She worked for some time, giving aid mainly to her own kind, as most of those others who entered their realm from above were already beyond the living world's grasp. As she swam about, she caught a glimpse of something crashing into the water. Unlike many of the victims of this battle who either sank or floated with an odd grace, their limbs in a poetic rhythm with the ocean, this thing was rigid and descended the depths in a definite curving path. At first she mistook it for a piece of debris, something cast from the wicked ship above. Yet when it made an arc in her direction, she recognized the form of a person.

Surprised, the alônn made her way over to the body. The further down it spiraled, the less rigid it became, until when she reached it, it was in that slow dance that all which became one with the waters performed. It was an elf, someone she had not expected in this battle, for elves did not seem involved with all that had happened. She knew little of the hatred these beings had for the Ice Skull and nothing of the profession this one had chosen.

She reached for him and caressed his face, thinking he had joined the others in the long hall. The skin was cold, oddly cold. Some enchantment had taken this one, a cold spell that robbed him of life and sent him to this watery grave. Cruel perhaps, but a kinder act than the barbaric hacking blows so many others received, coloring the waters with their spirit's blood.

But wait; did she notice the spark of life? She took his hand and felt the cold flesh warm, felt the elvish blood flowing. Joy filled her, her eyes opening wide. Wordlessly, she took this fair elf under her arms, and with all haste, she made her way to the surface. This one could not survive in her realm, and what care he needed had to come from the healers of the over-world.

There, at one of the lower piers, were several healers of the Benevolent Moon, who tended the infirm and wounded in the storm-battered world above. Already, many were lying about, some dead, some dying, and some being tended by the healers. One of the acolytes saw her approach, saw the one she brought, and quickly motioned to her. She neared, and he stretched his arms out to take her charge.

Harruk was the man who pulled the seemingly lifeless elf from the water. Though the battle still raged on the sinking and burning remnant of the cursed Ice Skull ship, with much of it taking place on the wharf, he and his fellow healers had rushed to the scene where they knew their services would be needed. They had hurriedly set up an area where they could treat the wounded, could serve the last moments of the dying, and set aside the dead for those who might wish to claim them.

When the blessed ladies of the deep brought this one, Harrok thought the last area would be his place. As he lifted the body from the water, the elf coughed up sickly brine and struggled for breath. Surprised, he motioned to another of his order, Holl, who came over and quickly began his work. The healer nodded in satisfaction, for if the blessed spirit in the Moontower approves, this one would be stolen from death's wicked grip.

As the healers worked above, fighting the driving rain in their own fight with death, the alônn returned to her own world where she could continue her work. Below the waves, she saw the sinking bow of that cursed ship above. It had separated from the rest of the vessel and was plunging to the bottom, dragging various kinds of debris with it. As it passed before her, she gazed into its depths, and to her surprise, saw the body of a dwarf lying within. He looked asleep, his eyes closed, his expression so peaceful. For a moment, she dared not disturb his serenity.

Then, she suddenly recognized the spark of life that yet remained within him. And like the elf before, this was one who could not survive among her kindred. He needed the dry above for life. She called out, and two of her sisters, Jarridoon and Nûwn, came swimming up. Wordlessly, the three passed into the wreck and quickly removed the tangled debris from about him. It took both Jarridoon and Nûwn to lift the unconscious dwarf away, while Asliana retrieved his sword. Normally, she would not have bothered with an implement of butchery, yet she perceived the good this dwarf had done and knew that he had ended the terror of the cursed one. This was his blade, and she knew he might need it.

At the surface, Harrok and Holl rushed over to pull the dwarf from water. With him on the deck, Holl turned and bowed to Asliana and touched the silver moon broach on his cloak in salute. The rustic alônn smiled and disappeared beneath the waves to continue her work.

The two men turned their attention to this newest ward. Though neither knew the dwarf's identity, they rejoiced that he would not be joining the silent rows. Theirs was an order of healers and diviners who served all groups in Crown, from the wicked to the saintly, turning none away. Even now, many of his companions were treating the scoundrel sailors and bizarre were-rat cultists who had survived the battle and were now grievously wounded. Harrok motioned to the devoted litter-bearers to quickly take the dwarf to the Moontower, where healing would be found. Though he had not witnessed the deeds on the ship, he, too, perceived this person's worth.

He watched as the dwarf and elf were carried through the driving rain up the streets that led to the tower. There, those of greater power could guard them from death's assault. However, his job was not in the blessed spire, but here, in the terrible storm, dealing with the results of the violence that was now waning. And though he did not know it, in his own very important way, he was now involved in the events that repulsed the wicked schemes of the Grey God.

Had he known, he would have been even more satisfied. The Benevolent Moon strove secretly to prevent another Demon Scourge, something not well known in Crown, and they would also be pleased to thwart the evil designs of that chaotic deity. The evil postponed on this day was as much a threat to the city as the cruel demons. He did not consider the importance of the day, which commemorated that terrible scourge. All the same, it was fitting that the Grey God was denied his own evil rampage on the day remembering the demonic rampage generations before.

But Harrok and Holl did not have time to consider the worth of this terrible fight. The storm-lashed dock was already filled with the grievously wounded. Men, were-rats, cultists, and sailors lay moaning, crying, and screaming. Though he knew these were wicked creatures, he did not care. He would strive even for them. And so, fighting back the driving rain, he returned to the duties at hand, knowing a long night lay before him.

*   *   *

Flames and smoke swirled through the empty atmosphere. To a being who had only felt soothing waves and dampness his entire life, this was hell. Worst of all, this sensation of cinders and soot seared and stung Alastar's mind, as well as his body. Scales molted into charred flesh as his iridescent hide blackened from the heat. His nerves cried out for healing, for an end to this torment. He did not deserve this inferno that wrecked his domain, splintering his chess board and melting his pieces! He had only tried to save his rook, his friend!

A soft splash sang melodically against his seared flesh. With his mind in shambles, Alastar held on to the only anchor of his existence: the hand-carved pebble within his palm. He cradled it tightly against his chest. This stone represented the culmination of his life's work and a victory that he valued more than life. As his favored chess piece, he could not relinquish the carved stone to the flames or to the deep. And so, chess master and chess piece slowly descended into the recesses of the pool.

A soft glow suffused the waters around the unconscious oracle. Little remained of his mental prowess, that which he had pitted against time and the darkness for a people he had never truly met. The once-searing flames ebbed into warmth, at once soothing and peaceful. Swirls of blue and white drifted around the murky vision of Alastar's mind. Then, the world shifted, and he found himself standing opposite a tavern. Fragmented images of the past, the myriad pieces of Crown's history, as well as glimpses into a strange and indescribable future flowed through his consciousness. These passed quickly, and he found himself once more looking upon the tavern's marker: a radiant woman, her eyes flooding the ground below her with tears. To his surprise, the sign smiled joyfully and spoke, "I'm so proud of you, my son, so very proud. Do not think you failed."

The half-lumilon stared blankly at the woman and said without any emotion, "But the Grey God walks the earth, and I couldn't save the warrior to stop him,"

Chuckling with foreknowledge, the woman's piercing eyes squinted more as she smiled, "Oh, my son, don't you see? The Grey God remains imprisoned. What's more, your friend lives! And so shall you."

"But the Veil!" Sorrow punctured his apathy and flooded his soul with despair. "The Veil is torn! I destroyed the Veil." Tears slid down his cheeks.

The woman reached out and pressed a smooth object against his chest: a brooch. It was a Healer's Stone, the birthright of the lumilon. It glowed softly and fused through Alastar's scaled breast. "No, my son. The veil lives...in you."

Her figure dissipated into the gloaming of the world around him. Before the subtle light fully possessed him, her voice caressed his heart with love as she whispered, "You are the veil, beloved…"

*   *   *

Captain Tardel Minruvak arrived at the scene of battle not long after the devotees of the Benevolent Moon, leading a squad of men from the Crown Watch. At their barracks, they had received word of the battle and plunged into the storm to discover what was happening. As they neared, they saw the brilliant explosion and watched debris, people, and parts of people being flung in every direction. All the troopers were amazed at the appearance of the ship, with its strange, wicked-looking, rib-like framework jutting above the water. Like the drowning remnants of some undead dragon, the ship caused them only the briefest pause before they pressed on. At the dock, they found a battle beginning to wane and encountered its remnants as the wounded were carried away or walked under their own power.

Disciplined and alert, Minruvak held his men back while he determined what was happening. It would not pay to enter the fray and hack down the innocent. He ordered his men to take up positions about the wharf and detain any survivors not being carried to the Moontower for healing, including the wounded who were not in danger of dying. He then set his command post up in a warehouse adjacent to the docks, where he could begin questioning the participants out of the driving rain.

Two planks were set atop some barrels as a makeshift desk. The unharmed were led to one corner of the building. Mostly they were seamen from the doomed ship, but among them were a few brawlers of the city who could not resist a good fight. To the other corner were led the wounded who could tend to each other. Minor bloody wounds and broken bones would not prevent these from talking. Some of the healers came in and worked to minister to the wounded, and they were not interrupted. All knew the public mission of the order, so their work would not be hampered.

Suddenly, one of his troopers called from the other side of the building, where a great hole had been torn in the siding. An alônn lay gasping in the wreck of a vendor's cart, terribly wounded. The trooper barked orders that the healers come quick. They came, and the broken body was gingerly removed and taken from the building. Another man lay near the destroyed cart, but this one seemed unharmed, save for his unconsciousness. He ordered the guards to drag this man to the "unharmed" section and have him await interrogation.

Meanwhile, more guards had arrived, and Minruvak ordered them to break up what was left of the fight. The monstrous ship had sunk at its berth, and only the upper rigging remained above the water. The only fighting left was on the dock, and it seemed only half-hearted as it seemed all the leaders of this madness were either dead or had fled. He doubted that any useful information would ever be gleaned from the lackeys left behind.

Outside, Holl and Harrok carried the grievously wounded alônn along the pier, to where his kindred were being lowered to the water's edge for return to the sea and care there. Though they had rarely worked on the alônn, they doubted much could be done for him. Like so many others, his light seemed all but extinguished. Soon, they guessed, it would go out altogether.

As they gingerly carried him, a form stepped from a building and stopped them. "Where do you take this warrior?" he asked. The two bearers recognized the face of another alônn, one who had been seen in the Moontower on occasion for reasons neither knew. He stepped over quickly and looked at the body, concern and a small amount of sadness registering on his face. Looking up, he said urgently, "Quellon think you are taking this one the wrong way. No healers down there can help. Give him to me, and I will care for him."

Holl and Harrok looked at him suspiciously for a moment but then complied. The alônn took the broken body in his arms and turned away, quickly making his way back into the city. Where he was taking the fallen hero, the men did not know. With one last look, the two returned to their own duties; their work was not finished.

The terrible storm that had lashed Crown for days, bringing worse weather with each passing day and flooding many of the lower parts of the city, began to ease. The driving rain had become a drizzle, and the tearing winds had calmed to little more than a strong breeze. Sailors of every kind worked to repair damage to their own vessels moored in the harbor district, while curious onlookers began to poke their heads out of windows and doors to see what the commotion heard over the storm had been. The fires had largely gone out, though a portion of the crippled ship still burned at the stern.

Captain Minruvak's guardsmen busied themselves searching the nearby wharves and taverns for any who might have slipped out of the riot before they arrived. A work party of seamen had been pressed into service by the watch to search for victims among the half-submerged ship. Many citizens came forward with lanterns and lamps to help in any way they could.

Suddenly, a cry was heard near the rear mast of the doomed ship. Minruvak stepped from his command post to see a number of sailors and watchmen carefully bringing a mangled body from the tangled debris. The men loaded the body onto a boat and rowed back to the dock, where other guards carefully lifted it and laid it on the decking.

Healers stepped over to the person to determine his wounds. As the captain turned to step back into the warehouse and resume interrogations, he heard several of the watchmen cry out a name. Not clear enough for him to understand, Minruvak turned back to see who they were shouting about. A second time he heard the name: Tenet.

Surprised, the captain stepped quickly town the pier to where the healers were busy working. He arrived to find the Queen's Intelligencer being carried haphazardly in the arms of several orderlies. The etherean was like something he had never seen before. Looking like an image of someone being reflected by a turbulent pond, Tenet was phasing in and out of the material plane while other parts of his body were distorting grotesquely for a moment and then returning to normal. Those portions would then phase out while other parts phased in and distorted. The effect made the captain nauseated, so he turned away.

Clearly, Tenet was in grave condition. Nothing could be done for him here; perhaps nothing could be done for him at all. In any case, the only chance this Queen's trusted servant had would be in the Moontower. Wasting no time, he called several of his most capable men and ordered them to take the etherean with all haste to the tower. His own were more vigorous than any of the litter-bearers he had thus seen, and Tenet certainly had high enough standing to justify their efforts.

So, what business had brought this most important of people to the brawl? Nothing he saw had indicated that this riot was of any importance. The captain, upon seeing were-rat cultists, common seamen, and alônn fighting desperately on a ship that had exploded, had assumed some dirty business but nothing all that great. He could not understand what the alônn might have to do with the Cult of the Grey

God, but then, the two groups were largely antagonistic in nature. Obviously, something on the ship was their goal, and perhaps with the ship's destruction, that goal was not achieved.

Minruvak felt nothing but disdain for the cult and its twisted followers, and he hoped that whatever he and his men had stumbled into, it had gone badly for the cult. Judging from the condition of the rats, his hopes were realized. How Tenet had become entangled in this mess, only he knew. Perhaps the captain would find out. The way the etherean looked, though, convinced Minruvak he would probably not.

Before he had a chance to ponder further, he spotted a cart being wheeled up the dock, pushed by two stout orderlies. When the cart neared, he ordered them to halt as he looked in. Lying on the cart, his giant arms and legs hanging out, was an oltreggan covered in so much blood and filth it seemed impossible for it to be alive. That it moaned in strange, guttural grunts was the only confirmation that the morgue was not its destination.

Just as Minruvak was about to allow the bearers to go on their way, presumably to the tower or another house of healing, he suddenly recognized the beast. This was the same thundering brute his men had taken prisoner many days earlier after a pretty nasty brawl involving unpaid debts. But, certainly this mindless creature was not part of the night's troubles? How had it even been released from his cell? The captain figured the oltreggan must have seen the fighting and tried to get in on the action, not unlikely for one of its kind.

Minruvak's first inclination was to order the half-dead brute to be dumped into the harbor for dead. Crown had no use for it, and if it were allowed to live, it would only end up behind bars after another brawl. Might as well save the citizens of Crown the cost of imprisonment. But, the captain was an honorable man, and while he had no use for this beaten and bloody creature, he could not really justify killing it. After all, he knew of no new crimes this oltreggan had committed and, while many disputed it, oltreggans were sentient beings, and so they could not be slaughtered out of hand.

Instead, he ordered the bearers to take it to the lock-house on Mariner Street. The surgeons there could tend to it in their fashion and certainly with better security than could be found in the tower. If it died, well, the captain had done all he could, right?

The captain turned and stepped down the pier to his command post.

The rain had almost ceased, and the wind was nothing more than a salty sea breeze. Arriving at the post, he walked inside and prepared for the long interrogations before him. With a sigh, he sat down at the makeshift desk. He called out for the first person to be brought forward. The bedraggled merchant found near the wounded alônn was led before him. Minruvak sighed, opened his record book, picked up his quill, dipped it into ink, looked up at the pitiful man, and began his questioning.

As the bearers took the mammoth oltreggan up the cobblestone street, they were met by a fellow member of the Benevolent Moon, an elf by the name of Alkarish. He was one of the diviners and not a healer. He raised a pale, long-fingered hand, halting them. Alkarish walked to the cart and peered at the hulk inside. His bright, keen eyes blinked once, and he turned to face the men.

"Where are you taking this oltreggan who is so harmed?" he asked in his clear voice.

"To the lock-house," said one.

"Is that our custom?" demanded the elf. "Do we normally send the grievously wounded to such a place?"

The two looked at each other and then back to Alkarish, "We were instructed by the watch to take him there. He is a criminal, we are told."

"Our order does not pass the care of one so hurt to others," replied the elf. "It is not our way to turn any away. The healers in the jail will do nothing for this one. We cannot allow him to die by passing him to others. Criminal or no, he is now in our care, and we will do for him. Had the watch wanted him in the lock-house, they should have taken him themselves. The devoted are not their servants. You have him, and so you must take him as your oaths demand."

Alkarish stepped ahead of the cart and its bearers and pointed down another street, one that led towards the Flats. "Follow me," he said, pondering briefly the guidance given him by the Oracle before this terrible night. This was the last of the five he was to bring to the Tower once all was completed that night. As he walked, unaware of the disaster at the Moontower, he wondered how Alastar could have known these five would all be grievously hurt.

Unwilling to disobey a diviner in their order, the two devotees lifted the handle of the cart and followed him. Though disregarding an order from the Crown Watch, they knew the elf was right. If the watch needed him after his healing, they could find him in the Moontower. It mattered little, though, for Captain Minruvak was far too busy with the survivors of the melee and had already forgotten about the bloody oltreggan.

*   *   *

As the last vestiges of lightening flashed, amber, bloodshot eyes snapped open. An odd, oft-kilter giggling echoed in a vast dark space deep beneath the streets of Crown. It began low and soft, but soon it was growing – just like the sounds of complete madness nested within it.

"I...I did it," the voice snickered to itself. It seemed perfectly content to talk to itself; it had done so many times before...when it was living. "Oh yes....I've...done...w...w...well!" Slowly, the red lines within the bloodshot eyes faded – and were replaced with black.

*   *   *

"Lady Kyrrava, there is a letter for you." The page swallowed hard; he did not want to anger his mistress.

"Well, bring it to me, lad! I cannot come to you after it!" the Queen's Champion snapped. She was not feeling well, and to add to her illness, she'd not heard from her charge in many days. Rumor of the explosion and fight in Deep Harbor was rampant across the city; news had reached the Castle and the Queen almost immediately. Lorelei's sister was demanding answers.

"Y-yes, m'lady," the page stammered. As he entered, the ferret leapt down from his shoulder, much to his relief. The lad, being raised in the city since birth, had never seen such a long, strange-looking rat; he feared it might bite him or scratch his eyeballs out. The creature bounded across the room and scampered up Lady Kyrrava's bedpost. A sealed note attached with a blue thread was slung across its shoulders. Tentatively, she took it, dismissed her page, and then broke the seal with blackened fingers. As soon as she began reading, her eyes widened:

Lady Kyrrava,

   Forgive the intrusion, m'lady, but I feel that I

must write to you in stead of your servant and my friend and brother, Tenet. While I, myself, am still not entirely sure of these events and their connections, I have summarized my suppositions regarding the recent dark affairs in Crown over the past several days and possibly weeks. I know you had assigned Tenet to investigate these events, only because he sought out my assistance, in the strictest of confidence, regarding the translation of some magical formulae. I feel that it is my bound duty to you and to my wounded brother-in-mind-and-heart to inform you thusly.

It is my firm belief that many steps were taken by high-ranking members of the Cult of the Grey God to put the pieces in place for another Demon Scourge. According to the research conducted by Tenet, as well as discussions shared with me in private, he would concur with this assessment. In fact, Tenet believed that a Demon Scourge was only the beginning of the impending threat upon Crown. It was Tenet's belief that a new Scourge upon Crown was merely the "appetizer" to a great banquet of sorrow, suffering, and evil that may soon befall Crown. It is my brother's firm belief that it was the Cult's ultimate intention to not only release demons upon our beloved city, but also the Grey God himself, in physical form!

We shall not know the true depth and breadth of this plot until we can again converse with the Queen's Man and learn what he has uncovered through his investigation. I only know a fragment of what he knows, I can assure you. Yet, this is the conclusion to which I come through all rational thought. We can only hope that Tenet will soon recover, but as a precaution, I urge you to hedge those within the Moontower together for the time being. It is apparent that there is some shadowy thread that tangles each of their futures together, and while I regret to say it, Crown's future may well lie tangled within that wispy thread as well.

As requested, I am still diligently searching for the book lost to you some time ago. I am sad to report, however, that it has been some time since I have heard from my man, Landon Quintar. I can only hope that, as Tenet *says, Truth and Goodness are watching over him and guiding his steps.*

May they watch over yours as well,
Galsarius

Lady Kyrrava finished reading and crushed the note in her bandaged hand. Black, clotted blood oozed from her wounded digits as a result of the violent gesture. Anger twisted her features and the only words that slipped from her clenched teeth were, "that...book!"

Flames leapt to life, completely engulfing both the hand of the Queen's Champion and the letter crumpled within it; Lady Kyrrava knew that she would do anything to keep these words from being seen by any...

*   *   *

Day came, and the citizens of Crown emerged from their dwellings and began the arduous task of cleaning up the debris from the terrible storm. Refugees from the flooded low-lying places, particularly the Flats, lined the streets and public courtyards holding their few belongings, waiting for the waters to subside. Those few revelers who had braved the elements to celebrate the Long Night stirred. Most of the taverns and grogeries were filled by those seeking news of the astounding happenings at the harbor as well as the now infamous demon fight and the strange disappearance of the Fiend Fighter. The events would be discussed, debated, and considered for many days, until some other event occupied the minds of the people.

None of it mattered to Taedrellia, who cared for a small group of survivors from the battle at the docks. One of the strange and wonderful lumilons, fair to look upon and pleasant to listen to,.many of her kind served as healers throughout Crown. Some of the very best served here in the Moontower, as members of the Benevolent Moon. The night before had maimed and killed many, and she and her fellow healers had been busy.

She was one of the most skilled of all the healers in Crown, her inherent powers being stronger than most of her kind. Yet, she did not rely solely on her innate energies to heal, for not even she was strong enough to heal so many of the hurt and wounded in such a way. In addition to her inner lumilon power, she added years upon years of lore gathered from across the entire world. Though the Moontower boasted the most diverse apothecary in all of Crown, her personal collection was itself more impressive than any of her fellow healers, save for the greatest.

This day after the calamity found her busy at work, taking care of a curious group of survivors, not only because they were so few among the large number of wounded, but also because of their makeup. She had five patients: an elf who had been brought in with severe frost bite, a dwarf who was burned, bleeding, and half-drowned, the etherean, Tenet, who was near death from wounds she still did not fully understand, an oltreggan who had arrived covered in so much filth that at first she had not recognized his species, and an alônn, who had suffered severe blunt trauma and deep gashes from the ship's explosion.

The elf and dwarf had been fairly easy, for their wounds were not so grave. The giant oltreggan and the alônn were difficult only in their nearness to the final crossing from this world to that of the dead. The Queen's Intelligencer, though, was something else, and he had required all her skills and innate abilities. He was an etherean, and they did not die in the way of other beings, but the strange damage she saw made her wonder if the conventions were true. And if he did survive, what form would he take? Would he be a being partially in this world, partially in the ethereal, never to take whole form again?

Taedrellia stepped lightly down the stone corridor, an ornate bronze tray in her hands. On the tray were several plain stone jars filled with various preparations, the creation of a few only she knew. She had used them through the night in various ways, and early in the morning, she had been forced to retire to her chambers to formulate some of the more perishable salves. Fresh tinctures in hand, she now returned to the room of healing for another course of treatments.

At the entrance, she paused, listening for any sound. She heard none, but that meant very little. He might have returned to question any of the patients who were awake, as he had several times during the night. He was Galsarius, the well-known mage from *The Blue Crystal*, and though his interest had been primarily directed towards Tenet, he had investigated each of the victims of the fight.

Inquiring about their condition, their names, what she might know about them, who would live, and who would die, Galsarius had gotten in the way many times while never offering to actually help her. The only one awake had been the dwarf, and the mage had gotten nothing out of him. Each time he left, he did so without as much as a word to her. When he returned, he announced his arrival with more questions. One time she had arrived to find him touching the waters of the alônn's healing tank, his eyes closed, as if trying to make contact with him.

She had ordered him back and had spent some time ensuring the water remained untainted. Taedrellia was not angry at his presence so much as exasperated that he did little more than get in the way without actually accomplishing his own goals. She knew he was there for a valid reason; his reputation was not that of a meddler. Yet, she could see nothing gained from his presence. The last time he came, she had advised him to be a bit more patient, that when more is known, she would send for him. He had thanked her and left. Had he taken her advice?

To her relief, she did not find Galsarius inside, only several beds, a stone slab, and a marble tank arranged along the wall, their feet pointing towards the room's center. Lying on or in them in various conditions were her charges. To her immediate left lay the dwarf, hands behind his head and staring into the ceiling. She had been told he was Farulazar the Fiend Fighter, a name she had heard before but a face she had never seen. He was obviously awake and bored. She stepped to him and wordlessly handed him one of her jars, a salve for burns both magical and physical. He had suffered several on his face and chest, in addition to numerous cuts, bruises, scrapes, and punctures over his body.

When he awoke during the night during the early treatments, he had resisted quite vigorously. Demanding first to know where he was, and then where his clothes were, it took a long time filled with gentle talk to calm him down and convince him that the treatments were necessary and that his clothes were being cleaned and mended. Even so, he refused any treatment unless he could apply it himself, and so she had compromised by giving him the salve and instructions on how to apply it. This morning, she did not try to alter the agreement.

Passing him by, she approached the elf, who still lay unconscious. He was naked save for a loin-cloth. Apart from minor cuts and scrapes, his skin was an almost uniform pasty-white that was thick and leathery.

In places it had cracked, revealing pink, raw skin beneath. She leaned over him, and jar in hand, applied a golden liquid to his skin, rubbing it in carefully. For a moment, the injured skin took on a healthy glow before fading once again to its ghostly pallor. It would take days to heal and would be painful, but it was not life-threatening.

In addition to his skin, his lungs had been seared by the bitter cold that had enveloped him, and that had been a cause of worry. He had survived the early anxious hours and now was improving steadily. Yet, treatment was still needed, and she dabbled some white powder in her hand and blew it into his face. In his sleep, he sneezed once, his breathing quickened for a moment, and then he returned to normal. Another day and his lungs would be healed.

Finished with him, she stepped over to the marble tank. Out of it flowed a violet mist that cascaded down the side before mingling with the air and disappearing. Looking in, she saw the alônn who had been brought barely alive from the wharves. He was bleeding from numerous deep gashes on his back, head, and chest. In addition, he was severely burned in various places, including along one side of his neck where the gill slits were almost swollen shut. He floated in the water, unconscious, but breathing normally. The lumilon sprinkled a handful of blue dust across the water and watched as it precipitated across his whole body.

With nothing else to do for the alônn, she walked over to the oltreggan covered in bandages and lying on the stone slab. Across his chest, waist, and legs were heavy chains that restrained him. His wrists and ankles were similarly clasped to heavy chains. Not willing to trust the strength of the iron alone, she had enchanted the links, and now they glowed with a green light. The restraints were not out of malice, but all that she had heard about his rampage through Crown made her cautious. His wounds were serious but were now healing without trouble. Indeed, he needed no more treatment other than time for his strong body to continue what she had started. She leaned down and whispered soft words in his ears to keep him asleep and then stepped quietly back.

She strode over to Tenet, who some called the Spymaster. His corporal body was bandaged in the same fashion as the oltreggan, though with far more linen, but it was suspended just above the covers in a softly glowing, flattened sphere. The etherean was phasing in and out, flickering like a dim candle. Worse still, the portions of his flesh that were not wavering in and out of the solid plane were bubbling and rolling like a simmering pot of porridge. Yet over the whole of the etherean's body, this effect was not constant; one moment an arm would fade while his face would seethe and stir, and in the next, all seemed well. This made the malady increasingly difficult to diagnose or treat.

Though not awake, he was not asleep, either. Taedrellia knew he was unconscious as only ethereans could be, but what struggles his body faced, she did not fully understand. What limited treatments she could administer had been applied early in the night. There was very little left for her to do save for observation. It was frustrating to her that nothing else could be done. But for Tenet, whether life, death, or some strange cursed middle ground awaited him, only the fates knew.

Finished with her tasks, she stepped away, tray in hand, and walked from the room. She would return several more times that day, and over the next few days, until she was finished with her work. Though some would be healed much sooner than others, particularly the dwarf and the oltreggan, she and her fellow healers were given instructions to keep this odd group together. Fortunately for her, with the serious healing over, she could pass on the delaying duty to the diviners. She was never good at lying. Taedrellia reached the end of the corridor and passed once again into her chambers, where she planned a small nap. After such a long night's work, she knew she had earned it.

* * *

He lay at the bottom of Deep Harbor, his body half submerged in a soft muck. A seaman by trade, he had worked the rigging on the *Winter's Claw* before its demise several days earlier. In those days, he had gone by the name of Dirvuk and was by all accounts an ordinary but capable member of the crew. For more than a decade, he had served on various ships belonging to the Ice Skull League, working for different captains. Most were elvish and most were the same: surly and demanding. Yet though he occasionally received lashes and had spent many a lonely night on deck fighting chill or storm, the sea life was the only he had known, the only life that brought comfort. Dirvuk had been as content as any sailor on the open sea.

But then the ship had come into port and had docked at Crown carrying the cargo wanted by so many. The battle had started, and he had drawn a cutlass from the rack to repel boarders, first the slimy slit-necked alônn and then the crazed were-rats who belonged to some sort of cult. His tally had been good: two of the fish-men and a handful of rats. Yet like so many of the crew, his personal measure of luck had not been adequate, and a spear had been thrust through his chest, tearing open his heart and ending his life. He had fallen overboard, but he was dead before he splashed into the turbulent waters.

There he floated for a while as the battle raged. Soon his lungs filled with water, though, and he slipped below the churning surface. When the ship exploded and broke apart, he was already on the bottom, mingling with the bilge. In the days that followed as he decomposed, his body began to swell until he doubled in girth. His bright blue eyes grew pale and bulged in their sockets, his hands thickened until each digit pointed out under the pressure, and his mouth opened as if to scream. The skin on his bloated back had split along the spine, revealing pale bone and corrupted flesh on which the crabs now feasted.

Dirvuk was not alone. About him were strewn corpses of every kind that had suffered an almost infinite number of terrible ends. There were many of his fellow crewmen, some showing gaping wounds, others charred from fire, still others dismembered from the explosion. There were many more were-rats in similar states, their beady eyes bulging in death, their tongues lolling thickly from their open mouths.

They were not alone. In the center of the grisly assembly it lay, silent after its own ordeal in the place where it had plummeted when the ship exploded and the hold split. It had been bathed in blood, had consumed its sacrifice, but the waters had washed it prematurely, and some of the potency of the spell was lost. Yet in the demise of the plans prepared for it, not all had been lost. Though not yet known in the world above, the cursed relic, the cause of the calamity above, was not destroyed.

For days, Dirvuk lay in the muck mere feet from the object, his body spoiling. Then suddenly, his bloated hand twitched, the fingers curling, and the skin on its back split, revealing tendons. Soon his arm flexed, pulling up and then relaxing. His ghostly head turned, his gaping mouth closed as if speaking, and his eye-lids strained to close over his bulbous eyes. He gasped like a fish washed up on the beach. A strange sound issued from his swollen throat. Soon, other bodies nearby joined in his macabre dance, silently moving their limbs, opening their mouths, some rolling over, others seeming to sit up.

For hours, the horrible scene played out as the terrifying corpses twitched and moved, not straying from their final resting places. Then, as if he was a strange leader of a decaying army, Dirvuk moved towards the relic, his unblinking eyes turning towards it. The sailor moved awkwardly through the water, his arms floating about in the undulating current. Soon, he was next to the strange object, where his body drifted once again to the bottom, resting on his knees as if to kneel. Through the night and into the next day, he was joined by scores of were-rats and sailors, until the relic was surrounded by an impossibly attentive audience.

The corpses stared at the relic as if in a trance, mouths gaping, hair waving in the water, their bodies moving back and forth in unison. Their bloated flesh ceased its corruption, remaining unchanged from the moment the strange object began to act upon them. As if acolytes in a bizarre cult, they waited in patient death for something unknown.

And so, the assembly waited through the day and into the night, followed by the next day. Then, on Darkday, a week after the explosion of the *Winter's Claw*, the silent crowd ceased its movement. The grisly audience leaned forward as if to hear a whispered word, their already pale eyes turning white. As if caught in a collective scream, their mouths opened wide, their hands dropped silently to their sides.

In the center of the macabre forum, the relic began a low thrumming, causing the murky silt to drift up and cloud the waters, hiding the devoted corpses. For a moment, all the waters in Deep Harbor stilled, the winds ceased, and those ships entering or leaving ports were becalmed as their sails sagged. Hundreds of fish turned about and floated to the surface, while the scavenging crustaceans blanched and became motionless. All color bled away, and the dead, for but a moment, were motionless. At the center of it all, the diseased beat faltered, slowed, and finally, the relic quieted. The dead raised their ghastly faces to the water's surface and then bowed in supplication to the relic. Then, silently, they arose and drifted towards the shore...

ABOUT THE AUTHORS

Nathan Ellsworth

Nathan is a hobbyist writer-errant currently residing in Georgia. He's enjoyed writing ever since high school, but he followed the path of the dollar and got his degree in engineering. Since then he's been writing on and off, but just for fun. He's only recently – since 2006 – considered writing professionally. He pays the bills through his engineering day job, so he spends a lot of time editing his work before he submits it.

He prefers writing science-fiction, fantasy, pulp, and hardboiled detective stories, and regularly tries to blend all his favorite genres.

Davis Riddle

Davis Riddle grew up in southern Alabama, the only boy among four sisters and the only grandson to carry the Riddle name. Possessed with the a love of the outdoors and an explorer's soul, Davis started backpacking before he was old enough to shave. Tied with his love of the mountains, where good hard stone could be found under foot, is a passion for experience.

Davis has hiked with nothing but a traveling kilt and a bed roll through the mountains, drank from running streams, bathed in roaring water falls, and slept in the wilderness in earshot of mountain lions. He has flown in a B-17 bomber, slept on a WWII battleship, swam salt-marshes, and had dinner on giant fortresses lost in the swamp. His explorer's heart has brought him miles down lonely bayous to explore forgotten ruins and kayaking across the mighty Mississippi, dodging alligators and ocean-going freighters to explore a disappearing 18th century Spanish fortress and a ghost town now lost to the world from Hurricane Katrina's wrath.

Davis is a Consulting Forester and president of his own firm, practicing in South Mississippi and the Florida Parishes of Louisiana. His daily experiences in swamp and hill continue to provide him with a wealth of experiences on which to draw for his writing. He is married with a wonderful son who already, at less than 3 years of age, tells stories of his Nanna's castle populated with dinosaurs and a daddy-knight.

Brannon Hall

Born Election Day, Nov 4th 1975, Robert Brannon Hall "elected" to pop out 19 days early. Incidentally the first and last time Brannon was early for ANYTHING. (Even this bio for this site was late!) Born and raised in the south in a small rule area along the outskirts of the city of Birmingham, Alabama, it became apparent at a young age that Brannon (or HALL, as he is most fondly called because of a certain "other white meat" that shared the same name as he did), was quite different from the other children around him. His imagination found root in books, art, and the world around him. Fascinated by art, his parents bought him a finger paint set at age 4 and from there, there was no turning back.

Hall's love of the arts grew throughout his high school years. Between writing and drawing, the imagination that so defined him as a child continued to grow as well.

Currently Hall lives with his beloved wife in a old castle in the highlands of Scotland with seven. (I did mention the wild imagination thing earlier, didn't I? Ok, so I don't live in Scotland and it sure ain't a castle but I DO love my beautiful bride!! Believe it or not, the seven cat thing is actually true! Don't ask, long story.)

By day, he is a mild-mannered graphic designer, a job he truly loves; not only for the work involved, but due to the people he works with, as well. By night he dons the multi-leveled hat of Husband, Illustrator, and Muralist. (They call me H.I.M.!...Please insert superhero pose here. Chest out, rippling muscles flexed, and cape blowing in the wind.... Image can be found in my mind. Please knock twice before entering...)

Corey Blankenship

Thrown harshly from the roost of normality at a young age, Corey ("Tsid" to his beloved gaming group) struggled to find a place in a broken world, clinging to the vestiges of imagination for comfort. If neither weather nor mandates prevented him, the creative youth would mount countless incursions into the perils of the "wild" frontier behind his home. These adventures, coupled with living in the majestic foothills of the Rockies and Adirondacks, implanted a love for sylvan beauty and mystery in the youth's heart.

Once he rose into adolescence, his world shattered once more to displace the child of creativity into a realm of harsh realities. The trials of middle school tore through friendships and dreams. The only intermission came from his first glint of hope: reality Himself, Christ.

Despite his surrender to Truth, this rogue found the next years lonely and painful. The world did not answer his illimitable queries and insatiable hunger to understand; similarly yearning souls did not appear to sate the longing for fellowship. Thus, the outcast dreamer found a single avenue for his tattered heart: writing. Poetry and prose, the reams of binders and blogs filled with the longings and dreams for fellowship, communion, understanding, peace, and (above all) love.

Brannon "Ashy" Hollingsworth

Born on Thanksgiving Day, 1972, Brannon "Ashy" Hollingsworth was a misplaced, idealistic child thrust into the harsh realities of growing up in the real world in the heart of the Deep South. Arising from a simple, honest background, Brannon always seemed different from other children and was forever reading, writing, drawing or exploring any patch of woods he could find. To those who knew him well, it seemed that Brannon was ceaselessly trying to escape the discordant scraps of reality around him, looking for passage back to whatever fairytale realm from which he had originated.

Apparently, Brannon never found a lasting road back; his childhood thankfully passed and he entered adolescence, during which some solace was discovered. Through a close, valued companionship with a tightly knit group of friends (from which the Wandering Men eventually sprang), Brannon received an introduction to two things that altered him irrevocably: true bonds of brotherhood and role-playing. These twin concepts became the corner stones for the construction of a new life which Brannon has endlessly toiled to complete. Leaving his home town, finding peace with God, attending college, remaining close to his friends, meeting and marrying his soul mate, having his children, forming his family and beginning his career as a freelance author have all been necessary and welcome additions to this construction, which is still on going today.

Currently, Brannon lives with his beloved wife, fantastic five children, and their hyper-intelligent border collie in a very small town in northern Alabama. By day, he works in a field for which he was not trained and performs tasks for reasons he does not fully understand, but apparently is very good at; by night, however, he is allowed to explore his first love: writing. It would seem again that Brannon is looking for those passages back "home". The sole exception is that now he searches for an entirely different reason; instead of looking to escape, he desires to show others the fantastical place that lies just beyond reality's ragged and threadbare borders.

Brannon's work to date has been for several D20 publishers including *Paizo Publishing, Sword & Sorcery Studios, Green Ronin Press, Bastion Press, Sovereign Press, Necromancer Games, Atlas Games, Fantasy Flight Games, Eden Studios, Skeleton Key Games, Dark Quest Games, Ambient, Inc.,* and *Citizen Games.* He has also been published in several industry periodicals such as *Dragon Magazine, Gaming Frontiers,* and *The EN World Player's Journal.* Brannon is also known on the internet as "the guy that started the Official Planescape Website, Planewalker.com", where he gained the pseudonym "Ashy", which has stuck ever since...

He, along with the other Wandering Men currently maintain their own website at http://www.wanderingmen.com.

If you found adventurous tales like this one to your taste, turn the pages for an exclusive preview.

Skein of Shadows, Book II
By the Wandering Men

Available 2008, wherever Dark Quest books are sold.

El'laa awoke from a most pleasant dream. She and Tenet had picnicked on the hills north of Crown and then made love as the sun set. He had held her tightly in his arms as they gazed on their beloved city, its towers and walls aglow with the fading light.

She was lying on a bed of cool linen, wearing a dressing gown of the finest silk. She smiled. Finally, she was happy. As the sun came up, she saw the surrounding bed chamber, their bedchamber. She was at home, at peace.

With a sigh, she started to roll over to get out of bed, but the sheets were tangled around her. She was trapped. She panicked and flailed, desperate to escape, to flee. With a mighty heave, she freed herself and stood, panting, over her marriage bed. Her head began to throb.

As she gazed about the room, the seemingly familiar objects turned sinister.

This is not right.

But it had to be right. This was where she lived with her beloved, her Ghost, her Tenet. Her head throbbed more as she thought of her lover.

This is NOT right.

Images began to assault her senses. She staggered backwards and screamed in pain. Her eyes seemed to be on fire. She saw the were-rat, the elven assassin, and the demon fighter. The chanting of the cultists merged with the cackling of Xigx. Her family, in chains, was being led towards the gallows and the burning spits...

Too much, too much. She screamed. She did not want to see these things, but she could not stop it.

She hit the cold wall and collapsed against it. Then, she saw him. Her beloved Tenet. She had been fleeing from him, racing down a dark tunnel. But her way was blocked, the grate was locked. She struggled with the lock, knowing she did not have time. She sensed his arrival, felt the cold steel of his sword on her neck.

She had tried to fight, but he had been too fast. His mind had seized hers. Again and again, he had entered her mind, rooting through her secrets and forcing her to give them to him. He had violated her mind, and once he had what he wanted, he had left something. He had forced love into her mind, had filled it with emotions she no longer felt. A gift, but not for her, for him...

El'laa suddenly awoke, sitting upright in her bed - her **real** bed, in her **own** chambers. Her stomach heaved, and she vomited on the plain wooden floor of her dwelling. Her entire body shook in protest as she strove to expel his presence. She ripped the dressing gown from her body and shrieked. She had to rid herself of his filth, cleanse herself from this violation. After a moment, she found herself lying on the floor, panting.

Standing, she walked, naked, over to her wardrobe and pulled out a pair of tight-fitting pants, a white shirt, and her normal green vest and dressed herself. As she did so, she considered the dream and its revelations. She remembered fully now the assault, the telepathic and magical rape of her mind, perpetrated by Tenet, the one who was supposed to be the servant to the truth. Yet, he had attacked her in such an intimate way, had planted the seed of a lie into her mind, and then had left it there to grow. Whether he intended her to fall for him again, or whether he merely had become sloppy by leaving the remnants in her mind, she did not know, nor care.

Dressed, she passed out of her abode and into the city. She had several tasks for the day. First, she had to garner what information she could with regard to the events leading up to the death of Szeethe and the *Idol*'s explosion at Deep Harbor. Following that, she would discover all she could about Tenet's whereabouts and his condition. With that knowledge in hand, she would begin moving pieces on her own chess board, biding her time, making her preparations.

And then, she would have her vengeance.

* * *

It had taken her the better part of two days to fill in the missing pieces. It had not been easy. Those cultists who were not dead or in hiding wanted her head for betraying them. Arastin was in the care of the Order of the Benevolent Moon, and she doubted he could have helped her much now, anyway. She knew Tenet was there as well and would try to kill him if the opportunity availed itself, but he was well protected. Besides, merely killing Tenet would, it seemed, be a blessing to him. No, she would do things to him that would be far worse than death. To complicate things even more, the Crown Watch was after her as well.

She had run out of friends and was running low on useful enemies. She needed a powerful ally, and there were none left for her in Crown. So, she turned north, chasing a rumor and her last hope for vengeance...

*   *   *

Na'akiros had fled Crown in pain, heading north towards the barren land he called home. His wounded arm throbbed incessantly, burning with an unquenchable fire. With every passing mile, it pained him more, until he could take it no longer. Landing on a rocky crag in the early dawn, he paused to succor his wound and assess his condition. He could not believe what had befallen him: he had lost his ship, his trophies, his gold...and his hand. With his ship had gone his men, his items, and his life.

He stared back to the south, to Crown, in a cold rage. Looking down at his stump of an arm, he knew he could not go home like this, broken and disgraced. At best, his dragon-kin would kill him and devour his flesh. At worst, they would keep him alive while they devoured his flesh. The Iceskull League did not forgive failure of any kind. The only way he could return home would be to claim redemption first. He would have to seek revenge and destroy those who betrayed him. Or, he would be forced to hide forever.

But, he could not take the first steps towards retribution and his return to the League in his current guise; his white scales were a death sentence if he were caught outside Iceskull territory. Only as an elf could he move about among the populations in this bleak and desolate land, where small fishing settlements and farming villages dotted the otherwise untamed wilderness. Na'akiros steeled himself for the changing. It was not comfortable under the best of circumstances, but in his wounded state, he could not imagine what pain he would endure.

He closed his eyes, arched his head upwards, and held his arms out to the side. Na'akiros focused on the arcane power within him, the one gift from his sire, and he felt his form begin to shift. His wings drew inward, and his face began to change, his teeth withdrawing into his mouth as his jaw shrunk in size and width. He felt his tail absorb and the scales begin to smooth. So far, so good. But, as his arms and legs changed into elvish form, the agony hit him full bore, driving his breath from his lungs. He fell to his knees, unable to bear the pain.

Na'akiros quickly returned to his half-dragon incarnation. His arm still ached and oozed around its cauterized tip, but he could breathe again. With frustration, he realized he could not change forms! Somehow his wounded stump, which still burned unnaturally, was preventing him from changing. How could he hope to begin his revenge in this form? Now missing one claw, how could he hope to grip a wand or cast a spell? How could he make the necessary connections among villagers or fishermen? How could he command a ship?

He roared in rage at the sky. Before he could even begin his return to Crown, before he could dish out retribution and return to his kindred, he would first have to heal his burning wound. That would take time and magic, yet his abilities seemed impaired. So, he would bide his time and marshal his strength.

To regain his vigor, he would hunt in the forests and towns in these northern lands. He would hide in caves and avoid drawing attention to himself. Those hamlets he ravaged, he would leave in utter ruin, its folk and livestock devoured. He would become an unknown scourge.

And so he did, for months, killing and feeding with a voracious appetite. As the time passed and with every meal, he gained some measure of strength, but his wound did not heal. Worse, it festered and spread up his arm. The fire had cauterized the wound, but now, it was eating into his icy-essence. Throughout the winter, his whole arm burned, and some days he would shake with fever. Even the inviting blizzards and northern gales did nothing to soothe him. By the earliest spring thaw, he could no longer use his arm. It hung limply at his side, an impediment to flight.

The longer he stayed in half-dragon form, the more his savagery increased. He found that his thoughts were less focused on revenge against the elven assassin, the Cult of the Grey God, Szeethe, and the alônn, and more on killing and pillaging - the primal urges of his kind. As his wrath blossomed, his ability to wield any kind of magic waned evermore, which only fed his rage.

To make matters worse, he was now a target. As his attacks had grown more brutal, his notoriety also grew. There was now a sizable bounty on his head. What had started out as bands of farmers with pitchforks had become parties of wizards and warriors, paladins and rogues. They were persistent, if inept. But with each battle, the opponents grew stronger. Still, he was not taken.

As spring waned, he had amassed quite a collection of trophies. He had lined the walls of his cave with the corpses of his foes, had piled their armor and weapons in great stacks. But, he was growing weary of these pointless games.

He had tried using the wands, amulets, and globes from dead heroes to heal his wound, but to no avail. While he remained in half-dragon form, Na'akiros's mind seethed with a fury that clouded his thoughts and made recalling the ephemeral incantations impossible. Though he could hold his elven form for a few minutes now, the agony remained too great for him to concentrate on the spells he required.

And so, Na'akiros found himself alone in his cave at summer's dawn, talking to the skin of a newly killed wizard, a mage of some strength that he had frozen before he flayed. He asked it for advice, and when it did not respond, mocked its silence. All the while, he brooded over his fate.

Suddenly, a voice called to him from the shadows, cold and yet strangely fiery, "If you really want vengeance, you'd do better to talk with the living."

He whirled around, sniffing the air and searching for the speaker. He could smell no scent, and his eyes could see no living creature. He reached out with his mind, listening for the faintest whisper of a thought. Even the most skilled wizard would sometimes be betrayed by a stray mental fragment. But there was nothing but a voice, and the mere sound taunted him. How could someone have gotten this far without detection? His rage built into frenzy.

"Calm yourself, Na'akiros. I have not come for battle but for talk."

"Speak then," he growled in his guttural voice, pacing the chamber and searching for the speaker.

"We share common enemies, my friend. Powerful, arrogant enemies. Alone, we cannot hope to touch them. Together we can bring them down. But first, you are in need of my aid."

With that, a slender form slipped out of the shadows in front of him and raised a spike of glimmering ice. Before he could let loose an icy blast, a white ray from the spike struck his lifeless arm. He felt the cold enter it once more, and the shriveled flesh began to pulse with life. The charred shell fell away as a scaly claw sprouted from the pinkish stump. His arm was once again whole. He lifted it over his head and stared with amazement.

Without a word, he became elven once again and stood naked before her. He examined the macabre gallery of corpses that lined his walls. He had to admit there was quite a variety to choose from. After a few moments, the stranger helped him select the naval garb from the body of a merchant captain he had plucked from a schooner along the coast, followed by a rather plain but expertly-balanced cutlass, and then a black ebony wand from his cache. He was now ready for the real battle.

"So, sorceress, to whom do I owe my rebirth?" he asked, caressing the wand in his newly-formed hand.

She smiled a wicked grin. "My name is El'laa..."

To Be Continued...

PLOTSTORMING.COM

for
Writers and Gamers
*

Friendly Community
Daily Writing Prompts
Entertaining Short Stories
*

Hone Your Writing
Receive Helpful Critiques
Enter Contests

Printed in the United States
201164BV00003B/400-450/A